RAV

MN00399194

"This book took ı
tures and the simple g
neighbors. Great read for kids young and old!"
—*Dave Ettinger, Sierra Publications*

"*A Good Day to Live* gives us a positive message, plain ole good manners, consideration for others, responsibility and honor, things we come in contact with everyday."
—*Kathryn Dean, COO, liaisonmanager.com*

"These stories remind us that life has consequences. But those lessons are delivered with a sense of humor from a wise sage."
—*Blair Fischrupp, EBF Designs*

"I'm hopeful and extremely grateful that Fred Garth has put the pen to situations all children will experience. This is exactly what I needed to read and share. I can't get enough of it."
—*Ridge Hails, Life Councilor*

"Many times I was moved to tears by the simplicity and beauty of the images that author Fred Garth paints for us."
—*Beth Slagsvol, Producer, Gryphon Pictures*

"I'm eagerly awaiting the next adventure! My family will have a copy of Fred Garth's next book as soon as it's off the presses."
—*Tracy Krause, housewife*

This book was written in its entirety by Fred D. Garth.
No previous printed versions have been published.
Excerpts have been available online since 2008.

Published by
Lost Key Publishing
7166 Sharp Reef
Pensacola, Florida 32507
www.lostkeypublishing.com

ISBN: 978-0-9823946-0-1

The text in this book is set in 11-point Times Roman

Cover design, book layout and maps by EBF Graphics.

Manufactured in the United States of America.

First edition March 2009.

750

PERDIDO—BOOK ONE:

A Good Day to Live

FRED D. GARTH

Mike —
enjoy!

Lost Key
PUBLISHING
Perdido Key, Florida

*This book is dedicated to
the child in each of us.*

*A special thanks to my wife, Blair,
who allows me to be myself,
even when I shouldn't.*

I also want to enthusiastically thank my favorite editors, Tracy and Robbie, for their support, encouragement, and keen eyes.

The Finding of Perdido

By Fred M. Scott

A puff came out of the windward.
A flurry—the wind went dead,
The moon broke through the flying cloud
And we saw the shoreline ahead.

Sand-dune following sand-dune
And just one tiny rift
So we headed for the breakers
Sail lowered, we let her drift,

We landed on an island—
Island we called Ono
And slept that night on her beaches—
Beaches whiter than snow,

Next morning we followed the channel,
Twisting and winding and slow,
Creeping around our Island—
Curious where it would go.

The water was clear and tranquil,
The shores were wooded and high,
And we felt a growing calmness
As point after point crept by.

And so we came to Perdido—
The bay that was lost and found,
Where human troubles grow dim and fade
And nerves forget to pound.

High bluffs breaking the skyline,
Pine flats, cedar and oak—
And we knew that we'd found our stopping place
Tho not a man of us spoke.

Thus was Perdido settled.
On its shores each build his shed,
And the King of Spain gave us our grants,
And the bay gave us our bread.

Poem printed with permission from the Fred Scott family

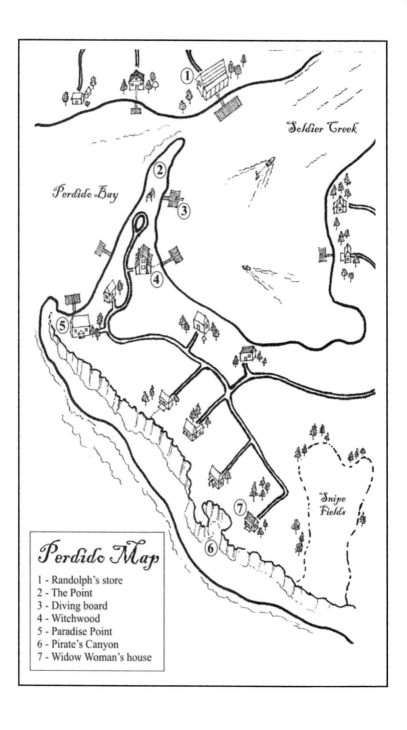

Soldier Creek

Perdido Bay

Snipe Fields

Perdido Map

1 - Randolph's store
2 - The Point
3 - Diving board
4 - Witchwood
5 - Paradise Point
6 - Pirate's Canyon
7 - Widow Woman's house

INTRODUCTION

If we're really lucky in this life, we can look back upon a place or a time when we were truly happy. I've stumbled into that luck from time to time and I just assumed that most others have too. Yet, as I've grown older and more aware (I didn't say wiser), I've realized that finding true happiness is more elusive than I ever imagined.

So when I decided to write this book I hoped to share a magical place that might evoke at least a moment of joy, like an Alabama summer breeze, soft gulf sand between your toes, or a dip into cool spring water. Those moments, along with the bizarre ways kids find to have fun, are what drove the storyline rather than some secret desire to make the *New York Times* bestseller list (although I wouldn't turn that down).

As it turns out, many of the people who've read the book have told me about some delightful place their family went on summer vacation in the Smoky Mountains or Lake Michigan or Colorado or California where there were no telephones or traffic jams and they were free to enjoy the simple pleasures of being with their family.

It's my sincere hope that you will relive the best of your past through Danny, Will, and Trout and the rest of the colorful characters you'll meet. Speaking of the which, I should note that even though this book is somewhat autobiographical, the characters are fictional. They are amalgamations of folks who've woven their way in and around the Alabama Gulf Coast over the course of more than a hundred years. In other words, if you think that character is you, it's not.

Please enjoy the book and I hope you'll rediscover that happy place inside of you.

Take care.

Fred D. Garth

CONTENTS

PART I

CHAPTER 1

Hunting Armadillos

Armadillos might be ugly, but they sure are dumb.
—Will Stapleton, 1962

Crab nets were not intended to catch armadillos. But it was the best idea Danny, Will, and Trout could come up with. The long handles seemed like they'd help, and the net at the end was about the right size. What the boys didn't account for was the tiny beast's surprising speed. Armadillos don't run like normal, godly animals. They bounce like four-legged kangaroos and scurry behind palmetto bushes faster than, well, faster than three twelve-year-old kids swinging crab nets.

Ono Island, a hot, mosquito-infested strip of land with nothing but sand dunes, scrub oaks, and malnourished pines, was the best place along Alabama's Gulf Coast to track the wily possum with an armored overcoat. The island was hostile to the senses, but for kids on a quest, Ono was the New World, devoid of parents or rules and chock-full of 'dillos.

It took thirty minutes for the Johnson Seahorse, 5 horsepower to chug the skiff southward across Perdido Bay, around the sandy tip of Innerarity Point to the north shore of Ono Island. From there, they could see the opening to the Gulf of Mexico just five miles away. Too far and too dangerous to explore without adult supervision, the Gulf could rip *Greenie* apart, rib by rib. In her day, she was a solid boat, but years of pounding waves and abusive older brothers had aged her. Now *Greenie*, simply named for her green wooden hull, hauled kids around the backwater where the seas were calm and a shoreline was always within swimming distance.

Greenie allowed them to be captains of their own destiny. Sometimes that meant scrapping with wild rodents. Armed with three crab nets, a hefty supply of potato chips, and a gallon of lemonade, the boys were ready for action. Shortly after they dragged *Greenie* onto the beach and tied her bowline to a pine tree, Will spotted the first critter burrowing under a palmetto root.

"There's one!" he shouted as he sprinted toward the oversized rat.

It's one thing when an armadillo is frozen in the headlights. It looks positively clumsy, slow, and stupid. Of course, when armadillos are dead on the side of the road with their rigor mortis feet in the air, they're even less imposing. But in the dunes with lots of scrub oaks and palmetto bushes to provide cover, the little buggers were downright agile—squatty gazelles of deep sand.

"Hot damn, they're fast," Will said after fifteen minutes, throwing his net on the ground in frustration. "Tell you what. Trout, you get on my left, and Danny, you get on the right. When we see one, we'll spread out, surround him, and bag his gray butt."

That was the answer: teamwork. Within minutes, Trout and Danny had cornered one by an oak tree. Will covered the rear flank. They moved in slowly, crab nets poised for the snatch. With its little head lowered, the creature stared at the boys through cold, suspecting eyes. Before they could strike, it took off and juked left past Will, right past Danny, then bounced away in a spray of sand. Crab nets flew but missed again.

For the next two hours, the boys tracked and chased. By the time the chips and lemonade were gone, the game was over. Score: Armadillos, 23, Boys, 0.

Nothing had gone as planned. They were covered in sand and sweat. They were tired and angry. Dejected, they packed up *Greenie* and left Ono Island behind them. But they were not beaten. Never underestimate the ingenuity and tenacity of a preteen.

Early the next day, Will, Danny, and Trout were back at Ono with a sixteen-foot shrimp trawling net. Cone-shaped for dragging behind a boat, it was the perfect armadillo trap. They hung it between two trees and camouflaged it with palmetto fronds. After an hour of chasing and herding, they finally wrapped up a big one. As it hissed viciously and wriggled wildly in the netting, the boys stepped back, wide-eyed.

"What are we going to do with it now?" Trout asked.

"Let's just watch it awhile and see what it does," Danny said.

"I say we kill it," Will said. "I've heard you can eat 'em."

"How we gonna kill it?" Trout asked.

Will took a mighty swing with an imaginary club. "Whack it on the head with the paddle."

Danny held up his hands and shook his head. "Wait a minute. We're not really going to eat it. Let's just let it wear itself out, then untangle it and let it go."

Will and Trout were already fetching the death paddle.

"We'll be back," they yelled as they disappeared around a sand dune.

Danny eased closer to the mesh, looking into the animal's hollow eyes and pointed snout. It was one of the ugliest of creatures God had ever dreamed up, and just as useless as far as Danny knew, but it wasn't worth killing. As he untangled the net, he realized the armadillo had already chewed a hole large enough to poke its head through. The little beast snarled at Danny as its sharp claws ripped at the netting. Using a pine branch, Danny spread the net just enough for the critter to squirm through and run off. Danny's father didn't know the boys had taken the net. Now there would be hell to pay.

"Hurry with that paddle," Danny yelled, hoping they'd never make it back in time. "It's getting away."

Like paratroopers, Will and Trout appeared in midair, flying from the crest of a sand dune. Will shrieked as he held the paddle over his head like an ax. The wooden blade must have broken the critter's neck. There was an awful squeal as its jaws clamped shut over its thin, red tongue. The boys had never heard or seen anything so horrible. Time seemed to stop, and a deep sadness swept over them as they witnessed death—a killing they were responsible for. The animal quivered for a few minutes, then lay motionless.

Without talking, Will scooped up the lifeless body with the paddle and carried it to the biggest oak he could find. Danny and Trout knelt on the ground and took turns digging the grave in the soft sand. After he slid the carcass into the hole, Will dropped the paddle and wiped a tear from his cheek.

"Lord," he drawled. "I'm sorry I killed that armadillo. I was just trying to knock it out. I swear."

4

Trout shot a glare at Will. "You can't lie to God."

"I'm not lying."

"But you already said you wanted to kill it," Trout said.

"Yeah, but I'm still sorry I did it."

Trout shook his head in shame. "We shoulda just let it go, like Danny said to."

"If you'd had the paddle, you woulda killed it, too," Will shot back.

"Would not."

"Would too."

Trout clinched his fists and moved toward Will.

Danny stepped between them and sighed. He'd seen them battle too many times. "Y'all just shut up," he said. "Fighting won't help that armadillo. It won't help us, either. Let's just go home."

Silently, they gathered their gear and loaded into *Greenie*. On that day, the glamour of armadillo hunting had lost its luster and a chunk of innocence had been chipped from the boys' childhood.

CHAPTER 2

Catching Shrimp and Trout

It's hard but it's fair.
—Mr. Walter Thornton, 1960

The boys were practicing flips off the pier when they noticed Danny's daddy inspecting the shrimp net and chewing harder than normal on his cigar.

"Damn it to hell," Mr. Walt snapped. "Somebody cut up my shrimp net."

He removed the stub and took a deep breath. Danny knew what was coming. With his head cocked slightly and his lips stretched across his teeth, Mr. Walt ripped his patented piercing whistle. It had singular meaning to all kids within range: Drop everything and come running, now! No bird dog had ever been better trained.

The three boys sprinted down the pier and arrived with several of Danny's breathless brothers, all awaiting instructions.

Mr. Walt held up the net. "Anyone know what happened to this?"

No one moved a muscle.

"I suppose a wild animal got into it last night. You boys think that's what happened?"

"I guess so," Will said. "Probably a possum or a coon."

"But how'd all that sand and those sticks get there?" Mr. Walt asked, never really expecting an answer.

The boys stood silently, hoping to avoid hard labor or a belt strap across their butts.

Mr. Walt finally dropped the net. "Okay. Danny, you go to my workshop and get some nylon string so we can patch this. Will, you and Trout stretch this net out on the grass, and let's get a good look at it. See how many holes you can find."

He looked at the older siblings.

"What were you boys doing?"

"Just playing cards," one said.

"Okay," he said. "Hunter, you get the ladder and clean the leaves from the gutter. Gar, you get the lawnmower going and cut the back-yard. Davis and Willis, get some hammers; we need to pull the nails out of those old boards that washed up on the beach."

Within minutes, the place had transformed from quiet summer re-treat to work camp. It didn't matter who was responsible for the net. Everyone paid the price. They were used to it. Working earned them playtime, not to mention gas for the boat. That was Mr. Walt's way. It didn't matter if you were a blood relative, a friend visiting for a few days, or a couple of kids strolling innocently down the beach. If some wood needed moving or a hole needed digging and you were nearby, he'd put you to work. In fairness, when the boat set out for fishing or if the water smoothed out for skiing, you were invited on that joyride too, as long as you'd put in your time. Mr. Walt was one of the first equal-opportunists.

They were just happy he hadn't summoned the mother of all jobs, the task that filled them all with stinky fear—cleaning out the wretched septic tank. That was the beast they dreaded more than death itself: being up to their waist in waste. Whoever got that sentence handed to them was, literally, in deep doo-doo.

As Danny fetched the string, he thought about that poor armadillo. He wished they had just let it go. Instead, they'd ripped the shrimp net and riled up Mr. Walt. Plus, they'd killed a perfectly innocent critter, even though it was mighty ugly. Danny rarely questioned Will, even when he knew they'd get in trouble. He'd follow Will into a burning house, and he figured Will would do the same for him.

Danny handed the string to his daddy.

"Thanks, son. Looks like there are only a couple holes. You help Will and Trout, and make sure you boys tie double knots. We don't want any shrimp slipping out of the net."

"Yes, sir."

Sewing up armadillo holes was tedious work. And the summer heat, even under the shade of an oak tree, made them long for a cool swim. But the boys worked without complaining. For one thing, they were as guilty as Al Capone. Mr. Walt knew it but didn't accuse them directly. Repairing the net was getting off easy as far as Danny was concerned. The icing on the cake was the possibility of an evening shrimping with Mr. Walt in the big boat.

When he worked them too hard, they had a lot of names for him—names whispered under their breath: Hitler, General Patton, or even Lucifer, when the Alabama heat seared them mercilessly. Affectionately, he was Daddy, Uncle Walter, Mr. Thornton, and a host of endearing terms from his wife, Miss Kitty. At some point, everyone, even his own kids, just took to calling him Mr. Walt.

"Boys, how's that net coming?" he asked.

"It's pretty much done," Danny said. "We even cleaned out the sticks that got into it when we … um, I mean, when whatever happened to get those sticks in it happened."

"Yeah, however that happened," Will chimed in. He and Trout both glared at Danny. What was he thinking? He almost blurted it out. Mr. Walt smiled and let it slide. If the boys didn't know it then, one day they'd realize that he knew their every move, no matter how slick they thought they were.

"Then, by golly, let's go shrimping. Who's in?"

The boys sprang up and danced around the net like monkeys. Shrimping was a treat, even though pulling in the net was Trojan's work. But the rewards far outweighed their blistered hands and sore backs. They'd get big fat blue crabs and more shrimp than they could eat, sometimes thirty or forty pounds. And sifting through all the weird sea creatures they dragged up was like delving into a world of aliens. They had figured out how to shoot squid ink at each other and the best way to inflate tiny puffer fish (by blowing into their mouths). That trick always made the boys giggle uncontrollably. And just the sight of a flounder with those bizarre eyes was worth the trip.

Maybe the best of all was what happened to all the leftovers. Inevitably, they were the makings of a massive pot of steaming gumbo they'd eat for days. So they donned their work gloves and dragged in the net time and again. As always, there were a multitude of brothers, sisters, and cousins to feed, and Mr. Walt's job, beyond slave driver, father, and friend, was provider.

Contrary to what white-collar snobs might expect, dragging a shrimp net behind a boat involved plenty of artistry. When the Styrofoam float tied to the back end of the net started to submerge, the boat was traveling at the proper speed. An experienced driver also kept an eye on the draglines to make sure the wooden doors were gliding through the water at the correct angle, keeping the mouth of the net open wide. Even if the speed was right, the net was spread symmetrically, and the tickler chain was gently bouncing along the bottom with absolute perfection, there was still one vital detail: You had to find the shrimp. And they didn't advertise.

Mr. Walt eased back on the throttle. "Okay boys, pull 'er in. Let's see what we've got."

The sun was settling low on the horizon, and nightfall was coming fast, a welcomed event that brought on more tolerable temperatures. Plus, they never knew what mysteries might be revealed under a dark, starry sky.

"You take the right side," Will said to Danny. "My arm hurts from all the net sewing."

"Okay," Danny said, always agreeable with his older cousin. He knew Will's arm was fine, but he didn't mind pulling the load, as long as it won him favor with Will.

Some said they were like brothers, but they were closer than that. Brothers, at least in the Thornton family, fought like wild dogs and tormented one another with fists, ropes, sharp-toed boots, and death stares. Danny and Will had their differences, but deep down they loved each other as much as a mother loved her child.

Trout wasn't a blood relative, but his family had an old cottage down the beach. As long as Danny could remember, Trout had been his best friend. Whenever Will was back home in Montgomery, Trout and Danny bonded even more. Friendship got more complicated in triplicate, but Danny made sure it worked out.

"Pull harder. You're getting behind," Will scolded. "We need to bring the doors in at the same time."

Danny tightened his grip but the rope slipped, burning across his palms. "I can't. I'm trying as hard as I can."

"Don't be a crybaby. Just pull."

A half a foot taller and considerably stronger, Will was barely breaking a sweat, while Danny gritted his teeth and tugged hand over hand. Mr. Walt eased off the throttle just enough for Danny to build his back muscles and some character.

"Come on, Danny," Mr. Walt said. "It's hard but it's fair."

Danny already knew pulling in the net was hard, but he wondered what was fair about it.

Mr. Walt cranked the wheel hard to starboard. "I see the doors. You boys bring the net around the motor. Watch that propeller! Don't drop it. Be careful. Will, help Danny with those doors. Okay, pull it in. Pull it *in*!"

Every muscle in Danny's back strained under the weight of the net and the tickler chain. With a grunt, he finally dragged the net over the railing, leaving the prize—the ball of shrimp and fish at the end of the net—for Will. *So much for fairness,* Danny thought.

Will caught sight of the net and slumped in disappointment. "Not much, Mr. Walt."

"Dump it in the bucket anyway, and let's see."

Will poured the meager catch into the twenty-gallon steel bucket. A few muddy sticks, a dozen or so shrimp, and a pile of jellyfish filled it up.

"Damn," Mr. Walt said. "Let's run down the bay a ways to that deep trough by Tarkiln Bayou. You boys get those shrimp and pull a few of those pinfish and croakers out. We might use 'em later."

They wanted to dump it all overboard, lose the shrimp, and save themselves from certain jellyfish torture, but Mr. Walt had put out an order, so they followed without question. As Trout reached for a shrimp, it jumped away, splattering tiny droplets of jellyfish venom into his face.

"Ouch," he yelled and fell backward. "It went in my eye."

Will chuckled. "Hey, goofball, once you grab it, you gotta close your eyes and pull it out quick."

"If you're so smart, you do it," Trout said. "My eye burns."

"I think you need the practice," Will said. "I'll just watch and give you advice."

"I need your advice like I need a poke in the eye," Trout snapped.

"Then you'd be blind in both eyes."

"I'll try," Danny volunteered as he pulled on his work gloves. "Will, can you shine the flashlight so I can see their eyes glow?"

"Got it," Will said. "I can handle this."

"Yeah, holding a flashlight is your kind of job," Trout said.

"Yep," Will said, unfazed. "And I'm good at it, too."

Mr. Walt already had the boat planed out and was focused on finding the elusive crustaceans while the boys tried to avoid too much jelly carnage. The fish and shrimp splashed around wildly, trying to figure out how they'd ended up in a galvanized bucket. Unfortunately for the boys, the brimming jellyfish soup sloshed on them, too.

Trout helped Danny dig into the slimy goop. The paltry total came to nine shrimp, hardly enough for a decent seafood platter. Their forearms burned, and they dared not rub their eyes or touch any part of their bodies. Even though they'd worn gloves, they'd learned to keep their hands off any exposed flesh or pay the price.

"I hope we get some shrimp on the next pull," Trout said. "I've had enough jellyfish stings for one day."

Danny leaned against the hull and stretched his back. "We will. I can feel it. Mr. Walt always finds 'em."

"Yeah, he does," Will agreed with a smile.

The motor throttled back quickly.

"Put her in, boys," Mr. Walt said. "Let's catch some shrimp."

Like seasoned commercial shrimpers, they moved in silent synchronicity, tying off the net, tossing the buoy, dropping the doors, and making sure the tickler chain was in place. For the next thirty minutes, they waited and hoped.

"Dump the bucket overboard when I turn," Mr. Walt said. "We don't want to pick those jellyfish back up."

Danny saw movement on the water as he dumped the bucket. "Dolphins!"

Trout rushed to the side. "I see four, no five. Wait! There are six, at least."

"Let's feed 'em," Will shouted while he collected a few stray fish that had fallen out of the bucket.

"Use those pinfish and croakers," Mr. Walt said. "That's why we saved 'em."

Pink light rimmed the horizon as the bay's surface faded into deep purple. Stars popped out in the eastern sky, and a fingernail moon hung overhead. Half a dozen dolphins cut a lazy path across the surface, nibbling on the fish the boys tossed out. They watched the show in awe, listening to a symphony of seagull squawks and the regular puff of air from the dolphins' blowholes.

"Whoa, look at that," Danny said. "They're glowing."

"Where?" Will and Trout yelled in unison as they sprang next to Danny.

"Look there." Danny pointed. "Under the boat. There goes one."

"Unreal!" Trout said. "It's like a comet."

Will tugged on Mr. Walt's shirttail. "Look, Mr. Walt, the phosphorus is out."

"It's so bright," Danny said. "Why is it lit up so much more tonight?"

"Well, boys, on a dark night like this," Mr. Walt explained, "the phosphorus seems to get really active. But you never know. It's one of God's mysteries. Sometimes the phosphorus glows, and sometimes it doesn't."

Growing up on the bay, they'd seen phosphorus many times before, but never as intense as that night.

"It's like a million lightning bugs," Danny said.

"Yep, same idea," Mr. Walt agreed. "Put your hand in the water and shake it around."

In a flash, the boys' hands were incandescent. They began drawing lines across the surface as if their fingers were sparklers.

"Try putting a fish in your hand and see what happens," Mr. Walt said.

All three boys scrambled around in the stern to find another fish. They'd already tossed out the ones they saved from the first haul. Trout spotted a tiny flounder stuck to the side of the hull. Holding it by the tail, he swished it in the water. In a few seconds, a white bottlenose bobbed up an inch from his hand. Wet, dark eyes looked directly at him. With that signature smile, the dolphin floated motionlessly, waiting for Trout to drop the fish.

"He probably won't take it from your hand, Trout," Mr. Walt said. "Just drop it."

The flounder was snatched from midair so fast it startled the boys. Then in a flash of phosphorescence, the dolphin disappeared.

"Whoa!" they all shouted.

For the next fifteen minutes, they found anything they could, even braved a couple of jellyfish tentacles, to attract the dolphins. Mr. Walt watched with admiration, knowing this was one of those experiences that would fertilize their Alabama roots—something he hoped they'd be able to share with their kids, too.

"Okay, enough playtime, boys. Let's pull in the net."

Trout stepped forward. He was due.

Will grabbed the bucket. "Let me move this out of your way," he said, leaving Danny to pull with Trout. "I'll pull in the next one." If luck was on his side, this haul would be big enough to take them in for the night. "Oh! And I'll hold the flashlight."

"Yeah, you're getting to be an expert at that," Trout said sarcastically.

"Watch it, butt face," Will said. "Somebody has to do it."

"You're the butt face, making us do all the work."

"I pulled it in last time so kiss my—"

"Okay, that's enough boys," Mr. Walt said. "Focus on getting the net in. You can fight like wild boars if you want when we get home, as long as I'm not around."

"Yes, sir!"

When Will's flashlight beam hit the net, they saw sweet success. As big around as a fifty-five-gallon drum, the ball of seafood they'd scraped off the bottom of the bay took all three of them to drag over the side. Hundreds of the tiny red eyes shined at them.

"Oh man, look at all those shrimp," Will said as they filled the bucket. "We hit the mother lode!"

"How much do you think we got, Mr. Walt?" Danny asked.

"Oh, I don't know. Looks like at least twenty-five, maybe thirty pounds. That ought to do it."

"*Yeeeeee-ha!*" Trout yelled. "We're gonna eat like kings!"

Mr. Walt cut the engine and tossed out the anchor. "Y'all put the net back out and let the current clean out the trash fish," he said.

A steady tide sucked the net behind the boat, washing away the pinfish, croakers, and baby crabs that hung in the webbing.

"I have an idea," Mr. Walt said. "How about a quick swim?"

The boys stared silently down at the dark water.

"Come on, boys. The water's warm, and if you open your eyes, the phosphorous will zoom by like you're flying through the stars."

"I'll go if you go, Daddy," Danny said, his voice shaking.

"All right. How about it, Will? Trout? Y'all in?"

"Okay."

As they dived in, hundreds of tiny lights swept over their corneas. Just like Mr. Walt said, they were flying through outer space passing stars at warp speed.

"Will, look at this," Danny said as he stirred the water with his hands and feet until they glowed.

"Cool!" Will said.

In a flash of light, a dolphin streaked under them and shot out of the water like a Roman candle. They cheered wildly as he splashed down in a spray of luminescence. Even Mr. Walt let out a hoot. Their bodies tingled in wonder.

Will floated on his back and looked up at the stars. The Milky Way arched over them in a blaze of light. *Folks who don't believe in God have never seen anything like this*, he thought.

Mr. Walt shook Will out of his dreaminess. "Where's Trout?"

"He was picking fish out of the net," Danny said.

"I told you boys to stay away from that net!"

Danny and Will swam to the back of the boat but couldn't find their friend.

"Trout!" they screamed.

Then Danny noticed the net jerking violently.

"Daddy, he's in the net!"

"Get in the boat, and pull the net in," Mr. Walt yelled as he dived under.

When Mr. Walt got to him, Trout wasn't moving. The last few bubbles of air had spilled from his lungs. Mr. Walt grabbed a wad of Trout's pants and, in one motion, tossed the boy into the boat. Danny and Will pulled in the rest of the net and saw the tickler chain wrapped around Trout's cutoffs. He'd fought hard enough to almost rip his pants off. But *almost* didn't count underwater.

Even in the darkness, he looked ashen. Mr. Walt knew how quickly the sea could take someone. He'd seen it happen. With calculated swiftness, he turned Trout on his side and pounded on his back. Then he shoved his fist into Trout's stomach. The seconds ticked off agonizingly slow as Trout's body lay limp at the bottom of the boat. Three more whacks on the back, and another solid punch in the gut. Like a fire hose, Trout threw up what seemed like twenty gallons of water. Then he gasped and threw up again.

"Danny, keep Trout on his side," Mr. Walt said. "We have to get him to Doc Jordon."

Mr. Walt jerked the anchor off the bottom and into the boat with two yanks. Mud from the flukes splattered all over the bow, but no one noticed. They were headed home at full throttle. At least Trout was semiconscious and breathing, but Mr. Walt had seen people lapse back into darkness. He was determined this was not going to be one of those times.

Will sat next to Trout and rubbed the hair out of his face. His forehead was clammy, and he could only force shallow breaths.

"It's okay, Trout," Will said. "You're gonna be fine. I know it for certain. Anyway, you're the toughest kid I know. Tougher than galvanized nails. And I'm really sorry I called you a butt face."

Trout's eyes twitched toward Will. There was a blackness Will had never seen in his young life.

CHAPTER 3

Doc Jordon Works Magic

There's not much a good shot in the backside won't cure.
—Dr. Josephine Jordon

Danny and Will sprinted along the beach to Doc Jordon's house, three lots down from the pier. Mr. Walt was close behind carrying the limp boy in his arms. Trout was ghostly pale. Always at the ready with her little black bag, Doc Jordon had a thriving practice in Montgomery but spent summers at the beach. Her vacation was interrupted regularly by barnacle scrapes, fish hooks, and rusty nails. Tetanus shots were a regular event along with a few stitches here and there. Her services were always free but rendered with a stern warning not to be such a fool and to be more careful next time.

As usual, Dr. Josephine Jordon, Miss Kitty, and a few neighbors were relaxing in rocking chairs on the front porch, sharing stories enhanced by a blend of gin, tonic, and fresh lemons. They'd heard the boat screaming into shore, then the boys yelling as they ran along the beach. By the time Mr. Walt bounded up the steps, Doc Jordon was waiting and wondering what cure needed to be rendered this time.

"What in the hell happened here," she said. "What damn fool thing did you boys do this time?"

They were accustomed to her accusatory tone. She was the only woman they knew who regularly cussed like a tugboat captain.

"Trout got hung up in the shrimp net," Mr. Walt said. "We were taking a dip and he got back where he shouldn't have."

"Somebody get the green oxygen bottle out of my closet," Doc Jordon said. "And make it fast."

She pulled out a needle and gave Trout a horrific shot in the butt. It didn't matter what the ailment, she always managed to work in a shot as part of the treatment. As they grew, the boys suspected she just liked sticking people. They could have had an extra large pimple and somehow she'd figure a shot into the healing process.

But Trout was bad off. Foam had started oozing from the side of his mouth and she clamped the oxygen mask on tight.

"One of you fools get me some damn bourbon," she demanded. "And hurry up with it. This boy needs help."

With the oxygen flowing strong, she raised his arms above his head a few times then passed that job off to Will.

"Keep that up just like I've been doing it," she said. "And pay attention, damn it."

Will pumped Trout's arms while Doc eased the boy to a sitting position. In one rapid motion, she yanked off the oxygen mask and poured a shot of bourbon down his gullet. At first Trout gagged, then he hacked hard for close to a half a minute. Doc slapped the mask back on him just before he took a gargantuan breath.

She pinched his cheeks so hard they turned purple. "Keep up that deep breathing Trout. Oxygen is just what you need. And we like seeing your pug face around here so don't let me down."

She poured another shot and handed to Mr. Walt.

"You probably need this as much as he does," she said. "Don't beat yourself up. These boys know to stay away from a shrimp net."

Mr. Walt threw the liquor back.

"Is he gonna be okay," he asked. "I mean really?"

"Sure, he's a tough kid. He'll be as good as new by tomorrow. Danny, you and Will go over to the Loxley's house and get Trout's mama. Tell her I'm keeping the boy here tonight."

Will and Danny stood by Trout like cypress stumps.

"Well, what are you waiting for," she said sternly. "Get the hell over there and get Trout's mama!"

By the time the screen door slammed, they were halfway down the driveway, bare feet kicking up a trail of dust. Doc Jordon held Trout's eyelids open wide and shined her flashlight into his pupils. She whacked his knees with a reflex hammer and took his pulse and blood pressure. If she'd been back in Montgomery, she'd be on the way to the hospital but the closest one was in Mobile, at least two hours away.

That's if the roads were all clear, they didn't have a flat tire and the car didn't break down. If he didn't improve by morning, they'd make the journey to Mobile at first light.

Doc Jordon waived Mr. Walt and Miss Kitty toward the front porch. "Trout, you keep sucking in that oxygen and try to relax," she said. "I'll be right back."

"He might have some damage," she said. "Too early to tell."

Mr. Walt dropped his chin to his chest. "Should we take him to Mobile?"

"It's too risky right now," she said. "I'll keep an eye on him tonight but if we need to go tomorrow we'll need to borrow Carlton's Lincoln Continental. It's the only car I know with air conditioning."

"I'll go see Carlton in a few minutes," Mr. Walt said. "You think a good night's sleep will help the boy?"

"Maybe, but we're going to have to watch him all night. He could go into a coma if that oxygen doesn't do the trick."

"I can stay with him," Mr. Walt said. "And I'm sure his mama will stay, too."

"No," Miss Kitty whispered kindly, "Honey, you go see Carlton then go home and get some rest. Doc and I will stay here with Trout."

Mr. Walt was seldom wrong, but in this case he'd misjudged Trout's mother to a significant degree. The boys had been back for an hour before Mrs. Lottie Loxley burst in stone faced and angry. A look of disgust spread across her face as she stood over Trout.

"Well this beats all," she finally said. "How long do you think he'll be laid up?"

"It's hard to say," Doc Jordon said. "He might be feeling okay tomorrow or it might be a week or God only knows."

"A week! It better not be a week. He'll be so far behind on his chores he'll never catch up. I never should have let him go shrimping. Well, I'll come back in the morning to collect him."

And just like that, she stormed off. Fortunately, Trout was too groggy to understand what was going on. But Danny and Will, and the rest of the folks at Doc Jordon's place, didn't breathe until she disappeared down the driveway.

"Poor Trout," Danny said. "He might be better off staying hurt for a while. If he wakes up too soon, she might just work him to death."

"Yeah," Will said. "It's like Mr. Walt said, she must have ice water running through her veins."

As Lottie Loxley strode down the tree-lined dirt road, hidden by the darkness of night, tears streamed silently down her cheeks. With her head bowed and her hands clinched tightly, she prayed that God would protect her baby boy.

CHAPTER 4

Change of Heart

God might make you well but I'm the one who gets paid.
—Dr. Josephine Jordon

They put Trout under a ceiling fan on the porch to keep him cool. Danny asked Doc Jordon if he could pull his bed next to Trout's so he could check on him from time to time during the night. She said that would be fine even though she knew Danny wouldn't wake up until he smelled bacon frying in the morning. As usual, those boys were worn out from a long day of swimming, shrimping, and this time, worrying. Will slid the head of his bed close, too. But his motivation was more about catching the breeze of the fan. Getting to sleep on a still, humid Alabama night was downright sticky and painful. A little air movement and the mesmerizing *whup, whup, whup* of the blades spinning cut the heat to a tolerable level.

"Danny, wake up," Trout said as he shook his arm.

The morning sun brushed across Danny's eyelids but he didn't move.

"What are you doing?" Will asked. "You can't wake Danny up like that."

"Oh yeah," Trout said. "I forgot."

Danny didn't just sleep, he got lost in his dreams. The boys could jump on his bed and sing *You Are My Sunshine* at the top of their lungs and Danny wouldn't move. They could punch him in the arm or pinch his nostrils shut and somehow he'd keep on snoozing. Way back when they were six or seven, Will somehow figured out the only way to wake Danny up was to blow into his ear. That did it. That or the smell of bacon frying.

Will had perfected the wake up puff. He could shoot a stream of air into Danny's ear canal from almost a foot away. He slid from his covers, blew a wisp into Danny's ear, and watched his cousin's eyes pop open.

"Hi y'all," Danny said. "Trout, you okay, buddy?"

"I think so. At least I don't think I'm dead but I'm really, really hungry."

"You're always hungry," Will said. "That's gotta be a good sign."

"Yep," Danny agreed.

They scrounged around Doc Jordon's kitchen and found some biscuits, butter, jelly, and milk. In the time it took Will and Danny to eat two biscuits, Trout gobbled up four, all of which were covered in a mountain of jelly. As he swallowed the last bite, Trout's face went blank. He jumped up, ran across the kitchen, and flung open the screen door.

Doc Jordon heard Trout's heaving guts and came quickly. "What in the devil's name is going on out here?"

Will ducked his head and looked down at the floor. "Uh, we just had some biscuits and stuff."

"And then he started throwing up," Danny said.

"Well, his system is messed up," she said. "He had all that salt water in his belly. Trout, when you feel like you're finished fertilizing my bushes, come in here and let me take a look at you."

Doc Jordon took his pulse and blood pressure and shined her light into his pupils.

"Looks like to me you're as right as rain, as long as you don't eat like a starving dog," she said. "Trout, drink plenty of water today— fresh water, that is. But remember, don't eat too much."

"Okay, I'll try."

"And one more thing," she said with a quirky smile. "No hard work. I'll tell your mama to keep you in bed today."

"Thanks, Doc Jordon," Trout said.

The boys sauntered as slowly as they could to Trout's house. Normally it was a short walk, but Trout had to stop twice to rest. He leaned against a pine tree and rubbed his belly.

"I'm still feeling pretty icky," he said. "And I'll bet Mama's mad."

Danny and Will glanced at each other. "Naw," Will said. "She'll probably understand."

"Ya think so?"

"Maybe yes, maybe no," Danny said.

As they rounded the big oak tree at the corner of Trout's yard, they could see Trout's mama standing on the front porch with her arms folded, her hair pulled back, and her sleeves rolled up. She was holding a broom.

"Get on in here, Trout," she commanded.

Danny looked up at the imposing woman and gathered as much resolve as he could muster. "Uh, Miss Lottie ..." he said.

"Yes, what is it boy? Speak up."

"Well, it's like this. Doc Jordon said Trout needed to rest today. You know, no chores and stuff like that."

Lottie Loxley stared down at the boys with a suspicious scowl. The woman came from dirt poor farm stock. Standing nearly six feet tall and with massive calloused hands that could crush six pecans at a time, she made kids quiver like Jell-O. But Danny's deep friendship gave him strength, especially because he was speaking the truth.

"Oh she did, did she?"

"Yes, ma'am. And she said for him to drink lots of water and uh, did I mention no chores."

"Yes Danny, you did."

"It's true," Will said, "Trout's still not right. We had to stop three or four times on the way over here for him to rest."

She pointed the bristles of her huge broom at them. "Well I'll talk to Doc Jordon about it and you boys better be telling the truth. Now go on. Skedaddle on home."

Danny and Will turned and ran as Trout crawled up the stairs. When he reached his mother's shins, he collapsed on the floor like an old hound dog wondering what fate awaited him.

"Trout," she said, "If you could walk home, I figure you can do some chores. I've been working my fingers to the bone this morning. I've got to splash some water in my face and clean up. Have the rake ready when I get back."

Trout didn't move until she had disappeared into the bathroom. He noticed that the fishing poles were gone and his no account brothers were all gone. Without thinking about what Doc Jordon said, he rummaged in the kitchen and scarfed down four pieces of fatty bacon his brothers had left on the counter. Then he remembered the water, so he drank two huge glasses full. As his mother came around the kitchen counter, Trout was spewing water and bacon into the sink.

"Oh my word," she screamed as she ran too him. "My baby!"

Perhaps it was an instinctual act of survival or Trout might have clearly understood his moment of opportunity. Either way, he slid down the face of the cabinet door and flopped on the floor.

She scooped him up and laid him in the bed.

"Trout, I'll get you a wet towel," she said, clearly shaken by the turn of events. "Don't move a muscle."

In Trout's mind, no kinder words had ever been spoken. After she'd wiped his face gently, she pulled back the covers and helped him crawl into the sheets.

"Rest now," she said softly.

He watched as she trotted to the front porch, her eagle eyes scanning the front yard. Soon enough she spotted Trout's oldest brother at the water's edge casting for fish.

"Willie!" she screamed as loud as he'd ever heard. "Git up here! Right now!"

Willie dropped his pole and sprinted to the house. "What is it, Mama? Is somebody hurt?"

"Yes, your brother is in a bad way. So, it's time for you to stop fishing and start working. There's trash that needs burning and garbage that needs burying. Go find the shovel."

"But Mama … those are Trout's chores. I was fishing and …"

She raised her hand in his face. "You can put a plug in it right there, son. Trout's resting, and there's work to do. That's final. Now get that shovel."

Her words drifted across Trout's young ears like sweet music. His pillow had never felt as soft as it did now. And his mind was crystal clear. With a grand smile across his face, Trout rolled over, closed his eyes, and figured he'd ride this train until the tracks ran out.

CHAPTER 5

The Contest

If you don't win, you lose.
—Mr. Walter Thornton

L unch at the Thornton cottage was as much of a social event as it was about filling their bellies with fried bluefish, black-eyed peas, sweet corn, and fresh buttermilk biscuits. Kids were allowed to wear bathing suits at the dinner table because, well, that's all they had. Their entire wardrobe for the summer consisted of a couple of swim-suits and three or four t-shirts. Even though bare feet and dripping wet bathing suits were acceptable attire at meals, they had to wear shirts—no matter how dirty—because that was the proper thing to do. Some of Mr. Walt and Miss Kitty's rules were weird even though their intent was honorable.

With more than a dozen family members seated at the table and at least ten conversations going simultaneously, Mr. Walt picked up his teaspoon and tapped the side of his glass. All eyes turned his way as the thunderous chatter quieted to the muffled sound of heavy chewing.

After he removed his reading glasses from his pocket, Mr. Walt un-folded an official looking sheet of paper. "The Mobile Country Club is hosting a swimming and diving competition during Labor Day Week-end," he read. "Trophies and cash prizes will be awarded to the win-ners."

Danny's eyes lit up. "How much can we win daddy?"

"Says here first prize is fifty dollars."

The kids erupted in wild hoots until Mr. Walt's firm spoon quelled the noise.

"There's a five dollar entry fee for each event," he said. "So if you don't win, you lose."

Danny was undeterred. "I'm not gonna lose. How do we enter?"

"Well now, that's the thing. We're not members of the Country Club but Carlton Lyons is. In fact, he gave me this letter. He's invited anyone interested in the contest to come to the swimming hole and try out. If he thinks you're good enough, he'll sign you up. "

"I'm gonna do it!" Danny said. "I'll spend five to win fifty anytime."

Will slapped him on the back. "Don't be so sure, cuz. Some of those country-club goobers are pretty good."

"Not as good as us."

"Sure they are. They have big ritzy swimming pools and fiberglass diving boards that spring them way up in the air. The only diving board we have is made out of old planks of wood."

"That means we'll do better on their fancy diving board."

Will shook his head. "Maybe so, maybe not, but I wouldn't be spending that fifty bucks until you win it. Anyway, I'd rather keep five dollars in my pocket than go to their stupid competition."

"Come on. At least you can try out," Danny said.

"I'll try out but even if Mr. Lyons says I'm good enough, I'm not going to Mobile. I hate country clubs."

"Then you can come and watch me win."

"We'll see."

Mr. Walt cleared his throat to continue. "One more thing, Carlton says he'll pay the five dollar entry fee to anyone twelve-years-old or under who can perform a one-and-a-half at the tryouts. So, I guess that means Danny and Will. He'll pay another five dollars for a gainer."

"A gainer?" Danny said. "That's impossible."

"Only if you think so," Mr. Walt said.

CHAPTER 6

Naked as a Tree

I think I broke my butt.
—Trout Loxley

That afternoon Will and Danny hid in the bushes under Trout's bedroom window. He was propped up on three pillows and his mama was spoon-feeding him chicken soup. Danny was anxious to tell him about the big contest at the Mobile Country Club.

"Man oh man," Will said, "Trout's never had it so good."

"Well, he did almost drown, ya know."

"Yeah, I guess so. But he's living in hog heaven—for now."

Trout heard them rustling through the leaves and saw Danny swatting at a wasp.

"Hey y'all. How's it going?"

"You boys come on in," his mother said sweetly. "Trout's doing much better."

"That's great," Will said. "Miss Lottie, we were wondering if we could take him for a short boat ride."

Trout's eyes lit up like two lightning bugs.

"I don't think he's up to it boys. He doesn't need to exert himself. Right now he needs rest more than anything."

"But he won't even break a sweat Mrs. Loxley. We'll carry him down to the boat," Danny said. "See, it's right down at your pier. And he'll just be sitting and riding. That won't take any energy. Then we'll bring him back all rested up."

Trout shined his biggest puppy dog eyes at her.

"*Please, Mama.* I promise I'll take it easy."

26

"Well, okay. But you boys be back well before dinner. Take a jug of water, and be sure Trout drinks a lot."

"Yes, ma'am."

Will carried Trout on his back while Danny pull-started the Johnson Seahorse engine. As *Greenie* skimmed over the smooth surface of Soldier Creek, the wind blowing across their young smiling faces, Trout felt a rare kind of freedom. Normally he'd be struggling with yard tools and sweating like a dog. But now, somehow, his shrimping misfortune had blessed him.

Upper Soldier Creek was actually more river than creek, about as wide as a blacktop county highway, and plenty deep to dive into from tall tree limbs. It meandered through thick stands of pine, cedar, and cypress trees that lined the edges and gave shade to garfish, mullet, bass, speckled trout, and the occasional gator. Snakes were plenty happy up there too but the sound of motorboats and kids laughing like crazed hyenas scared most of the wildlife away, including the snakes and gators. Osprey patrolled the skies and regularly swooped down to snatch up unsuspecting mullet, fish that were so dumb, even other fish didn't associate with them. This was especially insulting to the meager mullet because fish, as a whole, had brains smaller than a butter bean, according to Mr. Walt. Of course, many a fisherman would disagree with that notion considering they spent small fortunes on boats, poles, lines, lures, bait, live wells, and a multitude of instruments to outsmart the bean brains. Even with all of that effort, many a fisherman got skunked, usually because they didn't think like a fish. When and if they finally did hook one, the cost per fish was ten times what they would have spent at the fish market. And those were already cleaned and ready to cook. But that's altogether another story because the only thing the boys were fishing for was adventure.

In addition to an abundance of nature provided generously by the Almighty, Soldier Creek had one legendary feature that required man-made tools, nails, and boards. It was simply known as "The Tree." At least a hundred years old, The Tree leaned over the creek at a 45-degree angle, a perfect slant for hanging a rope swing. The smooth bark of the big cedar tree was easy on bare feet but its prickly greenery easily cut deep enough to draw blood.

The prior summer, Mr. Carlton Lyons had filled his fancy Chris Craft cabin cruiser with twelve kids, a forty-foot long, three-inch thick tugboat rope and some hammers for nailing up ladder boards. Within an hour, they'd nailed boards up the trunk and had tied the rope in place. Mr. Lyons even remembered to bring an old handsaw to whack off any limbs that obstructed the path of the swinging rope. Nothing smelled sweeter than fresh-cut cedar, which is why fancy closets and saunas are lined with the reddish wood. The boys could never have imagined it, but knowing about the cedar aroma/sauna relationship would play a major role in their lives many years later. For now, all they cared about was a thrill ride on a rope swing and a cool dip into the spring-fed waters of Soldier Creek.

They had a bounty of swinging and dismounting combinations and practiced them religiously. A low, large limb that jutted out of the side of The Tree was their launch platform. Like seasoned trapeze artists they'd pull back on the rope, hop onto the large knot and sail through the thick summer air. To warm up, they'd do simple stuff, like swinging out as far as possible and just pushing away from the rope for a feet-first splash down. There was nothing wrong with that. Plenty of rookies did it that way. But inventiveness sharpened every adventure and Lord knows they liked to push those edges. Their most common trick was a back-flip dismount. As if spinning blindly backward in midair was not enough, they were never sure if they were going to land in the water or in the branches of the giant crepe myrtle on the other side of the creek. Fortunately, the bush hung well out over the water so scraping it, or even punching right through it, was okay, save the scratches and cackles from everyone watching. Of course, going too far and smacking into the muddy creek bank was considered bad form.

Standing on the knot and doing a back flip was a harder stunt so naturally, in their minds, it was loads more fun. The absolute most challenging routine was the standing back dive because flying through the air upside down threw their balance off kilter. They not only had to worry about flying headfirst into that stupid spider-web-filled bush but the possibility of a belly flop or back buster haunted them.

The really crazy maneuvers involved multiple riders. One person would swing out and come back far enough for the second person to hop on and sit in the opposite direction. When it came back the second time with far less height, like a pendulum in a Grandfather clock that needed winding, the third person would have to do a full-on frog leap just to latch on. Misses, followed by embarrassing face-first splashdowns, were common. If they pulled off the tricky three-boy hook up, just for the sake of showing off, they'd do well-timed, one-two-three back flip dismount. Eventually the boys perfected the maneuver and regularly performed it for folks who came along on family boat rides, picnics, or some tree swinging of their own.

On the way to The Tree Danny filled Trout in on the diving contest in Mobile and the five dollars Mr. Lyons was offering. Part of their reasoning for going to The Tree, in addition to swinging on the rope and swimming in the cool spring water, was to see if they could do a gainer or a one-and-a-half from a high limb.

"Okay boys, let's have our own diving contest," Danny said. "First one to do a one-and-a-half wins."

"Wins what?" Will asked.

"Uh, I guess wins means being able to say you were first."

"Okay, and then we'll show Mr. Lyons and see if he'll pay us those five buckaroos."

Trout back flipped off a limb. "I'm in," he yelled as he flew through the air.

"Me too," Danny said.

Will scampered to a limb ten feet above the water. "Here goes," he said as he sprung off the limb, balled up, spun, and opened just in time to land flat on his face.

Trout let out a hoot from the water's edge. "That was uglier than a catfish's face," he said. "I'll show you how it's done."

"Me first," Danny said as he stepped onto a lower limb.

With a grunt, he threw himself forward but freaked out in mid turn. His arms and legs flailed as Danny landed on his back with a loud crack. Trout's crash was equally impressive. The water slapped his belly so hard that his zipper blew apart.

"Crap," Trout shouted. "I guess I don't need these pants anymore. I'll have to go naked."

Trout pulled off his pants and underwear and tossed them toward the embankment.

"Guys," Trout said. "I'm gonna practice another time and just go skinny-dipping right now."

Danny was still rubbing the sting on his back. "Good idea," he quickly agreed.

The tingling in Will's cheeks had barely worn off, and although he didn't want Trout and Danny to know it, he was glad to postpone their contest to another day. "Aw, y'all are a couple of sissies, but I'll go along 'cause I'm a nice guy."

"Nice guy with a beet-red face." Trout said.

Will wasn't listening. He'd already stripped and was scampering up The Tree as naked as a squirrel. "I'm gonna jump from the top," he giggled.

"Wait a minute, Will," Trout said. "Let's do a triple nekked jump from the top."

"Yeah!" Danny screamed. "Let's do it."

From the tiptop of The Tree, Will and Danny tossed their cutoffs into the creek next to Trout's. Will directed traffic. "Trout, you jump that way. I'll jump over there, and Danny, you jump toward the bush. Ready? One, two, three … *jump!*"

They flew through the air without a care in the world. Then they landed.

Will yelled first. "Ouch. I cracked my nuts!"

"It feels like Mr. Walt smacked my butt with a hickory branch," Danny said.

Trout rolled over in the water and moaned. "I think I broke my butt. And I'm pretty sure I just got an enema. That's gonna be *bad*."

The boys learned three lessons that day they carried with them for life. First and foremost, always cover their private parts in any kind of collision, even with water. Second, water was plenty soft when they were swimming, but it would slap their butts like a barber strap when it was flat calm. Third, cutoffs don't float.

Danny swam in three circles under The Tree. "Hey, Will, Trout, do y'all see my pants?"

"No," Will said. "Mine are gone, too."

"Mine, too," Trout said.

For at least half an hour, the boys dove into the dark tannic waters but came up empty-handed. The closest thing to extra clothes they had in *Greenie* was a few bulky orange life jackets.

As they sat naked in the skiff with sore privates, bruised egos, and at least one possible enema, they contemplated their situation. They were up the creek *with* a paddle, but not much else. Will didn't much care if folks saw him nude. He was proud of his body. But a sense of fear filled Danny. His privates weren't for public viewing. And poor

Trout agonized over his eventual confrontation with his mother. He was supposed to be taking it easy. That afternoon had begun with such promise. Now his future looked grim.

CHAPTER 7

Bees and Tees

A bad idea with good intentions is better than a good idea with bad intentions.

—Walt Thornton

"I've got it!" Trout said.

"Got what?" asked Danny.

"Tommy Lyons's sailboat."

"What about it?"

"It's anchored in the creek!"

"So?"

Trout smiled in satisfaction at his brilliance. "So, I'll bet we can find some clothes in the cabin."

Will looked perplexed. "Yeah, but where's Tommy?"

"He's been gone for like a month to England I think … to see some family castle or something goofy like that."

"Maybe he's gonna moon the queen," Danny giggled.

"Yeah and then steal her crown jewels," Will laughed.

"Whatever," Trout said, still focused on his unfortunate nudity. "But we can just borrow some of his clothes and get 'em back without anybody knowing the difference."

"Won't they be kinda big?" Danny wondered.

"*His* clothes will be," Trout said, "but he might have some kid's clothes, too."

"Okay, Trout. It sounds like a good plan to me," Will said, approving the burglary scheme and cranking up the throttle to full speed.

While Upper Soldier Creek was narrow, the lower part opened into a series of elongated bayous large enough for water skiing, sunfish sailing, or just good old-fashioned boat racing. Fast traffic played in the boys' favor that day; their nakedness was more of a blur. In fact, no one even noticed. From a distance, they looked liked they always did: shirtless, tanned, and bleached hair blowing in the wind. Just to play it safe, Will hugged the shoreline, and they draped life jackets across their laps.

Within minutes, they'd safely made it to Tommy Lyons's sailboat. Will maneuvered the skiff as inconspicuously as possible, hoping to avoid any eyes on land that might happen to be watching. Ya never knew. During summer afternoons, most of the beach cottages were filled with folks lounging in rocking chairs on the porch, enjoying the breeze, staring out at the natural beauty around them, and keeping one eye trained for a dolphin jumping or, even better, a humongous water-skiing tumble.

"I'll jump into the cabin real quick and look around," Trout said.

With cat-like quickness, he hopped on board, slid the hatch cover open, and disappeared down the companionway into the cabin. The clandestine mission was progressing well. Danny and Will kept a keen lookout for any approaching boats. The coast was clear.

Suddenly, from within the bowels of the cabin, an ear-splitting squeal erupted. Judging from the horrendous screech, Will and Danny figured Trout had seen a snake or a real-live ghost. The cavernous boat hull had a megaphone effect and Trout's agonizing shriek turned heads of everyone along the surrounding shoreline. A split-second later young Trout shot out of the cabin with a horde of wasps attached to his butt cheeks. A swarm of their friends followed close behind. Danny and Will flipped over the gunnel and into the water faster than terrified otters and held their breath until they turned blue. Trout splashed down and disappeared.

From land the wasps were, of course, too small to see. Observers watched with mild curiosity as a totally nude twelve-year-old boy slapped violently at his backside as he took a screaming leap from the stern of Tommy Lyons's sailboat in broad daylight. For reasons they didn't understand, an orange t-shirt was flying from his outstretched hand. Every so often, they'd see a torrent of hand splashing, and then a boy's head would pop up for an instant and go back under just as quickly. This strange behavior continued for quite a while, much to the puzzlement of witnesses. Everyone watching the show recognized

33

Greenie as it drifted slowly away from the sailboat. They were all too familiar with the mischievousness of the boys. Most of the time folks brushed off their antics as harmless childhood foolishness. But skinny-dipping during daylight hours was pushing the edge.

Danny, Will, and Trout weren't concerned with dress codes. Near panic, they figured on getting away from that sailboat as fast as possible. With their hands on the bottom of the skiff, they swam it toward shore, all the while looking back and forth at each other through underwater bug eyes. Trout's expression was clearly one of misery, but to his credit, he still did his part pushing the boat. Their collective fear, even though they couldn't speak very well underwater, was whether the bees had gone back to the sailboat or were following them.

Through a series of hand signals and semi-intelligible gurgles, Will convinced Danny to stick his hand up through the surface to test the danger level. With some trepidation, Danny poked a finger into the air. His hand, forearm, and eventually his head followed. All appeared safe, but there was still one small problem. All they had for privacy was one sorry wet T-shirt.

They were smart enough to push the boat away from the beach cottages and into Sawgrass Cove where there was nothing but an old ramshackle boathouse. The small slew, they always feared, was full of snakes and gators, even though they'd never actually seen any. At that point, fighting off real or imagined wild reptiles was worth the price.

"Let's just tuck in behind the boathouse," Will directed, "and climb onto the pier."

"How's your backside, Trout?" Danny asked. "That was a real sight seeing all those bees hooked onto your moon pies."

"Well, I'm glad y'all enjoyed watching me get stung!" Trout said. "I must have had twenty bees on me, and it still hurts like the dickens. Maybe y'all should check it out and see if the stingers are still in there."

Will's face twisted in disgust. "Check what out?"

"My backside."

"Why would we do that?" Will asked.

"Like I said," Trout insisted, "to see if the stingers are in there. Maybe you can pull 'em out."

"We'll look at your cheeks," Danny said, "but I'm not touching anything on your bony butt. That's just too gross."

Trout climbed up on the pier inside the boathouse and stretched out on his tummy while Will and Danny stayed in the water. A look of fear had spread across their faces.

"Well come on," Trout said. "I'm ready."

"Maybe we're not," Will said.

Danny eased onto the pier and examined the welts covering both cheeks from three steps away. "Don't see anything but a bunch of puffy red sting marks. If there's any stingers in there, I can't see 'em. And I sure can't pull out what I can't see."

"No kidding Albert Einstein," Trout said sarcastically.

"Well I can't! That's all I'm saying, Trout."

Will had no intention of playing butt doctor. He slipped into *Greenie* and stretched out on the seat to soak up some sun.

"Why don't you come closer so you can tell me how many stings I got?"

"Let's see," Danny said. "One, two, three, four, uh … is that one?"

"Where?"

"That one kinda by your right leg. Uh, did you have any other red spots back there besides bee stings? Any pimples and stuff?"

"Heck I don't know. I don't look at my butt everyday. Just count 'em!"

"Okay, uh, sixteen, seventeen, eighteen. I get eighteen. Nineteen if you count that zitty-looking thingy."

"That's a bee sting!"

"Doesn't look like a bee sting."

"Well maybe it was a small wasp."

"Maybe, but I don't think so."

"Okay. That's enough looking at my butt anyway. Thanks, I guess."

"You're welcome. It's not a pretty thing to stare at, I'll tell you that."

"Oh-KAY!" Trout snapped. "I can't help it if I got stung. At least I tried to get us some clothes."

Will lifted his head and glanced at Trout. "Yeah, you tried."

"I'd like to see you do better."

"Next time I will."

"Why don't you shut up, Will."

Danny spoke up to avoid a showdown. "So Trout, where were the bees anyway?"

"Well, when I got down inside the cabin everything was fine. I saw a stack of t-shirts and I grabbed that orange one. Then I opened up a cabinet, and all of a sudden I was staring at this huge wasp nest on the backside of that door. There must have been fifty of 'em. All at once they flew at me, and I turned tail and ran as fast as I could."

"But not fast enough," Will grinned.

"That's right smart mouth. I'm sure you could outrun a swarm of angry bees."

"Well I am pretty fast."

"Not that fast. The first one stung me before I even turned around to run."

"Maybe you shoulda fought 'em off," Will said. "You know, swatted at them."

"I did but there were too many. If you'd have been there, you'd have run, too."

"Maybe," Will said. Being confident and cocky was part of his nature and riling Trout up entertained him.

"I guess that's some more bad luck y'all." Danny said. "What are we gonna do now?"

"I know what I'm doing," Trout said. "I'm going to wear this t-shirt, sneak home and slip back into bed."

"What about us?" Will asked.

"You've got the boat. You can find something in somebody's boathouse or something. I'm going to slip through the woods and go home. I think I've had enough fun for one day."

"Okay, good luck Trout," Danny said. "We'll check on you later."

And with that, Trout disappeared into the oaks and pines with the orange t-shirt fashioned around him like a diaper.

He was right; they did have their boat. And, *Greenie* was more than mere transportation. She was a family member. Like most of their possessions, from shoes and winter jackets to bicycles and books, *Greenie* had been passed down from a throng of brothers and cousins.

In her prime *Greenie* was a fine wooden boat, one of the best built at the time. Mr. Walt caught many a Spanish mackerel, king mackerel, bluefish and shrimp from that boat. But time and pounding waves eventually get the best of wooden boats, no matter how strong the ribs or how many bronze screws you use for reinforcement.

By the time the boy's turn came to take care of *Greenie* she was missing a third of her ribs and another third were cracked. They patched many a hole but she still leaked shamelessly. Every morning around seven o'clock Will and Danny waded out to *Greenie* where she was tied to a piling. For the next twenty minutes, they bailed her out. During the day, they could simply drain the water that seeped in by going fast enough and pulling the plug. But overnight, she took on at least six inches and the weight of that had to be bailed. To Will and Danny, scooping out a little water everyday was well worth the reward. Mr. Walt and the rest of the adults hoped it was building character. The leaks, cracked ribs, and protruding screws didn't bother the boys in the least. *Greenie* was their escape and as long as the motor ran and the gas didn't run out, their adventures blossomed.

CHAPTER 8

Sneaking In

I'd rather be lucky than good.
—Trout Loxley

Trout emerged from the woods and hid behind a giant live oak at the edge of his yard. Getting into the house and sliding into the sheets undetected was going to be tricky with his eagle-eyed mother on the prowl. Plus any or all of his brothers could be slugged out on the couch waiting to be startled. Surveying the yard, he was happy to notice his two oldest brothers fishing on the dock.

He tiptoed across the pine straw and fallen piles of Spanish moss. The occasional crackle of dried oak leaves under his feet sounded like a siren to him but no one stirred. At the house, he peeked into his mother's bedroom window. Bingo! She was napping. But even from a dead sleep, she could hear a mosquito landing on a marshmallow.

Instead of opening the squeaky screen door, he decided to slither through the hole in the screen where a raccoon had chewed through two days earlier. The coon had made it to the kitchen counter and had already munched down three oatmeal raisin cookies when Trout's older brother had seen it, grabbed his shotgun, and blasted the animal to kingdom come, or, to be more precise, to the refrigerator door. Why his brother hadn't waited until the coon ran onto the porch was a question Trout asked himself over and over as he cleaned coon guts and fur off the fridge.

If Trout hadn't been laid up from his near-drowning accident, fixing the screen would have been at the top of his list of chores. Fortunately, none of his brothers was skilled enough to do the job without making it look as if a drunken monkey had gotten a hold of power tools.

The coon was a big daddy, but Trout still had to rip the screen slightly to fit through the hole. Once inside, he literally slid on his belly across the porch and into the bedroom he shared with two brothers. Finally hidden from his mother's view, he stood up, turned on the fan, and jumped into bed, right after he put on some clean underwear and hid the wet T-shirt under his bed.

"I didn't even hear you come in," his mother said just seconds after his head hit the pillow. "I must have been sleeping like a rock."

The muscles in his stomach tensed when he heard that voice. He played as if he was asleep.

"Wake up, sleepy head," she said. "You feeling better?"

Besides his throbbing buns, Trout felt okay, but he had no intention of letting that knowledge run free. He had already decided that acting a little goofy might win him another day or two.

"Trout!" his mother said sternly. "Wake up."

His body jerked and he rolled over slowly, peaking at her through saggy eyes.

"Hi, Mama," he said slowly. "What time is it?"

"It's time to get up," she snapped. "I think you've had enough rest."

"Are we going to church?"

"Church! Boy, it's not even Sunday. And you know what we do on those other six days? We work!"

"But I don't feel so good, Mama."

"What's wrong? Doc Jordon said you ought to be fine by now."

That was a good question. He couldn't tell her about the bees, but he had to think of something quick. He went for the old mainstay.

"My stomach hurts."

"Well then, get yourself up and go to the bathroom," she demanded. "And clean yourself out."

As he was making up the stomach story, he realized that his belly really was a little bit icky. The nude leap out of the tree, followed by the splashdown from Tommy Lyons's sailboat, had pumped a sizeable amount of creek water up his tailpipe and it had been percolating for a couple of hours now. His mother was standing over him and about to perform a full inspection when he realized that he'd better sprint to the toilet or things were going to get ugly.

"'Scuse me, Mama," Trout blurted, pushing past her and running into the bathroom.

Even with the door closed, the wretched sounds coming from within the bathroom shocked Mrs. Loxley.

"Goodness gracious," she said. "And I just thought you were trying to get out of working again. Come back to bed, son, and let me tuck you in."

That's when she spied his backside.

"*Oh my God!*" She screamed so loudly that his brothers almost dropped their fishing poles. "What on earth is that?"

"What is what?" Trout asked, knowing full well she'd seen his speckled bottom.

"Your behind is all spotted and red and swollen … *Willie!*" she yelled. "Run and get Doc Jordon. Tell her to come over here. Right *now!*"

The path from Trout's to Doc Jordon's house was getting worn out. The same could be said for Trout. Ever since the shrimping trip, God had thrown him curve balls. Bees stings, stomach problems, clothes sinking—he was starting to wonder what he'd done to deserve it all. The only bright spot was his reprieve from an endless list of chores.

The churn in his stomach intensified when he thought of Doc Jordon. She would certainly diagnose his condition as an acute number of common wasp stings. And that, he was sure, would set his mother off. He was supposed to be on a restful boat ride, not venturing into wasp hangouts.

"I'm okay, Mama," he said, "I just need a little more rest."

"I know, Trout, but we need for Doc Jordon to look at you. Something is just not right."

"Can't I just sleep? Please, Mama. *Please?*"

"After the doctor looks at you."

"Ow!" Trout moaned, thinking more about getting caught than about his queasy belly.

When Willie returned with news that Doc Jordon was nowhere to be found, Trout sighed happily. He once again began to relish his new-found position of comfort. Night was coming on, and his mother was already in the kitchen making him some chicken soup for supper. For him, the forecast for tomorrow was work free with plenty of rest under the ceiling fan. *Maybe God did plan it this way*, he thought. The preacher always said He worked in mysterious ways. And everything sure was strange around his house these days.

"This soup sure is good, Mama," he said with a satisfied grin.

"Don't eat too much," she called from the kitchen.

Just then, a head poked through the porch window.

"You'd better enjoy that soup," Willie whispered. "I'm tired of taking up all the slack on your chores. That's about to stop."

"Sorry," Trout said, trying to be sincere. "If I felt better I'd …"

"That Mr. Pitiful act might be working on Mama," Willie scowled, "but I ain't fooled by it. Your playtime is coming to an end real soon, Trout. Real soon!"

If it wasn't his mother on his back, it was his brothers. Trout wondered why it was so hard to please everybody. Just as he dozed off, he heard scratching on the screen. Danny and Will were outside.

"Hey Trout," Danny said, "we're going swimming at The Point. Can you sneak out?"

"I'd better not. If I get caught, my goose will be cooked, and so far I've been luckier than I've been good. But come by tomorrow morning. Maybe Mama will let me go for a little while."

"Okay. But we'll be there if you change your mind," Will said.

CHAPTER 9

Getting to the Point

The purposes of The Point Club, Inc., shall be for the social, cultural and athletic advancement of its membership.
—From the original By-Laws, State of Alabama, 1961

To outsiders, The Point was just a spit of sand separating Perdido Bay from Soldier Creek. For the boys, it was a place where they learned the nuances of the backstroke, freestyle, and butterfly; dives like the jackknife, inward half, and coveted one-and-a-half and gainer; and, eventually, the beauty and idiosyncrasies of girls. Far more than just a swimming hole, The Point was a safe haven where they spent hours chasing pinfish or playing *Sharks and Minnows* or just staying submerged up to their necks for hours on end to escape the midsummer heat.

By day, The Point was Perdido's social epicenter. By night, kids discovered how to build bonfires, find the position of the North Star, and roast hot dogs. They learned how, no matter how careful they were, sand always got between the bun and the dog. Nothing spoiled a meal quite like the gritty grains in their teeth. But when they were hungry enough, they'd eat it and enjoy it, sand and all. In due course, their education at The Point evolved into the art of flirting, overcoming the awkwardness of that first kiss, and what to tell an irate daddy when you brought his daughter home after midnight and smelling of beer. But those concepts were foreign to Danny, Will, and Trout. They were focused on more important pursuits, like how long they could hold their breath underwater or who was going to be the first one to win five bucks from Mr. Lyons.

Located at the dead end of the sandy road that connected a string of beach cottages, The Point was a private club, even though you'd never know by looking at it. Adorned with a flimsy pavilion capped with a green corrugated plastic roof and a roped-off swimming area with barnacles-encrusted buoys, it defined the beach-shanty look and never saw anything more than bathing suits, t-shirts and bare feet. If Polo shirts had been invented back then, they would have been banned along with manicured poodles and women with nicknames like Muffy and Tootsie.

Surrounded on three sides by water, the finger-shaped peninsula was generally overflowing with a passel of kids playing water games and gorging on watermelon. The boys usually spent a better part of half the day there and the occasional night swim, especially when the phosphorus was glowing.

As they neared the big pine tree with the faded "The Point Club" sign nailed to it, they noticed a glow from a bonfire. Never ones to pass up an opportunity to surprise unsuspecting fire watchers, they hatched a plan.

"Let's sneak up and throw pinecones at 'em," Will suggested.

"Okay," Danny agreed. "You mean, at 'em or around 'em."

"Well, I guess I meant around 'em but if we hit somebody, well, that's just bad luck for them."

"I don't know. One of those big pinecones to the head can hurt bad."

"Then get little ones if you want to. But I'm gonna find the biggest ones I can so I can scare the pee out of 'em."

Somehow, Will always came up with the perfect scheme. When it came to deviant plans, he had a gift. With a half dozen handpicked pinecones, they slipped into the water and moved in along the shallows as inconspicuously as a couple of gators. For a few moments, they just stayed at the edge of the beach to observe their prey. Three young girls sat on logs around the fire, chatting and giggling excessively.

In true invader form, Danny and Will were submerged above their upper lips and breathing through their noses. If some charcoal had been around, they'd have rubbed it on their faces. They recognized Elberta Weeks, an athletic but not particularly attractive girl, whose family rented a cottage for a couple of weeks every summer. The other two girls, apparently Elberta's guests, were newcomers.

When the time was right, Will raised a soppy pinecone and prepared to launch. Danny followed. Since every successful battle plan needs a general to lead the attack, Will took on the role. It was his plan, after all. He directed Danny to throw to the left of the fire into a group of bushes. Danny had an idea where Will was aiming but he dare not ask, even in a whisper, and risk giving away their position.

Will gave the nod and Danny heaved two cones toward the palmetto bushes. Just before they landed, Will pumped three monsters high in the air directly above the tin roof of the pavilion.

When Danny's cones hit the girls stopped laughing. "What was that?" Elberta's friend asked.

"Probably just an armadillo," Elberta said calmly. She was the expert, the experienced Perdidoite, but the idea of wild critters sneaking around in the bushes still put her on edge. Her friends were in a pre-petrified state when Will's cones crashed down on the roof like a rapid round of artillery—*bang, bang, bang*—and the three fire tenders sprung from their logs, screaming in cheesy, horror film fashion. In the same instant, Danny and Will burst out of the water and sprinted toward the fire, waving their arms and howling.

Elberta was startled at first, but quickly recognized the boys and turned an angry face to them. Her friends, on the other hand, had stumbled through the soft sand, tripped over a fallen tree and landed face-first into the sand.

Elberta called them back, "It's okay girls. Just a couple of nincompoops trying to scare us."

"Trying?" Will laughed. "Man I've never seen anybody move so fast in my life!"

"Yeah, I'll bet those two wet their pants," Danny giggled, "maybe you too Elberta."

"I most certainly did not. You didn't scare me one whit. Anyway, that was just plain mean. Y'all ought to be strung up and whipped within an inch of your life."

"Oh, lighten up, Elberta," Will said. "We're just playing."

"You coulda given one of us a heart attack or something," she said. "Wait 'til I tell my daddy what you did."

"Come on now. It's not that bad," Danny said. "You don't want to make your daddy hate us, do ya?"

"Maybe I do. Maybe he already does."

As the conversation began to heat up, Elberta's friends stepped in.

"Hi, I'm Grace … Grace Garland. This is my friend Georgiana. We're okay but y'all scared us to death."

"Sorry about that," Danny said. "It's just that we like to kind of initiate people when they come down here for the first time."

"Yeah," Will said. "We didn't mean anything by it. We were just having a little fun."

"I suppose it's okay," Grace said, "as long as you don't do it again."

And then she smiled.

Will and Danny stood transfixed for a moment as her auburn hair brushed across her neck and glowed in the firelight. Her eyes twinkled above soft cheeks dotted with sun freckles. They'd never seen a smile so enchanting or, if they had, they'd been so consumed with their own silly adolescent pursuits, they just didn't notice. But, that night, they not only noticed, their boyhood melted as if the fire had crept up their spines and burned against their hearts.

"Uh, naw. Uh, it's okay. We won't, uh, do anything like that, um, again," Danny babbled with a silly grin, still reeling from the sight of the goddess smiling at him.

"What he's trying to say," Will said smoothly, "is that we were just messing around and now that we know you, we'll be nice. The truth is we're nice guys."

Elberta let out a grunt of disapproval but Will pressed on.

"Anyway, my name is Will and this is my cousin Danny. Most people just call us Will 'n Danny, because we're always together."

"Or Danny 'n Will," Danny said.

"So which is it?" Grace asked.

"Which is what?" Will asked.

"Is it Danny 'n Will or Will 'n Danny?"

"I don't know, I guess it depends on who you're thinking about first," Will said.

"Hmm," she said. "I'll have to think about that one."

"It's the same thing," Danny said. "Danny 'n Will or Will 'n Danny. Either way is the same. We don't care," he giggled, "especially if you're calling on us to do something fun. When Mr. Walt yells for us … that's my daddy … everybody just calls him Mr. Walt, I'm not sure why … but when he's calling for us, it usually means we're gonna work."

Grace was touched by Danny's sweet nature but her spark had already floated toward Will. Danny was oblivious to it all. His thoughts were purely on her pretty hair and smile and nothing beyond that concerned him. In this game of chess, Will was already thinking six moves ahead. Danny was just admiring the queen.

Grace and Georgiana were happy to have two tanned beach boys to play with. Both were attractive and fit, Will with his gleaming blond curls and Danny with wavy brown hair bleached from endless days in the sun. Will had a confident swagger about him and a James Dean wild streak. Quieter than and as innocent as a fresh summer rain, Danny instantly endeared himself to the girls.

"So are y'all from Mobile too?" Danny asked.

"Yeah," Grace said, "we all go to St. Paul's School together."

"We might be coming to Mobile this summer," Danny said, "to be in a diving contest at the country club."

"The Labor Day Swim Meet?" Grace asked.

"Yeah, that's it," Danny said. "We have to learn a one-and-a-half first."

"Danny's all worked up about it," Will said, "but I'm not leaving Perdido to go to Mobile."

"Why not?" Grace asked.

"Because it's hot and nasty and I like it here better," Will said.

Elberta shoved Will over a log. "It's not that bad, doofus," she said.

Will sat up and brushed the sand off his forearms. "It is compared to Perdido, Elbutt-a."

Danny turned to the girls, hoping to change the course of the conversation. "Is this the first time y'all have been to Perdido?"

"Yes," Georgiana jumped in, "but Elberta's told us all about it."

Will stood up and puffed out his bare chest. "Well, then I guess you already knew about us."

"Yeah," Elberta said, "I told them there were some obnoxious butthead boys around that we could have fun ignoring."

Danny looked genuinely hurt. "Come on Elberta, that's not fair."

"I agree," Grace said. "I think they're cute."

The perpetual smile returned to Danny's face. "Thanks Grace, that's more like it."

Elberta grimaced at the thought. Boys had never paid her any attention except when she whipped them in sandlot baseball or running races. Now these two little twits were horning in on her friends. Of course, future debutants like Grace Garland and Georgiana Starlington weren't helping with all of their eye fluttering and compliments.

"I'm with Grace," Georgiana said. "If we'd have known you had such cute boys around we would have come over to Perdido a long time ago."

And that just ticked Elberta off. Her supposed friends had turned soft on her. Sure, they were two of the most popular girls in school but this was her turf and they were her guests. There was no way in the Alabama blue sky that she was going to be the fifth wheel. Then she had an idea.

"Hey Will, have y'all been doing any snipe hunting lately?" she asked with a wink.

"Uh no, Elberta, not this summer."

"Well I think we should see if we can catch some," she said. "Grace and Georgiana have never been."

Will fidgeted and dug a big toe in the sand "Are you sure Elberta?"

"I'm doggone sure!" she said.

"That doesn't sound like a good idea Elberta, I don't think anyone's catching snipe now," Will said.

She was throwing a giant monkey wrench into his romantic plans and he couldn't figure out why. If a few pinecones scared her friends, a late-night snipe hunt would melt them like butter and probably end any friendships she had.

"Well I think we should try," Elberta said. "We can't catch any if we don't try, right?"

"That is true," Danny said. "My daddy says that a lot."

Georgiana finally took the bait. "What's a snipe?" she asked.

That did it. Elberta had led them into temptation and Will just couldn't deliver them from evil. Georgiana had asked the question every scheming kid loved to hear. It meant they had a virgin snipe hunter at their mercy—an uninformed, non-indoctrinated snipe rookie who was about to ride on a one-way trip to an evening of terror. How could kids have so much fun and be so mean, all at the same time? It was one of those mysteries they didn't think about, they just did it. Will's romantic notions blew away in the breeze and he masterfully shifted from flirt to expert hunter.

"Well," Will started out, "a snipe is a bird."

"A fast bird," Danny added.

"That runs along the ground."

"And we catch 'em in paper bags," Danny said.

The boys were as smooth and polished as Shakespearean actors.

"They're attracted to noise …"

"Loud noise …"

"So we get out in this big open field …"

"Late at night …"

"And bang pots and pans together …"

"To make noise …"

"Because that attracts them …"

"We let one of y'all hold the bag …"

"While the other bangs the pot and pan and yells 'S*nipe, snipe, snipe*' …"

"And they come running out of the bushes …"

"Trying to find that noise …"

"Y'all keep banging the pots and yelling …"

"And here comes those snipes …"

"Right into your bag …"

As unbelievable as it sounded, their commentary was entirely convincing even though it was utter hogwash. But like their older brothers before them, Danny and Will were masters of hooking unsuspecting kids into the snipe hunt because they ran at least half a dozen expeditions each summer. Even though Elberta wasn't one of their favorite friends, she frequently brought fresh meat to the barbeque.

CHAPTER 10

Be Careful What You Wish for

A snipe is a real live fictitious bird.
—Will Stapleton

A successful snipe hunt requires a coal dark night, an ample helping of deception and an active imagination. But really, only two ingredients are absolutely essential. First and foremost are completely naïve friends. Second is the ability to spout off an endless string of outlandish yarns.

Danny and Will were both a little distraught that Elberta had shifted their evening from flirting to fooling girls. But it was an easy transition. The two were well experienced in the art of hoodwinking and, anyway, their skills at flirting were still green on the vine.

The hunting party set a quick pace down the dark, sandy road. Will and Danny stayed two steps ahead of the pack and never stopped yakking.

"I remember one snipe hunt," Will said, "on a night kind of like this one."

"Yeah, just a puff of wind out of the southeast," Danny continued, "and kinda muggy."

"Yep, that was it. We were sweating like cows at the slaughter-house. I think it might have been the exact same day as this one, last summer," Will said. "Yeah, we had a fantastic hunt. Caught fifteen snipe in less than thirty minutes."

"Actually Will, it was sixteen. Remember, that big ol' fat one followed us home 'cause the other ones were making such a racket inside the bag. And we nabbed him right after he ran into the screen door and knocked himself out."

"Oh yeah, I forgot about that. And, he was a meaty one. That was some good eating."

"So they really are good to eat?" Georgiana asked, already hopelessly hooked.

"Better than fried chicken," Danny said, knowing there was no higher praise in Southern cooking.

They raided Miss Kitty's kitchen to gather the necessary implements—paper bags, pots, pans, flashlights, wooden spoons (to whack the snipe on the head, of course), and anything else that seemed appropriate.

Mr. Walt walked in to check on the frantic tool gathering. "So you're going on a big snipe hunt, huh?"

"Yes, sir," Danny said. "This is my dad. Like I said, everybody just calls him Mr. Walt most of the time. This is Grace and Georgiana. They've never been snipe hunting."

"Well I kind of figured that," Mr. Walt said dryly then quickly added, "Because I've never seen you girls around here. Nice to meet you."

Snipe hunting was one of those rituals that had been passed down generation by generation. In his childhood days, even Mr. Walt had been duped by some older kids. And he'd led many a fresh kid on snipe hunts, too. His apparent endorsement added volumes to the snipe credibility.

"This is our first time to visit," Georgiana said.

"Well, let's hope it won't be the last," Mr. Walt smiled. "Now y'all don't catch too many. Leave some for the rest of us. We might go tomorrow night."

"Yes, sir," Will smiled. "We'll leave you a few."

"Nice to meet you, Mr. Walt," Grace said.

"You too. Have fun."

There were exactly seventeen cottages along the beach starting at The Point and running east to Pirate's Canyon. Beyond that, only vast woodlands and wide-open beaches bordered the bay.

The very last house was set off by itself, perched on top of a high bluff and inside a grove of gnarled scrub oaks. Unlike most of the well kept, open-air cottages with sprawling screen porches and board and batten cypress siding, this one was built of pee-yellow brick and had ramshackle shutters framing dingy windows. Whatever was inside was masked by dark shades.

Although they'd never seen her, the old lady living there was simply known as the Widow Woman. From the look of the house, yard work and fresh paint were against her religion. They figured she never even ventured into the sunlight. Their older brothers told them that the Widow Woman just lived on water and rats her cats caught for her.

Once they passed the Widow Woman's house, they were in the wilderness - acres and acres of flat and not particularly fertile fields of malnourished pine trees, some scrawny oaks and palmetto bushes.

Like her cats, the Widow Woman must have had night vision because her lights were never on. The quicker they passed her house the better. Unfortunately, the only way into the prime snipe hunting grounds was the sandy path that snaked its way past her house through the scrub oaks near the edge of the bluff.

They had no trouble selling their fear of the Widow Woman, because they were genuinely afraid that, at any moment, she was going to run out and toss them off the bluff one by one and put a frog hex on them. Never seeing the woman added to her eerie mystique, and they were sure she was a wild-eyed, frazzled-haired woman who could scare the hair off a dog with one look.

"Be quiet as we go by here," Danny said. "We don't want the Widow Woman to get us."

Grace gasped. "Who's the Widow Woman?"

"She the old crazy woman who lives here," Elberta said.

They knew the girls were going to have to come back by the house on the way home. Throwing a witch into the mix was the Tabasco in their snipe soup.

Once they were safely into the open field, they set up.

Will stepped forward and directed. "Okay, here's what we do. Grace and Georgiana are the catchers. Elberta, Danny and I will flush the birds out of the bushes."

"Right," Danny said, "one of y'all needs to hold the bag wide open and the other needs to stand behind her and bang those pots together like crazy."

"Where will y'all be?" Georgiana asked with a shiver in her voice.

"We'll walk around those bushes over there, bang on our pots and make a bunch of noise," Will said.

Danny hopped up and down, spun around and performed his best snipe impression. "That gets 'em all stirred up. They'll be confused and running wherever the noise is coming from."

Grace and Georgiana listened attentively but silently wondered what kind of madness they'd signed up for.

"When I give the signal, we'll we stop hollering and stop banging on our pots and pans," Will said. "That's when y'all need to start yelling and whacking things together as hard as you can."

Danny leaned in close to the girls and smiled. "And, just like that, those stupid ol' snipes will come running right into your bag."

"Some of them might miss the bag and run past you," Will said. "If they do, don't worry about it. They'll come back around if you keep making noise. And whatever you do, don't drop the bag. Ya need to keep a good hold on it."

Continuing the string of lies until the very end was essential. They'd seen kids abandon the hunt seconds before it started because, sure as the sunrise, it was downright frightening out there at night, in this strange place, near some crazy witch house. The truth was, by the time they arrived into the wilderness, the newbies never really cared about snipes; they just wanted to fit in. Instead of sitting in a pitch-black field, they'd rather have gone home where there were friendly people, soft drinks and working light bulbs. But once someone committed, the boys never gave them a chance to back out.

"Okay, you think y'all got it?" Will asked.

Georgiana whimpered. "I think so."

They'd heard that tone of voice many times before. She was primed and ready to be sniped.

In the confusion of endless directives and preparation, the girls didn't notice Danny stuffing both flashlights in his back pockets. Grace held the bag and Georgiana stood behind her with an old worn out black-eye pea pot in one hand and a wooden spoon in the other. Both of them wondered what in Sam Hill's name they were doing out there and how they were going to bang quick little birds on the head or keep them in a paper bag, all in complete darkness. But it was too late to try to understand. The hunt was underway.

For about two minutes Elberta, Will and Danny shook around in the bushes yelling, "SNIPE!" and whacking their pots. They made a terrific commotion. If the Widow Woman was home, she knew another snipe hunt was in progress.

"I see one!" Danny yelled.

"There goes two more," Will shouted.

As they neared the path past the Widow Woman's house, they fell silent just as they'd told Grace and Georgiana they would. Seconds later, they heard the girls yelling, banging, and sliding hopelessly down the slippery slope of snipery.

Danny, Will, and Elberta giggled all the way back to Mr. Walt's house. They'd pulled off another successful hunt. They could hear Grace and Georgiana's clamor almost the whole way home. As they got farther and farther away, the sound faded into the night breeze. The trio knew that soon enough, the girls would realize they'd been duped.

Grace and Georgiana did their best snipe calling and banging for almost five minutes.

"Ya got any yet?" Georgiana asked.

"Not yet. Keep banging," Grace said.

Another minute passed.

"How about now?"

"Nothing."

The seconds ticked by.

"Now?"

"Nope."

Georgiana cupped her hands around her mouth and yelled for Elberta. "Hey, we're not getting any Elberta. We haven't even heard any yet."

The cold silence washed over them.

"Elberta! You out there? Will? Danny? Where are y'all?"

Back at Mr. Walt's house, Will was mixing some chocolate milk. They laughed and jabbered about what might be happening in the lonely snipe fields.

"I'll bet Grace and Georgiana are sitting there hugging each other and trying to figure out whether to cry or die," Elberta said. "And they've definitely already wet their pants!"

"I'm sure they're worrying about that old Widow Woman," Will said.

"I would be, too," Danny said.

Their predictions were dead-on target, because they'd been in the same position before and had left so many others to wallow in their own anxiety.

Grace grabbed Georgiana's arm and shook it. "Hey, stop crying."

"I will if you will."

"I'm trying, but I'm too scared."

"Me too. Did they just leave us out here?"

"I guess so. Those jerks!"

"Why would they do that?"

"I'm not sure, but I kinda think that's the point," Grace said. "I don't think there's any such thing as a snipe. It's all a big trick."

"A bad, bad trick. What if we can never find our way back to the house? What if we die out here?"

"Georgiana, we're not going to die. They're probably just hiding behind those bushes over there."

"I hope so."

"*Elberta!*" Grace yelled. "You can come out now. The game is over."

"Yeah. We're ready to go home now. You really got us this time."

They waited, hoped, and called out until it finally became crystal clear that Elberta and the boys were neither hiding nor returning to escort them home. Grace's fear turned to anger. Their survival depended on it.

"Georgiana, they're not coming back. We have to figure out how to make it back to the house."

"Can't we just wait a little longer?"

"No. Don't you see? That's the trick, to scare us and make us cry and walk home. We just need to follow that path. Where are those flashlights?"

"I thought you had them."

"Those buggers took the flashlights, too. I can't hardly see anything. Can you?"

"A little bit. I can kinda see the path."

Fortunately, even on a moonless night, the sandy path through the pine straw shone like a chalk line on a blacktop road.

"Let's just try to walk," Grace said.

"I don't know if I can. Let's just wait a few more minutes."

"Georgiana, get a grip. We're on our own."

"Okay, you lead. I'll follow," she whimpered.

As they inched by pine trees and ducked under the twisted

branches of stunted scrub oaks, fear held a tight grip on them. Neither of the girls knew what critter might be hiding in the shadows. And, even if they made it out of the woods, they had to pass through the creepy dead gardens of a crazy woman.

"Once we pass that old Widow Woman house," Grace said, trying to build their confidence, "we're home free. The rest of the houses are all lit up."

"Maybe we can sneak by without her hearing us."

And just like that, they made it to the house that was shrouded in spookiness without dying. The tangled trees bent and creaked as the wind blew over the bluff. In fact, Grace was sure she heard the trees moaning. In the distance, through tall pines, they could see dim lights from the next house. They could soon breathe again.

Suddenly an intense beam of light smacked them in the face and a shrill voice screeched, "Stop right there!"

They both squealed and tried to run, but their legs had turned to putty.

"Who are you?"

It was *her*. The Widow Woman had them trapped, soon to be in her sharp claws. Their hair stood on end. Death was certain.

"I ... I'm Grace ... and, uh, this is my, my friend, Georgiana. We're sorry for being here, but we're lost and trying to get back to our house."

"We're not trying to cause trouble. We're just *lost*," Georgiana sobbed.

"I heard someone crying in the woods," the old woman said. "I guess that was you?"

"Yes, ma'am. We're just scared. Please don't hurt us," Georgiana begged.

"What? Why in heaven's name would I hurt you?"

"Because you're the old Widow Woman," Grace said.

"Oh, I see," the woman laughed. "Those conniving boys got you all scared of me. You don't have to worry. I'm harmless."

"You are?" they said in unison.

"Sure I am," she said. "Just because I live alone and keep to myself doesn't mean I'm some kind of witch or something."

The girls twitched when she said 'witch,' but she sounded almost like a normal person, even though they noticed several cats rubbing against her legs.

"In fact, I tell you what. You girls take this flashlight to help you get home. You can bring it back tomorrow. If I'm not here, just leave it on this table right here."

"Thank you," Grace said. "That would be great."

"I only have one condition," the woman said.

"What is that?"

"Don't you dare tell those scheming boys that I was nice to y'all. I like it better when they're scared of me. That way they won't come around and bother my little kitties and me. We do like our privacy."

"We promise. We won't tell a soul."

"Good. Now, how about a Coke and a cookie for the journey home?"

"That's okay," Grace said. "The flashlight will be fine. We'll bring it back tomorrow."

The cookies and drinks sounded good, but the woman's squeaky voice gave them goose bumps. Besides, it looked as if she hadn't brushed her hair in a hundred years.

"All right then. Run along, and maybe I'll see you tomorrow."

Back at Mr. Walt's house, the chocolate milk was long gone, but there was still no sign of Grace and Georgiana.

"You think they got lost?" Elberta asked.

"Probably," Will said.

"Maybe we should go look for 'em," Danny suggested. "I'm getting a little worried."

"They might have gone back to our house," Elberta said.

"That's true," Will said. "Why don't you go check there, and Danny and I will walk the path to see if we can find 'em."

For the past five years, Elberta's family had rented the old Rabun house, one of the first homes built on Perdido Bay in the mid-1800s. Most of the cottages were set within a stone's throw of the beach, but when old Mr. Rabun built his house, he tucked it back between two massive live oaks that were more than a hundred yards from the water. The view wasn't as good, and it seemed strange to everyone that the house was so far away from the beach; strange, that is, until a hurricane hit. Mr. Rabun's wisdom became obvious when most of the cottages sustained damage and his didn't lose a single shingle. Year after year, as more storms eroded the shoreline and people were forced to build retaining walls, Mr. Rabun let natural erosion bring the beach to him.

Even though the Rabun cottage was only two houses from Mr. Walt's place, it was completely hidden, being set so far back in the woods like that. So Grace and Georgiana snuck past Mr. Walt's without Elberta or the boys noticing. When Elberta arrived, she was met with two angry ex-friends. Elberta did her best to calm them down, pointing out that everyone at Perdido had gone through the same ritual at some point in their young lives. She recounted her snipe horror story, remembering to mention that she and her snipe partners had been blindfolded (some snipe have night vision and are, of course, scared by the sight of young girls' eyes). Grace and Georgiana finally calmed down after she served them some hot chocolate and convinced them that, in a bizarre way, being sniped was an honor.

"They only take popular people on snipe hunts," Elberta said, "because they can handle it. Maybe we can find someone else to snipe next summer. This is, if y'all come back down with me."

"We'll have to think about it," Grace said.

Will and Danny were slinking along the path, hiding behind trees and bushes along the way. They fully expected to spot Grace and Georgiana creeping along in blinding fear, at which point, they'd jump out from behind a tree and scare the bejeezus out of them again. Before they knew it, they were approaching the Widow Woman's lair.

"Maybe they're still out there in the field," Will said.

"I doubt it. It's been over an hour."

"We'll just have to check. If they're still out there, we can do the old pine cone toss at 'em."

"Yep, that we can," Danny said.

First, they had to slip by the witch. The thought of scaring the girls again gave them the strength to cross the den of death, but Will hesitated to listen for distant whimpering. All was quiet. He motioned for Danny to follow. They'd gone no more than four steps when suddenly a squeaky door flung open and banged against the house.

"I'm gonna *get you*!" squealed the woman as she leaped through the door, just ahead of fourteen wild, screeching cats.

Will and Danny had run from trouble many times during their young lives, but they'd never moved across the face of the earth as fast as that. Fear of being dismembered or turned to rats and fed to a horde of cats motivated them beyond human boundaries. They passed nine houses in an all-out sprint and didn't stop until they burst through Mr. Walt's screen door. They never, ever told a soul, not even each other, but both of them had to change their underwear that night.

CHAPTER 11

Wind Slapped

All good ideas have to be a little bit crazy.
—Trout Loxley

The boys wished Trout could have been on the snipe hunt. They had flung pure fear into those girls but no one was better at pumping people up about catching a fake bird than Trout. The problem was, his mother still had him under her big burly thumb and now they had to tell him about being terrified out of their wits by the Widow Woman. Or maybe he wouldn't find out.

"You know, we could just tell him about how much we scared those girls," Will said.

"Yeah, but if we don't come clean about the Widow Woman, he'll find out. He always knows everything that's going on. Plus, I'm sure somebody saw us running home like scared rabbits last night."

"I think we should take our chances and not spill the beans. He'll really rub it in."

"We'll see."

Danny glanced across the room just in time to see Trout pulling open the screen and crawling through the window. "Morning y'all! See about what?"

"Oh nothing," Will said. "We were just talking about our snipe hunt last night."

"Y'all did a snipe hunt? Doggone it. I can't believe I missed that. Who'd you take?"

"Couple of girl friends of Elberta's," Danny said.

"Grace Garland and Georgiana Starlington?" Trout asked.

"Yeah," Will said. "How'd you know?"

"I already met 'em."

"You meet everybody," Danny said.

"I guess I like to get around," Trout smiled.

"Wow," Danny grinned, "That Grace is some kinda good looking, huh?"

"Yep, she kinda made my heart flutter," Trout chuckled. "But Georgiana wasn't no fish face herself."

Will gave Trout and Danny a look that could have cut through steel. He'd already decided that Grace was *his* girl and he wanted to make sure they knew it.

"She was flirting with me like crazy last night. Y'all just stay out of the way. She's sweet on me," he said.

"That's too bad," Trout said.

"How come?" Will asked.

"'Cause they all went back to Mobile this morning."

"Really?"

"Yep, those girls were pretty upset. They talked Elberta's daddy into going home early."

"That's too bad," Will said. "'Cause we got 'em good last night. I want to know how they got back home."

"You think they might be mad at you?" Trout asked.

"They shouldn't be. The snipe hunt was Elberta's idea," Danny said.

"Where'd you take 'em?" Trout asked.

"Up on the bluff past Pirate's Canyon."

"By the Widow Woman house?"

"Yep."

"That's a good spot. Any sign of the old witch?"

Danny and Will looked at each other and wondered if Trout had already heard something.

"Naw," Will said. "The house was dark. I guess she wasn't home."

"Is that right?" Trout asked.

"Yep," they both said.

Trout could see that Danny was hiding something. He was a crummy liar. But Trout let it pass because he had big plans.

"Hey guess what I found?" Trout asked.

"What?"

"Some old World War II stuff of my dad's in the attic and there's a parachute in there."

"A real one?" Will asked.

"I guess so. I didn't really look at it too close."

"I can't believe your mama let you dig around in the attic," Danny said. "Isn't she making you stay in bed? You are supposed to be sick, you know."

"She went to town early this morning and won't be back 'til after lunch. I asked if I could just stay in bed and rest."

"That's great. You've got it good," Will said.

"Yep, this is the best deal I've ever had. She's got my brothers doing all my chores and I'm home free. Boys, this is the good life."

"So what are you thinking about doing with that parachute?" Danny asked.

"I'm not sure. I thought we could jump out of The Tree with it. But I'm not sure it's high enough. Or maybe we could go off the bluff. But I'd rather be over the water in case it doesn't open or something."

The boys sat in silence for a few moments and let their creative juices flow.

"Shouldn't we be trying to do a one-and-a-half?' Danny said. "That competition will be coming up soon and all we've been doing is snipe hunting and swinging from The Tree."

"I told you I don't care about that," Will said. "I wouldn't mind getting five dollars from Mr. Lyons but I'm skipping the fancy-schmancy, country-club folks."

"What about you, Trout?" Danny asked.

"Me?" Trout said. "I've got it!"

"Got what?" Will asked.

"The best idea for that parachute. We tie it on the ski rope and pull it behind the boat."

"Do what?" Will said. He'd never heard of anything so goofy.

"We make our own wind by pulling it behind *Greenie*," Trout smiled. "Instead of floating down, we make it float up!"

Danny bounced on the bed next to Trout. "You know, that just might work. And if it doesn't we'll just glide down into the water and won't break any bones or anything."

Will laughed. "Y'all are goobers. It won't work. A parachute is made to come down, not go up."

61

"It won't work if we don't try," Danny said. "If we get enough air underneath it, we might make it fly."

"Well, I'm not doing it."

Trout bounced up and touched the ceiling. "Look I'm flying already. Let's go!"

"Fine," Will said. "I'll drive the boat and watch you two idiots drown when you get all wrapped up in that thing."

"Don't be such a wet blanket. It might work," Danny said.

"And a mullet might run for president," Will laughed.

Danny and Trout didn't care if it worked or not. They just hoped something outrageous might happen. It was calculated danger, a euphemism that pretty much summed up their entire childhood. Pulling a full-sized parachute behind a powerboat was dicey but their new toy was only a reserve chute, not intended to give a man a soft landing, only keep him from shattering all his bones as he crashed into the ground.

The chute looked small, but that didn't stop them from building a harness out of old ski ropes and some rubber tubing they scavenged from Mr. Walt's workshop. It didn't look like much, but it had a crude seat and a rope with a fat knot to hang on to.

Only one location fit for their launching pad—The Point. The long, uncluttered spit of soft sand was surrounded by deep water so the chance of hitting a tree or head planting in the sand was low. By the time they built the contraption, got *Greenie* ready and made it to The Point, the wind was blowing close to twenty knots.

Will pull cranked the engine. "Who's going to be the first victim?"

Danny and Trout both stepped back and pointed to each other.

"Trout, it's your parachute," Danny said. "You can go first."

Even though shades of doubt crossed Trout's face, the dream of gliding with the birds filled him with hope. After checking all the knots, Trout gave the thumbs up. Will gunned the engine as Danny flung the chute into the air. Instantly, Trout became the victim of a tug-of-war, kind of like a cowboy getting yanked apart by wild horses. Strong winds dragged the parachute backwards while *Greenie* struggled to go forward. They'd reached a stalemate between nature and machine. Somehow Trout hung on as he dangled two feet above the water with skis hanging from his feet. Something had to give. Then it happened. The chute made a high sweeping roll like a giant windshield wiper.

With a jarring yank, Trout shot thirty feet into the air—a puppet at the hand of an old war relic. Amazingly, it looked like he had achieved cruising altitude and he hooted with nervous pleasure. Towering over the pine trees, he could see clear across the bay and all the way to the gulf.

Well I'll be dogged, Will thought, *that thing is actually flying.*

Danny waved his arms and sprinted down the beach. "Ride it Trout! Ride it!"

Then in a sudden and violent turn of events, the chute rolled again and plummeted down. Trout slapped the water so hard it laid him out flat. Instinctively, he hung onto the rope and stayed in the harness. Then the chute swept back into the air. Trout got sucked out of the water and, once again, flew amongst the seagulls. He dangled there for a few seconds with his head bobbing back and forth, then crash-landed again. The homemade harness blew apart. A dazed Trout clung to the rope with one hand. Before he let go the chute took to the sky again and flung the youngster ten feet up. He rotated head over heals and managed to twist his body into a sideways dive as he splashed down.

It all happened so fast that bystanders could only wonder if Trout was dead or alive. Danny dived in to rescue his friend while Will battled the renegade parachute as it jerked on *Greenie's* stern. When the wind gusted, it looked like the parachute might carry Will and *Greenie* into the stratosphere. Even with the little outboard engine at full throttle, *Greenie* was losing ground.

Folks on the beach yelled advice to Will.

"Cut the line."

"Jump out of the boat."

"Turn it downwind."

Will might have been apathetic about parachute flying but even twelve-year-old captains don't abandon their ships. He respected *Greenie* too much for that. Just holding the boat steady took all of Will's strength and concentration. If he jumped out, *Greenie* would surely tump over and sink. If he let go of the throttle to reach for the fishing knife, chaos would give way to disaster. As Will and *Greenie* fought an epic battle against the wind, Danny reached Trout floating gingerly on his back and moaning.

He looked up at Danny and smiled. "I flew Danny. I really flew."

"You okay Trout?"

63

"I don't think I'm dead but I know I flew like a bird. I could see clear to the gulf. It was beautiful."

"That's great Trout. But let me get you back to the beach"

Danny realized the impact had knocked the sense out of Trout. A look of bliss covered his face but his body was limp. Grabbing him under the arm, Danny swam them to the beach.

Will's muscles strained mightily as he waited for a howling gust of wind to pass. In one last-ditch effort, he gunned the engine and cranked it hard to the right. *Greenie* spun around downwind, and Will kept it at full throttle until the wind spilled out of the chute and it collapsed harmlessly into Soldier Creek. Will quickly gathered up the rope, grabbed the chute, and stomped it angrily into the bottom of the boat. He'd never experienced the relentless power of the wind that way. His body shook in fear.

Furious at Danny and Trout for their ridiculous idea, Will beached *Greenie* and flopped into the creek. "I told y'all it wouldn't work. Plus y'all almost killed me and *Greenie*."

"But it did work," Danny said. "I mean Trout flew for a few seconds."

"If flipping and flopping around like a rag doll is what you call flying, then sure, he flew."

"I did fly," Trout said as he lay motionless in the sand staring up into the clouds. "I really did fly. See those birds in the sky. I was up there with them. Hi, birdie. I see you little birdies."

"He's loopy, Will said. "We need to get him back home and into bed before his mama gets back."

"Good idea," Danny said.

"And you know what else?" Trout said.

Will rolled his eyes. "What Trout?"

"I did a one-and-a-half."

"How's that?" Will said.

"Before I let go of that parachute it slung me into the air. I flipped once and landed in a dive. That was a one-and-a-half."

Will looked at Danny for confirmation. "I guess you could call it that," Danny said.

"Maybe so Trout," Will said, "but being flung into a one-and-a-half ain't the same as actually doing one. You can't win the money like that."

"I have to agree with Will," Danny said. "You have to do it under your own power. I don't think Mr. Lyons would pay you five dollars on account of you getting helped by a parachute."

"Aw, y'all are just jealous 'cause I flew. It was amazing, just amazing."

Trout climbed in the boat still mumbling to the birds. As they pulled up to his pier, they saw a dreadful sight. His mother's car was already in the driveway and she was standing in the front yard with one huge hand on her hip and the other wrapped around the handle of a shovel. Her face was taut and flushed. They'd seen that look before and nothing good ever came of it. Trout almost floated across the grass as he approached her.

"Trout, I saw that whole silly episode," she said sternly handing the shovel to him. "If you're well enough to play, you're well enough to work!"

"I love you, Mama," he said as the shovel fell unattended to the ground. Trout didn't even notice. He walked right past her and said, "I flew like a bird, Mama. I really did." Danny, Will, and his mother watched as he went directly to his bedroom and climbed into bed.

Mrs. Loxley shot a death stare at Danny and Will who had already scurried back to *Greenie* and were high-tailing it to The Point.

"He's having a tough time lately," Danny said.

"Better him than us," Will said. "At least he's not doing all those chores."

"I'm not sure which is better, chores or almost killing himself."

"Well, he's not dead yet and you don't even have a chance to have fun when you're doing chores. So, I say he's better off this way."

"If you say so," Danny said.

Back at The Point, the wind was still blowing stiff. Before long, Danny and Will had figured out how to wrap the ski rope around the trunk of a tall pine tree and fly the chute like a humongous kite. Then Will had a brainstorm.

"Danny, get me the ski."

"Whatcha gonna do? Danny asked.

"I'm gonna ski across the creek with this thing."

"You're what?"

"Just get the ski."

Will attached a short ski rope to the parachute, and sure as the wind blew, he took off downwind at twenty knots. For the rest of the day they entertained themselves by slalom skiing on wind power. One would ski and the other would jump in *Greenie* to retrieve the skier for the ride back to The Point.

A small crowd gathered to watch the show, but riding the wind on a slalom ski was not as easy as Danny and Will made it look. Both expert skiers, they had to struggle to stay up when the wind slacked off and hang on for dear life when a thirty-knot gust whistled across the creek, hit the chute, and yanked them, ski and all, into the air.

During the entire event, a blond-headed kid with a deep tan sat at the edge of the water entranced with the new-fangled contraption. He watched the boys zipping across the creek and day dreamed about how to steer the chute. Drawing with a stick in the sand, the kid even sketched out a few of his ideas. Years later, that kid made a fortune when he invented a new sport called kiteboarding. Although Danny, Will, and Trout never knew that their old army parachute and vivid imaginations stirred the creative mind of a kid on the beach, the fact was, they were the very first people to ever ride the wind on a kite and a board.

CHAPTER 12

Why Do Mullet Jump?

There are some things God doesn't want us to figure out.
—Walt Thornton

On their way home, the boys spotted Trout sitting on the end of his pier staring across the creek.

"Hey Trout," Danny yelled. "How ya doing?"

"Better, I guess."

"That's good. Then whatcha doing on the pier?"

"Just thinking."

Will eased along side the dock. "About what?"

"About mullet."

"What about mullet?" Danny asked, figuring he was still dazed from head-smacking the water.

"Well, I've just been sitting here watching them jump and I was wondering why?"

"Why you've been sitting here or why they've been jumping?" Will grinned.

"I know why I'm sitting here smart butt. I've been wondering why mullet jump."

"Probably because a big fish is chasing them," Will said.

"Yeah, that might be it," Trout said. "But they sure do jump an awful lot. I'm not sure there's that many big fish to chase them."

"Maybe they're trying to catch mosquitoes for a snack," Danny said.

"Could be," said Trout. "But my dad said that mullet are bottom feeders and they eat worms and stuff out of the sand and mud."

Danny scratched his head. "Yeah, but they could also eat bugs if they had a mind to. They might swim along and look up into the air for bugs. Then when they see one—zoom—they leap out and grab that sucker."

Will laughed. "How could they see a tiny mosquito flying around? I don't think they see that good."

"How do you know?" Danny asked.

"I don't know for sure but I just don't think a mullet could see a little bug flying around."

"Well, I do," Danny said.

"You know what I think?" Trout said. "Well, y'all both might be right. But I think mullet jump because they can."

"Huh?" Will said. "'Cuz they can? What does that mean?"

"You know, kinda like a dolphin. They jump sometimes just for the pure fun of it. And I think mullet might do the same thing. Maybe they just ate something real tasty or they saw a pretty girl mullet and they're jumping for joy. If they could scream, I'd bet they'd be going, *'Yeeeee-ha!'* when they jumped."

Will shook his head. "Trout, that parachute ride knocked the ever-loving sense right out of you."

"Well, why not?" Trout said. "Fish might like to have fun just like us."

"I guess it's possible," Danny said.

"Y'all are both cracked," Will said. "And Trout's brain is water-logged."

"Maybe it is but that parachute flying is why I think they jump for fun because when I was up in the air, I felt as light as a feather and free like I've never felt before."

"Maybe we ought to tie a mullet on that parachute," Will said, "If they like jumping so much, they'd love that."

"You don't have to be a smart ass about it," Trout said.

Danny face crinkled in deep contemplation. "But how will we ever know?" he said.

"Know what?" Will asked.

"How will we know the real reason mullet jump? I mean, we all *think* we're right but we're not really sure who's right."

"I guess it's one of those mysteries like that city of Atlantis," Trout said. "Maybe we'll never know for sure."

"Or who even cares," Will laughed. "Mullet jump because they jump. It doesn't matter why. They just do it."

"It matters to me," Trout said.

"That's because you whacked your head today," Will said.

"No it isn't," Trout snapped.

"Yes it is."

"Hey," Danny said. "Y'all quit arguing. Maybe Mr. Walt will know. Let's ask him."

Will slapped Danny on the back. "Good idea, cuz," he said. "You're always thinking, aren't you?"

"I guess so."

"I'm thinking, too," Will said.

"About what?" Trout asked.

"About blueberries."

"Blueberries?"

"Yep, if I'm right about the mullet, Trout has to snag me a bag of those blueberries from his mama's freezer."

"You're on," Trout said. "But if I'm right, you have to do my chores for one whole day."

"But you're not doing chores," Will said.

"I am now. As soon as I woke up from that nap, Mama told me that my honeymoon was over. She was almighty upset because somebody told her all about us getting on Tommy Lyons's sailboat."

"Who told?" Danny asked.

"One of my no-count brothers."

"That dawg!" Will said.

"Yeah, and then she saw me up in that parachute. Starting tomorrow, I'm back on the chain gang."

"Okay then," Will said, "we'll ask Mr. Walt about the mullet and see who's right. I can taste those blueberries already."

"You better hope so, because Mama has a list a mile long for me tomorrow."

***

"Well, boys, that's a question folks have been contemplating for many years," Mr. Walt said. "And to be honest nobody really knows for certain why mullet jump."

Will hung his head. "They don't?"

"Well, there are many theories, of course," Mr. Walt said he as rubbed his chin.

"Like what?" Danny asked. "Catching bugs?"

"I think they're trying to get away from a big redfish or maybe a dolphin," Will said.

"Yeah, a lot of folks would agree with that. There's lot of big fish eating little fish under that water and dolphins do love to eat mullet. So, it's possible they jump to save their skin, so to speak."

Will danced a victory jig around the screen porch. "I knew it. I *am* right."

"Not so fast there bucko," Mr. Walt stopped him. "I said it's possible that's why mullet jump but I didn't say it was a scientific fact."

"Well what do you think daddy?" Danny asked. "I think they're jumping for bugs."

"Yep, they might catch a bug or two when they jump."

Danny beamed with pride. "Really?"

"Sure. And not just bugs in the air but sometimes they might eat bugs that are on the surface of the water, like a trout does in a mountain stream."

"Yeah, I never thought of that," Will said.

"Some people believe mullet jump because they're trying to knock parasites off of their skin."

"What are parasites?" Danny asked.

"Well, kind of like how ticks or fleas get on dogs, parasites are tiny critters that get on fish. Maybe mullet jump to knock them off."

"Wow," Danny said. "Do we have parasites too?"

"No son. You're safe. But there's another reason mullet might jump."

"What it is?" Will asked.

"Well, some folks say they jump just for the fun of it."

Will slapped his hand across his knee. "Well I'll be danged. Really, Mr. Walt? Come on, that's just too hard to believe."

"Why is that?"

"I just don't think fish, especially low down mullet, know anything about having fun. I mean they're fish. They swim, they eat and we eat them."

"Yeah but how about dolphins," Danny said. "They jump for fun, don't they?"

"But dolphins are smart," Will said. "Mullet are stupid."

"How do you know they're stupid, Will?" Mr. Walt asked.

"I just know they're stupider than dolphins."

"Why is that?"

Will tugged on his earlobe and thought for a moment. "Well, I can catch mullet in a cast net but dolphins swim around the shrimp net all the time and don't ever get caught."

"Now that's where you're mistaken, son. Sometimes commercial shrimpers catch dolphins in their big nets. So maybe it's just the size of the net that matters, not that a dolphin is that much smarter than a mullet."

"But they teach dolphins tricks in aquariums," Will said.

"That's true Will. And, you're probably right that dolphins are smarter. But that doesn't mean that mullet are stupid."

"I don't know, Mr. Walt, it's just hard for me to understand how a mullet can have fun."

Mr. Walt leaned back in his chair and smiled. His expression was gentle but serious. "Will, there are many things in this life we'll never completely understand, like heaven and hell and God's way of doing things, but we still believe in them."

Will contemplated Mr. Walt's wisdom. He was right about heaven and all that, but Will still didn't believe a mullet could have fun. Plus, it meant he wasn't going to win the bet with Trout. Then he wondered how they were going to settle up because he didn't lose either. Will decided to give it one last shot.

"So Mr. Walt, let me ask you this: If you had to pick just one reason why mullet jump, what would it be?"

"I don't think I could pick just one."

"But say if your life depended on it and you had to pick just one thing or you would die, what would you pick?"

"That's a situation I hope I'll never be faced with, son," he chuckled.

"Yeah but what if it did happen, I mean just somehow?"

"I tell you what Will, I don't think I'm going to give you the answer you want, no matter how many ways you ask it. So, here's my final answer. You ready?"

Will slunk down in his chair. "I guess so."

"Nobody really knows why mullet jump," Mr. Walt began, "but they probably do it for a lot of different reasons—some we know about, and some we don't. Smart people solve puzzles about the world every day, puzzles like how deep are the oceans or what is the elevation of the tallest mountain. But thank goodness there are some phenomenons men may never solve, keeping them forever as strange and wonderful mysteries mankind may pursue with great curiosity and creativity. And that's my answer. End of story."

Will kicked at the floor. He didn't like it, but he knew he was just going to have to live with it.

"I still think I'm right," he mumbled to himself as he left the room.

When Danny and Will showed up the next morning, Trout was already burning some brush and raking leaves toward the fire.

Trout threw a board on the fire and turned to Will. "Well, what did Mr. Walt say?"

"He said we were all right," Danny said.

"Huh? How can we all be right?"

"Well," Danny said, "he said the mullet probably jump for a lot of reasons—for fun, to get away from a redfish, for bugs, and something about parasites."

"What are parasites?"

"Some kinda bugs that get on fish. Like a tick."

"Fish have ticks?"

"No. *Like* a tick. I don't really understand all of it 'cept it's another reason they might jump."

Will had heard enough. "Would y'all shut up about ticks and stuff? The thing is, either we both win or we both lose."

"I say we both lose," Trout said. "That way you can help me with my chores, and I'll sneak a bag of those blueberries for us."

As much as Will hated to work, he loved those blueberries.

"Okay, Trout, what do you want me to do?"

"It doesn't matter to me. I've got to cut the grass, sweep the leaves off of the roof, fix that busted screen door, and cut all of those sticker vines off the fence. That's just for today."

Will laughed. "That's all, huh? Buddy, you *are* back on the work train."

"Yep, so you pick."

"I guess I'll cut the grass," Will said.

"I know I wasn't in the bet," Danny said, "but I'll do something. I can chop those sticker vines."

"Y'all come back in half an hour," Trout said. "Mama's about to go up to the Superette to get some groceries. You can help then. She'd kill me if she found out."

With all three boys working together, they buzzed through Trout's chores by early in the afternoon. When Trout's mom returned earlier than expected, a tactic she used regularly to catch her kids off guard, the boys were swimming in the creek. Suspicious of how Trout had finished his chores, she called him up to the house.

"Trout," she said. "Since you finished so fast, you can start on tomorrow's list. In fact, I have it right here."

"But Mama, can't I just swim for a little longer? I've been working like a horse."

"You can have another fifteen minutes," she replied sternly. "But first I have some food in the car that needs to go in the freezer."

"Yes, ma'am," he said.

Since it was on the porch where anybody, even raccoons, could get to it, the freezer stayed locked. Of course, Lottie Loxley was no fool and she knew the biggest threat to her frozen goods were her wily sons. She didn't rule out the quick hands of Danny and Will either so the key was hidden where those boys would never look—her makeup case.

Normally she supervised Trout when he loaded the freezer but a long ride in the car coupled with a cold Dr. Pepper had the lavatory calling.

"Trout, get all that food stored and I'll be right back."

When the opportunity fell into his lap, he took it, quickly slipping a half-gallon package of frozen blueberries into his swimsuit. As he bounded down the steps toward the water, his mother called.

"*Trout!*"

"Yes, ma'am?"

"Come back up here. I want to go over this list with you."

"Can I swim first?"

"No!"

Trout quickly looked down to see if the package was bulging in his shorts. Fortunately, his t-shirt hid the stolen berries and his swimsuit held the bag firmly in place. But the tight swim trunks worked against him in other ways. He was starting to feel the chill of iced blueberries

73

pressing against his privates. As he climbed the porch steps, Trout had a strange jiggle in his walk. His mother had locked the freezer and was studying the list of chores.

"Let's see," she said. "What could you do this evening before dinner?"

"It doesn't matter, anything's fine with me," Trout said quickly.

"Hmm," she contemplated. "I don't really want to start painting the porch this late in the day. Maybe you could ... no, not that."

"Mama, can we do this after I swim?" Trout begged. He was worried about freezing his hot dog and the pain was getting intense.

"Just a minute. What's your hurry?"

"I just want to swim before Will and Danny have to leave."

"Okay, just give me a second. Let's see here ..."

"Mama, *please!*" he pleaded.

"Calm down, Trout. Don't be so impatient. You're starting to make me angry."

Trout knew he had to shut up and bear the pain. Biting his upper lip, he stood like a soldier waiting for his assignment.

"I've got it; you can start scraping the barnacles off the bottom of the boat. You're going to be swimming anyway. So that works out just perfectly."

"Great, I'll go start right now."

His feet barely touched the ground as he sprinted across the yard and flung himself into the water. The sharp stinging subsided slowly as the soothing warm creek sloshed around him. After he got the sweet taste of blueberries in his mouth, Trout forgot about his pain altogether.

Danny and Will had watched the whole scene play out from the shade of the pier. As they feasted on the bounty, they all giggled uncontrollably.

PART II

July

CHAPTER 13

A Good Deed

Sometimes life is a long row to hoe.
—Big Johnnie Showers

Freddie Showers sat on his front porch holding six pork chop bones. In the distance, a white mutt scratched a shallow hole in the dirt. Like Freddie, the dog had a pork chop bone too but it dangled from his slobbery mouth.

"Git over here, Spooky!" Freddie yelled.

The dog's head jerked up and looked Freddie's way.

"Come on. I got another bone for ya."

In a flash, the mutt dropped the bone, kicked some dirt on it, and lit out toward Freddie. He reared back and flung another bone. "Get it, Spooky! You know you ain't nothing but an old mutt."

Freddie laughed as the dog tumbled across the dirt after that bone.

"You sure are dumb. That bone ain't gonna run off. It ain't no possum."

For the next hour, Freddie and his dog played chase the bone. It was something they did whenever Freddie got enough bones from his mama and the other mamas in the neighborhood. He was about to sling the last bone when a big silver Chevrolet rambled down the dirt road. Dust swirled up behind the shiny car. Spooky took off after it, barking up a storm.

"Git back here," Freddie shouted. But the dog wasn't listening this time. Chasing a car was just too much fun and besides, he was tired of chewing on bones.

The sun shimmered across the hood as the Chevy turned on Freddie's driveway and eased up to the house. Lottie Loxley rolled her window down to yell at Freddie and his dog.

"Freddie, would you please get this dog off my car?"

"Yes, ma'am, Miss Lottie. Spooky, git yer smelly butt off of Miss Lottie's car."

With his front paws scraping at the door handle, Spooky yelped a racket.

Freddie walked up and slapped the dog's nose. "Would you shut up? I'm sorry, Miss Lottie, but he does like to chase cars."

"It's okay, Freddie. We have dogs, too. I know how they act."

"Yes, ma'am, but he's usually real friendly. Don't take no offense at this, but I think he just likes to get after rich folks. I don't know why that is. Maybe he can smell 'em."

Lottie Loxley smiled at Freddie. "It's probably because he's never seen me around here. I'm just unfamiliar."

"Yes, ma'am. I'd say that's got to be part of it. He's not used to seeing fancy cars either."

"Well, that explains it. I'm sure he'd like me if he got to know me better."

"And if you gave him a pork chop bone. He'd like that, too."

"I don't happen to have any bones with me at the moment, Freddie. But next time I come, I'll be sure to bring a few."

"Next time?"

"Yes, Freddie, I hope to be coming up here from time to time."

"How come, Miss Lottie?"

"I'll explain it to your daddy. Is he home?"

"Yes, ma'am. He's out in the back tending to the vegetable garden. I'll run and fetch him."

"Great. Maybe you can take your dog with you."

Spooky had been sniffing around Lottie Loxley's feet and had even nipped at her ankle. Not that she was scared. Growing up on a farm with hogs and goats had taught her to use her huge feet as weapons. She didn't want to have to hurt Freddie's dog, but if the mutt had gotten vicious, she'd have kicked him halfway to Mobile.

Big Johnnie, as they called Freddie's daddy, was a jack-of-all-trades. He could rebuild an engine, frame a house, design a septic field, build furniture, and throw a cast net over a school of mullet better than Wallace Flomaton. The man was strong enough to lift up a car by the bumper if a tire needed changing and he didn't take kindly to slick talkers . When a door-to-door salesman called him poor white trash for refusing to buy a life insurance policy, Big Johnnie grabbed the man by the collar and threw him into the pig pen. No other insurance agents ever called on Big Johnnie.

They were poor but proud. The money Big Johnnie made doing odd jobs kept his family in shoes and the small plot of land he worked yeilded plenty of food for his family, the neighbors, and some extra veggies to sell on the side.

At the top of his list of many talents was growing some of the tastiest vegetables in Baldwin County. Unfortunately, Freddie didn't inherit any of his daddy's abilities. To Big Johnnie's constant disappointment, Freddie's greatest skill was talking up a storm and throwing pork bones to Spooky.

Big Johnnie knocked the dirt from his overalls as he ambled toward Lottie Loxley. Freddie and his dog followed close behind.

"Howdy, Miss Lottie. What can I do for you?"

"Nothing, Johnnie. I'm actually here to do something for you."

Johnnie looked at her with a skepticism that had been sharpened over many years. The beach folks never came around unless they wanted something. In fact, the last time he saw Lottie Loxley she asked him to haul off an old refrigerator that wasn't worth anything. She acted as if she was doing him a favor when she said he could have it for free. The last thing Big Johnnie wanted was a useless appliance but he took it anyway because occasionally she hired him for jobs that actually paid real money.

"Unh huh and what might that be Miss Lottie?"

"Well, you know my boys are growing up and I have some children's books they don't read anymore. I thought you might want them for Freddie."

Big Johnnie didn't know if she was serious or just trying to be mean. "I don't know why you'd give them books to Freddie, Miss Lottie. You know he can't read."

"Well that's something else. I figured I could come up here once a week and teach him."

"Why would you want to do that?"

"I don't know. I guess I just think Freddie needs to learn to read. Every child should know how to read."

"I agree with you on that but Freddie just didn't take to reading no matter how hard we tried to teach him."

"For one thing, I know he's smarter than folks give him credit for. Some kids just have trouble reading. I can spend extra time with him and give him another chance."

Big Johnnie smacked more dirt off the back of his pants and thought about her proposition. He couldn't figure out why she was trying to be so nice and, the truth was, he didn't trust her.

"Well, what do you say John. It can't hurt. Let me give it a try. If he doesn't start learning, I'll stop trying. Nothing ventured, nothing gained."

"Okay," he said. "Freddie ain't doing nothing anyway 'cept messing with that old mutt. Have at it."

She turned to Freddie, who'd been listening curiously the whole time. "Did you hear that, Freddie? I'm going to teach you how to read."

"I tried real hard, but I just couldn't do it," he said.

"Would you be willing to try again?"

"I don't know. Why should I?"

"I tell you what. Every time you learn a few words, I'll bring you some of my famous homemade peach ice cream."

Freddie lit up like Spooky chasing a bone. "Okay, I'll try again!"

"Marvelous," she said. "I'll come back tomorrow and we can have our first lesson."

"Can you bring some of that ice cream?"

"Not only that, I'll bring a bone for your puppy."

As she drove away, Big Johnnie watched his son tangling with Spooky in the dirt and wondered what had gotten into Lottie Loxley.

"She's got a long row to hoe," he said. "A long row."

CHAPTER 14

The Game of a Name

She was smart, pretty and rich—a dangerous trifecta.
—Walt Thornton

Thousands of years ago in ancient Greece, men began naming their warships after women. Like their wives and mistresses, boats shared their souls and routinely consumed particularly large sums of money. In modern times, pleasure boats pay homage to the fair female with names like Sweet Lucy, Caroline's Chariot or simply, The Other Woman. Perhaps the gentle, smooth lines and the love and meticulous care required to keep boats on an even keel is why female names are appropriate. Besides, there's nothing at all romantic about naming a boat Billy Bob or Frank. That's just dumb.

Perdido boats were no different. Some went beyond gender and had clever names like the fishing boat, Reel Fun, or the racing sailboat, Blew By-You. Others were less imaginative as was the Perdido Princess, the boat that carried mail and supplies to local waterfront outposts.

Since all of the cottages in Perdido were vacation homes, folks took to naming them, too. The tradition began with the very first home built near Soldier Creek in 1892 by a fellow named Colonel L.B. Hatch. A veteran of the Civil War, Hatch constructed a grand home with massive columns, wide porches and a wandering driveway lined by towering oaks. He named it Rambler's Rest because that's where he finally settled and invited old friends to come and rest awhile with him. He raised three daughters and a son there and passed on parcels of land to them when he died. Most of them built houses of their own and carried on the naming legacy.

As the Montgomery crowd descended upon Perdido around the turn of the century, they devised their own set of clever names. Overextended financially, one family named their cottage Cantafford but disguised the meaning by pronouncing it *CANT-uh-frd*, with the emphasis on the first syllable instead of the last. That way, it sounded like a grand old family name.

One of the original cottages, Dumbiddy, was probably a reference to a mother-in-law or ex-wife. Mr. Walt and Miss Kitty's cottage, Paradise Point, was self-explanatory, as was Doc Jordan's Breezehunter. But the most famous, in both name and reputation, was Witchwood. The only home with waterfront on Perdido Bay and Soldier Creek, Witchwood was old, spooky and, because of a somewhat sordid past, undoubtedly haunted.

When the boys passed by Witchwood on their way to The Point during daylight hours, it just seemed like a big old beach cottage. But at night, there was no place scarier and no house they'd run past faster, except the Widow Woman's.

One night as they sat around a roaring bonfire at The Point, Danny posed the question. "I wonder why they call it Witchwood."

"I know," Trout said. "My dad told it to me one time."

"So how come?" Will asked.

"I'm not sure I want to tell it. We have to walk by it tonight you know."

"So," Will said, "you gonna be a scaredy cat if you tell it?"

"Heck no! I was just trying to protect y'all."

"Don't worry about me," Will said. "I can take it."

"Me too," Danny piped up. "I don't scare easy."

"That's not what I heard."

"What do you mean?" Danny asked.

"Oh nothing, except about the snipe hunt the other night."

"What about the snipe hunt?" Will asked.

"Well, I talked to some folks up on the bluff and they said y'all came running by their houses so fast, they thought a bobcat was chasing you."

"We were racing," Will said. "Haven't you ever raced?"

"Sure I've raced but not all the way from the Widow Woman's house."

Danny and Will knew Trout had their number. Somehow, he always knew everything. When he wasn't working under his mama's iron rule or getting into mischief with Will and Danny, Trout just loved to ramble through the woods and along the beach taking in all that nature provided. On those long walks alone, he'd inevitably bump into folks along the way. They'd chat and he'd get all the gossip: what family members were visiting, if they were going to rent their house and, most importantly, if they had any cute girls staying with them. More often than not, he'd get invited in for a snack and a cold drink or even lunch or dinner when his timing was right. Of course, he always had impeccable timing and a tummy that stayed as tight as a tick.

"Well we might have gotten a little scared by the Widow Woman," Danny admitted.

Trout laughed. "A little?"

"Well, maybe a lot. If you'd have seen her …"

"You mean you actually saw her? In the flesh?"

"Did we ever," Will said. "She came running out with all of her cats and she was screeching at us like a wounded owl."

"I thought she was gonna snatch us up and skin us alive," Danny said.

"Oh my gosh," Trout said, "I can't believe you really came face to face with her."

"Not for long. We turned tail and took off like a bunch of wasps were after us," Will said with a chuckle.

"Un huh. Is that so? Well you got me there. I guess I do know all about that. And boys, I know one more thing: I'd have been right there with y'all running like a scared puppy, too."

"I know you wouldn't have stuck around to count her cats," Will said.

"No way."

"So now that you know all about us almost getting snatched up by the Widow Woman, tell us about Witchwood," Danny pleaded.

"Alright, if y'all survived the Widow Woman, this ought to be a piece of cake. Well, it's like this. Back a long time ago, maybe a hundred years I guess, a man and his wife moved down from somewhere up north. Chicago or Illinois or something, I think. And they bought the house from the people who built it. Well, they lived there for a few years, then one day the man just kind of disappeared. The wife told everybody that he moved back home but people started wondering 'cause he loved to fish and hunt around here and always said he hated Chicago. They were pretty old so she told everybody that for all she knew he had died up there in the cold winter. But my dad said that neighbors had heard them fighting and stuff so they started getting suspicious."

"Yeah, so what happened?" Will asked. "Did she kill him?"

"Just listen, I'm trying to tell you. Some fella from Mobile came over on a hunting trip with a couple of guys and their bird dogs. They rented a house down the beach for a couple of weeks and it turns out he was some kind of sheriff or something. Well, one morning they heard all kinds of barking and the dogs had gotten after a coon. They chased that coon right into the woman's house and the coon climbed into the attic."

"Oh God," Will said. "They found the husband in a steamer trunk in the attic, didn't they?"

"No! And if you don't quit interrupting I'm not gonna tell you."

"I'm sorry. Go ahead."

"Well those dogs ran in the house after that coon and the old woman was trying to run 'em all out. So the sheriff guy came in with his buddies to try to help, but by then, the coon had wedged his way behind the paneling in the bathroom. And the dogs were going crazy. Sure enough, those men popped off a board of that paneling and had their shotguns ready to shoot that coon when they saw some kind of hidden closet and inside was a bunch of those big ol' gallon glass mason jars. The first one they saw looked like it had a human hand in it. And, sure enough, when they looked closer they found her husband all cut up and packed in those jars."

"I knew it," Will said. "She killed him and cut him up."

"That's the creepiest thing I ever heard," Danny said. "What happened to her?"

"Well, first of all, they shot that coon and calmed the dogs down. Then they took the old woman away to jail. My daddy said she claimed she didn't do it."

"Sounds like she was as guilty as sin," Will said.

"Well, that's where the story gets even wilder. She told the police that her husband had been some kind of real bad criminal in Chicago and that's why they moved down to Perdido. They were trying to hide out from some mobsters who wanted him dead. So she said they must have killed him and put him in those jars when she was gone one day or something. So when they checked on the man, it turned out that he really was some kind of gangster and folks really were trying to kill him."

"So what happened to the woman?"

"They let her go because they never could prove she did it."

"And she came back to the house."

"Yep and she lived there for a good while after that and always wore some long black dress and a black veil. And my daddy said he remembers seeing her but she never talked to anybody. They'd just see her walking around on her porch sometimes."

"That's weird!"

"And listen to this, daddy said that at night with the moon was full, she'd row out to the middle of the creek and folks could hear her kind of howling at the moon. After she died, they sold the house and the new owners named it Witchwood."

"Is that really true," Danny said with a tremble.

"My daddy says it is."

"I believe it," Will said. "I mean why not? That is a perfect place to hide out if you were in trouble and running from the law. Maybe those gangsters killed that man but I still think it was his wife. Heck either way, I guess it drove her crazy."

"Yep, a crazy old witch. That's why they say that sometimes during a full moon her ghost goes out on the creek in a rowboat and howls at the moon."

"You mean like tonight?" Danny asked. "Look over there."

Will and Trout looked east across Soldier Creek. At that very moment the full moon, as orange and a pumpkin, was rising out of the pine trees.

"Now that's a weird coincidence," Danny said. "Think we'll hear her tonight?'

"I don't know," Trout said, "but when we go by Witchwood I'm gonna be running."

"Me too," said Danny.

"You guys are a couple of chickens," Will said. "She's dead and gone. Even if there was such as thing as ghosts, they can't get you. Not like the Widow Woman can. She's real."

"You can walk as slow as you want," Trout said. "I'm still gonna run."

As the night wore on the boys roasted a few marshmallows, told more stories and took a short swim. Eventually, when the moon had climbed up the sky and turned icy white, they had to walk home. From The Point, they passed by three houses before coming to Witchwood. Along the way, their senses were acute to every sound—a possum digging in the woods, tree branches brushing together and waves lapping on the shore. Suddenly a large redfish splashed near the bank and they froze.

"What was that?" Danny whimpered.

"Just a fish splashing," Will said quietly. "It's not a stupid ghost."

His words were unconvincing, lacking their usual conviction. For all he knew, maybe it really was a phantom paddle churning through the water.

"I don't see any lights on," Danny said as the road curved and Witchwood came into sight. "Okay Trout, you ready?"

Trout was already kicking up sand. "Let's go!"

Will stood steadfast for a few seconds until a great blue heron flew over and let out a deathly screech.

"Wait for *me*," Will yelled as he broke into a full sprint in a split second. He was catching up fast when a flash of intense light hit their faces and stopped them dead in their tracks. Danny fell to his knees and skidded face first into the sandy road. It took a few seconds for the boys to figure out that they were looking into the headlights of a car.

"Hey guys," someone said as they stepped from the car, "whatcha doing?"

"Uh, just going home," Will said.

"You sure were in a hurry."

"Stuart?" Trout asked.

"Yeah?"

"Oh man, are we glad to see you. When did y'all get down?"

"Just now," he said, "not more than thirty seconds ago. Daddy's over at the power pole turning the electricity on."

Just then, they heard a loud click, and Witchwood lit up inside and out.

"Got it," Stuart's father yelled.

"Why'd you hit us with those headlights?" Will demanded.

"I heard some commotion down the road, and I just wanted to see what it was. I guess I found out."

"Well what'd you think it was?" Will said.

"I don't know, maybe a possum or a wild hog or something."

"Next time be more considerate. You blinded us."

"Sorry."

Stuart Felder's family had rented Witchwood the prior summer. The same age as the boys, Stuart looked forward to getting to know them better since they knew all the best fishing holes, places to ski and far off lands to explore. In the short time, he'd hung around with them they'd lived large. Back home in Mobile, Stuart had plenty of close friends. But they didn't leap from cypress trees or take kids snipe hunting. Stuart had been initiated into sniping on his last night at Perdido and he passed the test with flying colors, meaning he didn't hold a grudge. He figured it as a right of passage into the Perdido circle of deep friendships.

His dad, Dr. Thurwood Felder, was one of Mobile's most prominent surgeons and meticulous in every way. His thirty-foot Hinkley sailboat was a classic wooden vessel with divine lines. Painted with precision and without a single tarnish on the bronze hardware or even the slightest blemish in the varnish bright work, the *Water Lilly*, was appropriately named for his lovely wife. As one would expect from a surgeon, the sailboat was obsessively immaculate. She was in better condition than replicas gracing mantle pieces in million-dollar mansions. Absolutely consumed with the *Water Lilly*, Dr. Felder was often accused of spending more time on his yacht than with his wife and kids. In fact, if they wanted to see him, they'd go out to the boat where he'd be polishing metal, cleaning the cabin and touching up paint. Everyday from about two o'clock to four, the Felder family would hang out on that boat and maybe, if everything was spotless and the wind wasn't too strong, they might even take the *Water Lilly* sailing.

"Hey, y'all. Want to come in for a Coca-cola or something?" Stuart asked.

"Sure," Trout answered.

"Y'all need some help carrying stuff in?" Danny asked.

Mrs. Lilly Felder appeared on the porch. "That would be great honey," she said. "There are some bags in the trunk you boys could bring in. I'll fix you some lemonade. How does that sound?"

"Great," Will said as he stared at her in awe. As they say, the good doctor had robbed the cradle and Lilly, his second wife, was twenty years his junior. At thirty-two-years-old, she still possessed the beauty-queen qualities that had first hooked Dr. Felder. She was an ideal match for his sailboat. Both had beautifully classic lines and both were scrupulously maintained. Even at twelve, the boys recognized her stunning good looks and shapely body. As they sipped on lemonade, they admired her golden brown skin and shiny lips. Eyeballing her was something they looked forward to during the next two weeks.

"Hey, y'all want to play Sardines?" Stuart asked. "My sister brought some friends down. They might want to play, too."

Will looked at Lilly out of the corner of his eye hoping she might play too but he knew that was just a boyhood dream. "Good idea," he said. "Let's do it."

Stuart cupped his hands and yelled toward the back bedrooms. "Hey Ellis, y'all wanna play Sardines?"

"We'll be out in a little bit," his sister said.

Stuart's paternal twin, Ellis was a budding beauty in her own right. Fortunately, she'd gotten her mother's good looks. Stuart got his father's brains.

Ellis rounded the corner with her companions.

"Hi guys, these are my friends," Ellis said, "Grace and Georgiana."

"Well I'll be a dead mullet," Will said. "It's the snipe twins."

Grace and Georgiana smiled slyly at the boys.

"We didn't expect to see you but it's sure nice seeing y'all again." Danny said.

Ellis and Stuart turned to the girls. "Y'all know them?" Stuart asked.

"Well, kinda," Grace said. "We came down for a few days earlier this summer with Elberta Weeks. We ran into 'em a couple of times."

Ellis was perturbed. "Is that so? You never mentioned that when you called me about coming down with us?"

Will laughed. "They called *you*?"

"Actually, I did call," Grace admitted. "Georgiana and I had such a good time we wanted to come back."

"Ain't that something?" Will said. "Well then, welcome back."

A frown dug deep into Ellis's face. Grace and Georgiana were popular, part of the in crowd, and she thought this was their way of inviting her into the inner circle. Now it appeared they were just chasing boys.

Trout stepped up to Georgiana and extended his hand. "I'm not a cousin or anything, I'm just a friend. My name is Trout. We met real quick right before y'all left that morning with Elberta."

"I remember," she said with a wink. "Nice to see you again."

Trout blushed and giggled. "Even better to see you."

"Okay, enough with the mushy stuff, do y'all know how to play Sardines or what?" Will asked.

"I don't," Grace said.

"Me either," Georgiana said.

Will stepped forward to explain. "It's real easy. It's just like hide-and-seek but instead of everybody hiding and one person looking, it's the other way around."

"Yeah," Danny followed up. "One person goes and hides and then everybody else looks for him."

"Then," Will said, "when you find the person who's hiding, you get in there with him."

"After a while," Danny said, "they'll just be one person left looking and everybody else will be crammed together in the same hiding place."

"That's why they call it Sardines," Will said.

"So, when you pick a hiding place, make sure it's big enough to fit everybody," Danny said. "Like under a bed or in a closet."

"And you have to be really quiet when you're hiding together so the other people looking won't hear you. Any questions?"

The girls understood. They were smart, pretty, and from an affluent neighborhood in Mobile, a dangerous trifecta, as Mr. Walt would say.

Fortunately, Dr. Felder was at *Water Lilly* removing the tarp so she'd be ready to launch in the morning. He never would have approved of Sardines. It involved too many kids with the potential of upsetting the quiet order of things.

"Oh yeah," Will said, "We have to turn out all of the lights."

"You're kidding, right?" Grace asked.

"Nope," Will said. "That's the way it's played."

The girls didn't need to hear Trout's rendition of why the house was named Witchwood because the old place oozed spookiness. With dark wood paneling on the walls, floors and ceilings, antique furniture and eight-foot doors that all creaked on their hinges, Witchwood and haunted fit together like its tongue and groove floors. From the living room, a skinny door opened up to a steep and narrow stairwell leading to the attic where ghosts and goblins surely lived.

"One more thing," Will said. "You can hide in the attic, too."

The girls squealed quietly and prayed that no one would actually venture up there.

"Okay, unless Stuart wants to be "it" first," Will said, "I'll do it."

"Go ahead," Stuart said. "Be my guest."

The pale moonlight was blotted out by thick Spanish moss hanging from giant oaks that surrounded Witchwood. There was a blackness so deep they had to feel their way along the walls to get from room to room. Will snuck away while the rest of them huddled together in the middle of the living room slowly counting to fifty. He knew exactly where he was going to hide.

Lilly sat on the front porch admiring the full moon under the breeze of the ceiling fan. Practically a kid herself, she loved listening to their conversations and games. She would have joined in except that Thurwood wouldn't approve of it. Everything came with a price.

"48 ... 49 ... 50," Danny said. "I'm gonna check out the attic."

One of girls gasped just thinking about going up into the coal darkness. Slowly they spread out. Will had slipped through a small opening in the wall of the master bathroom where the infamous mason jars had been discovered. Although it gave him a chill thinking about body parts in jars, he figured Trout and Danny would only search the dead man's room after they'd looked everywhere else.

The blond curls on Will's head rubbed the ceiling of the tiny space. Barely as big as a broom closet, Will could hardly spread his arms out. He knew it was going to be tight but that was his plan.

While Trout, Danny and Stuart had set out alone, the girls stuck together to explore one room at a time. Will heard their voices in the master bedroom as they looked under the bed and felt inside the closet. Ellis led them into the bathroom where they checked behind the shower curtain. She knew about the weird little alcove by the sink but was too scared to step into it. The darkness and silence was overwhelming.

"What's back there?" Grace whispered nervously.

"It's just a small closet with a couple of shelves," Ellis said.

Georgiana quivered and squeezed Ellis's arm. "How far back does it go?"

"A few feet but I'm not stepping in there," Ellis said. "Georgiana, you reach in and see if he's in there."

"No way. You do it."

"I can't," Ellis said.

"Hush y'all!" Grace whispered. "I'll do it. I just hope nothing grabs me."

Will held his breath as he listened but almost laughed at how frightened they were. As she reached in, Will pressed himself against the wall but her fingers brushed against his shoulder. Goose bumps ran up her arm but she suppressed her instinct to scream. Grace had already figured out the game.

"Nope, he's not in there," she said. "Let's check another room."

They followed Ellis blindly out of the bedroom and slid along the living room walls until they stumbled on the doorway into their bedroom. As they went in, Georgiana turned to grab Grace's arm. She groped into thin air.

"Grace, where are you?"

Silence.

"Grace?"

Silence again.

Even though the space was cramped, there was plenty of room for Grace and Will. As Ellis and Georgiana shuffled around the living room, Grace had turned back silently and crawled in with Will.

"Maybe she found Will," Ellis said.

"Or goblins got her," Georgiana shivered. "This is too scary!"

"If she found him, it was either in the living room, the bedroom or the bathroom. Let's go back. I'll check the living room; you check the bedroom and bathroom."

It didn't take long for Georgiana to find Will and Grace. And now with the three of them in there, there was barely enough room for one more. When Georgiana didn't return from the bedroom, Ellis retraced her steps and heard giggling inside the bathroom. She squeezed in quietly. Will's plan had worked even better than he hoped. Wedged between three cute girls, he had turned the scene of a fabled murder into his slice of heaven. He loved this game.

Trout bumped into Danny on the stairway to the attic and his heart almost stopped.

"Crap, I didn't even see you," Trout said.

"Sorry, but I didn't see you either. You can go on up and look, but I don't think he's in the attic," Danny said.

"Did you check in that little storage room?"

"Yep."

"Well I'm gonna go look anyway," Trout said.

"Have fun."

Stuart was crawling under the dining room table checking between chair legs when he heard a bump against the wall. He eased over to put his ear to the paneling and heard voices through the boards. Within a minute, he was trying to wedge himself in with the others but he could only get half his body inside. Will had one arm around Grace's waist; another draped over Georgiana's shoulder and a smile from ear to ear. Every time someone shifted, they all giggled then tried to calm each other down.

A chill ran down his spine when Danny entered the master bedroom. He didn't want to go in that bathroom. All he could think of was a bony hand of that dead man reaching out and grabbing him around the neck. Goose bumps popped up on his arms and neck. When he finally got the courage to poke his head into the bathroom, he heard snickering and he knew he'd hit pay dirt. He breathed a sigh of relief but with Stuart already sticking out into the bathroom, he could only lean up against the wall.

Inevitably, the game had come down to one player. As Trout lurched around in the attic, he noticed that unmistakable silence, even deeper than the blackness that surrounded him. The realization hit him. He was the last one looking; a solitary soul in a bloodcurdling and, undoubtedly haunted house and perhaps the next victim of Witchwood's deadly past. Fear of the dark and creepy unknown began to smother him and Trout scurried quickly downstairs. For a moment, he sat on the living room couch hoping to hear his friends. But there was only the sound of Spanish moss brushing against the house like witches' brooms sweeping across the porch. Dark shadows writhed on the windows and fear tightened its grip around him. He staggered out of the room thinking some fresh air would help. Suddenly a massive dark figure moved silently across the porch draped in a flowing dress. *It's the Witch of Witchwood,* Trout thought. *And she's coming to get ME!* His mind and body went numb, his legs weakened and as the living room lights flashed on, he collapsed. From a sitting position on the floor, Trout looked up at Dr. Felder standing in the doorway carrying a mainsail over his shoulder.

"What the devil is going on here?" Dr. Felder asked. "Why are all the lights off?"

"They're playing Sardines honey," Lilly said as she breezed in from the porch. "The lights have to be off."

"Son, are you okay," he said looking at Trout withered on the floor.

"Yes, sir, you just scared me."

"Sorry Trout, but I didn't know what was going on. Where is everybody else?"

Will, Stuart and the girls scampered out of the bedroom chattering like monkeys.

"That was scary," Stuart said.

"Yeah, great hiding place," Ellis said. "How'd you think of that one?"

"Oh, I don't know," Will said. "Just lucky I guess."

He winked at Grace and Georgiana. "Y'all want to play again sometime?"

"Sure," they smiled.

"But you know what we really ought to do," Trout said finally composing himself.

"What?" Danny asked.

"Well, let me ask this: Has Ellis ever been snipe hunting?"

CHAPTER 15

The Second Worst Job

A productive man is happy and a happy man is productive.
—Walt Thornton

Life around Perdido Bay was always about self-reliance. The cottages had running water and electricity but that's where the luxuries stopped. That is, if you call indoor toilets and light bulbs luxuries. No one had television, newspaper deliveries, garbage service, city water or sewer. Water came from the well, waste went into a septic tank, and everyone dealt with garbage in their own way. At Mr. Walt's house, paper got burned, old food was tilled into a garden, and cans and bottles were buried in the garbage pit. He didn't know it and wouldn't have appreciated being called one, but Mr. Walt was an early environmentalist. Not because he wanted to be. It just made sense.

The garbage pit was notorious because the boys had to dig a new one at the beginning of each summer. Mr. Walt would pick a spot way off in the back yard out of sight and smell of the house. Back there, the sun seemed to be more intense and the cool breeze was blocked out. He'd hand out the shovels and come back every thirty minutes or so to check their progress and to make sure the heat and humidity hadn't melted their brains. The only good aspect, if there's anything positive about digging a giant hole in the ground, was the sandy soil. That made it fairly easy to dig. On the other hand, Mr. Walt liked humongous garbage pits. The rule of thumb was six feet deep, six feet long and six feet wide.

"Still needs to be a little deeper," he'd say on his inspections or, "make it wider on that side."

It didn't take long for the boys to figure out that grave digging was not a career they wanted to pursue.

"I wonder what's gonna happen when some scientist digs one of these garbage pits up in a million years," Danny said.

"They'll probably realize we ate a lot of peanut butter and jelly," Will said as he stopped to lean on his shovel.

"Are you goofy? The labels won't be on there anymore in a million years."

"Yeah but they might find some petrified peanut butter or something."

"I think the worms and critters will eat it all by then."

"Maybe so," Will said still rubbing his chin contemplating petrified peanut butter.

"Hey, keep digging Will. You've taken four water breaks and gone to the bathroom twice. I've been digging the whole time."

"I can't help it if I have to pee. It's all the water I'm drinking."

"Yeah, but I've dug twice as much dirt as you," Danny said.

"Not twice as much."

"Well more. Anyway, we can go swimming when we finish."

"Fine," Will said, "but I'm not gonna kill myself digging."

"You're not gonna die by working hard."

"You don't know. I heard about this man who was working in the lumberyard. He picked up a huge board, and his heart just exploded. Folks said it sounded like a cherry bomb. He fell over dead as a doornail."

"He was probably old and fat and shoulda been in an old folks' home. You're twelve!"

"Still, I don't want my heart to blow up."

"If it does," Danny laughed, "at least we'll already have your grave dug. I'll just cover you up with some dirt."

Will resented Danny's badgering. He wasn't lazy; he just liked to pace himself. If they had time to go for a boat ride or a swim later, that would be fine. If not, that was fine, too. Danny didn't think that way. With each shovel full of dirt, he imagined diving into the cool water. Motivated by future rewards, Danny dug relentlessly. Talking about it was a waste of precious time so he turned to the pit and continued to dig.

Mr. Walt's shrill whistle pierced the muggy heat and the boys knew one of them had to show up fast.

"You go, Danny," Will said. "This will give me a chance to catch up on all the digging you did."

Will seemed sincere but they both knew that being summoned by Mr. Walt was a crapshoot. If he needed help working on the boat, that could mean a cool dip in the bay. But they feared the ickiest, nastiest job of all: cleaning the septic tank. Of all chores, whoever showed up for that job would be better off in hell. Digging out the septic tank was not just stinky and grueling; it undoubtedly caused traumatic damage that would ooze into future psychotherapy sessions. Not to mention, the smell stuck to their skin for days, so they'd be stuck at a separate table for meals until the odor subsided.

Danny rolled the dice and answered the call. Without looking up from his digging, Will said, "I think I hear someone taking the top off the septic tank."

Danny froze for a moment but noticed Will's wry smile. Then as quick as a rabbit, he sprinted to Mr. Walt. Danny was the first to arrive, even though being first didn't win him any rewards. Seconds later two cousins and a brother showed up. Mr. Walt showed no signs of appreciation for their promptness mainly because when he whistled he was totally focused on the task at hand. Handing out prizes didn't help get the job done.

On that particular occasion, Mr. Walt had pieces and parts of the old Yazoo lawn mower spread across the grass. His hands were greasy and two knuckles were bleeding. It was a typical scene. Those huge hands were a patchwork of scabs and bruises and the fifteen-year-old lawn mower had been rebuilt more times than the red ant piles it regularly blew apart.

"Danny, grab that long screwdriver," he said without looking up. "You other boys get back to what you were doing."

"Got it," Danny said.

"Okay, put it in the spark plug cap. I need to see if we're getting power to the plug."

"Like this?" Danny asked obediently.

"Yeah. Make sure it's up against that little metal cap inside. Let me know when you've got it."

Danny poked the screwdriver into the rubber cap until he jammed the tip against the metal ring that normally fit snugly on top of the spark plug.

"Now what?" he asked.

"Just hold it steady," Mr. Walt said as he grabbed the pull chord and gave it a yank.

"*Yeeeooowww!*" Danny yelled when the jolt of electricity shot up his arm. It scared him more than it hurt him, but the shock still knocked the screwdriver from his hand.

"Well, we've got a spark," Mr. Walt said analytically, still staring at the Yazoo mower. The fact that he'd just mildly electrocuted his son took second fiddle to fixing the decrepit grass cutter. This was essential problem solving, not babysitting. "Okay Danny, now put the cap back on the sparkplug."

Danny was still shaking random electrons out of his hand and wondering if Mr. Walt was going to zap him again.

"Uh … is it gonna shock me again?" he asked.

"Not if you hold the rubber cap. Um, you alright boy?"

"Yes, sir. That just surprised me. I didn't know it was gonna shock."

"Yep. That's how it works. When I pull the chord, it sends electricity to the spark plug, the spark fires off the gasoline and this old machine cranks to life."

"Un huh," Danny said stupefied.

"Now you watch the spark plug real close to see if it sparks when I pull the chord again. I promise, it won't shock you."

Mr. Walt yanked on the pull chord and Danny saw little blue flames flickering at the business end of the plug.

"It's sparking," he said.

"Good. That means we just need to make sure she's getting gas."

Danny watched in awe as Mr. Walt tinkered with the choke, cleaned filters, and made sure all the gas lines were clear. Within minutes, he had the old mower put back together.

"Okay Danny, give her a tug."

On the second pull, the ancient Yazoo coughed to life, shooting noxious blue smoke from its rusty muffler. Mr. Walt stepped back and admired his work. The old beast could still whack a lot of grass.

"So how are you and Will coming on the garbage pit?" Mr. Walt yelled over the clamoring engine.

"Almost done daddy," Danny yelled back. "Maybe another hour or so."

Mr. Walt cut the engine, tilted his head and let out another whistle. "Get on back to the pit," he said. "Somebody else can cut the grass."

As Danny ran off, he saw several boys sprinting around the corners of the house. *Grass cutting victims*, he thought. He knew why Mr. Walt asked how much longer they had on the pit. If he'd told him they were finished, he'd be pushing that Yazoo right now. And with three acres of back yard, that was one brutal job. The truth was, Danny wasn't sure how much longer it would take to finish the pit, especially since he'd left Will in charge. One thing he did know for sure, Will wasn't doing much digging while he'd been gone. Most likely, he was sitting by the pit drinking water from the hose.

As he approached the garbage pit, Danny's suspicions were confirmed. Will was nowhere to be found. There was plenty of shade in the woods and he figured Will was escaping the relentless sun. Then he heard a dull cough from deep inside the hole. Danny ran to the edge of the pit and saw Will spread out at the bottom with the shovel across his chest and brown foam bubbling from his mouth. With one leap, he landed next to Will for a closer look. Will's eyelids were fluttering and his eyes were rolling back in his head. Danny slapped his cheeks.

"Will, Will! Wake up!"

More foam poured from his mouth and Danny couldn't tell if he was breathing or not. He felt Will's neck and wrist trying to find a pulse—something he'd learned in Boy Scouts—but all he noticed was that Will was cold and clammy. *That's too weird*, he thought. *It's ninety degrees outside, and he's cold.*

Danny tried slapping Will's face again, and even shook his head around, but got no response. He'd seen someone do mouth-to-mouth resuscitation, but Danny's mind was racing too fast to try that. Instead, he yelled for Mr. Walt. But that old Yazoo could drown out the sound of an atom bomb. He didn't want to leave Will alone, but his last choice was to run to the house for help. As he leaped from the hole, Will coughed. Danny looked back and saw even more foam gurgling out. He also thought he saw Will's arm move behind the blade of the shovel. At the same time, it looked as if Will was grinning slightly.

Before he ran for help, Danny snuck slowly around the back rim of the pit. Will's hand was wrapped around a can of Coca-Cola behind the blade of the shovel. Will lifted his head to see if Danny had gone. He took another sip of Coke and laughed at his cleverness.

"You *turkey*!" Danny yelled and jumped down on top of Will, knocking the Coke can into the dirt. "You scared the crap outta me!"

Will grabbed the Coke and held it out to Danny. "Wanna sip?" he said with a smile.

Danny shoved him back down into the dirt.

"I thought your heart had exploded like that fat man's at the lumber mill."

"Sorry about that," Will laughed, as he let more brown Coke foam run down his chin.

"But how'd you make your face cold?" Danny asked.

"I just poured water from the hose on my face and hands. When I saw you coming, I jumped in the hole, took a big sip of Coke, and started choking."

"Well, I thought you were dying for sure."

"Serves you right for working me so hard."

Danny shot him a glare and grabbed a shovel.

"You haven't seen anything yet," he promised. "Let's just get this finished so we can go swimming."

"Okay," Will said. "You win. But seeing you jump around like a wild animal was the funniest thing I've seen all day."

Danny shot him a death stare. "Whatever it takes to keep you working, cuz."

CHAPTER 16

Mr. Randolph's Store

When I got rich, somehow I became a genius.
—Wallace Flomaton, 1961

Typical Perdido cottages had two basic kitchen appliances—a refrigerator and stove. Fancy kitchens even had a toaster. Radios, record players, TVs and other such devices were considered ridiculous extravagances. Mr. Walt did keep an old weather radio handy that repeated tide information and the weather forecast every ten minutes.

To listen to a bona fide radio, folks went to Mr. Randolph's Store. The old RCA radio scratched out a little country music, a few news reports from the outside world and the occasional night baseball game. Thing was, most people were too busy fishing, sailing or swimming to sit around listening to a radio. By day, that is. At night the store cranked up the action—some cold beers, a little penny-ante poker and when the radio signal was clear enough to play a particularly good song, maybe even some dancing. The "back room" even had a couple of slot machines there were kept very secretive among the men.

Built on pilings over Soldier Creek and wrapped in a wide pier for boats to tie up, the store also served as fueling station, grocery store, hardware store and Post Office since the supply boat dropped the mail there. If Perdido had a town hall, Randolph's Store was it. But even that center of activity didn't have a telephone. Carlton Lyons, the self-declared patriarch of Perdido, had the only telephone around. And that was only used to deliver urgent news. Of course, in those days there weren't many burning issues. America was between wars, no one flew on airplanes and email was a half-century away from consuming every-one's lives. Travel was slow, on bad roads, and folks arrived when they got there. Family and friends were "set to show up around Friday or Saturday and maybe Sunday if something slowed them down."

Watches and calendars just got in the way of enjoying the slow pace of life. If it hadn't been for an informal Sunday morning church service on the beach, the summer would have all blended into one long Saturday. Time didn't matter to anyone except the men who had to shuttle back to Montgomery to make a living.

Mr. Randolph had come to Perdido from Selma, Alabama. A skinny, somewhat sickly man, he'd been told by his doctors that he only had a year or so to live. So he decided to spend his last days in heaven on earth, fishing, shrimping and breathing the fresh sea breeze. He built the store and ended up running it for thirty years much to the amazement of medical science. Fresh fish, salt air, sunshine, crabs and shrimp apparently agreed with him, as well as everyone else who came to Perdido.

Fishing boats coming back from the gulf pulled into Randolph's Store to fuel up and show off their catch. It was considered mandatory to brag excessively, tell wild fish tales and enjoy a cold beer. Monster king mackerel or loads of fifty or sixty bluefish were proudly displayed on the dock for gawkers. The obvious question being, "When's the fish fry?" The answer usually followed, "tonight."

Danny, Will, and Trout were on the diving board at The Point try-ing to work up the nerve to try a one-and-a-half. They'd talked a lot about the diving contest but so far that's all they'd done. After their ex-perience at The Tree, their enthusiasm for diving had faded.

In the distance, an inboard engine revved loudly. Wallace Floma-ton's fishing boat was cruising in. Perdido boasted lots of great fisher-men, but Wallace was the guru. Being that The Point was less than a hundred yards' distance from The Store—a distance they swam without breathing hard—they decided to see what he'd caught.

Trout stroked quickly toward the ladder. "Let's race," he said, with Danny and Will already close at his heels. Three slippery boys laughing and wrestling on a ladder was enough grounds for strong parental dis-approval, not to mention the "No Horseplay" clause posted on The Point Club rules at the pavilion. But the boys were actually careful in their ladder fight—not because of any written rules or threats from parents. No, they'd learned by experience that falling, then sliding down a barnacle-encrusted piling could ruin a perfectly good day. The razor sharp crustaceans had sliced open their feet, toes, knees and hands enough times to keep their horseplay down to pony size.

Trout and Danny made it up the ladder first and sprinted toward the tip of The Point, which pointed directly at Randolph's Store. Even though he was last up the ladder, Will was a faster land animal. As Will overtook Trout, he shoved him aside then yanked on Danny's swimsuit to take the lead. All was considered fair in racing because winning was the prize. Points were not awarded for good sportsmanship.

Even though Will could move across the soft sand the fastest, it was a proven fact of nature that he was slower in the water. It didn't make sense, what with his lanky arms, big hands and all, but the truth remained that Trout and Danny always beat him in swimming races. Maybe their strokes were faster and more compact or they just had less body to drag through the water. Whatever the reason, it balanced out the competition. With Danny and Trout two steps behind, Will launched himself off the end of The Point in a gangly Superman dive. Two more splashes followed and the water leg of the race was in progress. Danny and Trout edged closer to Will as they freestyled gracefully across the bayou. They were careful not to pass too close to Will or he'd latch on to one and leave the other to win. To avoid the dreaded gator grab, Danny swam wide left and Trout swam right hoping to evade Will's clutches. With about fifty feet to go, the boys were neck and neck. A dozen folks gathered on Randolph's pier to watch the impromptu contest. They knew how competitive the boys were and took pleasure in their all out efforts. Even Wallace Flomaton stopped piddling with his fishing gear for a moment to witness the finish. Secretly, everyone had a favorite kid he or she was pulling for.

Three boys in a dead heat with their arms and legs and thrashing made quite a commotion. Then, suddenly they all disappeared completely. When the water got shallow enough, they entered the final leg of the race—running along the bottom. As quick as otters, they dived down to the sand four feet below and literally torpedoed underwater, pushing with their legs and keeping their bodies six inches off the bottom. From the pier, folks could see three shadowy shapes churning along as streamlined as dolphins. Coming up for air—even once— would cost them the race. Like a missile launched from a submarine,

Will rocketed out of the water and onto the pier in one motion just two seconds in front of Danny and Trout. Barely beaten, they stayed in the water and caught their breath. Will danced a few victory steps before he back flipped off a piling back into the water. Somehow he always moved across the sand faster, whether it was high and dry or under four feet of water.

Not that he needed the added publicity, but the race highlighted Wallace Flomaton's arrival. A first-class sea dog and a master of all things related to boating, Wallace naturally drew attention. As a young man, he'd won three Olympic medals in sailing, he held countless Alabama fishing records, and he could navigate anything that floated through whatever weather God threw at him, even though religion was an issue Wallace avoided. Famous far and wide for his accomplishments, he was, unfortunately, also known for his astounding ability to drink abundant amounts of alcohol. At sixty years old, Wallace was a living legend. Too outlandish and grizzled to be called *Mr.* Flomaton, everyone knew him simply as Wally.

"Damn good race, boys," Wally boomed. "Looks like Will kicked your young asses once again."

Danny and Trout didn't answer. Nor was Wally expecting a reply. He made proclamations that didn't need to be acknowledged, and his stories were outrageous—some true, some not, but all were heavily embellished.

"How many did you catch?" Trout asked.

"More than a few, but not all of 'em," he said. "We left some dumb ones for the rookies."

Trout climbed on the pier. "Did you catch a hundred?"

"Not quite. Probably forty blues and three nice kings. One of the kings is bigger than you boy."

"Really. Can I see it?"

"Sure," he said and motioned to one of his fishing protégés to show off the prize.

Like most legendary seadogs, Wally had a loyal following of men—young and old and mostly wealthy—who hoped to learn from the master. They'd bring food and drinks and gladly pay for fuel just to rub shoulders with him. Brash to the bone, Wally would bark commands at them as if they were greasy deckhands. They'd bring him beer, clean the fish, wash down the boat, and, if he asked, cook his dinner and iron his shirts. The role suited him, especially in his older days when most of the money he'd made as a younger man went into cocktails and hefty alimony payments.

A fortyish Wally wannabe from up north somewhere held up a fifty-pound king mackerel for the boy's inspection.

"Wow," Danny said, "that's the biggest one I've ever seen!"

"I believe that, son," Wally said, "but it's no state record like the one I brought in three years ago."

"How big was that one?" Will asked.

"Almost twice the size of this one, ninety-seven pounds."

"Is that the biggest fish you've ever caught?" Trout asked.

Wallace Flomaton let out a howl of laughter aided by the three beers he'd already pounded down since they arrived at the pier.

"Oh hell no boys! Are you kidding? I've caught blue marlin that could chew you up and spit you out. I've caught tarpon that could eat that king mackerel in one bite."

"So what's the biggest fish you've ever caught," Trout persisted.

He slugged on his fourth beer and dropped into a foldout chair while three underlings scrubbed and hosed off his boat. The situation was well under control and Wally's ego was starting to puff up.

"Well, I'll tell you boys a story about the biggest fish in the ocean. It's a fish bigger than you can imagine."

"How big?" Will asked.

"You just sit there and listen and I'll tell you," he said.

"We'd gone about a hundred miles offshore, just past the continental shelf and we were in six hundred feet of water so clear and blue we could see schools of fish swarming under the boat. Dolphins had been jumping by the hundreds and we'd filled the boat up with every kind of fish.

"I put on my best marlin rig and we were trolling in an area where I'd caught marlin before. But this time I let out a hundred yards of extra line and told the captain to ease off the throttle so the lure would dive extra deep. All of a sudden my lure got slammed and the biggest blue marlin I'd ever seen came out of the water thrashing and trying to shake the hook."

Wally's masterful storytelling already had the boys as still as gravestones and hanging on his every word. "Well sir, I grabbed that pole and gave it a yank with all my strength to set the hook. I knew by first glance that this was a world record blue and he was mine. He dove and started to run, so I loosened the drag a tad and the line spun out faster than I'd ever seen. I yelled at the captain to back up at full tilt. Luckily, it was as slick as glass so we didn't have any waves slapping against the stern. We were going in reverse so fast, you coulda skied backwards. It was truly masterful steering by that old captain. He and I were working like a well-oiled machine, and slowly but surely, I started reeling that fish in.

"Every time he got close enough to the boat so we could see him, he'd sound straight down a couple hundred feet and the fight would go on. I got him twenty feet from the boat a dozen times and he took off every time. Finally, after six hours of fighting that giant blue, I wore him out. I gotta tell you boys, I was plum wore out too, but not too much to get him in the boat.

"So just as I pulled him along side of the boat, the captain climbed down out of the wheel house and got ready to gaff him. Neither of us wanted to let a dumbass deck hand gaff that fish. He might knock him off the hook. Plus, the blue was too big for a lesser man. I mean a real monster.

"Wouldn't you know it, when he was a few feet away he rolled on his side and looked up at us. That fish was so tired he was almost dead. For a couple of seconds our eyes met, that fish and I knew the end was near. Well, right then he opened his mouth and the hook just popped out. Don't ask me how, but it did. We were just out of reach to gaff him. The captain yelled up at the first mate to back down real, real slow. We only had a few moments before that fish regained some strength and swam off forever.

"Well boys, that first mate's eyes were as wide as a moon jellyfish and his hands were shaking. He hit the throttle a little too hard and we slid right past that fish. I said to everyone, 'hell no, I ain't gonna loose this fish' so I eased over the side real quiet like, swam over and wrapped my arm around his giant head. I figured I could just swim him over to the boat. The captain had the gaff ready so he tossed me a line and just as I grabbed it, I felt a shiver go through that fish. I cursed at God because that world-record blue was coming to life. Just then he put his head down and dove with me still hanging on."

Wally stopped right there and took a long, slow drink of beer. The boys had a million questions at the tip of their tongues but they kept their traps clamped shut.

"So I hung on as tight as a bull rider as that fish went deeper and deeper. Just when I thought I was gonna drown, it turned and shot out of the water. He was trying to throw me off but he couldn't. I was a man possessed with near immortal strength. And, the old blue wore himself out again. I yelled at the captain and he came over at full speed to get me and that blue marlin. But by the time he got there, the fish dove again and, once again, I hung on. We flew out of the water and slapped down so hard that I almost lost my grip. But I didn't. And here came the captain again to get us. But, sure enough, the fish dove again. And I hung on again."

The boy's mouths hung open so wide an apple could have rolled inside. They hadn't blinked in three or four minutes and they were hardly breathing. A few men who weren't tending to Wally's boat had gathered around.

"And then boys," Wally paused. "And then … and then that fish started pulling on my leg …"

Wally took a swig of beer and burst out laughing so hard beer spewed from his nose. "Just like I'm pulling on yours," he hooted.

For a few moments, Wally stared dead in their eyes to soak up their reaction. The boys sat quietly dazed, trying to process what he'd just said. Pulling on their legs? Then one by one, they realized that Wally had hooked them just like he did that state-record fish. They'd swallowed the bait—hook, line, and stinker. Wally was still howling when he marched into Randolph's as the master fisherman *and* storyteller. He was damn good and he knew it, as long as his underlings kept buying him booze.

"Hey Wally, nice fish," Mr. Randolph said from behind the counter. He tossed his empty bottle into the trashcan. "Thanks."

"Another beer?" Mr. Randolph asked. "Or how about a tonic water to cool you off?"

"You know vodka goes well with tonic water," Wally proclaimed as if he was simply enlightening anyone within earshot of the many useful qualities of tonic water.

"So would you like a vodka tonic?" Mr. Randolph asked dryly.

"Well, now that you mention it. I mean, if you insist, I guess I will."

"Fine," Mr. Randolph said. He'd played Wally's ridiculous game before. Unfortunately, he knew it led to a long night of drinking, more of Wally's tall tales and another disgruntled wife. A Wally disciple, still dripping with suds from washing down Wally's boat, approached the counter.

"I'd like an ice cold Coca-Cola please."

"Ya know," Wally prophesized, "bourbon goes well with Coca-Cola."

Mr. Randolph just smiled and handed the man his Coke.

CHAPTER 17

Fishing the Breakers

You can't catch a fish without a line in the water.
—Mr. Walt Thornton

Wisps of white smoke glowed in the dawn light as Mr. Walt puffed on a fresh cigar and surveyed the bay. Without a breath of wind blowing, the water was flat calm. There was nothing he liked better than a smooth boat ride just before sun up. And, getting to the gulf at sunrise, just as the fish woke up, was part of his formula for success. That meant leaving the dock around five-thirty with a piece of toast and a cup of orange juice. Eggs and bacon took a backseat when there were fish to be caught.

After hearing about Wallace Flomaton's big day, Mr. Walt was anxious to add more fish to his freezer. With a horde of hungry mouths to feed at Paradise Point, stocking up on fresh meat was basic survival. The strong tide shifts had turned on a feeding frenzy and the window of opportunity to load the boat was wide open.

Still young and impressionable, Will and Danny were two of his favorite fishing mates. They worked like the devil without complaining too much and each one always tried to catch the most fish. Mr. Walt happily spurred on the competition between them.

"Danny's got two more fish than you," he'd say, and sure enough, Will would reel the next fish in faster. Or he'd use size to keep them battling. "Danny, I think Will has the biggest fish so far," he'd say. And without fail, Danny would sharpen his focus. Winning was deeply rooted in the boys, something that had developed during childhood years of card games, races and anything else that ended with a winner

107

and a loser. Mr. Walt used any motivation that caught more fish to feed the masses.

On the brink of their teens, the boys had reached a milestone that summer. Instead of staying in the main cottage, they'd been granted access to the Back House. Set back a hundred feet from the water, the Back House was hidden under a massive live oak on one side and a few magnolias on the other. Originally built for a housekeeper, back when a woman from Montgomery would come to help with chores, the Back House was just one bedroom and a bathroom. Eventually, it became a private cabin for kids.

The hinges squeaked as Mr. Walt pulled open the screen door. Will cracked an eyelid but Danny, the comatose sleeper, didn't flinch. Mr. Walt snuck across the room silently and leaned in close to Will purposely blowing a puff of smoke in his face. The smell of a cheap Dutch Masters was an ugly way to start the day.

"You want to go fishing?" he whispered with another dose of smoke.

Will tried to avoid the smoke bomb. "Ugh. Ask Danny."

Mr. Walt crept across the room and gave Danny the cigar treatment. He didn't have to blow in Danny's ear. The smoke did the trick. Will heard some mumbling but was already tumbling back into dreamland.

"Danny, ya wanna go fishing?"

Danny moaned at Mr. Walt. "Uh, I don't know. What did Will say?"

"He said he absolutely wants to go," Mr. Walt lied.

"Okay, then I guess I'll go."

"Good, alright then boys get up. The fish won't wait for us."

As he left, he flipped the light switch on and turned off the fan. That would do it. Mr. Walt had been playing his little game of one boy against the other all summer. It was years before they figured out his trick. Of course, it wasn't like he was asking them to cut the grass or clean the gutters. This was fishing for God's sake. Plus he knew that Danny and Will were inseparable. Whatever one did, the other followed as much out of friendship as competition. Neither of them wanted to miss an adventure because it might be the day they saw a school of manta rays leaping ten feet out of the water or the time they caught two monster king mackerel at the same time or the harrowing escape when a waterspout chased them across the bay. It had all happened before and the boys didn't want to miss the next wild ride.

On the boat ride out, Danny munched on a banana and watched the red ball rising slowly but steadily from behind the pine trees. "Daddy, why do we always have to leave so early?"

"Because we catch the fish when they're having breakfast," Mr. Walt said. "Then we have *them* for lunch."

"But why don't we fish when they're having lunch?" Will whimpered.

"Why are y'all complaining? You're usually thrilled to go fishing."

"We are thrilled," Danny said. "But we'd just like to try fishing during the day sometimes."

"Boys, like I've told you many times before, fishing is best at sunrise and sunset. In the morning, the fish feed because they're hungry from a long night and in the evening they feed because they know they're in for a long night, just like us."

"Well, I just wish they ate lunch too, just like us," Will said. "It doesn't seem fair."

"Life's not always fair boys. You have to seize opportunities, like catching fish when they're biting."

"Or when the wind is right?" Danny asked.

"Correct," Mr. Walt said and recited the old limerick. "Winds from the east, fishing is least. Winds from the west, fishing is best."

"What if there's no wind, like now?" Will asked.

"That's okay too," he smiled. "But, you'll see, when the wind comes up later this morning, it'll be out of the west. Mark my words."

Once they arrived and started catching fish, Mr. Walt knew that the boys would turn back into fun-loving twelve-year-olds glad to be on an adventure. Just being in the game was enough for Mr. Walt, because he was a maniacal fisherman.

As they eased out into the gulf he was chewing the stub of his Dutch Master's cigar and scanning the horizon, looking for any signs of fish—birds diving into the water, a group of boats circling around a school of fish or, best of all, the churning white water of big fish feeding on baitfish.

When he fished, he liked to wear one of those beat up old golf hats with the wrap-around brim. Never a T-shirt man, Mr. Walt preferred a button-down, oxford shirt that at one time looked good with a coat and tie, but had since been stained with fish guts and motor oil. His plaid swim trunks exposed solid legs that once captained his high-school track team. And, of course, he was barefooted, because that's how folks fished. As they passed under the Alabama Point Bridge, Mr. Walt's senses were on high alert.

"There are some boats fishing the breakers for blues," he said. "Y'all wanna catch some bluefish?"

"Sure," they said in unison.

"Will, put a spoon and a yellow duster on your pole. Danny, you use a spoon and a red and white duster."

They sprung into action like a couple of Navy swabs. In less than a minute, they had their poles rigged for blues and were letting out line. Of the many fish that live in near-shore waters—blues, Spanish mackerel, pompano, skip jacks, hard tails—they mostly wanted blues and Spanish. With beautiful yellow spots that glowed against platinum skin, Spanish were coveted because they had no scales, a feature the boys liked when the time came to clean them. Despite their good looks, Spanish put up a pitiful fight. They'd hit the lure with a bang then surrendered to the pull of the boat, skipping along the top of the water like a tiny surfboard. On the other hand, bluefish were meaty, angry buggers that fought for their lives both in the water and after they were yanked into the boat. They flipped and flopped even after they were tossed in the cooler whereupon they rattled around and slapped their tales against the cooler walls, throwing blood everywhere. Even though Spanish were easier to clean, the boys favored bluefish. The heart-pumping adrenaline rush outweighed the pain of scaling them later.

Spanish and blues had more differences besides just their skin and temperament. Spanish fed on schools of tiny menhaden that stayed in deeper water. Most of the time, blues patrolled the sandbars. That threw the threat of breaking waves into the mix. In deep water, waves merely created that gentle rolling motion that lulled people to sleep or made folks with weak stomachs turn green and puke. Seasoned fishermen got perverse satisfaction out of seasick newbies by thanking them for chumming the water.

Sandbars, on the other hand, were where waves transformed from harmless undulating water to steep, frothy battering rams, adored by surfers but dreaded by fishermen tracking blues. But that was the drill. To catch blues, they had to spar with the breakers. And every so often, a wave would break over the bow, throwing thirty or forty gallons of refreshing seawater into the boat.

"Hang on," Mr. Walt would say. The boys knew from the tone of his voice whether to get ready for a cool splash or a butt-busting whopper. When the fishing was hot, they'd have bluefish literally swimming in the bottom of the boat, a floating fiberglass aquarium. They caught them so fast, there was no time to throw them in the cooler. Or the cooler was chocked full. Or both.

As they trolled into the breakers, three other boats were reeling in blues as fast as they could catch them. Without delay, fish hit both Will and Danny's lines. They pulled them in, yanked them over the gunnel, and got the hooks out without losing a finger to the blues' razor-sharp teeth. But it was never fast enough.

"You can't catch a fish without a line in the water," Mr. Walt barked for the millionth time.

When they had a fish on the line, he'd ride them hard.

"REEL," he'd command. "Reel faster! Don't lose him. You're gonna lose him. Come on! Get him in the boat. Don't bang him on the side of the boat! You're gonna *lose* him!"

The boys rarely failed to land the fish. But to Mr. Walt, fishing was not just sport. It wasn't the relaxing stress-reliever doctors prescribed to their patients.

"Go fishing, try to relax a little," the docs said to stressed-out patients. "Rejuvenate your spirit."

No, this was essential hunting and gathering because Mr. Walt knew there were fifteen, or twenty-five, or maybe thirty cousins, sons, daughters, uncles, aunts and people who claimed to be cousins, back at home to feed. Simply put, catch and release was not a concept that would have gone over well with him.

Rule one of avoiding lethal waves was to fish perpendicular to the breakers so the boat wouldn't flip over. "That always ruins a good fishing trip," Mr. Walt would say. Rule two was to cruise over the waves when they were still just smooth, low rollers, before they peaked, broke, and smashed into the bow. In an ultimate act of trust, Will and Danny always faced backward to keep vigilant eyes on their lines. Mr. Walt drove and generally looked in the direction he was going. What worried the boys was the fact that Mr. Walt was constantly diverting his attention from the immediate danger of the waves in search of more fish. He'd be scanning the horizon for birds feeding and checking for other boats catching fish. He'd look for jumping fish, ripples in the water, dolphins feeding, blood slicks and anything that could put more fish in the cooler.

"Hang on!" Mr. Walt said with a slight sense of urgency. The bow rose, the wave passed, then the boat dipped into the trough and plowed into the next wave. The thin wall of water that splashed across their backs actually cut the July heat nicely. And, just like that, another two inches of seawater poured in for the fish to enjoy. As the wave passed, Mr. Walt prompted them.

"Get ready, we're going through the school. Catch one!"

As if they didn't know. This was their thousandth fishing trip and they were as good as any two first mates in the entire state of Alabama. But he was the captain and captains barked orders. They were kids. Kids took orders.

In the corner of his eye, Danny saw commotion at the helm and Mr. Walt did a weird, jerky little dance.

"Damn it to hell," he yelled, yanking his foot up. It was one of his favorite expressions but not one to be taken lightly. Danny saw blood streaming from his little toe as he continued his Irish jig with an angry bluefish. The fish, undoubtedly unhappy about being hooked in the mouth and yanked into the boat, had taken its angst out on Mr. Walt's toe. And a bluefish was nothing to scoff at. They had piranha-like teeth and jaws strong enough to crush titanium. He was lucky the fish didn't just nip off the whole toe for a snack. Mr. Walt kicked and stomped, and eventually the blue shook off and darted away looking for a way out or maybe another nibble. As he tried to stop the bleeding, Mr. Walt made a decision.

"Danny, pull the plug. Let's drain this water out. Will, put those fish in the cooler. We're getting out of the breakers."

He had spoken none too soon but unfortunately, not quite quickly enough. Danny sloshed around in the stern groping for the plug as Mr. Walt wrapped a piece of oxford shirt around the jagged flesh of his toe. Suddenly Will squealed in a voice approaching a six-year-old girl's.

"*Mr. Walt! Look out!*"

There are times in life when you know you're screwed, when injury is unavoidable, like when you hear a strange cracking sound and look up to see tree limb plummeting toward your forehead. You know there's going to be blood and stitches, and you can only hope to survive to have fun—or fish—another day. Unfortunately, this was one of those times.

The face of the wave crested at ninety degrees as the bow of the nineteen-foot *Glaspar* rose nearly straight up. Clinging to the bow like a spider monkey, Will grimaced in anticipation of impact, while Mr. Walt gunned the engine trying to power through the wave. His effort was valiant but futile as the wall of water slapped the bow so hard that Will took flight as if a giant tennis racket had swatted him. Danny and Mr. Walt could only watch as he passed over their heads with his arms and legs flailing. He looked a lot like a seagull with broken wings spinning in their sockets. And he fell just as fast. For an instant, the boat was vertical, literally bobbing on the stern. Danny fell onto the 85-horsepower Evinrude outboard that saved him from going overboard. Mr. Walt dangled from the steering wheel with blood trickling from his toe.

The seconds dragged by as everything unfolded with cosmic clarity—Will splashed down into the gulf; Mr. Walt hung vertically with a death grip on the steering wheel; the fishing poles crashed down around Danny; and the Evinrude submerged halfway, gurgling to stay alive. Then, suddenly and miraculously, the boat fell forward and landed with the clapping sound of a canon. The ever-reliable Evinrude didn't stall and Mr. Walt never relinquished his vice grip on the steering wheel. He quickly steered safely into deeper water where he and Danny checked their limbs for deep gashes and compound fractures.

Will had belly-flopped into knee-deep water and was running toward the boat with the look of terror etched into his twelve-year-old face. Mr. Walt had lost his glasses and his hat but somehow still chomped the nasty Dutch Master's stub between his teeth. Tragically, in one fell swoop, all of the fish had washed out of the boat and back to their homeland.

"Damn it to hell," Mr. Walt scoffed. "We lost all the fish."

Will stood at the edge of the sandbar wondering if he should swim for the boat or not. Then Mr. Walt spotted the cooler tumbling in the breakers, spilling the rest of the catch.

"Will," he yelled. "Quick. Grab that cooler. See if you can save some of those fish."

But they all knew the attempt was pointless. Mr. Walt's hat floated into calmer waters where he retrieved it, the cooler and a shivering Will. His glasses were most likely in the custody of a large bluefish. Not one to be defeated, especially considering the hungry crowd waiting back home, Mr. Walt took a deep breath and looked at the boys.

"How are y'all feeling? Everybody okay?"

His questions were strictly rhetorical and Will and Danny knew as much. Their hearts were racing, their bodies in shock but they knew what was coming next.

"All right boys, grab a pole. You can't catch a fish if your line's not in the water."

Two hours later, they'd caught enough to feed the family. They had survived the trauma, and everyone feasted on fried blue fish, hush puppies, silver queen corn, and black-eyed peas. Even though they fed everyone, neither Will nor Danny was considered a martyr. In fact, fishing with Mr. Walt was more like being a victim. But it was always exhilarating, and more often than not, they loaded the boat with fish. And, if Will and Danny didn't pull in the fish, there were a dozen or so brothers or cousins who would happily take their places. Life at Perdido was always about pitching in, being a small part of the whole to make life comfortable. The reward was a boat full of gas to explore the unknown, ski until their muscles ached, and, of course, fish like a young Wallace Flomaton.

CHAPTER 18

That Aqua Velva Smell

I don't care if you're poor, you can still be clean.

—Kitty Thornton

The thrill of catching fish was always tarnished by the nasty job of scaling and cleaning. Folks with delicate constitutions would turn green at the mere smell of fish. The boys were immune to fish stink because that aroma lingered on their skin all summer, especially after a hearty round of chopping off heads and pulling out guts.

Once they were in the sink, the fish had to be submerged underwater so the scales wouldn't fly all over the room. Inevitably, someone would pull a fish too far out of the water while they were scraping and sure enough, they'd get pelted in the face with dime-sized scales—most of which instantly stuck to the target. After scaling a few fish, Will and Danny's chest, tummy, face and hair would be caked in more scales than the fish.

But that was just the opening act, leading to the real blood fest—splitting their bellies and pulling their smelly guts out. Of course, when they got bored, the boys would dig out a few eyeballs and scare the daylights out of some of their younger cousins. Anything to break the monotony. Although they loathed the job, they didn't complain. Just like all of their chores, they did their duty because it had to be done and Mr. Walt demanded it.

Will tugged on some bluefish guts. "If I ever thought about being a doctor that cuts people open, all of this fish cleaning has cured me of that hair-brained idea."

"You think people smell this bad when doctors cut on 'em?" Danny asked.

"If they cut open their guts they would," Will said.

"That's just nasty," Danny said. "I'd never be a doctor."

"Me neither. So besides a doctor that cuts people open, what's the worst job you could have?"

Danny thought about it for a second. "I know, working in a funeral home with all those dead people."

"I think I'd rather do that than this," Will said. "At least dead people wouldn't bleed like these blues."

"That's true. And if you messed up somehow, it wouldn't be that bad."

"Why not?" Will asked.

"'Cause they'd already be dead."

Will laughed. "That's a good one."

They had caught exactly twenty-eight fish and divided them equally into fourteen each. If they worked hard, they could finish in an hour or so. Even though poking around with eyeballs and checking out fish livers gave them some relief, it did drag out the job. Mr. Walt always seemed to walk in right when they were goofing around.

"Y'all get back to work," he said sternly, "we have a lot of hungry mouths to feed."

Even though they were secretly thinking about how hard they had been working they responded with a crisp, "Yes, sir", and ramped up their efforts. The bucket they were filling up with heads and guts had become a vicious brew. And, for God's sake, neither of them wanted to tote that bucket down to the bay and load up the crab trap. That was the final insult, shoving all the heads and guts into the crab trap's bait cage.

In the kitchen, Ethel May Brackin, a veritable soul-food gourmet, was mixing up a dry batter for the fish and heating up the cooking oil. She'd just pulled a fresh batch of biscuits from the oven and was having to smack the hands of everyone who passed by.

"Git your hands out of my biscuits," she scolded. "They're for lunch."

"Hey Ethel," Danny said. "I got an idea, hit 'em with the cast iron skillet."

She glared around the kitchen for any potential thieves. "I just might do that."

"Ethel," Will said, "can you do us a favor?"

"Depends on what it is."

"Just pick a number, either one or two. Danny and I will try to guess it."

"How come?"

"Because whoever loses has to load up the crab trap."

"Why don't you both do it? That'll make the job half as hard."

"Because the winner also gets to eat one of your biscuits."

"Not before lunch you don't."

"Alright, but can you still pick a number."

"Okay then," she said. "Got it."

"One," Will said.

Danny spun his head around. "Wait a minute. I was gonna pick one. How come you get to go first?"

"'Cause I'm the oldest."

"Well that's not fair, is it Ethel?'

"I don't suppose it is."

"Then who gets to go first?" Danny asked.

"Let's do rock, paper, scissor," Will suggested.

"Okay," Danny said, "One, two, three!"

Danny threw out a rock and Will showed scissors. With his fist clinched, Danny crushed Will's scissors.

"Alright!" Danny exclaimed. "You load the crab trap."

"Un unh," Will said. "That was just to see who got to pick first on the number thingy."

"No it wasn't. Why would we do one game just so we could do another one? That doesn't make sense," Danny said.

"Well, that's what I thought we were doing. I didn't understand so it's not fair."

Danny wondered if Will was confused or just trying to avoid the heads and guts. He suspected the latter. Then Danny noticed Ethel winking at him.

"Okay," he said. "But I won so I go first. I pick the number two."

"What?" Will said, stunned. "If you were gonna pick two anyway, why didn't you just go along when I picked one. That's just dumb."

"No it's not. It's called principles."

"That's goofy."

"It doesn't matter. Ethel, who wins?"

Ethel lowered a fish into the boiling oil. "Uh, I was thinking of the number one so I guess Will wins."

In shock, Danny dropped his knife. The blade stuck into the wood floor next to his right big toe. He was sure Ethel had winked at him.

Will looked down at the knife. "That was a close one, cuz. You almost had matching toes with Mr. Walt.

"No lie," Danny said as he leaned over and yanked the knife out of the wood. "How 'bout we do best two out of three?"

"Two out of three? I just won fair and square."

"Yeah, but I won the first round and let you off the hook. You owe me."

Ethel had already tuned them out. She'd heard their foolish banter for years and figured they could work it out without her help. Besides, cooking for that crowd was demanding enough and she had to get busy pulling the first batch of fish out of the fryer. Will was considering giving Danny his two-out-of-three when Mr. Walt stomped onto the back porch.

"What in Sam Hill's name is this all about? I could hear you boys from the front yard."

"We're trying to decide who has to load up the crab trap," Danny said. "I won the first round and Will won the second, so I want to do a two-out-of-three."

"No, that's not it, Mr. Walt. Here's how it happened. Danny won the rock, paper, scissors, but that was only to see who—"

Mr. Walt held up his hand. "That's enough boys. I have an easy solution."

"What?" Will gulped.

"You're both gonna load the trap. Now get going and quit arguing."

"But …"

"No buts. All I want to see is your backside on the way out the door. Danny, you carry the bucket, and Will, you wash it out when you're done. Now *go*!"

When Mr. Walt raised his voice, they moved with the speed of a bluefish riding a breaker.

"It's not fair," Danny said.

"Well, buddy, that's something we can both agree on."

Their hands were already encrusted in fish guts so loading the crab trap wasn't a matter of smell. Just having to cram the heads and guts into a chicken wire cage was disgusting. But the promise of fresh crabmeat softened the task.

Back up at the house, Ethel's home cooking filled the kitchen with hearty aromas. The smell of her fresh baked biscuits and fish frying was enough to make a dog cry human tears and beg for just one bite. Will and Danny were starving too but their hands had a stench that no amount of soap could scrub off.

"Hey Danny," Will said. "I have an idea. Maybe we could put some perfume on 'em."

"Think that'll work?"

"It's worth a try."

In the bathroom, they smelled some of Miss Kitty's sweet perfumes.

"I don't want to smell like a girl," Danny said. "Let's try some of this stuff."

Setting proudly on the vanity was Mr. Walt's coveted Aqua Velva aftershave. They covered their hands generously in the blue tonic and rubbed it in.

"It's smells okay," Will said scrunching his nose, "but my hands still smell like fish."

"Mine too. Let's put some more on."

No matter how much Aqua Velva they used, the fish odor still prevailed. Then they realize they'd created a monster—fish stink with an Aqua Velva kicker. In the first place, Aqua Velva already had an uncanny smell—kind of a burnt pine, musk and mouthwash blend that could curl up a man's nose hairs. Combining that with dead fish produced an odor that could drive rats out of a sewer pipe. During lunch, they were banished to the back porch where a downwind breeze blew the stink away from the house. Ethel set up a table for them next to the fish-cleaning sink. As she walked away, she fanned the air in front of her face. "Y'all smell worse than a dog's breath after he ate a coon carcass."

Each time they put their hands near their mouths to take a bite of fish or biscuit, that ungodly smell rushed up their nostrils and ruined what should have been a delicious lunch.

"I'm gonna sit on my hands," Will said. "Maybe that'll work."

Danny did the same to cut the smell to a tolerable level. Then they proceeded to bury their faces in their food and eat like common dogs. When Mr. Walt checked on the boys, they had food from their eyebrows to their chins. Usually a stickler for proper table manners, he couldn't help but smile this time.

"Before I tell you boys what a fine job you did today catching those fish and cleaning 'em, could you please wipe all that food off your faces?"

Will thrust his hands at Mr. Walt. "We *had* to eat that way. Smell this."

"I already have. From across the room. But you need to clean up now. Anyway, we all appreciate your hard work, especially considering our run in with that big wave today. But remember this, there are a lot of things in this world you just can't get rid of quickly, like a bad haircut, obnoxious neighbors, fire ants and the smell of dead fish. The sooner you learn to accept things you can't change, the happier you'll be. Oh, and one more thing. In the future, for God's sake, stay away from my Aqua Velva."

CHAPTER 19

Soul Food Saint

Clothes well hung is ironing half done.
                                —Ethel Brackin

Born and raised in rural south Alabama, Ethel May Brackin had two loves—cooking and fishing. She was an expert at both skills, neither of which was hindered by her sixth grade education. Although book smarts were never afforded to Ethel, she was as honest as the sun was hot and a flawless judge of character. Tinkering in her garden or cutting her own grass soothed her spirit but when given the choice, Ethel would be wetting a fishing line in pursuit of tender white trout.

With rich chocolate skin, a happy round face and thick black hair pulled into a bun, she turned a lot of men's head as a young woman and she'd even tried marriage once but she "ran that scoundrel off after two weeks." After quitting men, her companions became stray puppies she'd take in and a few chickens to keep fresh eggs on the table.

Barely five-feet tall and with hands and feet smaller than one of Santa's elves, Ethel might have been short but she was long on keeping Will and Danny in line when they stepped out of bounds—especially in her kitchen. Even though she never had a lot of money, she was one of the happiest souls on earth and quick to flash a wide smile. Of course, it was a smile tilted slightly by a wad of snuff—another one of her loves—that always occupied a lower corner of her bottom lip.

Over the years, Ethel had gained a few strands of gray hair and a couple of wrinkles but so had Mr. Walt and Miss Kitty. She was forever trying to teach Mr. Walt how to cook cornbread and seafood gumbo, but he could never duplicate her flavors. When she tried to help him with cornbread, he would end up more confused than when they started.

"Ethel, how much baking powder do I put in?"

"Just two pinches," she'd say as her tiny fingers sprinkled the powder into the mix.

"But Ethel, how much is that, a teaspoon? Half a teaspoon? Can we measure it?"

"You don't need no teaspoon," she said. "It's just two pinches."

"But what if I'm making more cornbread than we're making now?"

"Then you add more pinches. It ain't *that* hard to understand Mr. Walt."

Although he could whip up some tasty waffles and cook a rib eye steak to perfection, Mr. Walt was better off fixing broken things and ruling over his child labor force. And while he took care of his domain, Ethel and Miss Kitty, women from vastly different worlds, grew to be great friends planning meals, keeping the house clean and doing their best to quell the roiling tide of kids constantly flowing through Pleasure Point.

In their efforts to stay cool, Miss Kitty and Ethel would roam the house barefooted and dressed in loose fitting cotton dresses. Neither of them cared about being stylish when they could be comfortable instead, as was evident by the frayed dish towel they draped over one shoulder to wipe the sweat from their faces during a bout of housework. If not for their hair and skin color, folks might have taken them for sisters.

One of the early pioneers of duct tape as an all-purpose tool, Ethel had reinforced the bottoms of the fenders on her 1950 Chevy with two layers of the silver tape. Partly to keep rocks from banging into her fenders but mostly to cover up the rust showing through the white paint, the duct tape had been placed with such artistry that from a distance it looked like special-order chrome trim. The tape framing the back window also gleamed proudly on sunny days and when summer thunderclouds burst open, the rain was banished from Ethel's prize possession.

After almost two weeks without rain, the corn farms were beginning to take on the color of wheat. Finally, three days of heavy rain brought relief to the crops but sent the boys into a fit of stir craziness.

"Ethel, when do you think this rain will stop," Will complained. "We've been stuck inside for days."

Ethel grinned as she looked Will dead in the eyes. "Boy, the Lord can't seem to please you no matter how hard he tries. When it was sunny, you complained that it was too hot. Now we're getting a nice cool rain, and you're upset about that, too."

She flashed a big snuff smile and laughed so hard her cheeks shook. "Y'all boys are just a mess. You got to learn to make the best of what the Lord gives you."

They considered her wisdom for a moment. She was right, of course, but they'd never looked at the world that way.

"Y'all just better enjoy this rain 'cause it's gonna get hotter than the devil's workshop in a week or two."

"How do you know that Ethel?" Danny asked.

"Well, I've been studying on it. You know, I've been looking for signs. One thing I know is this, when the pecan leaves are bigger than a squirrel's ear by the first of June, that's a sign that we're gonna have a long, hot summer."

Danny and Will looked at each other with silly grins. "Squirrel's ears?" Danny asked.

"That's right. You gotta keep an eye on the natural way of the world. I catch a lot of fish, right?"

"Yep," Will said.

"It's because I can think like a fish thinks. I study on the tides and watch the way the water moves and where the bait is gonna hide. Once I figure it out, I can catch fish."

Danny hung on her words. "So Ethel, can you think like a squirrel too?"

"It's not exactly the same thing but I do watch 'em real close 'cause they help me predict the weather. You always gotta check up on the trees and the animals that lives in the woods and see what they're up to. That's the way the natural world works."

Fascinated with Ethel's insight, Danny wanted to know more. "So when the squirrel's ear is small in June it means it's gonna be hot?"

"Could be. Or it might mean we're gonna get a nasty hurricane this year," she said. "Now that's what I'm really worried about."

"Wow Ethel," Danny said. "How'd you figure all that out?"

"Oh, I didn't figure it. A lot gets passed down from folks who learned about the world before they had radios and television."

The boys had heard stories about hurricanes hitting Perdido but that was before their time so Ethel's predictions didn't disturb them.

"Ethel," Danny said. "I know how we can make the best of what the Lord gives us. I know the perfect place to be right now while we're getting all this rain."

"What are you thinking?" Will asked.

"I can't believe we haven't already thought of this."

"Pigland?"

"You got it. Let's go."

Miss Kitty walked in with a broom as the boys were scrambling to leave.

"Where are y'all going?"

"Pigland, Aunt Kitty," Will said. "It ought to be good and wet."

Ethel just smiled knowing that she was going to get some peace and quiet.

"Ethel, there's a lot of sand on this floor," Miss Kitty said. "The boys must have tracked it in."

"Well, if you put some shoes on, you wouldn't feel it. It don't bother me."

Miss Kitty smiled. "I was thinking we might sweep the floor."

"Oh, I see. Well I was about to cut up some chicken for supper."

"Either way, you cut chicken and I'll sweep or vice versa."

"Well, you better sweep because you know I've been down in the back and the doctor told me to stop sweeping for a while."

"But Ethel, you were out cutting your grass yesterday with that push mower."

"Yes I was. The doctor said I could cut grass, but no sweeping."

Miss Kitty burst out laughing. "You're kidding, right?"

"No I'm not."

"You mean sweeping is worse than pushing that old mower of yours?"

"Well see, it's a different motion, pushing and sweeping. When I sweep I twist all up and that's what hurts."

"Okay Ethel, you win. I'll sweep. You're better at cutting chicken anyway."

"You're right about that. Oh, and those boys dropped some cracker crumbs under the table. Don't miss those or we'll get ants."

Miss Kitty flashed at crooked glance at Ethel. "Thanks for the advice but I won't tell you how to cook if you don't tell me how to sweep."

"No need to get all huffy," Ethel said. "I'm just trying to help."

CHAPTER 20

In the Land of Pigs

We won't know unless we try.
—Danny Thornton

Due to eons of pounding rain and erosion, the coastal landscape of South Alabama was almost as flat as one of Ethel's corn-meal pancakes. But in some areas along the bay, bluffs had been carved by years of wave action, revealing colorful layers of sand, clay, and sandstone. Vibrant pinks, purples, oranges and reds were exposed on the sheer face of majestic Red Bluff, so named because, when seen from a distance, the colors blended together into a reddish hue.

Passing boats marveled at Red Bluff's beauty, especially when the afternoon sun glowed against it. But standing next to it and digging their hands into the pliable clay was infinitely more fun. Whether or not the clay was pure enough for a potter's wheel or a kiln didn't matter. The boys were more likely to make little balls for throwing at each other and unsuspecting beach strollers. Occasionally, when creative urges set in, they'd make ashtrays and round slabs so they could squish in impressions of their hands. Then they'd scrawl in the date with a stick or rusty nail to memorialize the event.

The clay stayed moist because the ground water soaked through the sandy soil until it hit hard pack. Then it mixed with the clay and flowed along the denser layers until it spewed out of the bluff, either as artesian springs or little bitty, crystal clear waterfalls. Sometimes, when they were thirsty to the point of dehydration, they'd cup their hands and catch the trickle for a sip. The taste was tolerable but not worth filling a canteen with.

All of that water and clay combined in lots of different consistencies, from the pure stuff for making sculptures to the yuckiest muck New Age spas smear on rich folks. For the boys, the muckier, the better. And the sloppiest clay made the best material for building a steep, slippery slide down Red Bluff.

The exact location of the slide depended on where the spring water gathered in small pools. Just like a hose on a water slide, the natural trickles kept their clay slick and moist. The slides, the springs and the pools of sloppy clay all combined to make up the world they called Pigland. Just below the edge of the bluff was their favorite Slop Hole. Big enough for five or six kids to squish around up to their knees, the Slop Hole was full of slimy, watery goop. A handful of the slop would splatter as big as a dinner plate when it was thrown squarely against someone's back. Plenty of spring water flowed into the Hole, making it perfect for flopping in and knocking a few degrees off the intense summer temperatures.

In a feat of childhood ingenuity, the excess water from the Slop Hole was directed down the hill and fed into the speed slide. That kept the clay soft, wet and scary fast. The slide twisted, turned, and eventually made it all the way down to where the clay layers of the bluff met with the white sand of the beach. Best of all, all that water created a primeval muck pit at the bottom of the slide where they'd splash into and completely cover their bodies in gunk.

Of course, calling it sliding was a bit of a white lie. The slope was so steep and slippery, that they'd rocket downhill so fast they'd skip along until they either flew completely off the course or crashed down into the muck pit. They caught lots of airtime on the way down.

Will toted a bucket full of moist clay to fill bare spots. "Y'all use this to patch that top section," he said to Stuart and Trout who had been invited to help repair the slide and share in the fun.

Danny was busy digging out rocks that could slice through their cutoffs and into their tender buns. "Hey Trout, can you help me get these rocks out."

"I'm filling the bucket for Will," he said. "Get Stuart to help you."

"He's working in the Slop Hole."

"Stuart, can you help Danny?" Trout yelled up to him.

"I'm trying to build a canal from the Slop Hole to the slide."

"He needs to keep doing that," Will said. "We need more water."

"It's okay, I got it," Danny said.

Building a slide took a plan and a lot of work and more Indians than Chiefs so Will proclaimed himself the boss. The other boys didn't mind because the rewards—wild adrenaline rushes and clay-caked bodies—made working for Will worthwhile.

Will slapped a ball of clay into a rock hole. "I think that's got it. Let's use our butts to make a gully."

"We've got to make it kind of like one of those toboggan runs," Danny told Stuart, who was a Pigland rookie. "'Cause we don't want to fly off the slide."

"Why not?" Stuart asked.

"Look at all those rocks, doofus," Trout said. "You don't want to whack into those at high speed."

"Well, then why didn't we build it straight down?" Stuart asked. "Why does it have those curves in it?"

"We had to keep it where the clay was," Danny explained. "That's how we always do it."

Will smiled slyly. "Plus the turns make it more fun. As long as you don't end up in the rocks."

"That's what I'm saying," Stuart said. "I don't want to get hurt."

"You won't as long as you stay on the slide," Trout said. "Don't worry about it."

"I don't know about this," Stuart said.

"Just watch us," Danny told him. "In fact, you can just watch if you want to."

"But if you don't slide, we're gonna tell those girls you're chicken," Will laughed.

Stuart pointed an encrusted finger at Will. "If you do it, I'll do it."

"Another thing," Will explained, "Watch out for the rocks sticking up from under the clay. Danny tried to dig 'em all up but he might have missed one or two. And hitting a rock going that fast, will slice your backside wide open."

"And there's nothing worse," Danny said with a wide grin, "than a cut on your butt."

Even Stuart laughed at that one.

"You better believe it," Trout told him. "One time, a rock cut me right on my butt hole and Doc Jordon had to put in two stitches. Talk about embarrassing. Plus, it hurt for a month, especially when I...well, you know."

"What?" Stuart asked.

"When he made a poop," Will said. "He didn't want to bust a stitch."

And with that troubling image fresh in their minds, they climbed to the top. One by one, they pressed their bottoms into the slide and inched down the slope, using their feet and hands to save them from an out-of-control plunge.

"When we're sliding down," Danny explained, "we always stick our legs up in the air. Never, ever put your feet down!"

"Okay, but why not?" Stuart asked.

"Because you'll catch a heel and it'll spin you around backwards," Danny said. "Trust me, you don't want that."

When they'd made the trough deep and wide enough to keep their butts in the track, they were ready for some real live test runs.

"Okay, who wants to go first?" Will asked.

"Me!" Trout yelled. "I'm always the test pilot!"

"If Trout lives," Danny said dramatically, "I'll go second."

"Stuart, you can go third," Will said. "I'll go last once it's all smoothed out."

"Only if those two don't die," Stuart smiled.

"*Yee-ha!*" Trout screamed as he bounced down the slide all the way to the muck pit. He liked first runs since the clay hadn't been smoothed out yet, so they were always the bumpiest.

"Geronimo," Danny yelled as he took off. Being the smallest, he was able to hunch down, stay in the groove and make a humongous splash into the goop.

"Good run!" Will said. "Go for it Stuart."

"*Help!*" Stuart squealed as he picked up speed faster than he expected. Watching Danny and Trout wasn't the same as actually doing it himself. He couldn't believe how fast he was sliding. His eyes bugged out in shear fear, and his arms flopped around like a rag doll. Then, despite Danny's adamant warnings, Stuart made a classic beginner's mistake and tried to slow down by planting his foot. As quick as a greased pig, he spun upside down and backwards. The boys laughed uncontrollably as Stuart skipped down on his back pointing headfirst at the muck pit. Twice his entire body went airborne with his legs sticking straight up into the air and only the top of his head bouncing on the racecourse.

129

It was hilarious and, at the same time, an amazing contradiction of gravity.

"*Yaaaaaaaaaa!*" he screamed, just before his whole body disappeared into the goop at the bottom. The sound was something like a giant fist punching into a vat of mashed potatoes. Will, Danny, and Trout rolled on the ground laughing so hard their bellies ached. Then they noticed that Stuart was still submerged waist deep in the gumbo, with his feet sticking straight up.

As Danny ran over, Stuart started kicking his legs and slapping his arms in the muck. Danny grabbed Stuart's feet and managed to pop his head out of the clay. When Stuart surfaced, he coughed, spit, and wiped the clay from his eyes until he could see daylight. After he figured out he was alive, Stuart let out a long, low warrior's yelp.

"*Yow!* That was amazing," he yelled. "I'm going again!"

At that moment, Stuart became a certified lifetime member of the Perdido boy's club. Weaker kids would have run home crying to their mamas and in fact, some had. But Stuart passed his initiation with honors. He took everything Pigland could dish out and still wanted more.

"My turn next," Will said. "Stuart, you're after me."

For the next two hours, the boys slipped and slid until they barely had the strength to climb back to the top. Every so often, when the clay covered every inch of their skin and had gotten into their ears, eyes and between their teeth, they'd jump into the bay to wash off. A milky cloud would erupt around them as the clay dissolved into the bay water. When they were rested and clean, they'd go back to wearing out the slide and themselves. After they were too tired to slide again, they hit the Slop Hole to cool off, rest, and recuperate.

Will leaned back against the bluff and pushed his legs deeper into the goop. "Well looky there: victims."

"Can you tell who it is?" Danny asked.

"Looks like my sister and her friends," Stuart said.

"Perfect," Will said. "Let's make some clay balls."

Danny grabbed a handful of clay and rubbed it on his face and neck, "Quick, get camouflaged."

Strolling innocently down the beach, the girls had no idea they were being stalked. The boys were hunkered down behind a row of bushes with their skin and hair covered in clay. At their feet, they'd placed a dozen freshly formed clay bombs ready for launch.

"I think they're both cute," Grace said as she dragged her toes through the sand. "Will's kind of cocky but I just love that curly blond hair."

"Me too," Ellis said, "but if you had to pick between them, who would you choose?"

"I don't know," she said. "Danny's so tan and those blue eyes just shoot right through me. And he seems like a really nice guy."

"So who?" Ellis persisted.

"I'm not sure yet. I think I want to get to know them a little better before I decide. But I'd let either one of them kiss me."

"Me too!" Ellis squealed. "I'd be happy either way."

"Well," Georgiana jumped in, "if you want to know what I think …"

"Maybe we don't," Ellis said with a smile.

"I don't care, I'll tell you anyway. I think Danny and Will are really neat and all that. But I like Trout the best. Y'all might think he's kinda goofy but I just think he just likes to have a good time."

"I'd say goofy is more like it," Grace said.

"Say whatever you want," Georgiana said, "but I want to go out with someone who makes me laugh and is always doing fun things. I'm not as interested in all that kissing like y'all are."

"If you're not now, you will be," Grace said.

"Well until then, I'll stick with Trout. Hey what was that?"

The girls spun around as they heard a loud *splat* behind them. At their feet, they saw a strange, pink splotch in the sand. Chunks of clay had splattered onto the back of Grace's leg and she reached down to wipe it off. "Gross! Where did that come from?"

Just then, another blob crashed down next to Ellis. She glared up at the bluff and noticed movement behind the bushes. Then she spotted four more clay rockets flying toward them. In a flash, Ellis bolted down the beach, kicking up sand with each step.

"RUN!" she yelled.

Grace and Georgiana didn't ask why, they just took off at full speed behind her. But it was too late. The boy's ambushing techniques were as fine-tuned as military sharpshooters. They'd bombed so many unsuspecting beachcombers that they had their distances and trajectories down to a science. They'd also been bombarded more times than they could count by older brothers, cousins, neighbors—basically whoever was hiding in the bushes and looking for victims. In military parlance, Pigland was the high ground and the beach was the kill zone.

Ellis escaped a direct hit because of her quick thinking and fast feet but Grace got smacked on the shoulder and Georgiana took a projectile between her shoulder blades. Both girls screamed as they continued running for their lives, hoping to avoid a mud shampoo. When they were finally out of range, they stopped to scrape off the muck. Grace and Georgiana were whimpering and wondering what had just happened. One minute they were giggling and talking about boys and then, without warning, they were sprinting out of a war zone. Not that getting hit was painful. The soft clay flew apart harmlessly. But the clay was messy and the whole episode scared them so badly that Grace was in tears.

"What just happened?" she sobbed.

"We were attacked. Probably by Danny 'n Will," Ellis said. "Those boys can be big trouble."

"Where were they? I didn't see anyone," Georgiana asked.

"I think that's the place they call Pigland. I've never been up there but I've heard about it."

"Pigland?" Georgiana said. "You mean they have pigs up there?"

"No silly. It's Pigland because they flop around in the muck and stuff like stupid pigs."

"But why would they throw clay like that?" Grace asked.

"Because they're boys," Ellis said. "You wouldn't know because you don't have a brother. But they probably think it's funny."

"Well this is a brand new bathing suit," Grace said. "I think it's ruined."

Ellis reached over and wiped some clay off. "It'll be fine. The clay comes off pretty easily. Let's get you in the water and wash it out."

As they soaked in the bay, the girls heard loud hoots and howls coming from Pigland. Then they saw a spray of chalky water splashing high into he air and four boys covered in clay emerging from the muck pit. They were shoving each other around and giggling as they walked toward the girls. Grace had removed her bikini top to wash the last bits of clay out.

"Hey, what are y'all doing?" Will asked. "Skinny dipping?"

"No we certainly are not!" Grace said. "We're washing the clay off that some no-class baboons threw at us."

The boys hopped around and made their best monkey sounds.

"Yep, that would be us," Stuart said.

"Well, it wasn't funny," Ellis scolded.

"We sure thought it was," Will said. "Y'all ran so fast you should be on the track team?"

"You could have hurt us," Grace said. "In fact, a piece of clay flew into my eye."

"Sorry about that," Danny said, "it washes off real easy. We didn't want to hurt anybody."

"Yeah," Trout said, "we were just playing with y'all."

"Aw they're not hurt," Will said. "They're just trying to make us feel bad."

"Did it work?" Grace asked.

"Nope. I don't think so."

"Now you know," Danny said, "when you walk by Pigland you have to be on guard because there's always a chance that somebody's hiding up there."

"It's a little too late for that, don't you think?" Grace said angrily.

"It's never too late," Will said. "Because next time you'll run past Pigland."

"Well, the name is certainly appropriate," Grace said. "Y'all acted like spoiled little pigs!"

Her sharp tongue straightened them up momentarily. They usually didn't have any problems arguing with girls, but they'd never met a girl as pretty as Grace.

"Hey, really, we're sorry," Danny said, realizing the girls were fired up. "Maybe we can make it up to you."

"And how's that?" Ellis asked.

"What do y'all think?" Danny asked his tribe members. "Want to show them the slide?"

"That's a great idea," Trout said. "Why don't y'all come on over and see Pigland. We'll give you the grand tour!"

"What do you think?" Ellis asked her friends.

"I don't think so," Grace said emphatically.

"Me neither," Georgiana agreed.

"Looks like we'll pass this time boys," Ellis said.

"Oh come on," Danny begged. "We said we were sorry. It's really fun."

"Maybe you'll think twice about being mean to us next time," Grace said.

"Jeez," Will said, "you sound like my mother. Suit yourselves. Come on guys."

As Will turned and walked back toward Pigland, he was followed by Trout and Stuart. But Danny gave it one more chance.

"Come on girls," he pleaded. "Pigland is a Perdido landmark. Ya gotta come see it."

"We'll wait until y'all leave," Grace shot back.

"Okay, see ya later," Danny said as he ran to catch up with his buddies.

"Girls," Ellis said after the boys were out of earshot, "I have a fantastic idea!"

Will sat in the Slop Hole and watched the girls walking down the beach.

"Boy, we really ticked them off," he said. "They sure can't take a joke."

"Yeah, I don't think there's much chance of getting sweet on that Grace girl," Danny said. "She hates us now."

"Too bad, 'cause she sure is good looking," Will said.

"Back home," Stuart said, "she's the most popular girl in the school. Some high school kid asked her out but her mom wouldn't let her go."

"Wow," Will said. "Really, a boy from high school?"

"Well he was only a freshman. But still."

"I believe it," Danny said.

Trout was busy building a clay nose on his face. "You know, I think I like Georgiana the best," he said. "She's sweet."

"And as dumb as a post," Will said.

"Maybe I like 'em dumb," Trout said. "But I don't think she's as stupid as you think she is."

"I think she is Trout," Will said. "And come to think about it, y'all might just be a perfect match."

"What does that mean?"

"She's dumb and you do stupid stuff all the time. See, y'all are made for each other."

"Hey!" Trout said. "Take that back!"

"Why should I? If it's true?"

Trout clinched his fist and leaned toward Will. "Is not!"

"Y'all calm down," Danny said.

"He needs to take it back!"

"No way," Will said.

As the tension in the Slop Hole boiled over, the girls watched quietly and fought back their giggling. They had climbed up the bluff and doubled back with an arsenal of gushy clay bombs ready to bombard the boys. Just before Will and Trout's spat erupted into a full-blown wrestling match, the girls leaned over the edge of the bluff, let out battle screams and peppered the boys with loads of clay.

"*Ya!*" Ellis yelled as she rifled a shot into Will's chest, then whacked Trout in the tummy. Grace and Georgiana fired off bomb after bomb as the boys scrambled to get out of the way. Fortunately, for the boys anyway, the girl's ammunition ran out quickly. The Slop Hole, on the other hand, was a clay bomb warehouse.

Within seconds, the boys were fighting back. Their endless supply of blobs pushed the girls into retreat away from the edge of the bluff and out of sight. Having been involved in many epic Pigland clay fights, the boys had seen the girl's tactic before. Stuart watched as Trout, Danny and Will began blindly lobbing cannon balls up over the edge. Most of their tosses plopped harmlessly on the ground but a few missed the girls by inches.

Grace ran over to one of the duds. "Pick them up," she said. "It's more for us." Georgiana and Ellis gathered second-hand clay bombs and war raged on. This time it was the girls who had the high ground allowing Grace to splatter both Will and Danny relentlessly. Even though Georgiana might not have been the brightest star in the sky, she had an arm like a high-school quarterback. The boys dodged as best they could but Georgiana splattered them relentlessly.

"Okay, we give up. Y'all win," Will said as he motioned to Danny, Trout and Stuart to stop.

"We call a truce," Danny said. "The war is over."

As they'd done in past clay fights, the boys could have climbed up the bluff for a face-to-face confrontation with the girls but they figured this was their chance to reconcile with the fair maidens.

The girls walked skeptically to the edge behind Georgiana with her arm cocked and loaded. They fully expected to be hit with another round. But they had to smile at the sight of four clay-smeared boys standing in knee-deep muck with open arms and empty hands. A friendly armistice was reached.

"Why don't y'all climb on down," Trout said. "Now we can show you Pigland."

"Okay," Grace said. "Since we're even."

"Right," Georgiana said. "And don't mess with us any more or we'll just outsmart you again."

The boys looked at her and giggled.

"Why are y'all laughing?" she asked.

"Don't pay them any mind," Trout said. "They're just goofy."

The girls' fascination with Pigland lasted about five minutes. They tried the slide once and decided that was plenty, especially after splashing into the muck pit and completely messing up their hair with gooey clay.

"This is really kinda gross," Grace said. "I think I've had enough clay on my body for the rest of my life."

"Me too," Ellis agreed. Y'all can stay and play but I'm ready to clean off."

'That's fine," Will said. "Let's go for a swim then we can show you around Pirate's Canyon."

"What's Pirate's Canyon?" Grace asked.

Will and Danny pointed down the beach at a high peninsula protruding from the bluff.

"That's it over there," Will said. "Where the bluff kind of sticks out."

"Okay, but will we get dirty again?" Grace asked.

"Maybe a little bit," Danny said, "but Pirate's Canyon is mostly sand and what clay is there is all dried up."

"Yeah," Trout said. "It's great for climbing. And there are some ledges where we can jump off into the sand. It's really neat!"

"Sounds like fun," Georgiana said.

"Yeah, but do we have to jump?" Grace asked.

"You don't have to jump," Danny said, "but I tell you what, you'll want to check out our treasure chest."

Suspicion filled Grace's face. It sounded like another trick to her.

PUBLISHING

This book is being sent
as a gift to you by
Vicki Campbell

Merry Christmas!

"A treasure chest? Like what? Old coca-cola bottles and some fish bones?"

"Not old bones and bottles," Will said. "If we say we have treasure, we're not lying. It's valuable stuff."

"Well then, what do you have Blackbeard?" Grace shot back

"You'll just have to come see to find out, Missy Prissy," Will said. "Maybe we will."

"It's okay with me if you don't."

"Fine," she said as she turned and waded into the shallow water.

The narrow promontory that jutted out from the bluff to form Pirate's Canyon was, in itself, a spectacle of geological beauty. It reached almost forty feet into the air and curved away from the bluff then circled almost all the way back forming a deep gorge surrounded on all sides by high bluffs layered in multicolored sand and clay. The pastel pink and purple clay along with soft snow-white sand created a natural and magical scene. The boys named the bow-shaped peninsula the Camel's Hump because time, hurricanes and driving Alabama rain had rounded off the clay. The top was shaped more like a giant turtle shell but Camel's Hump was much more poetic than a dull old turtle, even if it wasn't quite as descriptive.

The top of the hump was an ideal perch for scouting the beach and large enough for four or five boys to sit on and contemplate their next adventure. A winding, narrow entrance opened into a kind of hidden amphitheater. From a kid's point of view, the place was custom built for burying stolen treasure.

As they approached Pirate's Canyon, Trout started running.

"Follow the leader," he hollered as he scrambled up the steep slope toward the top of the Camel's Hump. Will, Danny, and Stuart were right on his heels but the girls took their sweet time and picked their way up the cracked clay slope.

"Isn't this cool?" Danny said as they all made it to the top. "Look how far you can see down the beach. We see dolphins and stuff from up here all the time."

"It's pretty," Grace said. "But it's kinda crowded up here."

"Then come this way!" Trout said and he was off again. The girls stood rigid as they watched each boy scamper gingerly across a thin ridge of hard clay that bridged the gap between the hump and the sheer face of the bluff. None of the boys stumbled but little clods of clay broke off under their feet and plummeted down the steep slope.

"I'm not going over there," Ellis said.

"Y'all are crazy," Grace agreed. "We're staying here."

"It's not that bad," Trout said. "Try it."

"I'll give it a try," Georgiana said as she inched her way off the hump.

"Just don't look down," Trout said, "and stay balanced."

Georgiana held out her arms for balance and, without the slightest hesitation, walked straight across.

Wow, an arm like a quarterback and the balance of a gymnast, Trout thought. *That's a girl!*

"That was easy," she said. "Y'all try it."

"I'm more interested in seeing that treasure Danny and Will talked about," Grace said.

"Yeah, let's see those valuable jewels," Ellis said sarcastically.

"Okay," Will said. "Here's the fastest way down."

And with that, Will launched from a ledge and landed on a sandy slope twenty feet below, sinking in up to his knees.

"Geronimo!" Danny shouted. It was his favorite daredevil yelp. As he soared through the air, Danny spread his arms and legs wide just for show, then dug in two feet from Will. Trout and Stuart jumped in unison and punched into the sand just behind Will and Danny.

"Jump, Georgiana," Trout said. "It's a perfect place to land."

"*Ma!*" she screamed as she sailed through the air. Trout watched in total adoration as she plopped down next to him and fell into his arms.

"You okay?" he asked as he helped her up.

"I'm perfect," she smiled. "That was neat."

Grace and Ellis climbed carefully down into the canyon, complaining the whole way. Only Danny waited.

"Where'd everyone go?" Grace asked.

"They're heading to the back of the canyon to the treasure cave. Come on."

As they strolled beside the vertical canyon wall Grace looked over Danny. He *was* the nice one and he seemed comfortable with who he was.

"What did you yell?" Grace asked. "It sounded like you said, 'Your Honor Oh' or something like that."

Danny laughed. "That's funny. I said, 'Geronimo'."

"What's that?"

"Geronimo was this Indian a long time ago. He was some kind of hero. I think the Calvary pinned him up at the edge of a cliff. Instead of surrendering, he jumped off the cliff. Then all the other Indians did the same thing and they yelled Geronimo's name as they fell."

"Did they die?"

"Sure they did but it didn't matter to the Indians. They liked to say that it was a good day to die. That's the way I look at it. If I died today, it would be a good day to die. That's why I yell 'Geronimo' just like those Indians did."

"But you don't *want* to die, do you?"

"Nope, of course not, at least not anytime soon. But if I did, today would be a good day."

"I see what you mean but that's a weird way to look at it."

"I don't think so."

"What I mean is that if it's a good day to die then it's an even better day to live."

Danny thought about that for a few seconds. "Ya know what? I guess you're right. It *is* a good day to live. Come to think of it, that is a mighty fine way to look at it."

Grace smiled at him. "I'm glad you think so."

"I do. In fact I'm gonna change my whole way of thinking because, well heck, I'm not an Indian anyway."

Danny hopped onto a small ledge, threw his arms in the air and jumped into a pile of sand next to Grace. "Today is a good day to live," he yelled.

Grace laughed. "You're funny."

"And fast too," Danny said as he took off to catch up to Will. "Come on, follow me."

Will crouched next to a low cave at the base of the bluff. Before he crawled in, Will and Danny checked around and scanned the rim of the bluff just to make sure no one was spying on them.

"So where's this famous treasure?" Ellis asked.

"You'll see," Will said as Danny helped him move a pile of large rocks, dig down into the sand and pull out an old metal cigar box. For effect, Will placed it on a rock and slowly wiped the sand from the top. The girls crowded in closely, their minds churning with anticipation. For all they knew these crazy, carefree boys did have jewels hidden in that box. Dr. Felder had even told them stories about pirates hiding out in Perdido Bay.

Will played on the girls' curiosity and acted like the top was wedged on tight.

"I can't seem to … oh, I think I'm getting it … *argh!* … it's stuck, no … I think it's coming," he said.

As he struggled with it, the girls' eyes grew wider and they leaned in closer. *What was it going to be*, they wondered. *Gold? Diamonds? Money? Maybe a little of everything?* No one breathed, until suddenly Will flung the metal top at the girls and yelled, "It's a snake!"

The girls screamed and the boys burst out laughing. Will quickly put the top back on and with a giant grin on his face, he stared dryly at the girls.

"Now that was just mean Will," Grace said. "Come on. Show us what's in the box."

"On one condition," he said.

"What condition? You already promised to show us," Grace said.

"I know but if I'm gonna show y'all our treasure, you have to agree to something."

"We're not going skinny dipping with you if that's it," Grace said emphatically.

"Hmm, I didn't think of that. But that's not it. I'll show you the treasure if you let us take y'all to the Spanish Graveyard tonight."

"A graveyard?" Ellis asked.

"The old Spanish Graveyard," Danny said. "It's really scary and there are graves more than two hundred years old."

"Okay, we'll go," Ellis said quickly. "Just show us the box."

Will looked at Danny for approval. He nodded his head. "Go ahead and show 'em."

The girls crowded over the box as Will removed the top.

"Is that money real?" Grace asked.

"Sure is," Danny said. "Real *Confederate* money."

"How much is it worth?"

"Well, that's the thing," Will said, "Mr. Walt said Confederate money's not worth the paper it's printed on."

"That's too bad, has he seen it?" Ellis asked.

"Naw," Danny said. "We just asked him about Confederate money one day and he told us that after the war, it all became worthless."

"But we still like to play with it," Trout said. "And make believe we're rich."

"Where'd y'all find it?" Grace asked.

"There used to be an old shack back in the woods," Danny said. "Some old fella named Curtis lived there and kept to himself. It kinda burned down a few years ago and that old man never came back. After it burned, we dug around and found all kinds of old stuff buried under the floorboards. There were uniforms, letters, medals and this money."

"We took some of the money and a few medals too," Will said as he dug under the bills and pulled out two war medallions.

"That's neat," Grace said. "What else do you have?"

"Will, show 'em the arrowheads," Danny said.

"Okay. These here are real arrowheads. We found 'em right here in the sand in Pirate's Canyon."

Georgiana squinted at the arrowheads. "I didn't know that Confederate soldiers used arrowheads," she said. "I thought they used guns."

"Georgiana!" Grace said. "Don't be silly. They're Indian arrowheads."

"You mean the Indians fought in the Civil War?" she asked, trying desperately to piece her history together.

"Uh, no, they didn't," Danny said, as nicely as he could. "These arrowheads were here before the Civil War. Probably even before Columbus discovered America when there was nobody but Indians living here."

"Why that's just fascinating," Georgiana said. "Just fascinating."

Will dug to the bottom of the box. "This is our favorite," he said. "It's some kind of whistle on a cross. But it has a lot of rust on it from being in the water, I guess. Danny found it one day when we were jumping into the sand. He landed right on it and cut his foot."

"Does the whistle work?" Ellis asked.

"No, it's all clogged up," Danny said. "We tried to clean it but it's real fragile so we just figured we'd leave it be."

Grace picked up the crucifix by its thick encrusted chain and examined it. "Wow, it's really heavy. I bet it would be pretty if you cleaned it up."

"Maybe we will one of these days," Will said.

The vertical part of the cross had been expertly fashioned into a boson's whistle. The figure of the Savior hanging from the crossbeam was hidden beneath a crust of rust. The boys had no idea that the chain and crucifix were several hundred years old and had been lost by a Spanish sea captain when his ship and the rest of the fleet went down in a hurricane. Will carefully put the money and valuables back into the box and covered it with sand and the rocks.

Will looked at the girls and put his hand over his heart. "Do your hand like this," he said, "and promise that you'll never ever tell anybody about this."

"We promise!" they agreed.

"If you tell anybody," Danny said, "we'll leave you at the Spanish Graveyard for the ghosts to get you."

CHAPTER 21

Crabbing at the Gulf

The best way to pick crabmeat is to let somebody else do it.
—Brewton Stapleton

Danny and Will were launching themselves off the end of the pier attempting to nail a one-and-a-half. Mr. Walt watched briefly through the screen door as they did face plant after face plant after belly flop. Carlton Lyons's tryouts were coming up, and neither of the boys was close to claiming the five-dollar award.

"Danny!"

"Yes, sir?"

"Can you check to see how many crabs are in the trap?"

The boys immediately raced over and lifted the cage out of the water.

"Five," Danny hollered back.

"Okay. You boys come on up."

That was all it took—a direct command from Mr. Walt to shift from one competition to another: foot racing. Danny churned through the knee-deep water toward the beach while Will, being taller, climbed up the pier. By the time Will contorted his lanky body onto the pier, Danny had already reached the shore and was sprinting toward the house. Mr. Walt chewed on a fresh cigar and watched with a smile. *Those kids do love to race,* he thought.

Will's long legs helped him make up ground, and with one flying leap, he broad jumped from the pier all the way across the beach. Although Will was gaining on him fast, this time Danny's lead was too much. Danny quickly touched the wooden stairs leading up to the porch

143

and threw his arms up in victory. As the boys caught their breath, Mr. Walt explained the plan.

"Ethel and Miss Kitty want to make gumbo and we need more crabs."

"If we put more meat in the trap we might have enough by tomorrow," Danny said.

"Well that's a good idea son. We'll do that. But the problem is they want to make gumbo today."

"What are we gonna do?"

"Well there's more than one way to skin a cat, ya know."

"Mr. Walt, why would somebody want to skin a cat?" Will asked.

He thought about it for a second. "You know Will, that's a real good question. I really don't know. But, my point is, there are other ways to catch crabs. We don't have to wait for them to crawl in the trap. I want y'all to go crabbing in the gulf."

"Yes, sir!" Will hollered. "When can we go?"

"Right now. Y'all go get the crab nets and see who else you can round up. Ethel is packing your lunch."

Within the hour, *Greenie* was chugging across Perdido Bay with five expert crabbers—Will, Danny, Trout, Will's brother Hunter and Danny's brother Gar, both of whom were sixteen. The weight of five kids along with a full tank of gas and a cooler stuffed with ice and soft drinks put a hefty drag on that old 5.5-horsepower engine, and they plowed along at around five knots. They knew it was a far cry from rowing to the gulf like the old timers always talked about. Back then, the trip was usually a two-day expedition. Folks would take tents and gas lanterns and pray that the wind would blow the mosquitoes inland. The advent of outboard engines relieved a lot of pain from the trek to the gulf. But the boys had experienced hardships of their own.

"Do y'all remember that old silver 2-horsepower motor grandpa had," Hunter asked.

"Kinda," Will said.

"I barely remember it," Danny said.

"Trout did you ever go with us to the gulf back then?" Hunter asked.

"Nope, I never did."

"Well we'd leave at sunrise," Hunter explained, "and if we didn't have motor trouble we might make it to the gulf by noon."

144

"We always had motor trouble," Gar said.

"Well that's true. But the trip took so long we'd only get a couple of hours to body surf or catch crabs. Then we'd have to pile back in the boat and head home."

"They always timed it so we'd leave the gulf on an incoming tide so we wouldn't be fighting the current," Gar said. "If we were lucky we'd make it by dark."

"By the time we got home we'd be completely blistered by the sun," Hunter laughed. "And covered in salt and sand and all crowded together. Everybody would be pretty much miserable. It was bad."

"Yeah, that's why we only did it once a summer," Gar said. "It'd take us a week to recover."

Will, Danny, and Trout listened in awe. To them, the older boys were Gods. The four years that separated them were like eons. And the amazing things they did—gigged stingrays, swam across the bay or jumped off the Alabama Point Bridge—were truly supernatural. One day, they'd grow to be like them. That made them proud.

And even though *Greenie* was bogged down, completing the twelve-mile journey to the gulf in just two hours seemed like nothing. It gave them time to swig cold drinks, eat a PB&J and learn about things they couldn't figure out, like girls.

"Hey Hunter," Will said. "When did you first start liking girls?"

"I don't know," he said. "I guess I was about your age. Maybe younger."

"Heck," Gar said. "Most kids waited but I had a girlfriend when I was in second grade."

"You did?" Danny asked.

"Sure did," Gar smiled. "But I was the only one. All my friends hated girls back then and made fun of me."

"I'll never forget," Hunter said. "Her name was Stephanie Snod-grass."

"Snodgrass!" Will laughed. "I'd hate to be named Snodgrass."

Danny giggled, too. "No kidding. Hey, come here *Snod*grass."

"Yeah, it was a weird name but I didn't care. She was the best-looking girl in the school," Gar bragged.

"We used to tease him though," Hunter said. "Remember, that rhyme?"

"I remember I hated y'all for doing that."

Hunter launched into the ditty like they were eight-years-old again.

Gar and Stephanie, sitting in a tree

K-I-S-S-I-N-G.

First comes love; then comes marriage.

Then comes little Gar in a baby carriage.

The boys howled like it was the funniest thing they'd ever heard.

"Did you ever kiss her?" Will asked.

"Nah, we were too young but we did hold hands. I took her to Saturday matinees and stuff."

"So Gar, have you ever kissed a girl?" Danny asked.

Gar smiled. "Of course I have."

Will flashed a curious look at Hunter. "You too?"

"What do *you* think? We both have girlfriends, goofus. That's what we do. We go to the movies, we go to football games, and we make out."

"What's it like?" Danny asked.

"It's nice," Gar explained. "You know, you put your lips on her lips and you kiss."

"And that's it?" Will asked. "Doesn't seem so special to me."

"That's not completely it. Y'all know what a French kiss is?" Hunter asked with a sly grin.

"A French kiss." Will said. "What's that?"

Trout, Danny and Will were mesmerized. The older boys were opening doors they never knew existed.

"Well," Hunter said. "It's when you're kissing a girl and you slip your tongue in her mouth."

The boys rolled off their seats into the bottom of the boat in utter shock. "Yuck!" Danny squealed as he writhed among the life jackets. "That's disgusting. Why do you do that?"

"Because that's a French kiss," Gar said. "It's just part of kissing."

Will's face had contorted into a horrific scowl. He shook his body and blinked his bulging eyes as if he was getting electrical shock treatments. "But why do you put your tongue in there?" Will asked. "That's just sick!"

"No it's not," Gar said. "Then she puts her tongue in your mouth."

"*Ick!*" Danny continued wriggling. "Does she have too?"

"You want her to," Hunter said.

"Not me," Will said. "I'll kiss but she can keep her tongue in her own mouth."

"Just wait until y'all get older," Hunter said. "You'll be French kissing just like everybody else."

"I'm with Will," Trout finally spoke up. He'd been imagining a girl's tongue in his mouth and had sucked down his soft drink in three gulps. "She can keep her nasty old tongue away from me."

Hunter and Gar laughed at the boys. They were young but eventually, like all teenagers, they'd come of age and do things they once considered disgusting. That was growing up. That was life.

Fortunately, their adventures at Perdido, like crabbing at the gulf, diverted their minds from girls and French kisses. That day, they had a perfect distraction—the clear waters of the Gulf of Mexico.

The transition from the bay to the gulf was as different as earth and sky. With a placid shoreline of protected inlets lined with pines and oaks, Perdido Bay had a calming effect on folk's souls. The bay was born of fresh water with inviting shallows and gentle rolling waves. The tide eased softly in and out without rip currents or crashing waves.

The Gulf of Mexico was none of that. The relentless sun beat down on miles of barren beaches and the surf pounded its shoreline without remorse. Brackish bay water gave way to crystal clear pure salt water where scary monsters roamed. Sharks, manta rays and sea turtles made their home in the gulf. The bay was refuge for harmless shrimp, mullet and trout.

Many of the sea critters moved effortlessly between bay waters and the gulf. Dolphins wandered from the far reaches of Soldier Creek to miles out into the gulf. Flounder, stingrays, redfish and, unfortunately jellyfish inhabited a dual existence, along with lots of other species. God had not built a divine wall to keep the bay and gulf separated. But, the fact remained, venturing into gulf waters was entering a completely new universe with far more dangers and sometimes greater rewards.

Hunter stood in the bow as Gar navigated. "Do you see the pass?" Gar asked.

"Mr. Walt said to try the east side," Hunter said. "He said it was deeper over there."

"We might have to get out and push the boat over the shallow parts of the sandbar," Gar said.

A vast field of shifting sand separated the gulf from the bay. The combination of wind, waves and tides constantly changed the sandbar so that each passage into the gulf began with a search for a channel deep enough to get a boat across. *Greenie* could pass through water only a few inches deep but larger boats were forever getting stuck as they picked their way across the shallows.

Hunter pointed to the port side. "That looks like a good way to go. I see a deep trough where we can anchor. Will, get the anchor out."

"It's ready."

"Okay, chuck it."

They watched the anchor sink through the clear gulf water and dig into the sand six feet below. With the incoming tide flowing slowly toward the bay, it swung *Greenie* around and set the anchor.

"Let's wait and make sure she's set," Gar said. "It's a long swim back home. Y'all grab the nets and spread out. Will, you and Danny and Trout can take turns carrying the crab bucket."

With *Greenie's* anchor holding firm, they swam to the knee-deep part of the bar where they could chase down skittish crabs. The shallow sandbar extended out into the gulf for a half mile and along the beach even farther. Spread in front of the boys were acres and acres of pristine sandbar covered in crystal clear water and strange sea creatures.

"Look for a brown spot on the sand about the size of a potato," Hunter said. "Sneak up on it and then snatch it."

"They'll either bury themselves in the sand or they'll take off," Gar explained. "If they dig in, just put the net on top of them and scrap 'em out. But if they take off, try to chase them toward somebody with a net and double team 'em."

Unlike fishing, which required a certain amount of finesse—what lures to use, how fast to troll, where to fish—crabbing was more about simple stalking, a boy with a net versus a critter with sharp claws. The chase was often chaotic since crabs could zip along the bottom at surprising speeds. But they were rarely as fast as a pack of untamed boys. When they'd surround one and the crab determined that escape was futile, it could somehow slip its entire body under the sand in the blink of an eye. The sight of a dark crab disappearing under pure white sand that fast was an amazing thing to witness but with six spindly legs, a pair of claws and a weird pair of flipper legs in the back, a crab had the benefit of ten digging tools. In one instantaneous motion, they'd use their hind legs to make a pocket in the sand and their six pointed legs to shove their body backwards under the sand. Somehow, they'd tuck their pinchers out of sight, too. Occasionally, part of their shell, about the size of a quarter, would remain uncovered. That made it easy for the boys to drape the net over the crab and drag the scrappy little bugger from its hiding place. If its disappearing act were absolute, as the crab undoubtedly hoped, the boys would make an educated guess with their nets and either snag the crab or run it out of hiding. Either way, they'd usually bag it. Sometimes a particularly wily crab would choose the only possible escape route - deep water. When the boys got in chest-deep water, they just couldn't keep pace with a run away crab anymore. And even if they could, they'd eventually lose sight of the moving tater as it faded into the blue.

"There's one," Danny yelled as he flung his net into the water. "Got him!"

"I got one too," Will howled, "Trout, bring the bucket. It's a big un."

"Look out for those claws," Trout said. "They're huge! Don't let that one pinch me."

As they scooped the crabs off the sand, they flipped the net over and dropped them into the bucket. Crabs were some of the ugliest sea critters the boys had ever seen, not to mention angry and aggressive with their claws.

"He doesn't want to let go," Will said as he tried to shake the crab out of the net and into the bucket. "Those are some strong claws."

"Keep shaking it," Trout said. "He'll let go."

"Here comes one Danny," Hunter said. "He's headed right for you."

Danny positioned his net. "I see him."

Just as he was about to scoop, the crab moved. Danny yelled and jumped straight up as the crab zipped between his feet. "I missed him. He's fast! Get him Will."

Will had finally gotten his crab into the bucket and swung his net around. But the crab slammed on the brakes, turned and took off the other way.

"Wow, he *is* fast! And he's coming right back at you," Will said to Danny.

"I'll get him this time."

But this particular blue crab had different ideas. It charged at Danny's right foot with both pinchers snapping wildly.

Danny jumped straight up. "Hey! He's after me."

The crab's pinchers clamped shut just as Danny jerked his leg out of the water.

"He almost got me. He missed my toe by a gnat's hair."

Undeterred, the frantic crab rushed at Danny's left foot. Danny yanked it up a split second before disaster. And, once again, the crab zeroed in on the right foot. Danny hopped from one foot to other and squealed as the crab raced back and forth. Finally, Danny realized that the crab was going to eventually latch onto his foot or something worse if he happened to fall and expose more tender regions of his body to the crab's jagged claws. There was only one thing to do. Danny dropped his net, yelled "*Help!*" and took off in a full sprint across the sandbar. Just as Danny scampered off in a panic, Hunter's net crashed down and scooped up the irate crab.

"Got him!" he said. "You can come back now Danny. This little crab won't hurt you."

Will and Trout were flopping around in the shallows and cracking up. "Run Danny run. A crab's gonna get you," Will said.

"Well look at that," Hunter said as he held up the crab. "No wonder she was so mad. It's a mama crab."

Will pointed at the crab's underbelly. "Gross, what's that orange stuff?"

"Eggs," Hunter said. "She's about to lay her eggs. We've gotta throw her back anyway."

"We can't keep crabs with eggs?" Trout asked.

"Nope," Gar said.

"Why not?"

"Well goofus, if we took all the pregnant crabs there wouldn't be any more next year. They gotta have babies."

"Oh, I guess so," Trout said. "Can I touch the eggs?"

Hunter held the crab up. "Sure but don't poke at 'em, just touch 'em."

He fully expected Trout to reach under the little beast. Everyone knew not to dangle a finger near a claw. Or so Hunter thought. Just as the tip of Trout's finger poked the eggs, the she-crab clamped down with the force of a vice-grip.

"*Yow!*" Trout yelled and jerked his hand away. But she hung on tighter and slipped from Hunter's hold. The more Trout tried shaking her off, the deeper her claws dug in.

"Put it down in the water," Hunter said quickly. "She'll let go."

Normally, when a crab was dropped back into the drink, it would release whatever it was clamped on—a rope, a net, or, in this case, Trout's pointer. He jammed his hand underwater. But the mama crab decided to make Trout pay. Instead of releasing Trout's finger, she reached over with her other claw and hooked into more flesh.

"Ow!" he screamed. "She's got my pinky!"

With both pinchers dug in, she tugged, twisted, and worked his fingers over. Trout kept his hand underwater and shook as hard as he could, hoping she'd give up. But that crab was mad. Soon she drew blood.

"What do I do?" Trout pleaded.

"We'll have to pull her claws off," Hunter said. "Lift it up."

The sight was creepy. A gnarly blue crab with a half-dozen crusty barnacles on her back and, apparently, a deeply seated mean streak, was locked on. Not only was she grinding through his skin, but she was wedging his fingers apart as if she wanted to pull them out of their sockets. For all she knew, Trout's hand was some kind of fleshy crab killer, and she was fighting to save her babies.

As Hunter reached for her claws to twist them off and end Trout's excruciating ordeal, she let go, plopped into the water and sped away. Trout clutched his fingers and inspected the damage. Fortunately, the blue crab's claws were not razor sharp or Trout would have ended up with two bloody stubs. Instead, the cuts were shallow but the bruises would be deep. Gar went back to the boat for a rag to tie around the wounds. Trout was demoted to lowly bucket boy for the rest of the hunt.

"Y'all watch me," Hunter said to the younger boys, hoping to avoid future mishaps. "There's only one way to hold a crab so that it can't pinch your fingers. First, you use a stick or something to hold them down and then you grab their back flippers with your thumb and forefinger, like this. Once you have a good hold on it, you can pick it up."

Hunter demonstrated the universal crab grab and lifted up a particularly large male. It clawed viciously at Hunter's fingers but could never quite reach them.

"See," he said, "he's trying to get me. And it looks like he might but they just can't reach that far back."

"I already know how to do that," Will said.

"Me too," Danny said.

"I just wanted to make sure so you won't do what Trout did."

"Don't worry," Will said. "I know better than that."

"I know now," Trout said sheepishly. "And I don't think I'll ever forget."

"Probably not," Hunter said.

"If it makes you feel any better," Gar said, "Everybody gets pinched sooner or later."

"Really?" Trout said.

"Sure they do Trout," Gar said. "But, I'll tell you what, that was the nastiest crab pinch I've ever seen."

"Me too," Hunter said. "That's one you can tell your kids about."

Trout grinned slightly and puffed out his chest. He'd taken a beating and had survived to tell the tail. At least he could take pride in that.

It took the five of them an hour to catch seventy-three keepers. Including all the pregnant ones they had to throw back, they'd netted more than two hundred. Mr. Walt didn't tell them how many to keep but as far as they knew he always wanted as much seafood as they could get. Unfortunately, the cooler and five-gallon bucket couldn't hold all the crabs so Trout just dumped the rest into the bottom of *Greenie*.

"They can't climb up over the side of the boat," he said.

"I guess that's as good a place as any," Gar told him. "We'll just gather 'em up when we get home."

As they climbed into the boat and pulled the anchor, the boys noticed Hunter and Gar with their eyes locked on the Alabama Point Bridge.

"What do ya think?" Gar said.

"Let's do it," Hunter replied.

"What?" Will asked. "Y'all gonna jump off the bridge?"

"Yep," Hunter said as he steered *Greenie* to the beach.

"We've gotta jump where it's plenty deep," Gar told the boys. "So we'll be out in the middle of the pass. Y'all come pick us up after we jump."

"The tide's still coming in," Hunter told them. "So it'll push us toward that little island over there."

Will looked at the massive concrete bridge towering over their heads. "Hunter, I want to jump too," he said.

"Me too," Danny quickly followed.

Trout held his wounded fingers in silence. He'd had enough action for one day.

"No way Will," Hunter said. "It's too high."

"But we've jumped out of The Tree a million times," Will said.

"Yeah, but the tree is only about twenty feet high. The bridge is more like forty," Gar said.

Will stomped his foot on the bottom of the boat. "We can make it."

"No!" Hunter and Gar said in unison.

"Mr. Walt would kill us if he found out, even if you didn't get hurt," Gar said. "Plus, right before we left he made a point to tell us not to jump off the bridge."

"We won't tell," Will said. "If you let us jump, too."

Hunter pinched the back of Will's neck and looked him dead in the eyes. "Listen squirt, it ain't gonna happen. Got it!"

"Ouch! Okay, I got it."

"Good. Y'all wait here and come get us after we jump," Gar said.

The boys gawked at Hunter and Gar as they walked along the bridge to its highest point then stepped up on the railing. A couple of cars passed by and slowed to watch.

Hunter walked along the railing for a better position. "It looks deep right over there."

"You want to go first?" Gar asked.

"Sure. Here goes nothing."

Hunter leaped, let out of howl and splashed down in the middle of the dark water. As he bobbed up, he yelled up to Gar.

"I just barely touched the bottom. Come on!"

"You hit?" Gar hollered.

"Just a little."

Gar hesitated for a moment. The last thing he wanted to do was drive his foot into the hard sand.

"Come on. Jump!"

There was no turning back. Gar aimed for the deepest water he could see.

"That's unreal," Danny said. "It really is high."

"We could do it," Will said.

"I think Hunter and Gar are right," Danny said. "It's too high for us."

"Not me," Will said.

Gar shot through the water and hit the sand hard. He'd jumped on top of a sand bar. His ankle bent radically and something snapped.

He bobbed up and moaned.

"You okay? You missed the best landing spot."

"Yeah, I know. I think I broke my ankle."

Moments later Will pulled *Greenie* along side. "That was amazing!" he said

"Yeah," Danny said. "Unbelievable."

Trout noticed a grimace on Gar's face. Maybe the pain in his fingers increased his sensitivity to other victims. "Are you all right, Gar?"

Hunter helped Gar grab a hold of *Greenie's* railing. "He hit the bottom. He might have broken his ankle."

"You need some help getting in the boat?" Danny asked.

Gar winced as his foot scraped along the sand. "I think I'll just hold on. Pull me over to the beach."

Will eased the boat back to the shore so Gar could sit in the shallow water and check his ankle.

"It's already swelling up," Hunter said. "Let's head on home. You can put your foot in the cooler until we get back."

Gar hobbled into the boat and gingerly lowered his foot into the ice water. A bluish color had already surrounded his puffed-up ankle. Even with the intense pain, he knew the worst was yet to come. "Mr. Walt's not gonna be happy," he said.

"Yeah," Hunter agreed. "But maybe it's just a sprain."

After he helped Gar get comfortable, Hunter poured a couple of buckets of gulf water into *Greenie* so the crabs would stay alive until they made it back home. The on-board aquarium seemed to suit the crabs just fine. They hunkered down between the wooden ribs and kept their beady eyes fixed on the boy's feet, which were propped up on the seats out of reach from the treacherous claws. Every so often, one of the boys would shift their legs and dozens of claws would pop out of the water, snapping desperately for a piece of big toe or maybe an Achilles tendon. But Trout's episode had the boys on edge. They feared the death grip. None of them, especially Trout, wanted to lose a toe.

As Red Bluff came into view, the waves in the middle of the bay began to build. The crabs sloshed back and forth and they sensed their chance to escape or, perhaps, nip some young flesh. Will kept the throttle pegged as they surfed down a large rolling wave.

"Slow down!" Hunter yelled. "We're gonna flip over and get attacked by a bunch of angry crabs."

Will throttled *Greenie* back to a manageable speed.

"Let's bail this water out," Hunter said. "We'll be home in five minutes. Those crabs can live that long without water."

"Y'all do it," Trout said. "I'm not sticking my hands down in that water."

"Fine," Danny said. "Will and I can do it."

Using their bailing buckets, Danny and Will scooped the water, each time narrowly missing a host of angry claws.

"Look out for that one," Will said as a crab snuck up behind Danny's hand. "I'll get him with the paddle."

Wildlife was always in grave danger when Will wielded a paddle. He slapped a few aggressive crabs into submission but one latched onto the paddle and held fast. Will banged it on the bottom of the boat until its claws popped off.

"Stupid crab, that'll teach him."

Gar grabbed Will by the arm. "Watch it with that thing. You're gonna hurt somebody and I don't want it to be me."

As they eased up to the pier, they saw Mr. Walt walking down the front yard to see how the boys had done. They all knew he'd be proud of their success. That was the greatest reward they could ever ask for. That and a steaming bowl of Ethel's gumbo.

Gar slipped out of the boat into the shallow water where he could stand on one leg unnoticed. He quietly gathered crabs and tossed them in the bucket.

"How'd you do?" Mr. Walt asked.

"We got seventy three," Danny said proudly.

"That's great!" Mr. Walt said. "Now we just have to clean 'em."

"Can somebody else do that?" Will begged.

"Everyone has to pitch in, even y'all."

"Aw," Will said. "That's not fair."

"Not true, young William," Mr. Walt corrected him. "It's hard … but it's fair."

Mr. Walt cocked his head and ripped off a shrill whistle. More help was on the way. As they unloaded the crabs, the boys were peculiarly quiet. Mr. Walt's fatherly senses detected something. "So was it fun?"

"It was great," Hunter said. "Tons of crabs, clear water...we even saw some stingrays."

Mr. Walt figured he'd throw out an educated guess. "So who got pinched?"

The boys stopped gathering and wondered how he knew. Trout held up his wounded hand. "I did. A big 'ol crab got my pinky and this finger, too."

"Same crab?" Mr. Walt asked.

"Yes, sir."

"That sounds like a nasty one. Everything else okay?"

"Yes, sir," Gar lied, hoping he could limp undetected. The last thing he wanted was Mr. Walt's wrath and getting stuck with the chore he'd regret forever. In fact, he could almost smell the septic tank.

"Well that's just great, boys. Good job. Miss Kitty and Ethel will be thrilled. And I'm glad y'all had fun."

A pack of brothers, sisters and cousins came dashing toward the pier wondering why Mr. Walt had summoned them.

"We've got some crabs to clean here. If you've never done it, any of these boys can show you how. When you're finished bring 'em up to the house."

Anyone who has ever wondered why crabmeat is so expensive has never cleaned and picked a crab. The job is messy, tedious and disappointing, considering so much effort yields so little meat.

The kids didn't realize it but crab cleaning was a perfect metaphor for success in life. There were no shortcuts that ever worked out well and a big pile of meat could only be built with many small pieces. It took patience and persistence—more good traits to mold their characters.

Will held up one of the biggest crabs they nabbed and showed it to some younger cousins, "First thing you do," he said, "is pull off the pinchers so they can't pinch you."

"But you have to grab 'em both at the same time," Danny said. "If you just grab one, they'll get you with the other pincher."

Will looked slyly at Trout. "Yeah and you do NOT want to get pinched. Isn't that right Trout?"

Everybody laughed. They'd already seen Trout's fingers.

"That's right. And how many times have you been pinched Will?"

"None today," he said. "How 'bout you?"

"How about ever?" Trout said.

"I got pinched a few times when I was a little kid and didn't know any better," Will said.

The tiny cousins giggled. Trout decided to let that one slide.

"Just show 'em how to clean the stupid crab," Trout said.

"Okay. So once you get the claws off, you grab their legs on one side of the body and rip the shell off, like this."

Will demonstrated by slowly pulling off the shell revealing a squishy mass of yellow and brown guts.

"That's gross," a young cousin said. "What's that?"

"Those are the guts," Danny said. "That's what we're cleaning."

Will held up his index finger. "You take your finger and dig the guts out. Once you get most of 'em, put the body into the water and slosh it around. That gets the rest of the guts out."

"Is that it?" another cousin asked.

"Not quite," Will said. "You pull these little things off ..."

"What is that?"

"It's the mouth and eyes and stuff."

"Disgusting."

"Then you twist off the legs," Will said.

"Don't yank the legs out or you'll pull good meat out with it," Danny interrupted. "You have to twist 'em off."

"Yeah, twist 'em off," Will said. "The last but most important are the Devil's fingers," Will said.

"What makes them so special?"

"Well, for one they taste real bad," Will said.

"And they're poisonous," Danny added.

"If I eat 'em, will they kill me?" asked a cousin.

"If we're lucky they will," Will said smiling. "Then they'll be more food for the rest of us."

"Hey!"

"I don't know if they'll kill you but they might make you real sick so be sure to pick all of the Devil fingers off."

"Why are they called Devil fingers?"

"I guess because they look kinda like fingers," Will said. "Stop asking so many questions and just pull 'em off. That's it."

"What next?"

"Only thing left is the cooking and eating," Will smiled.

Although they didn't realize it, Devil fingers were not really poisonous. But they had the unappetizing consistency of little hairballs so the poison myth saved plenty of perfectly fine gumbo from getting thrown out to the raccoons. The Devil fingers were actually the crab's gills that filtered life-giving oxygen from the water.

"Ethel," Danny hollered, "we got your crabs. Seventy three of 'em."

"Lordy mercy," she said. "That's real fine boys. Just put 'em in the sink."

"How's that gumbo coming?" Will asked.

"It's ready. I just need to put in the crabs and shrimps."

"Ethel, are you gonna put all those crabs in there?" Danny asked.

"Heaven's no boy. I'll put in what I need, and the rest we'll just boil up for eatin'."

"Could y'all please give me a hand?" Miss Kitty asked as she was busily cracking the crab bodies in half.

"Sure, Mama," Danny said.

"I guess so," Will sulked. He'd been catching crabs, cleaning crabs, teaching kids how to clean crabs and now he had to handle those dadburn crabs again. He wondered if he'd ever get to eat them.

"Y'all have done this before, right?"

"Yes, ma'am," Danny said. "But can you show us again?"

"Sure honey. Just grab it with both hands and snap it in half like you would a graham cracker. Then we'll pile them in this bowl."

Miss Kitty worked quickly. She and Ethel were used to pumping out lots of food in a short time and she broke three crabs to every one the boys did. They ran through all seventy-three crabs in five minutes. As they finished, Ethel pulled a batch of fresh biscuits from the oven and casually placed two on a plate. Steam puffed out of the bread as she cut open the biscuits and smothered them with gumbo.

"Here y'all go," she said, "a little treat for all your hard work."

"Thanks Ethel!" Will said, digging in with both hands. "Mm, that is some kinda good Ethel."

"Mm-mmm," Danny agreed. "Ethel, how'd you learn to cook so good?"

"So *well*," Miss Kitty corrected him.

"I guess I was just born with a gift," Ethel smiled. "And, Lord have mercy, I do love cooking. That's the thing—if you don't love your work, you won't never be no good at it."

The boys were too engrossed in Ethel's food to ponder her wisdom. Danny wiped his mouth with the neck of his T-shirt. "We love your cooking, too, Ethel."

"Yep," Will said. "You must be the best cook in the whole state of Alabama!"

"Probably the whole United States," Danny said.

Beaming with pride, Ethel dumped the crabs into a massive pot. She knew her cooking brought lots of smiles and contentment. As she stirred the crabs into the mix, Ethel figured Miss Kitty could keep the gumbo from burning while she headed to The Point for some sunset fishing. She grabbed a fresh can of snuff, smiled, and eased out the back porch screen door. The white trout were waiting.

Miss Kitty put out three humongous bowls with the rice, gumbo and biscuits—enough to serve more than twenty cousins, brothers, sisters, aunts and uncles who had appeared from all corners of the house. With a stack of bowls, napkins and spoons at one end of the table, supper was strictly self-service. As the lively horde chattered, laughed and filled their bowls, Mr. Walt tapped his spoon against a glass pitcher of tea to bring instant silence and bowed heads.

"Bless, oh Lord, this food to our use and us to thy service. Keep us ever mindful of the needs of others. We ask, in Your name. Amen."

"Amen," the crowd said together.

Without missing a beat, Hunter piped up. "Amen, brother Ben … killed a rooster … shot a hen."

Even though she'd heard the post-blessing ditty since childhood, Miss Kitty laughed softly. "You know, Daddy used to say that all the time."

Danny and Will perked up. "Is Grandpa coming down this summer?" Danny asked.

"I hope he does," Will said.

"We'll see," Miss Kitty said. "I hope so, too."

The deafening yakking and giggling that shook the walls of Paradise Point before suppertime had suddenly fallen to a low hum of two-dozen folks gulping down biscuits and gumbo. Now the only words spoken were a few garbled compliments between swallows.

"Mm, that's good."

"Delicious."

"Best gumbo I've ever tasted," Miss Kitty said with a smile.

All the kids giggled because everything Miss Kitty ate, unless it was flat out rotten, was the "best I've ever tasted." But she might have been speaking the God's truth that night. If Ethel's gumbo could quiet that boisterous bunch, the food had to be blissful.

As was customary on a night of picking and eating crabs, the long table had been covered in newspaper. It helped soak up some of the crab juice but mostly made cleanup quick and easy. As they meticulously broke the crabs apart and dug out the sweet white meat, everyone just dropped the shells on the newspapers and moved on to the next claw or body. When the feast was over, they rolled up the paper tablecloth and, presto, cleanup was complete. As Mr. Walt philosophized bluntly, "newspapers are good for two things—lies and crab shells."

To keep from wasting all the paper napkins in the house on one meal, Miss Kitty put out several large bowls of water for folks to dip their hands in when they got too sticky and covered in pieces of shell. But the napkins still went fast.

Mr. Walt cleared his throat and looked directly at Gar. "Looks like we need more napkins. Gar, would you go to the kitchen and get some?"

Gar's ankle was throbbing badly but the feast had temporarily taken his mind off of the pain. He'd managed to sneak to the supper table among the crowd without anyone noticing his limp. If he went on a solo trip to the kitchen for napkins everyone would see that he was lame, especially Mr. Walt.

"Uh, yes, sir," Gar said as he shot a glance at Hunter.

"I'll get 'em," Hunter said, jumping up from the table. "I'm closer."

"Thanks, Hunter, that's sweet," Miss Kitty said, oblivious to their conspiracy.

Acting as if everything was in order, Mr. Walt wore his best poker face. *No need to cause a scene*, he thought.

When the gumbo fest was over and every rocking chair and couch was filled with folks rubbing their full bellies with pleasure, Mr. Walt strolled to the porch and lit a fresh cigar. As usual, Miss Kitty led the kitchen cleanup crew, who couldn't stop talking about how delicious the meal had been.

Hunter, Gar, Will and Danny were deep in a game of Hearts when Mr. Walt eased over.

"Hi boys. Good job on those crabs today," he said. "We all appreciate the work you did."

"We had fun," Danny said. "We'll go again anytime you want us to."

Will looked up, "Yeah, as long as somebody else cleans 'em."

"You know it doesn't work like that Will. Everyone pitches in."

Will dropped his head into his chest. "Catching crabs is fun but cleaning 'em is too hard."

"That's life, boys. Sometimes you work hard; sometimes you have fun. Get used to it. But I came out here to ask y'all something. Did you ever hear the story about those old pilings out in the bay?"

"A little," Hunter said. "Something about a runway for seaplanes."

"That's right," Mr. Walt said. "Back during the war, the military taught pilots how to land airplanes on the water right out here in Perdido Bay."

"And the pilings marked the runway?" Gar asked.

"Yep. Of course, there were more pilings back then. Most of them are gone now."

"What happened?" Hunter asked.

"Some of them rotted. Time and the waves wore out some others. Then Hurricane Baker finally knocked the rest of them over back in 1950. What you probably don't know is that they also built a big tower at the far end of the runway."

"What for?" Gar asked.

"Well it was kind of a control tower where the flight instructors could watch and so forth."

"What happened to it?"

"They tore it down."

"How come?"

"Well, after the war was over, the military stopped taking care of it and the thing got kind of dilapidated."

"Is that why they tore it down?" Gar asked.

"That's part of it I guess. But the main reason is because kids used to climb up on it and jump off."

"Did you ever do it?" Hunter asked.

"Oh sure. It was great fun."

"How high was it?"

"Pretty high, probably thirty or forty feet, I guess."

"I wish it was still there," Hunter said. "When did they tear it down?"

"Well, one summer we came down and the storms had pushed a lot of sand around it. There had always been deep water on one side of the tower but a couple of sandbars formed so it got pretty tricky knowing where to jump."

"How shallow was it?"

"Just a few feet deep in places but well over your head in others."

"Did anybody get hurt?" Gar asked.

"As a matter of fact, your Uncle Brewton broke his leg."

"Daddy broke his leg!" Hunter said. "Really?"

"Sure did. Broke it bad. Compound fracture. You know, when the bone sticks all the way out through the skin," Mr. Walt said, using his thumb like the bone shooting through his leg.

"Aw, that's gross," Danny squealed.

"Gives me the willies," Will moaned. "Poor daddy."

"The fact is, he could have bled to death but the bone just missed the artery in his leg. He was out of commission for a long time. I think it still hurts him sometimes."

"Daddy never has told us that story," Hunter said.

"He's not real proud of it. His daddy, your granddaddy, saw how shallow it had gotten and insisted that we stop jumping off that tower. But Brewton did it anyway."

"Did he get in trouble?" Hunter asked.

"What do you think?"

"I think he did."

"You're right. It was two years before he was allowed to come back to Perdido. For the next two summers he stayed in Montgomery and worked at the farm."

"Because he hurt himself?" Hunter asked.

"Not so much because of that. He got punished because he disobeyed his father. We did lots of crazy things when we were growing up—just like y'all do," Mr. Walt said, looking Gar and Hunter dead in the eyes. Will and Danny sat quietly and listened intently, knowing not to speak while Mr. Walt was lecturing. "All kids are gonna do that. And that's okay to a point."

"It is?" Gar asked sheepishly.

"Sure, up to a point. But what's absolutely not acceptable is being deceitful, lying, or disobeying. If you're going to make anything of yourselves in this life, you have to start with one thing: honesty."

The boys sat in awkward silence as Mr. Walt took a long puff from his cigar and let them stew in their own thoughts.

"Y'all think about that," he said as he walked away.

When he was far enough away Hunter leaned close to Gar.

"Ya think he knows?" he whispered quietly, not taking any chances that Mr. Walt might hear him.

"Are you kidding?" Gar said. "Of course he knows."

"But how?"

"I don't know how. Sometimes it seems like he knows what we're gonna do before we even do it."

"I know what you mean," Hunter said.

"He's kinda like God," Danny said. "He knows everything."

"Seems like it," Will said.

"We're gonna have to fess up," Hunter said. "And the sooner the better."

Gar shook his head. "I don't know. We'll get in trouble for sure."

"We probably already are. Mr. Walt's thinking of a nasty job for us, I guarantee it."

They sat in silence for a minute until Gar perked up. "Okay Hunter. You're right. Let's fess up."

Right on cue, Mr. Walt strolled through the door to the porch.

"Daddy," Gar said with a beaten dog look on his face. He hoped calling him daddy might win a little sympathy. "Today, after we finished crabbing, we jumped off the bridge and I hit the bottom pretty

163

hard. I don't think I'm gonna be able to walk very well for a day or two. I'm sorry."

"Hmm. You did, huh? Let me take a look at you."

Mr. Walt moved Gar's ankle gently and poked around the bone. The swelling was bad and it was hard to tell if anything was broken.

"I don't think you've broken any bones," he said. "But let's keep a close eye on it and get Doc Jordon to take a look tomorrow. She's a far better judge than I am."

"I really am sorry," Gar said.

"Me too," Hunter said.

"I tell you what Gar, you can help Ethel and Miss Kitty with the kitchen and cleaning for the next few days. In fact, Ethel's bringing down a couple of bushels of peas tomorrow. You can shell plenty of peas and stay off your ankle."

"Yes, sir," he said with a grimace. Shelling peas was as boring as watching dust gather on a windowsill. But he was still at Perdido so he had no complaints.

"And Hunter, tomorrow we need to …"

Hunter winced. He expected the worst. "We need to what?" he asked.

"We'll talk about it tomorrow." Keeping Hunter in suspense was the opening act of his punishment.

Not the septic tank, Hunter thought. *Please not the septic tank.*

"Oh, and boys," he said as walked away.

"Yes, sir."

"Thanks for telling me the truth. That showed a lot of character."

"You're welcome," they said, both too shaken to resume their card game. Will and Danny smiled. Not getting in trouble was comforting. Plus, with Mr. Walt focused on working Hunter's and Gar's fingers to the bone, they could probably spend the whole day water skiing

CHAPTER 22

A Flippin' Success

Life is all about timing.
—Carlton Lyons

The boys were right. The next morning Mr. Walt got Hunter and Gar out of bed at daybreak. Gar hobbled to the porch where an overflowing bushel basket of snap peas waited for him.

"Gar while you shell those peas, Hunter can help me on the roof," Mr. Walt instructed. "Hunter, get that old mop and the five-gallon bucket of black tar. We can patch the seams in the tin before the sun gets too hot."

Hunter wasn't happy about working on the roof with tar that would inevitably get all over his skin and in his hair. Then he'd have to endure the gasoline clean-up treatment. At least Mr. Walt was right about getting an early start. Being up on the roof during midday was a perfect way to melt brain cells and get a sure-fire skin roasting. Yet, even before seven o'clock, the temperatures were already in the mid-eighties and the humidity was nearing a hundred percent. As far as Hunter was concerned, Gar was getting off easy being able to sit under a ceiling fan and avoid hard labor.

Will and Danny scarfed down a bowl of cereal and headed down to *Greenie* to bail the four inches of bay water that had seeped though overnight. If they left her unattended for two days, she'd have sunk hard to the bottom. Mr. Walt had patched her more than a dozen times but finding every little seep and weep was impossible. At that point in her old age, morning bailing sessions were just part of the routine.

"I need my cup of coffee in the morning," Mr. Walt told the boys, "and *Greenie* needs to be bailed. That's just the way life is."

Will cranked the engine and pointed the bow toward The Point while Danny kept scooping out water. They had decided that it was high time to learn a one-and-a-half and earn those five dollars. And they knew Mr. Lyons always took an early morning swim at The Point.

When they putted up Trout was already on the diving board talking to Mr. Lyons, who was making circular hand motions as he explained the dive.

"Hey, wait for us," Danny yelled.

"You better get up early if you want to beat me," Trout said.

"We'll see about that," Will said.

A former and proud University of Alabama diving champion, Carlton Lyons knew that a forward one-and-a-half was an advanced dive for kids their age. Still, he'd watched them grow up since they were crawling around in a playpen and he had faith in their abilities. They just had to overcome their fears. That's where his coaching came in.

Even at age fifty-two and toting a healthy potbelly, Mr. Lyons could still perform a perfect one-and-a-half. With ballerina-like pointed toes, he'd slice through the water without the slightest splash. And while his soaring swan dive was an act of sheer grace and beauty the boys were most impressed with his seemingly simple jack-knife. He'd fly straight up into the air and touch the tips of his toes without bending his knees. Then, as quick as a switchblade, he'd open up and become board-rigid for his entry into the water. Try as they might, the boys could never keep their knees from bending. Their jackknives usually turned into head-smacking, upside-down cannonballs.

"Boys," Carlton Lyons began, "a one-and-a-half is just a forward flip with a dive tacked on at the end. You can do a flip, right?"

"Right," Trout said.

"And you can do a dive, right?"

"Right," Danny said.

"Then all you do is put the two together. Just stay in your tuck a little longer than normal and open up for the dive at the end."

"Sounds easier than it is," Will said.

"Not really son. You just have to believe that you can do it and you will."

"But we've tried," Trout said. "And we keep doing belly flops."

"Well then you're almost there boys. Just stay in your tuck for another split second and you'll have it. Who's first?"

Will stood next to the diving board. "I guess I'll go," he said.

Mr. Lyons stepped in front of him. "First, let me demonstrate. Boys, just do what I do."

With one fluid motion, Carlton Lyons bounced, spun and opened at the precise moment for a picture perfect dive. As always, the boys were impressed.

"Now, do exactly like I did," he said.

Will's attempt was the best he'd ever done. Instead of a belly buster, he split the surface at a forty-five degree angle and avoided the dreaded splat of naked skin on flat water.

"Excellent job Will," Mr. Lyons said. "Just a hair further and that would have been a fine dive."

Danny and Trout were encouraged by Will's success. It wasn't the first time he'd broken tracks for them to follow and it wouldn't be the last. Will's accomplishments became their goals.

Trout's stout legs sprung off the board with precise timing and he spun quickly - actually too fast - and he forgot to come out of his tuck until the very last second. Instead of a one-and-a-half, Trout did a one-and-three-quarters.

"See there, boys," Mr. Lyons said. "You can easily make it far enough around. In fact, if Trout had stayed in his tuck, he'd have probably done a double flip. Performing a one-and-a-half is like life—it's all about timing. And, of course, figuring out exactly when to open up."

After watching Trout and Will do so well, Danny popped onto the diving board and ripped off a slightly crooked one-and-a-half. Instead of cutting through the water at a ninety-degree angle, his body was slanted closer to seventy-five degrees and he threw out a large splash.

"Bravo, young Daniel," Carlton Lyons cheered. "Too much splash, but otherwise, that was nearly flawless."

Within fifteen minutes, the boys had slammed the door on the dive. They'd figured out their timing and were hitting it three out of four times. Every so often, they'd miscalculate and smack down hard, but their confidence was soaring, not to mention they were each five dollars richer.

Mr. Lyons clapped his hands and smiled. "A deal is a deal, boys. Come by my house later today, and I'll dole out your money. And, if you're interested, I'll sign you up for the competition in Mobile. However, I do have another proposition for you."

"What's that?" Will asked.

"Well, remember my offer about learning the gainer?"

"It's another five bucks, right?" Will said.

"Uh, yes, but I have another idea," Mr. Lyons said. "In addition to the five-dollar prize, I'll sweeten the deal."

"With what?" Will asked.

"You're all business today, aren't you Will?"

"I guess so Mr. Lyons. I just don't want you to make me go to that country club."

"I wouldn't force you to do anything you didn't want to do son, even though you'd probably have fun at the competition. However, I'm sure there are other things to motivate you that don't involve going to Mobile."

Carlton Lyons scratched his chin. He wanted to spark the competition with something grand. As his eyes wandered over to *Greenie*, Carlton's light bulb lit up.

"How's this. The winner gets to use my little *Boston Whaler* for a whole week. I'll even provide the gas and oil."

"Oh my gosh!" Trout screamed. "I'm gonna win that!"

"Keep on dreaming, Trout," Will said. "It's mine."

Thirteen feet long with a 25-horsepower engine, the little *Whaler* was an enormous upgrade from *Greenie*. It ran upwards of thirty miles-per-hour and even had a steering wheel. Wrapping their young fingers around that stainless steel wheel was harnessing raw power. They could envision themselves at the helm, jamming the throttle down and running circles around *Greenie*.

"Do we have to try a gainer now?" Danny asked. "'Cause I think I'd like to try later, you know, so I can keep practicing the one-and-a-half."

Will agreed. "Yeah, can we save that for another day?"

"Sure, boys. It's a standing offer. The first one who successfully does a gainer will get to be the captain."

"Will you teach us?" Trout asked.

"Whenever you're ready, I'll be happy to teach you."

Danny pouched out his lips in deep contemplation. "Mr. Lyons, do we have to know how to do a gainer to be in the competition in Mobile."

"No, son. I think you'll do fine with the dives you have in your repertoire right now, especially if you perfect that one-and-a-half."

"Great," Danny said. "Because I want to go and win that fifty dollars."

Mr. Lyons eyed Will. "Son, are you sure you don't want to go? Are you in or out?"

"I'm out like a cigarette butt," he said. "Country clubs are not my thing."

"Suit yourself," Mr. Lyons said, "but I still have five dollars with your name on it and my boat when, and if, you boys can do a gainer."

"I'll be looking forward to captaining your *Whaler* soon," Will said.

Trout pushed Will aside. "Not if I have anything to do with it," he said.

"Don't forget about me," Danny smiled. "I was the first to do the one-and-a-half, you know. I might as well be the first to do the gainer."

Mr. Lyons couldn't help but grin. He loved competition, and the boys defined that spirit. Fortunately, he had the money and toys to stoke the fire between them.

"Just let me know," he said. "I'll have her gassed up and ready."

CHAPTER 23

Rocking on the Water

Anything is doable, if somebody just does it.
—Trout Loxley

Five dollars richer and cockier than usual, the boys were feeling downright invincible. They needed another challenge to further pump up their egos or pop their balloons. As they'd done many times before, they loaded *Greenie* with skiing gear and headed to The Point for a day of dragging themselves at the end of a rope. They'd asked Mr. Walt about using the round piece of plywood he'd cut for Miss Kitty's breakfast table. Turned out she changed her mind and wanted a square table. The boys figured they'd try to ride that scrap of wood. It seemed like a good idea at the time.

"Just bring it back," Mr. Walt said. "Miss Kitty might change her mind again."

Trout rubbed his face from his forehead to his chin. "How're we gonna ride this thing."

"Just like the one-and-a-half," Will said, "we try and try again."

"Like the little engine that could," Danny smiled.

"Yeah," Trout smiled. "And I say these little Injuns need to do some skiing today."

"Did you say, 'engines' or "Injuns" like Indians?" Danny asked.

"Injuns, like Indians."

"Trout, the story is about a train engine, not Indians. You know, 'I think I can, I think I can' and all that."

Trout rubbed his face again. "Oh, I thought you were talking about some kind of Indians."

"You've never read *The Little Engine That Could*?" Will asked.

"Well, I've heard of it but I guess I never read it."

"That's too bad," Danny said. "It's a good story. Maybe we have that book around the house somewhere. Anyway, it doesn't matter—engines or Injuns—let's do some skiing."

As *Greenie* nosed into the beach, Will formed a plan.

"I tell you what," he said. "Once we get up on it, spinning around will be easy."

Danny jumped out of the boat and spun like a top. "It might be hard to stop it from spinning since there's no skeg on it."

"We'll sure find out," Trout said.

Danny was apprehensive about the unknown. He didn't want to seem like a wimp, but he was scared to try their new toy, so he played the part of the considerate cousin.

"Hey, Will," he asked, "Ya wanna go first?"

Without hesitation, Will said, "Sure," as he dived into Soldier Creek. "I'll give it a shot. I'm gonna start out on my stomach then try to get up on my knees. If I make it that far."

"You'll try to stand up," Danny said, finishing the thought.

"Right," Will said, "but what do we call it?"

"Call what?"

"This hunk of round wood we're gonna ski on."

Trout scrutinized the thing. "Well, it's round. We could call it The Circle."

Will laughed. "That's dumb," he said.

"I know," Danny said. "We can call it The Disk, like on a record player."

Trout and Will leapt in the air in agreement. "That's perfect," Trout said.

As Danny gunned the engine, Trout watched the disk shoot out of the water and quickly skip out of control. Somehow, Will hung on to the rope with one hand and the disk with the other. "Slow down!" he screamed. But it was too late. The front edge dug into the water, the disk dove, and Will flew fifteen feet in the air, flipping twice and splashing down face first. Danny and Trout laughed hard. Trout hollered, "You okay?" just to be courteous.

"Don't go so fast," Will said. "You're gonna kill me. The disk has to stay back at an angle or it'll nose dive."

"Okay. I'll start real slow," Danny said, "and you give me the signals."

The signals, as every skier knew, were straightforward. A thumb's up meant go faster; a thumb's down meant slow down and the universal okay sign meant the speed was just right. A finger cutting across the neck like a knife meant "Stop," and another finger meant "I'm gonna pay you back when I get to drive the boat."

Greenie chugged along with a huge wake while Will managed to stay in control. He spread the double-handled ski rope apart so he could wrap his fingers around the edge of the board. Pretty soon, he'd made it to his knees and was able to hold the rope without hanging on to the disk. It took a while but he managed to climb up to his feet.

"Yee-ha!" he screamed. "I got it!"

"See if you can spin around," Danny yelled.

Will twisted back and forth to get the feel of the thing. That disk was squirrelly—

kinda like standing on a big lazy Susan. Spinning around, he decided, would be safer from his knees.

"Go for it!" Trout prodded.

"I'm gonna!" Will yelled back, "when I'm good and ready."

The spin move was all about balance and keeping the board at a consistent angle to the boat. Leaning too far forward would catch an edge. The rider would get flung off the board, twist and turn randomly through the air and then flop into the water. Sometimes pain was involved. Embarrassment always lingered nearby. But experimental skiing and falling went together like black-eye peas and turnip greens. Just like bailing *Greenie*, it was part of the deal, until they tamed a new apparatus.

At slow enough speeds, the water was plenty soft. Later in their lives when barefoot skiing was among their bag of tricks, hitting the water at forty miles per hour was a lot like bouncing across a parking lot, without all of the scrapped-off skin. They'd skip and cartwheel until they slowed down enough to actually sink. Falls like that usually resulted in twisted necks, sore backs and more than a few smacked gonads. But with only five-and-a-half horses in *Greenie's* little engine, their stumbles were mostly harmless unless the wooden disk whacked them in a bad spot.

It took a while for Will to work up the nerve to spin around. That first fall was still fresh in his mind. On his first attempt, he yanked the rope for some slack and spun. He reached around his back, caught one handle and made it around—halfway. Keeping the disk in a perfect position, Will was able to ride backwards without crashing until he gained enough confidence to let go of the rope handle with one hand and spin back around.

"I got it. It's easy," he said. Then, in one steady motion, he spun all the way around. An hour later a new competition had developed. The game was to stand up and see how many times they could spin around continuously without falling off. Will held the record at thirty-four revolutions. Each time Danny got past twenty, he got dizzy, started laughing and wiped out. Trout kept losing his balance on his second or third rotation.

"I don't know how y'all do it," he said in frustration.

"It's all about balance Trout," Danny said. "Keep trying."

After he determined that he couldn't beat thirty-four, Danny decided to work out a new maneuver. "Watch this," he shouted as he spun around backwards. From his knees, he put his head on the disk, spread his hands and grabbed both sides of the disk. Slowly but steadily he lifted his legs. As Will and Trout pulled Danny by The Point, Doc Jordon and Miss Kitty sat under the pavilion enjoying the breeze and some lemonade. They stared at Danny as he stood on his head and rode that round wooden disk across the water.

"What will those fool boys think of next?" Doc Jordon asked.

"Lord only knows," Miss Kitty smiled. "You know, that was supposed to be my breakfast table."

"Then why in Sam Hill's name are they doing that with it?"

"I decided I didn't want a round table so I guess Mr. Walt let them use it."

"Well, I'll be damned," Doc Jordon said.

A sly grin spread across Trout's face when he noticed the women at The Point "I've got an idea," he said, "but it's a little crazy."

"Nothing to do with a parachute I hope," Will said.

"Nope but remember that old rocking chair on our pier?"

"The one with the seat knocked out of it?"

"Yep, let's get it."

Outlandish ideas come naturally to clever minds. In fact, they popped into Trout's crafty brain whether he wanted them to or not. Acting on those ideas was where the road split. For Trout, crazy ideas called for action and rarely did one go untried.

"I don't think you can do it," Will said.

"Just watch me."

Putting a rocking chair on a round disk and dragging it behind *Greenie* sounded impossible, but that just made it more appealing for Trout. Getting up with the rocking chair setting in the middle of the disk wasn't the hard part. Trying to keep the disk from spinning sideways when he tried to sit it in proved to be the real challenge. He started out with the chair in the middle of the disk. Then Danny put the boat in gear just to create a little tension and keep the whole contraption from sinking. As the disk and chair moved along ever so slowly, Trout stuck one arm around the chair's leg to keep it from getting washed off when Danny gunned the engine.

"Ready," Trout yelled. "Hit it!"

Three falls in three tries got Trout frustrated and he kicked angrily at the chair as he crashed down for the third time.

"Maybe it is impossible," he said.

"I told you so," Will grinned.

That did it. Trout had something to prove. He couldn't spin like Will but if he could pull off this stunt, it would become Perdido legend.

"Just keep the boat going straight and steady," Trout said. "Don't go too fast, don't turn and don't hit any waves."

"Anything else?" Danny asked. "Want Will and me to pray for you?"

"If you think it will help," Trout said.

"Help him Jesus," Will said sarcastically. "We all know he needs it."

On the fourth try, Trout was completely focused. His slender muscles strained as the boat took off and he struggled to keep the chair on the disk. With most of the weight in the center of the disk Trout climbed up on one knee and hugged the chair like he'd just found his lost dog. Slowly he slid his left leg over the arm of the rocking chair and inched his foot in front of it. Some oncoming waves sprayed water into Trout's face and the disk hobby-horsed wildly. But he stayed on.

"Hey Danny, watch it."

"I am watching it. I can't stop the waves."

With slow precision, he moved his butt over the arm of the chair and his right leg followed. With both feet firmly on the disk in front of the chair, he squatted toward the seat without touching it. Any major shift in weight would send him flying with the chair close behind. The thought of getting whacked in the back of the head by a rocking chair kept him focused.

Trout held the rope handles steady and lowered his butt closer and closer to the seat. When he was perfectly balanced, he sat down.

"Yee ha," Danny shouted. "You did it."

"Well, I'll be a dead mullet," Will said. "He sure did."

He hooked the rope handles on two screws jutting through the chair arms and cruised along hands free. Pretty soon, he was relaxing with his hands behind his head. Trout figured he was ready for the big show so he flashed the okay sign and motioned Danny to head toward The Point. A watermelon smile spread across his face as he thought about showing off for an audience. *They'll be talking about this one for a long time*, he thought.

By the time *Greenie* closed in on The Point, a half a dozen women had joined Mrs. Kitty and Doc Jordon for lemonade. They'd also brought a mess of kids, who were running wild, building sand castles and doing tricks off the diving board. An eight-year-old boy looked up when he heard *Greenie* coming around the corner toward them.

"Look," he said pointing, "what's that?"

"I don't know," another kid said. "Looks like an old lady skiing on a rocking chair."

From a distance, the flat wooden disk was undetectable. But the rocking chair was unmistakable. Trout, in his never-ending quest to outdo Will, had jammed a book, a big floppy hat and an umbrella into the rocking chair. When he got comfortable and balanced, he stuck the hat on his head, opened the umbrella and started reading the book. Holding the umbrella steady was tricky but *Greenie* was barely pushing ten knots. As he buzzed past The Point, folks who didn't know better saw a little lady skiing on the rockers of a chair. Mouths hung open and, for well over a minute, the mob of kids and women on The Point stopped everything they were doing and stared at a spectacle they could never have imagined seeing. Many of them tried to figure out exactly what they were witnessing. Whatever it was, all of them were amazed and a good bit perplexed. But no one, not for one second, took their eyes off of Trout as he performed his newest act of controlled goofiness.

Miss Kitty and Doc Jordon grinned at the sight of boys reaching the highest peak of enjoyment and using some pretty ingenious creativity.

"Well would you look at that," Miss Kitty said seizing the opportunity of a lifetime. "Will said he was going to teach Miss Lilly Felder how to ski on a rocking chair but I never thought she'd do it."

"That's Lilly Felder?" a woman gasped. "You mean Dr. Felder's wife?"

"Absolutely," Doc Jordon smiled. "I hear she's a real daredevil."

"My goodness," another woman huffed, "I wonder what the doctor thinks about her parading around like that?"

"Oh," Miss Kitty said, "she's just having a little fun. I'm sure he doesn't mind."

"It looks like she's reading a book," someone said.

"I think she is," another woman acknowledged.

"I hope it's not my copy of *Pride and Prejudice* I let her borrow. All that water will just ruin it."

Kitty and Doc enjoyed letting the women get worked up over the antics of other men's wives. But they didn't want it to go too far.

"You think we should tell them?" Miss Kitty asked Doc Jordon.

"Tell us what?" a woman asked.

"That she, uh," Doc Jordon paused. She hated to ruin a good joke. And this was as good as any. "Yeah Kitty, just what is it that you want to tell them?"

Without hesitation, Miss Kitty grinned and said, "Well, you know, that it can't be *Pride and Prejudice* because she read it last summer."

Doc Jordon smiled. "Yes, as a matter of fact she did. I remember it well."

The women were confused by the whole conversation but mostly they were shocked that a doctor's wife would be out doing silly ski tricks with young boys when she should be taking care of her own children.

As suddenly as they'd come into view, the boys disappeared around a bend in Soldier Creek. From The Point, the sound of *Greenie's* engine began to fade. The kids returned to swimming and diving with a strange image burned into their minds. Danny and Will were itching to try the rocking chair trick but they knew it would be better to wait for another day and a new crowd at The Point. Even though the entire event lasted just a few minutes, the skiing rocking chair story became an instant legend just like Trout knew it would.

"I never thought you'd do it," Will admitted.

"I just kept saying 'I think I can'," Trout told him. "You know, like that Injun book y'all talked about."

Will and Danny smiled. They were happy to have Trout as a friend.

CHAPTER 24

Country versus Country Club

Character is what you are; reputation is what you try to make people think you are.

—Walt Thornton

As far as the boy's skiing talents were concerned, riding the disk on a rocking chair really wasn't all that peculiar. They'd skied on paddles, seat cushions, and pier boards, not to mention getting pulled on the slalom by a parachute. If a dead alligator floated up, they probably would have tried to ride it, too. Fortunately, that never happened.

When they landed back at The Point, charged up about Trout's rocking chair success, a crowd of kids had gathered. Normally the boys bragged about their skiing accomplishments to each other. Now they had an audience. Unlike the lemonade ladies, the youngsters knew who was behind the rocking chair scheme so they fired off their questions.

"Trout, how'd you do that?"

"Why didn't the rocking chair come off?"

"How'd you hold the umbrella?"

"When are you gonna do it again?"

Trout held up his hands. "Calm down y'all. We can't answer all this stuff."

"Yeah," Danny continued, "if we tell our secrets then everybody could do it."

"A trick like that takes years and years of practice," Will said.

"Not to mention a lot of skill," Danny said.

"And plenty of try-try-again, too," Trout said.

178

They were feeling exceptionally proud of themselves because they'd retained top dog status around Perdido. *Greenie* wasn't fancy but, like them, she got the job done.

As they quelled the crowd of kids, they suddenly heard a racket coming across the bay. Danny and Trout ran up the beach to see a ski boat heading toward The Point at high speed.

"That guy better slow down," Trout said. "He's coming in hotter than a firecracker."

"Get outta the water," Danny yelled at some kids swimming too far from the beach. "That boat's gonna crash."

Parents scrambled to pluck kids from the water. Folks flopped on the beach and watched in horror. Just before the speeding boat plowed onto dry land, the driver jammed the throttle into reverse, spun a half circle and stopped her perfectly dead in the water. A slight breeze kissed the boat against the beach as gentle as a leaf falling to the ground. A muscular boy in khaki shorts, a Polo shirt, and Docksider shoes stood up from behind the helm and admired his navigational skills. With a cocky grin, the boy strutted to the bow of his boat and grabbed the anchor. "Hey you there," he yelled to Trout. "Put this anchor in the sand for me."

Will was already standing at the gunnel with a look of disgust painted across his face. He shot a death stare into the boy's eyes. "You can keep that anchor in your boat, Bubba," Will said. "This is a swimming hole, not a race track. You coulda killed somebody."

"Yeah, well, nice to meet you too, buddy," the boy said sarcastically. "And I didn't hurt anyone, did I? Anyway, as you just witnessed, I can drive a boat better than almost anybody."

Will examined the fiberglass hull's smooth lines and the shiny new 50-horsepower Evinrude engine. "More like a kid with too much boat and not enough brains," he said.

The boy laughed. "That's funny, coming from a country bumpkin. By the way, could you take your hands off my boat? The grease is messing up the gel coat."

Danny and Trout sized up the boy. He was about Will's height, maybe even an inch taller, and had the long muscles of a competitive swimmer. A fistfight between them might go either way, but Danny and Trout were ready to jump in to help if the shouting turned to blows.

Will shoved the boat off the beach. "Fine," he said, "we don't want your kind around here anyway."

"That's too bad," the boy said, "because I'm here to meet some friends."

"Who?" Will asked.

"None of your beeswax," the boy said. "Oh, well guess what? You're in luck, here they come now."

Will turned to see Grace, Georgiana and Stuart jogging down the beach toward them.

"Hi Rodney," Grace said, "good to see you."

"You know this goober?" Will asked.

"Uh yeah," Grace said, "he's one of our friends from the country club."

Will slapped his leg. "Oh, that explains it. He's one of those country club weenies. Just so you'll know, he almost crashed his boat into the beach. He coulda killed somebody."

The girls looked horrified. "Rodney, did you?" Grace asked.

"Of course not. I didn't hurt anybody. This redneck just doesn't know a good boat driver when he sees one."

"Look bud, I've been driving boats all my life …"

Rodney Farber was eyeballing the only other boat on the beach, *Greenie*. "What boat," he chuckled, "that old clunker?"

"It's a good boat," Will said.

"Sure it is," Rodney laughed. "Ya wanna race sometime."

Will stepped toward Rodney's boat with his fists clinched but Grace grabbed him by the arm. "Y'all stop it. This is our friend Rodney. We invited him over. His family has a house in Gulf Shores. Rodney, this is Will and that's Danny and Trout over there. They're our friends, too."

"Trout?" Rodney laughed. "That's his name?"

"It's a nickname," Georgiana said. "And, he's nice. They're all nice."

"Whatever you say," Rodney sneered. "Now do you girls want to go for a ride in a real boat? Sorry boys, I only have room for four and I don't take rednecks anyway."

As the girls climbed into Rodney's spit-polished ride, they smiled and sadly waved goodbye to the boys.

"What a dink," Will said. "He's lucky Grace stopped me from whipping his butt."

"Sure is," Danny said. "Trout and I were ready, too."

Will jerked his head around. "Thanks but I coulda handled him myself."

"He looked pretty stout," Trout said. "You mighta had your hands full."

Will had tuned Trout out. He was scratching his head in deep thought and looking toward Mr. Lyons's boathouse. "You know," he said, "I have an idea."

Danny recognized the tone of Will's voice. It sounded a lot like trouble. "What kinda idea?" Danny asked.

"Well, Mr. Lyons is gonna let us use his little Whaler so why don't we just borrow it now?"

"But he's not around," Trout said.

Will popped Trout on the back of the head. "Exactly," he said. "He's gonna let us use it when we do a gainer. Might as well get a head start."

"I don't think that's such a good idea," Danny said. "Isn't that kinda like stealing?"

"Stealing is when you take something forever. This is just borrowing."

"Yeah, but without permission," Danny pointed out.

"I don't think he'll mind," Will said. "Plus, he probably won't even find out. We can just go whoop that Rodney jerk in a race up the creek and take the *Whaler* back when we're done. Simple as that."

Danny shook his head. "You're on your own this time, cuz. I'm not gonna risk getting in trouble."

"How 'bout it Trout?" Will asked. "You a scaredy cat, too?"

"Uh well, how long are we gonna borrow it?"

"Just long enough to try show up that country-club snob. I might even let you drive."

Still pumped up on his rocking chair trick, Trout had a hard time refusing.

"Okay, let's just do a quick run and put the boat back like we found it."

Will shook his head in agreement. "That's all I'm saying."

At precisely the same time Will and Trout were initiating their scheme, Mr. Lyons' niece and nephew were arriving from Montgomery. At breakneck speed, they slipped into their bathing suits and dashed to the boathouse to go riding in their Uncle Carlton's *Whaler*. They'd been waiting for that moment all summer. When they returned to The Lyons' Den to tell him his boat was missing, all hell broke loose.

Trout and Will had just caught Rodney and the girls as they were easing slowly into the winding narrows of Soldier Creek. The *Whaler* blew past them so closely that a wall of spray soaked the entire crew.

"Hey, watch it you crazy rednecks," Rodney yelled.

"Come on son," Will laughed. "Let's race now."

When he shoved the throttle forward, Rodney's boat nearly shot out of the water. In seconds, he was on Will and Trout's tail and trying to pass as they wound around the narrow turns. Will jockeyed back and forth to block any chance of getting passed up. He knew that backwater like the back of his hand and took the inside track on every turn. But Rodney's boat was faster on the straightaways.

As Will jerked the steering wheel back and forth to stave off the rocket behind him, Trout leaned in close to him. "Go around the island and take him over that sandbar," he yelled into Will's ear.

As they approached, Will swung wide and then cranked a hairpin turn around the tiny sawgrass island. Like all first-timers, Rodney turned too late and ran hard aground on a sandbar. His fancy motor jacked up and spewed wet sand.

"Nice race," Will yelled over his shoulder. "See ya!"

Trout and Will putted slowly back up the creek. They knew it was gonna take all four of them to pull that boat off the bar. In open water though, that boat was like a missile. By the time Will made the final turn toward The Point, he could hear Rodney Farber's boat coming … and it was hauling ass.

Carlton Lyons was not one to cross, especially when he was about to take his post-cocktail, afternoon nap. He summoned everyone he could to find that boat. It didn't take long. When Will and Trout came screaming toward The Point at full throttle with Rodney riding inches from their stern, they saw Mr. Lyons standing on the diving board with his white hair mussed, his face blood red and his fists dug into his hips. They knew right quick that their fate was cast in concrete.

Rodney eased back on the throttle and turned back up the creek with the girls. Will and Trout had no choice but to face the man. With their heads hanging lower than a beat dog's, Will eased the *Whaler* toward Mr. Lyons.

"I'm very disappointed in you boys. I thought we had a deal. You could use my boat when you accomplished a gainer. I'm upset that you felt like you could use my property without my permission. Now get out."

"I'm sorry Mr. Lyons," Will said. "I just thought …"

"You obviously didn't think Will. You know the difference between right and wrong and what you did was wrong."

"Yes, sir, you're right."

"You're damn right, I'm right."

As his niece and nephew climbed into the boat, Mr. Lyons stormed off the pier. Suddenly he stopped, turned and yelled to Will and Trout. "And one more thing, our deal is off. No diving competition in Mobile, no five dollars for the gainer, and no use of my boat. You've ruined all of that."

Danny listened from a distance. Anger welled up inside of him. He told them not to take Mr. Lyons's boat and now his chances of winning fifty dollars were shot.

CHAPTER 25

Sharks and Minnows

The harder I work, the luckier I get.
                                    —Walt Thornton

"Y'all messed up royally this time," Danny said.

"I'm sorry, cuz. I guess we shoulda listened to you."

"Ya think?"

"At least I skied on those boards," Trout said.

"Aw shut up, Trout," Danny said. "You shoulda known better."

"Sorry, Danny," Trout said. "There's nothing we can do about it now."

"What do you mean? You can both go down to Mr. Lyons's house and apologize. And you better beg him not to tell Mr. Walt, or he'll work us to death."

Will's eye's bulged out. "You really expect us to do that? Mr. Lyons is really mad."

"And he's probably mad at me, too," Danny said. "Y'all need to tell him I tried to talk you out of it."

Trout was feeling bad about the whole event. He was even a little bit guilty for letting Will take the brunt of Mr. Lyons's lecture.

"I'll go talk to him Danny," Trout said. "I deserve whatever I get."

Will splashed angrily at the water. "I guess I will, too."

"Don't be mad at me, Will. You're the one that stole his boat."

"Borrowed."

"Whatever you say but you're the one who got us in trouble, not me."

"Okay," Will said. "If we agree to apologize to Mr. Lyons, can we

184

play a game of Sharks and Minnows first, then do it?"

"Sure," Danny said. "That would be okay."

Danny really wanted them to take care of their apology but, the truth was, Sharks and Minnows was too much fun to pass up. And if Will, Danny, and Trout were involved, all the other kids at The Point wanted to play, too.

The object of *Sharks and Minnows* was simple - to swim from Point A, the pier, to Point B, the floating rope thirty feet from the pier. One person, the shark, was "it." Everybody else was a minnow. When the shark was ready, he or she would say, "Go." As the minnows swam for the rope, the shark tagged as many as possible. The tagged minnows became sharks. Those who made it to the rope untagged went back to the pier to try again, against the growing shark population. As the number of sharks grew and minnows dwindled, getting from the pier to the rope got trickier.

The first round or two were always boring for Trout, Will and Danny. Getting past one or two sharks was too easy. But they lived for the ultimate challenge of being the very last minnow up against a large school of hyperactive sharks. Outsmarting nine or ten sharks took skill, cunning and some serious lungpower for slippery underwater tactics. And if, against all odds, that last minnow made it to the rope without getting caught, their reward was getting to set all of the sharks free and earning serious bragging rights.

Inexperienced minnows would simply dive off the pier and stroke for the rope. They might even swim underwater in a predictable direction. Easy targets. Expert minnows, on the other hand, like Will, Danny, Trout and their older brothers and sisters knew that misdirection was the key to escape. As soon as their bodies disappeared into the brackish creek water, there was no telling which direction they might go.

One of their favorite tricks was to swim to the bottom, stir up the sand, and muck into such a dark cloud that nothing could be seen. Then they'd slip out of the smoke screen along the bottom until they were directly under the rope. A quick rocket off the bottom with an outstretched hand to the rope was almost foolproof.

Will preferred to swim under the pier and pop his head up behind a piling. He'd hide there, catch his breath and watch the confused sharks wondering how in the world he could stay underwater for so long. Sometimes he'd make his way to shallow water, climb back onto the pier, sprint to the diving board and soar over outstretched hands trying to tag him. The key was to sail through the air like superman, hit the water at a shallow angle then glide safely to the rope.

Trout had the uncanny ability to fly. Or so it seemed. He'd launch off the diving board with reckless abandon and sail all the way to the rope. Half the time, he'd spin out of control in mid-air. Back busters were common and he scraped himself up on the rope a lot. But Trout never cared about hurting himself, as long as he landed on the rope.

They'd use anything to set the captive minnows free—swimming out of bounds, breathing through a grass reed or, if they could, walking on water. Like any contest they had, everything was fair in *Sharks and Minnows*.

The game was just beginning when Stuart showed up.

"Look who's coming," Danny said.

"Uh oh," Will said, looking toward the pavilion. "Competition."

"Yep. But at least Stuart doesn't know all of our tricks," Trout said

Will chuckled. "Maybe not but I know all of your tricks."

"And we know all of yours too," Danny said.

"Not all," Will said. "I figured out a couple more."

"Well, maybe I did, too," Danny said.

Will laughed again. "You did not."

"You never know. When I make it to the rope, you'll find out."

"Oooo," Will said sarcastically, "I'm really scared."

"You should be."

"Let's just play. Stuart, are you in?" Will asked.

"You bet I am."

"You just have to help us get each other," Danny suggested.

"I don't need any help getting Will," Trout bragged.

"Don't be so sure big shot," Will said. "I have new tricks."

"Do I look worried?" Trout asked.

"You should be."

"Just shut up and let's play," Trout said. "I'll even be *it* first."

In the first round, Trout's strategy was to snag as many little kids as possible. He tagged four and recruited them into his shark army.

"Okay, you two kids go after Will and you two go try for Danny. They're gonna stay underwater all the way to the rope so keep your heads down and stay near the rope. I'm gonna get Stuart this time."

"Not if I can help it."

"You can't," Trout said cockily.

Stuart has been watching and learning. He surprised Trout by diving left but swimming underwater to the right and coming up under the rope.

"You got me on that one," Trout told Stuart. "You're starting to figure this out."

Will and Danny made it to base easily. Trout managed to snag three more kids and huddled everyone up together. "Okay, this time we all go after Stuart," Trout whispered. "Just leave Will and Danny alone. We'll get them next time."

Stuart had no chance. With seven kids and Trout after him, he only made it halfway to the rope before two kids grabbed his ankle. Trout and Stuart schemed for the next round.

"Who do you want to try for?" Trout asked Stuart.

"Who's better?"

"It's about the same," Trout said. "They're both slicker than owl poop,"

"It's your call," Stuart said, "doesn't matter to me."

"Will's just a tad slower in the water," Trout whispered. "Let's go for him."

Even with the whole gang on his trail, Will managed to hide on the bottom and swim around a fat piling that the rope was tied to. He slipped up the backside of the pole and grabbed the rope, as the school of sharks looked on stupefied. Danny easily cruised to the rope untracked.

"One more time," Trout said. "You two kids guard that piling. The rest of you go underwater and look up. Stuart, you and I can just chase his skinny butt."

Trout spotted Will under the pier hiding behind his favorite piling. Stuart closed in on one side and Will dived deep. As quick as a tadpole, Trout gave chase and touched the bottom of Will's foot just as it was disappearing in the deep water.

"Got him," Trout yelled as he popped up. "One down, one to go."

All of the kids cheered. To them, catching Will was like bagging a world record fish. Plus, they were happy just to be involved in an epic game of *Sharks and Minnows* with three masters of the game. And if, by some wild stroke of luck, one of them got Danny, they might tell they're own children about it one day.

187

"I'll go after him and everybody else spread out," Will said confidently. "I know every trick in his book."

Now that he'd been snagged, Will assumed the role as Chief Shark. "Stuart, you keep watch under the pier. Trout, stay out of bounds by the big piling and you kids cover every inch of that rope so he can't grab it."

Trout spit a stream of water through his front teeth. "Who died and made you boss?"

"You did," Will said calmly. "He's my cousin and I know him better than you do."

"But he's my best friend."

"Okay friend, do you have a better plan?"

"No but I don't like the way you took over."

"Sorry but if we want to catch him, I know best."

"Okay everybody," Trout said sarcastically, "Mr. Fat Head knows best."

Trout glared at Will but deep down Trout knew Will was right. Danny figured his chances were slim and none. He had a few seconds to come up with something totally unique.

"Give me a minute to catch my breath," Danny said as he tried to cook up a plan Will didn't know. Then he noticed where *Greenie* was nosed on the beach. He considered the distance. Probably a hundred feet away, *Greenie's* stern stuck ten feet out into the creek. Nobody had ever tried to swim that distance. Even if he could make it that far underwater, he might get lost on the way. If there was ever a time to go for it, that was it.

Beyond *Greenie* were several more boats lined up on the beach. If he made it to *Greenie*, Danny figured he could just sneak from boat to boat, all the way around the tip to the bay side of The Point. Once he was behind the pavilion, they'd never find him. Maybe he could sneak past the pavilion, across the beach, down the pier and then make it safely to the rope. Or maybe not. There was only one way to find out.

"You ready?" Will asked.

"Yep," Danny said as he stood at the edge of the pier.

"GO!" Will yelled.

Danny took a deep breath, relaxed and casually stepped feet first off the pier. To swim a hundred feet underwater, he knew he had to stay calm and keep his movements slow and steady. No one would expect him to swim in that direction so he didn't worry about being caught in mid water. Not yet anyway.

Judging his direction wasn't easy. With no reference point, he might be swimming into deeper water. But his mental compass was on track and suddenly the sloping sand from the shore came into view. Staying about ten feet deep, he used his arms to slowly pull himself along the sand. The tightness in his lungs was growing stronger and but he knew to stay relaxed as long as possible. He strained to see the foot of *Greenie's* engine.

With each stroke, his lungs burned and the veins in his neck throbbed to the beat of his heart. Nothing but sand. Two pinfish shot past his face and he watched them zipping toward shallow water. With his stomach muscles cramping and his air used up, he saw it. With all his strength, Danny shoved his body off the sand, slipped under *Greenie's* hull and came up as quietly as he could on the other side.

He gasped for a full minute and listened to the sounds of the game.

"You see him?"

"Is that him?"

"Check behind those pilings."

"Where is he?"

"Has anybody seen him?"

Danny peaked around the stern and chuckled. Will was standing on the end of the diving board with his hands on his hips surveying the area. The board was their throne, the center of the universe from which everything could be seen. And with a quick bounce, Will could cover ninety percent of the swimming area.

"Check over there," he directed, "and right there."

Danny took a long, slow breath and headed for the next boat. It took him five minutes to pop from boat to boat and around the tip of The Point. With each passing moment, the sharks spread out further. The more he thought about it the more he realized that his chances of getting all the way to the rope were low. So he watched and waited for the perfect window of opportunity. Time was on his side.

"Nobody's ever been gone this long," Trout said. "Ya think something happened to him?"

"I don't know," Will said nervously. "He's got to be somewhere."

"Could he get stuck on some molecules?" Stuart asked.

"On what?" Will asked with a perplexed look.

"You know, the molecules on the pilings."

"You mean 'barnacles'"? Will asked.

"Oh yeah. I guess so. I meant barnacles," Stuart said with a silly grin.

"You're a serious goofus," Will laughed. "Molecules!"

"Well could he?" Stuart asked again. "Like could his bathing suit getting hung on a nail or some barnacles or something?"

"I don't know. You kids check under the pier anyway," Will yelled, still not wanting to give up his perch on the diving board. "Trout, you and Stuart check around on the bottom."

"We already have," Trout said.

"Do it some more."

"You do it," Trout argued.

"Okay, I will," Will said.

Five more minutes went by. Will, Trout, and Stuart were getting worried. There was no sign of Danny. Something had to be wrong. Will made the kids walk up and down the beach in the shallow water. Trout and Stuart dived to the bottom time after time looking for anything.

Will's mind began to spin out of control. His cousin was missing and he could feel a knot forming in the pit of his stomach. Almost in a panic, he swam to the beach and waded toward *Greenie*. Maybe Danny had snuck over and climbed inside the boat. Nothing made sense. Danny was too much of a water bug to get in trouble. Not at The Point. He had to be somewhere.

As Will placed his hand on Greenie's bow, he rolled every possibility around in his mind. He calculated the distance to the pier then he scanned the boats pulled up on the beach. Suddenly it all became crystal clear.

Danny knew his one slice of a chance had come. Will was far enough away from the pier and the kids had spread all over the beach. A few had even lost interest and were making sandcastles. Quickly and silently, he slipped from the water and sprinted across the beach toward the pier. At that precise moment, Will's brain cells sparked. He spun around to see Danny tiptoeing in fast motion across the sand. As he bolted toward Danny, Will yelled, "There he is."

Will and Danny closed in on the pier from different angles but Danny had a step on him. As Will dived and stretched his long arm for Danny's foot, he high jumped over Will's fingertips. Crashing chest

first into the sand, Will yelled for Stuart and Trout.
"Get him!" he yelled.

But they were exhausted and floating in No-Man's Land, halfway between the pier and the rope. With their last bit of strength, Stuart and Trout swam toward the rope in hopes of cutting Danny off. But he was too fast. In one leap, he broad jumped from the edge of the pier to the tip of the diving board. A monstrous bounce launched him fifteen feet through the air. Stuart and Trout lunged for him. A split second after Danny's hand touched the rope, Trout grabbed him by the ankle.

Danny hooted victoriously. "I made it!"

Walking slowly down the pier, Will spit the sand out of his mouth and smiled.

"You really did come up with a new trick," he said. "That was a good one."

"Told you I would."

"You sure did."

"And I think I had y'all a little worried too," Danny said.

"Not for a minute," Will said. "I knew you were okay."

"Sure you did," Danny grinned.

From that day on, the boys parked *Greenie* a little closer to the pier. In the years to come, they used Danny's plan on many unsuspecting Sharks. It worked every time.

CHAPTER 26

Diving for Whalers

A gainer is life's literal leap of faith.
—Carlton Lyons

Will and Trout were too young to grasp the irony of stumbling into a place called the Lyons' Den. Nonetheless, they forged onward soaked in fear and hesitation.

A steady warm breeze blew from the southeast and the gentle sound of lapping waves on the shore filtered through the giant live oaks on the grounds of Mr. Lyons's estate. They found him under the shade of one of those big trees, stretched out in a hammock with a white cotton sheet pulled up to his chin and his head resting softly on a feather pillow. A paperback novel was opened across his chest. Will was certain he detected a smile on the man's face.

Trout leaned in and gently poked an arm. "Mr. Lyons," he whispered.

One eyelid flickered and a low moan resonated from Carlton Lyons's throat.

"Mr. Lyons?" Trout said as he pushed his finger deeper into the man's thick skin. "We're here to apologize, uh, for borrowing, I mean, taking your boat today."

This time the twitching eye opened halfway.

"Mmm, huh? Wha? Hmm?"

"It's us, Mr. Lyons," Will said. "Will and Trout."

"Un huh."

Will continued. "We're really, really sorry, and we hope you'll forgive us."

The other eye opened slightly "Mm huh. Yes, that's fine, boys. Umm."

"And Danny, uh, Danny tried to talk us out of taking your boat, so I guess you shouldn't be mad at him," Will said.

"That's right," Trout said. "Don't be mad at Danny. It was our idea—mine and Will's."

Carlton Lyons dug his head deeper into his pillow and pulled the sheet tighter to his chin. "Okay boys, good … y'all … mmm … okay, good."

Will and Trout turned and hustled across the lawn. They'd apologized just like they said they would. The last thing they heard before they broke into a full on sprint was Mr. Lyons snoring like a crosscut saw.

"How'd it go?" Danny asked.

"Great," Will said.

"So did you really talk to him?"

"Of course we did," Will said.

"Where was he?" Danny asked.

Trout hesitated but spilled the truth. "In the hammock, taking a nap."

"And you woke him up?"

"Yeah," Will said. "We poked at him, then we apologized, and he said it was fine, and we left."

"Just like that?" Danny asked.

"Yeah, just like that," Will said.

Danny looked at Will with the skepticism of a cat sizing up German Sheppard. "We'll see," he said as he bounced high and ripped off a one-and-a-half.

An hour or so later, Mr. Lyons slowly eased his way up the sandy road. The boys were still knocking the eyes out of their newest dive. He stopped for a moment and watched from the shade of a large pine tree. After a long draw on his lemonade, Carlton Lyons smiled. *Damn, those boys really are good*, he thought.

"You boys are doing a fine job," Mr. Lyons said as he strolled out on the pier.

They froze. "Uh, thanks," Danny said.

Will looked up from the water at the towering yet tubby figure above him. "We, uh, came to see you Mr. Lyons."

"I know you did, and I appreciate it. In fact, I heard every word you said."

Danny watched grins spread across Will and Trout's faces. "You did?" Trout asked.

"Yes, Trout, I did. Look boys, here's the thing: if you do right by me, then I'll do right by you. That's the way the world works. So don't do anything stupid again."

"Yes, sir," they all said in unison.

"Okay then. I guess I'll accept your apologies and reinstate the offer. Five bucks for the gainer, and I'll also enter you into the dive meet. That is, if you want me to."

"I do," Danny said. "If you think we can win that prize money?"

"You'll have a real strong chance. I've seen a lot of diving competitions in Mobile and Montgomery and the top divers your age are still doing back flips, inward dives, swans, that kind of thing. Gainers and one-and-a-halfs are unheard of."

Will looked disgusted. "You know why I don't want to go? They make you wear those grippy swimsuits at country clubs."

"They do?" Danny asked.

"Yeah," Will said. "And everybody can see your weenie and everything?"

"They can?"

"Sure they can," he said, pointing at his privates. "Your willie bulges out right here. Anyway, country clubs are for sissies."

Trout climbed up the ladder and shook the water out of his hair. "Maybe they are sissies, but winning fifty dollars ain't something to sneeze at."

"Yeah," Danny said. "Trout is right."

Will shot a stream of water through his front teeth. "Y'all go ahead," he said. "I'll take The Point and my cut-offs any day."

Mr. Lyons grinned. "You know, they give out big trophies, too."

"See," Trout said, "trophies, too."

"I'd like to win a trophy," Danny said. "I've never won anything."

"Same difference," Will said irritably. "It's still a bunch of stuffy goobers
at a country-club swimming pool."

Will didn't realize that Mr. Lyons was a founding member of the Mobile Country Club. Steeped in Southern tradition, Carlton Lyons was courteous enough not to embarrass Will with that news flash. Besides, the man loved teaching them. His son never showed any more interest than flopping in with his knees bent and legs spread apart. That kind of undisciplined diving made Lyons's skin crawl. That his own flesh and blood shunned the art of diving was an insult to him and, as far as he was concerned, a sign of weakness. But, these boys were eager students.

"I tell you what," Mr. Lyons said. "In The Point Club competition, no grippy swimsuits are allowed."

"That sounds good to me," Will said.

"Here's my deal," Mr. Lyons said, "Do an acceptable gainer and the little *Whaler* will be back in your possession, this time with my permission, for a period of one week."

Trout threw himself off the pier. "But that's the hardest flip there is."

"Physically, it's actually a lot easier than a one-and-a-half," Mr. Lyons said. "But mentally ... well, it's all mind over matter."

"I'll try it," Danny said. "If that's the only way to win that boat."

"Good boy," Mr. Lyons said.

Trout looked up from the water. "Okay, I guess I'll try it, too."

Will had no choice. If they were in, he was in.

"Before we start, let me give you boys a few pointers."

They sat on the diving board as Mr. Lyons smoothed his gray hair back and adjusted his bathing suit around his bourbon and barbeque midsection. With white deck shoes, a matching belt and his golf shirt tucked in, he looked like he'd stepped right out of a cartoon. His voice drawled out for a nautical mile, but it was filled with the confidence of old money, new cars, and a young wife.

He cleared his throat and began his lesson in Lyons' Wisdom and Philosophy of Diving. "You see, boys," he began, "A gainer is life's literal leap of faith."

They wrinkled their faces and wished they could just get on the board and try the stupid dive. But diving was his passion and he wanted to drive home the significance of what they were about to attempt.

"You face forward and jump away from the diving board," he continued, "but you flip backward toward it. You're rotating blindly in reverse, never certain whether or not your head is going to smack the board as it whizzes past."

As he slapped his hands together for effect, Will's body jerked. He was already day dreaming about Ethel's gumbo.

"The gainer is completely unnatural yet at the same time poetic; as beautiful to the observer as it is to the performer."

As he spoke, he became more animated. His hands twirled as if they were the diver and he gazed into the sky preaching his religion.

"From the low board, technique is everything," he stressed. "Your knees kick up into a tuck, which is essential for a fast spin. And the landing is all timing. There's no time to see. No time to think. Just primal instincts."

His voice had gotten so loud that folks on the beach had started to listen. His face had turned a deep shade of pink. Danny marveled at the contrast between his white hair and flushed face and wondered if he was going to just keel over right there on the dock. Trout listened with devout attention while Will just thought about the hunger pangs in his belly. He needed some food before he died of starvation, or boredom. Whichever came first.

"You unfold, hoping to God in Heaven that your feet are pointing down. You're grimacing just in case they're not because when you're performing a dive as intricate as a gainer, a mistake is far worse than your run of the mill belly flop. An over spin delivers a full on, red-skinned back buster. Not to mention a seriously bruised pride."

At least the boys could relate to belly flops and back busters. They were all too familiar with red skin from bad landings. But "primal instincts" and "bruised pride" didn't register. They just sat there respectfully thinking about that little *Whaler* and hoping he'd finish soon.

"Then suddenly you slice into the water like a sharp blade, perfectly vertical, with your hands tucked by your side and your eyes focused on the horizon. And, just like that, it's over."

As he finished his diatribe, he hung his head and sighed.

"Did you say it's over?" Will asked.

"Yes."

"Then can we dive now?"

"No, I meant the dive was over. You know, my description of the dive. That's what's over."

"Oh," Will said undeterred. "So does that mean we can dive now?"

Carlton Lyons collected himself and realized the boys had tuned him out. He was prone to ranting and, fortunately, he knew it.

"I'm sorry boys, I got carried away," he said. "I'll do a gainer and show you how it's done."

He slipped off his shoes and shirt and got into position.

"It's step, step, spring," he said, "then you kick up your knees, tuck, turn and open.

And just like he said, he took two steps, bounced and nailed a flawless gainer.

"Whoa," Trout said. "That was great."

"Yeah," Danny said. "But he came kinda close to the board. I *really* don't want to hit my head on the board."

"Know what? I think I can do it," Will said. He just needed to see the mechanics in action. It looked easy enough.

Will stood on the diving board rubbing his hands together. "Okay here goes," he said.

"Stay in your tuck," Mr. Lyons advised. "And don't let your fear take over."

"Yes, sir," he said.

"Remember, step, step, spring and kick your knees up."

"Okay, yes, sir. Thanks."

"Mind over matter," Carlton Lyons persisted.

"Yes, sir!" Will said irritably. "I got it!"

Mr. Lyons finally shut up as Will followed his instructions exactly - step, step, spring, knee kick—until he got to the stay-in-your-tuck part. At the highest point in the air, barely a quarter of the way around, fear squeezed his heart and Will's body sprawled open. Eight feet above the water, Will's legs kicked wildly and his arms flapped. With his front side pointing to the sky and his backside facing the water, Will plummeted down. Trout and Danny were hoping to see a world-class back buster. Somehow, just before he slapped the flat water, Will managed to twist his shoulders down and land in a kind of crooked half dive. He saved his skin, but the spectacle alone had folks from the swimming area to the pavilion yucking it up. Danny giggled nervously. His turn was coming.

Trout and Danny turned to see what was going on. They'd heard some kids hooting and hollering and what sounded like a car rambling down the sandy road to The Point. Stuart, Ellis, Grace and Georgiana sat with their feet dangling from the back gate of Lilly Felder's station wagon. As she cruised along, the kids made lines in the sand with their toes.

"Hey Will," Danny said. "The girls are here."

Will was taking plenty of time swimming back to the ladder. Even though he showed courage trying the gainer first, putting on an air show like that was still embarrassing.

"Who, Grace and Georgiana?" Will asked.

"Yep," Trout said with a smile, "and Stuart and Ellis."

"And guess who brought them?" Danny asked. He knew Will had a crush on Lilly Felder.

Will felt his heart skip a beat. "Stuart's mom?" he whispered anxiously.

"Yes, sir-ree," Danny said. "Your true love."

"Shut up!" Will said. "I just think she's pretty."

"Love, love, love," Trout teased.

"Y'all just shut up about that," Will said. "Besides, I told y'all before that I'm kinda sweet on Grace."

"You still are?" Danny asked. "Because I am, too."

Their eyes locked for an awkward moment. Neither one of them had anticipated that one. Competing for a girl wasn't like a swimming race across the creek. Too many emotions were involved. It could get complicated, if not downright ugly.

"Hi y'all," Stuart said, "what's up?"

Danny and Will hardly noticed Stuart. They were still ruminating about the Grace situation.

"We're trying to learn the gainer," Trout informed him.

"Whoa. That's a hard one," Stuart said. "Can anybody do it?"

"Will tried but bailed out in mid spin," Trout said. "It was pretty funny."

"I'm sorry I missed that," Stuart said.

"Danny and I are next," Trout said nervously, as if they were standing in line for the guillotine.

"Hi boys," Grace hummed as she sauntered onto the pier right past Danny. "Good to see y'all again."

Trout and Danny stood in silence as she hopped onto the diving board and performed a simple but stylish dive.

Mr. Lyons nodded in approval. "That was mighty pretty," he drawled. "Mighty pretty."

"Thank you," Grace said. "I'm on the swim team at the Mobile

Country Club."

Will almost choked on his tongue. "The swim team at the country club?"

"Yes, is something wrong with that?" Grace asked.

"Will thinks country clubs are for sissies," Trout said.

"Oh really? Well, I'll have you know, we have some of the best swimmers and divers in the state of Alabama and we're not sissies," Grace said.

"I'm sure you're not," Will said trying to save himself, "It's just that I'd rather swim in real water like Soldier Creek with fish and dolphins and stuff than in some swimming pool with a bunch of kids peeing in the water."

"Some people aren't lucky enough to live here all summer," Grace shot back. "A pool is better than nothing, especially an Olympic-sized pool."

"I guess you're right," Will said. So far, he wasn't racking up any points with her.

"In fact, our friend Rodney is one of the top swimmers."

Will's face tensed. "Oh yeah Rodney. So, did y'all have fun riding in his fancy boat?"

"Yes we did, thank you very much," Grace said. "It was very enjoyable."

Trout dove off the pier and swam to the beach to meet up with Georgiana. They walked up the pier together chatting and giggling the whole way.

"Trout said y'all were learning the gainer. I think that's really brave," Georgiana said as she stepped onto the diving board. She stared off into the distance for a few seconds. "Hey, what's a gainer anyway?"

"It's a really hard flip," Trout said. "Kind of a back flip."

"Oh," she said. "Have you done one yet?"

"Will tried it," Danny said, "Trout and I are gonna try next."

Georgiana stepped back onto the pier.

"I want to see," she said.

Trout took her arm gently and led her back to the diving board. "No, you go ahead. It might take us a while to get up our nerve."

"Okay," she said and kind of tip toed off the end of the board, jumping feet-first and squealing on the way down.

"What's she on, the baby-pool team?" Will asked.

199

"Don't be so mean," Grace said.

"I'm just saying …"

"You're just being mean, that's all," Grace said. "If you can't say something nice, don't say anything at all."

"Geez, you sound like my Aunt Kitty."

"Good, she must be very wise."

"I guess," Will said. "Come on Trout, you're next."

Trout was thinking about winning that boat and impressing Georgiana all at the same time. But he couldn't get the image of Will's lame duck attempt out of his mind. As he stood on the board, doubt rushed into his mind.

"You can do it Trout," Mr. Lyons said. "Believe in yourself."

He barely heard the encouragement. By the time his feet touched the end of the board, his mind was log jammed in panic. All Trout could remember was something about kicking up his knees. He flew blindly into the air, rolled slowly backwards and crashed down flat on his back. The all too familiar slapping sound of an epic back-buster echoed across the water, followed by a sympathetic, "*Ow!*" from everyone watching.

"That one hurt," Will said. "It was mighty ugly."

"Ah-yah," Trout moaned as he surfaced.

"Oh Trout, are you okay?" Georgiana asked as she dog paddled awkwardly toward him.

"I'll be fine. It's not the first time I've landed on my back. Just the first time when I was trying a gainer."

"Next!" Will yelled sadistically as he looked at Danny. Since he and Trout had busted, Will knew what was coming. Watching Danny was going to be fun.

Danny wrung his hands as he replayed Mr. Lyons's instructions. He tried to focus but seeing Will and Grace chatting shot a tinge of jealousy into his psyche. Or course, if he had heard their conversation, he'd have known that Will was rapidly slipping down the drain. Yet, just the sight of them floating next to each other made Danny think they were as happy as two peas in a pod.

"Kick your knees up and tuck," Carlton Lyons said firmly. "It's just a flip. You can do it."

This was his only chance to win that boat. If he flopped instead of flipped, he was sure Will would make it on his next try. With his natural athletic abilities, Will rarely messed up the same thing twice.

"Can you show me one more time?" Danny asked Mr. Lyons.

"Sure Danny," Mr. Lyons said as he stepped onto the board. "Okay, here we go. It's really as simple as this: step, step, bounce, kick and tuck."

And once again, Carlton Lyons impressed the small crowd that had gathered to witness the show.

Danny hopped onto the diving board immediately after Mr. Lyons. He figured if he went quickly, it would be fresh in his mind. Somehow, he shoved most of the fear out of his thoughts, took two steps and bounced high. His knee kick was late but adequate. He balled up into a tight tuck and spun sluggishly backwards. The slow-motion gainer seemed to take forever but before he splashed down, Danny made it almost all the way around. With the tendons in his neck tensed and his chin jutting out, a stream of water shot up his nose. But he'd made it. That gainer would have been a joke at the country-club swim meet but Danny didn't care. He had a date with a *Boston Whaler.*

"I did it!" he hollered. "Yee-ha!"

For a moment, Will considered challenging the flip but Mr. Lyons was already clapping and congratulating Danny. His cousin had won that round fair and square.

"That was great," Will said. "Good job, cuz!"

"Thanks," Danny said. "It really was easy. Just kick and tuck, like Mr. Lyons said."

"Great job, son. Now let's see you other boys do it."

Will and Trout's pride was at stake. There was no way in God's good name they were going to leave The Point without learning the gainer. In all of the excitement, and as Trout and Will swam to the ladder for another try, Grace glided slowly toward Danny.

"That was very brave," she said. "I'm impressed."

"Thanks," Danny beamed. "It's no big deal."

"What other dives can you do?"

"Oh, a back flip, a one-and-a-half ..."

"Really, a one-and-a-half?"

"Sure, Mr. Lyons taught us that one, too."

"Then you should definitely come over to Mobile and enter the Labor Day competition," Grace said. "With a gainer and a one-a-a-half, you'd have a good chance of beating Rodney."

"Uh oh, is he a diver too?" Danny asked.

"He swims *and* dives."

"If you really think I could beat him, I'd sure give it a try. But, like we said, Will doesn't like country clubs."

"I do think you could win. And if Will doesn't want to come over you can just come by yourself. I'll be there cheering you on."

As Grace spoke Danny's heart melted. He could hardly imagine being in a diving competition with Grace in his corner. Not to mention winning the fifty-dollar prize.

"So is Rodney kinda like your boyfriend or something?"

"He'd like to be and I like him too but I guess I'm keeping my options open."

Danny grinned bigger than a slice of watermelon. "I'll come to Mobile Grace," he said. "You can count on it."

During the next two hours, Will, Trout, and Danny worked on their gainers. As Danny had predicted, Will made it around on his second try but Trout pounded his back with one back buster after another.

"Remember, I think I can, I think I can," Will said to Trout.

"But what if I think I can't?"

"Then you'll never do it," Mr. Lyons said. "First you have to believe in yourself."

That didn't always come easy for Trout. Dangerous stunts like jumping off ledges at Pirate's Canyon were more his speed. But one trait he'd learned was persistence and he kept trying until his back was as red as a possum's tongue. Worried that the boy was going to sustain permanent bruises, Mr. Lyons suggested that Trout take a break.

"We'll try some more tomorrow," Mr. Lyons said, "when your mind and body are well rested.

Trout was embarrassed but happy that Mr. Lyons let him quit. "Okay," he said with his head hanging low.

"You'll get it," Georgiana said. "I'm sure you will."

Trout smiled. At least somebody believed in him.

"I think y'all should all come to the swim meet," Grace announced. "It would be lots of fun and you might just win all the trophies. What about it?"

"Not me," Will said. "Send me a post card 'cause I'll be right here enjoying myself."

"That's silly Will," Grace said. "You'd have fun."

"I'd rather get bit in the butt by a gator."

"Fine then, I guess Danny will win everything."

"That's okay by me," Will said.

"Me too," Danny grinned.

Trout cupped his hands and squirted a stream of water toward Georgiana. "Are you gonna be there?" he asked.

"Sure, I always go."

"Well, maybe I'll come on over with Danny. I don't want him to win all the trophies. That is, if I can get permission."

"That would be real nice," she smiled.

CHAPTER 27

Fiberglass Meets Wood

Only believe half of what you see and none of what you read.
—Walt Thornton

Lilly Felder sunbathed topless on their sailboat every afternoon from two to four. The boys knew this for a fact because, after they heard the rumor, they had borrowed Mr. Walt's binoculars. When Stuart wasn't around, they'd focus in on her and wait patiently for her to sit up to adjust her towel. They knew what they were doing was wrong but like Will said, "How could something that pretty be bad?"

Anchored in the middle of Soldier Creek, the *Water Lilly* was too far from shore for the naked eye to see her nakedness. As long as no boats were passing by, Lilly Felder felt comfortable exposing her gifts of nature to the sun. She loved the freedom from her role as the stoic doctor's wife, not to mention the warm breeze wafting across her bare skin. Apparently, Dr. Felder also had a loathing for tan lines—just another one of his many obsessions.

Without a doubt, his deepest fixation was the *Water Lilly* herself. She was more than a sailboat; she was a showpiece. Most days, while Lilly worked on browning herself evenly, the narcissistic doctor touched up paint, braided lines, washed off bird poop and polished his brass. Sometimes the boys wondered who he loved more, Lilly or *Water Lilly*. And Will's youthful crush on the woman included a healthy disdain for the doctor.

"He doesn't treat her nice," Will was always saying to Danny and Trout. Sometimes he'd even ask Stuart about his stepmother.

"So, where did your step-mom grow up?" he'd ask. Or, "Does she like that boat as much as your dad does?"

To Will's great pleasure, Stuart was happy to talk about her. And the boys loved to listen. They were impressed that she actually swam out to the boat to sunbath. Not that it was so far; they swam ten times that distance every day. But most of their parents and aunts and uncles just lounged around in the water. If they were going anywhere, they rode in a boat.

Lilly was different. Not only was she ten or twenty years younger than the other adults but she liked the exercise and solitude of swimming alone. Naturally, Dr. Felder was not interested in wasting time swimming when he could ride out to *Water Lilly* in his dinghy, the *Lilly Pad*.

After she'd dropped Stuart and the girls at The Point, Lilly waded into the water and swam out toward the sailboat. Will watched her briefly and even thought about the binoculars in the forward hatch of *Greenie*.

After two hours of diving and swimming, the boys were easing over to *Greenie* to ride home. Stuart and the girls were gathering their towels and waiting for Mrs. Felder to return from her fun in the sun. Out in Soldier Creek, a ski boat full of Navy guys pulled a fellow sailor.

The Naval Air Station in nearby Pensacola was a bastion of young sailors who generally spent their free time guzzling beer and chasing girls. As fate and misfortune would have it, Carlton Lyons's wayward nephew, Monroe Miflin, had been assigned to the Navy's flight school to learn how to fly jets. The prospect of Monroe at the helm of a flying machine was terrifying to everyone who knew him. In a span of two years, between the ages of sixteen and eighteen, he'd wrecked five cars, run over two dogs and blown off part of his thumb with a homemade bomb. After he filled the ping-pong ball with gunpowder, the fuse accidentally lit as he dripped hot wax on it, hoping to make it waterproof so he could blow up some mullet. Trouble always lingered in the corners of Monroe's life because his mind worked that way.

If the military hadn't been in the middle of ramping up, Monroe and his reconstructed thumb would have never been admitted into the service, much less flight school. But the Navy had eased their standards and his family was thrilled. They hoped, no, they actually prayed diligently every night, that some far off outpost like Okinawa or the Philippines needed an American renegade of his caliber. But luck was not on their side when Monroe was concerned. In recent months, Carlton Lyons had been Monroe's surrogate father and he was not pleased when the Navy let him roam free.

That particular afternoon, Monroe and a group of his rowdy flyboy buddies were doing what Navy recruits were expected to do. They were getting sloppy drunk and raising hell. They were also dragging skiers behind Mr. Lyons's fancy twenty-one foot fiberglass ski boat. The waves they generated and their foul-mouthed screaming sent Lilly below to the cabin. She had no intention of sharing her fair skin with a bunch of drunken sailors. Before she was able to sneak below deck, Monroe steered the boat near enough for the sailors to glare at Dr. Felder's shapely wife.

"Hey honey," one of the Barbarians yelled. "Come on and ski with us, sweetie pie."

"Yeah baby, we'll be nice and gentle," another one hollered.

The rest of them guffawed and chugged more beer.

Will and Danny had noticed Monroe and his deranged buddies but paid him no mind. They'd known him forever and considered him a hopeless loser—someone who set a perfect example of what not to be when they grew up.

Because of all the waves Monroe was kicking up, the boys didn't even attempt to take *Greenie* for a ride or try to ski. Plus, they didn't want to end up like one of those dogs he'd whacked.

Danny was standing on the diving board about do one final gainer when he heard the explosion. At first, he thought Mr. Randolph was firing his cannon. But he usually only did that on the Fourth of July. Danny turned just in time to see the fiberglass ski boat cutting dead center through the classic, thirty-foot wooden sailboat. The mast seemed to fall in slow motion as the bow of the ski boat rose up, severed the deck, and kind of crunched back down through the hull.

Much to Danny's amazement, the *Water Lilly* sank immediately. Most folks at The Point were confused. They'd heard the explosion but weren't sure why. Before the mast even hit the water, Will and Danny were swimming toward *Greenie*. Like clockwork, they shoved off the beach, cranked the engine and sped away, without even considering waiting for Trout or Stuart. Neither hesitation nor contemplation mixed well with emergencies, especially that one. Will and Danny reacted instinctively arriving on the scene in less than thirty seconds.

As they closed in at full speed, Will yelled, "I'm going in." Before Danny even eased off on the throttle, Will took a deep breath, dove in headfirst and disappeared under the wreckage. Danny cut the engine and jumped in after him.

"There's a lady in there," Danny hollered but Monroe and his crew were in shock. He'd managed to reverse the boat off of the *Water Lilly* but had apparently forgotten about the dark-haired woman they'd yelled rude flirtations to. He'd spent a lot of his life dreaming up plausible excuses for his stupid stunts but this time his mind was jelly. Dogs and fender benders were one thing. People's lives were altogether another.

To Monroe and his cronies, it all happened so fast. The skier fell and bounced violently across the water. Monroe turned to watch as his drunken gang laughed uncontrollably and gloated at their friend's misfortune. Unfortunately, Monroe didn't notice that he'd steered his uncle's boat on a deadly course.

Life jackets and cushions bobbed among large chunks of wooden deck and floating debris. The mast, with its spider web of stays and halyards, slowly sank and tangled into the rubble. The *Water Lilly* had quite literally been sliced in half. The forward half, attached to the one-ton lead keel, had quickly plummeted ten feet to the muddy bottom. The back half remained semi-submerged at the surface.

With his heart pumping pure adrenaline, Will swam down and saw the bow section still intact but settled on the bottom. *She must be inside*, he thought. Without hesitation, he kicked his feet and swam inside the cabin. As surreal as it was—air pockets still leaking bubbles, books still on the bookshelf and framed pictures mounted on the cabin walls—Will didn't even notice. He was searching desperately for Lilly and she was nowhere to be found. Dragging himself forward, he slipped his body through the doorway leading into V-berth. Still nothing.

He'd been down for almost two minutes when nature slapped him with the reality that he needed air. His lungs burned in throbbing pain. Reluctantly, he turned and bolted out of the broken hull. Danny had followed and watched him go into the forward cabin. As Will shot past him, they surfaced together.

"I didn't see her," Will said breathlessly.

"Me neither," Danny said.

"Let's swim around the outside of the boat, maybe she wasn't inside."

"Okay," Danny said. "I'll start on the port side, you take starboard. We'll meet at the bow."

As quickly as they had surfaced, they dove again and circled the front half of the *Water Lilly*. When they came to the bow, they surfaced again.

"She's got to be somewhere," Will said. "I'm going back inside."

"I'm coming with you," Danny said.

And, once again, they entered the severed main cabin and V-berth. If she'd been in there they would have quickly spotted her. The classic schooner just wasn't that big, especially since the back half had been cut off. This time Danny pulled his way into the forward cabin. He hoped to find her but prayed that he wouldn't. The thought of seeing a dead person frightened the daylights out of him. As he swam to the forward tip of the cabin, daylight faded into darkness. Danny couldn't see anything so he groped around in all directions. As he ran out of air, he peeked into the head. She wasn't there either.

Will and Danny surfaced and lingered there.

"What now?" Danny asked.

"I don't know."

Monroe Miflin had climbed onto the bow of the ski boat and was surveying the carnage he'd created.

"Hey, what are y'all doing?" he shouted down to the boys.

"We're looking for Lilly Felder, you stupid idiot," Will screamed at him. "She was on board when you hit the boat."

"She was?"

"She always sunbaths after lunch," Will said. "Why don't you and your stupid Navy goons get down here and help?"

The drunken fog in Monroe's mind was beginning to clear and he recalled the woman on the sailboat.

"Oh my God!" he said. "Everybody, get in the water. We need to find that lady."

His intentions were admirable but his crew was hopeless. Dazed and drunk, they splashed around among the remains of the *Water Lilly* barely able to stay afloat.

"Why don't y'all get back in that boat," Will yelled. "One of you idiots is gonna drown and we're sure as hell not gonna save your sorry butts."

"The boy's right," Monroe slurred. "We can't do anything else."

"Yeah," Will said as he began to sob. "I think you've done enough."

At Witchwood's pier, Carlton Lyons cranked the engine on his *Boston Whaler*. At least twelve folks were crammed on board, included Dr. Thurwood Felder. As they cruised up, Will looked at the doctor through tearful eyes.

"We couldn't … Dr. Felder … we couldn't find her," Will said, barely able to utter the words.

He burst out crying. "We tried, we really tried."

"Find who?" Dr. Felder asked.

Will immediately shook out of his hysteria. How could that man be asking such a heartless question? Had he forgotten that his wife was onboard? A surge of anger welled up inside of him and just as Will was going to cuss the man up and down and call him every bad name he knew of, he saw her standing behind her husband.

"Oh, do you mean my wife?" Dr. Felder asked. "She's fine. She's right here. Unfortunately, I can't say the same about my boat."

"I was swimming back in when it happened," she said to Will. "Y'all must not have seen me."

"Thank God," Will whimpered. "I thought you were …"

"It's okay Will," Lilly said. "I'm fine."

He smiled at her, turned and swam toward *Greenie* sobbing.

Dr. Felder glared at Monroe as he floated among the junk, clinging to the biggest piece of jagged deck he could find. No one was quite sure whether he was trying to save a piece of the boat from sinking or just keeping himself afloat. To Monroe it just seemed like the right thing to do at the time.

"Is this your boat, sir?" Monroe asked with stiff military inflection.

"It *was* my boat," Dr. Felder replied in an unusually calm voice.

Nothing else was said. And nothing more needed to be said. Everyone knew that was Monroe's day to live in infamy. For the rest of the crowd, they had witnessed a nightmare in broad daylight. And as much as he liked sailing, Dr. Felder never replaced that boat. He had a replica made of the *Water Lilly* for his mantle and used the insurance money to buy a ski boat—a fiberglass ski boat—for Stuart and Ellis.

In a cosmic twist of fate, Monroe Miflin went on to become a decorated Navy fighter pilot and won a box full of medals in Vietnam. In a strange way, he found his calling that day. Life at Perdido had a weird way of steering folks in the right, or wrong direction.

PART II

August

CHAPTER 28

The Little Whaler

Bad ideas come cheap.
—Wallace Flomaton

Danny bounced up and down with excitement.

"Here's where I keep the gas," Carlton Lyons said to him. "Use as much as you want."

"Thanks, Mr. Lyons."

"No, thank you for working so hard on that gainer. You deserve it."

Danny grinned at Trout and Will as he tapped his finger on the two hundred gallon steel tank. He could hardly control his giddiness. Not only did they have the *Boston Whaler* but an endless supply of fuel to go with it.

"I might even let y'all drive," Danny laughed.

"Whatever you want to do," Mr. Lyons said. "You're the captain."

Even with gas available at Randolph's store, Carlton Lyons stockpiled his own fuel for his fleet of boats, cars, tractors and lawn mowers, to cover for the frequent times when Mr. Randolph's tanks ran dry. If grass needed cutting, he didn't want to wait for a shipment to arrive. He wanted it taken care of pronto.

Located halfway between Witchwood and Paradise Point, the Lyons' Den, as one would expect it to be named, was not the typical Perdido beach cottage. Mr. Lyons had built himself a full-blown estate. With its sprawling porches and lofted ceilings, the main house looked majestically over Perdido Bay. It was surrounded by a perfectly manicured lawn. A long driveway weaved through ancient oaks dripping in Spanish moss and two dozen majestic magnolias planted by Carlton

Lyons himself. Partially hidden in the woods was a large barn for his tractors and lawn tools. Adjacent to the barn was a guesthouse that he built bigger than most of the beach cottages dotting the shores of Perdido Bay and Soldier Creek. During the summer, several of Mr. Lyons employees stayed in the guesthouse with their wives. The men kept the grounds immaculate while the women cleaned and cooked. Outsiders considered the situation a throwback to the days of slavery, and in appearances, there were similarities. However, Carlton Lyons paid his staff well and most of them worked for him for thirty or forty years, after which he took care of them better than his own flesh and blood.

"Cookie," Mr. Lyons said, "can you help these boys with some gas and oil?"

"Yes, sir, Mr. Lyons."

They'd known Cookie for ten years. A regular fixture during summers at Perdido, Cookie was in charge of keeping the machines running, the grass cut and the woods cleared of underbrush and broken limbs. More than six feet tall with Herculean muscles, Cookie put the fear of God in many a redneck. He worked shirtless most of the time to beat the heat and remind folks of his extraordinary strength. If the boys ever got into a tangle, they were happy to call him a friend.

"Y'all come on," Cookie said, snatching up the ten-gallon gas tank without flinching.

"Whoa, how much does that weigh?" Danny asked.

"Oh not too much," Cookie smiled. "You wanna carry it?"

"I think it would take all three of us," Danny said.

"Probably so," he laughed.

The little *Boston Whaler* was tied to the Lyons's family pier, along with a wooden skiff, a Chris Craft cabin cruiser and the now-infamous ski boat that Monroe Miflin had used as a high-speed ramrod. Two men were putting the ski boat on a trailer for a trip to the repair shop. Even though it didn't crack wide open like the *Water Lilly*, the impact mangled the bow rail and busted out a chunk of fiberglass. The resilience of fiberglass was just one reason wood was becoming passé as a boat building material. Fiberglass didn't rot, break or get water logged. And, as far as they knew, it lasted forever.

For the moment, the boys had all but forgotten Monroe Miflin's horrific crash. Their attention was on the little *Whaler*. As Cookie filled the gas tank, Mr. Lyons briefed them.

"Go ahead and get in," he said. "It's pretty simple. Just pump the bulb on the gas line and turn the key."

"Make sure you have it neutral," Cookie reminded them. "Or it won't do nothing."

Will jumped to the stern and quickly pumped the black bulb as Danny settled into the driver's seat and worked the gears back and forth.

With one hand on the steering wheel and the other on the key Danny turned to Will, "Ready?"

"Ay ay, captain," Will said with a salute.

The engine fired off on the first try and idled quietly. Giant smiles spread across their faces. Trout scampered to the bow to untie the line.

"That's all there is to it," Mr. Lyons said. "Y'all have fun."

As he stepped from the boat, Cookie grinned at Danny. "Be careful and don't run into any sailboats."

The boys chuckled but Carlton Lyons found it hard to enjoy the humor. He and Dr. Felder weren't on speaking terms at the moment.

When Danny jammed the throttle forward, the boat almost shot out of the water. Wide grins were etched in their faces as they raced across Soldier Creek to The Point. The first thing they wanted to do was show off their new toy. After that was fully accomplished, they could set out on an adventure.

"Where's *Greenie*?" Danny asked, as they approached the swimming area.

"I don't know," Will said. "Hunter and Gar had it. Maybe they went up the creek."

"Let's go!" Danny shouted as he cranked hard on the steering wheel. The little *Whaler* hugged tight on the water, threw up a wall of spray and instantly changed directions without losing speed.

"Yee-ha!" Trout yelled. "This thing is fast!"

As they rounded the corner, *Greenie* came into view. There sat Hunter, Gar and Trout's brother Willy, plodding through the water only a knot or two faster than they could swim. With twice the weight *Greenie* was accustomed to, the best she could do was plow along and put out a massive wake.

Gar happened to turn around just as the little *Whaler* launched over *Greenie's* wake, flew completely out of the water and cleared the opposite wake.

"*Yow!*" Trout screamed with wild-eyed glee.

Danny held a firm hand on the wheel. Then he whipped the boat around, gunned the engine and skyrocketed back across the huge wave. By then, Hunter, Gar and Willy were staring at them with jealous contempt. Just to rub it in deeper, Danny literally ran three circles around *Greenie*. They laughed riotously while the older boys could only think about getting them home and whipping their little butts.

On the next pass, Hunter slung a seat cushion that flew just inches over Danny's head. Gar chucked a life jacket that connected with Trout's chest and Willy splashed water at them with the paddle. He considered using the paddle to spear his younger brother, but, as mad as he was, that still seemed excessive.

After taunting the older boys sufficiently, Captain Danny and his jolly crew sped away toward The Tree.

"We can go swing on the rope, jump a few times and leave before Hunter and them even get there," Danny exclaimed proudly. "Because …"

"We have the fastest boat," Will sung out.

"Let's do it," Trout laughed.

The sun sparkled across the water and glowed on their smooth, tanned skin. As they sped across Soldier Creek with the wind whipping through their hair and brushing over their faces, the boys were consumed with joy. Their freedom and friendship mixed with nature's ultimate playground and a high-speed boat had pushed their blissfulness to the limit.

"I don't know how heaven could be any better than this," Danny grinned.

"This *is* heaven!" Trout shouted.

Will squinted at the streaks of sunlight breaking through the clouds and wondered about heaven. He agreed with Danny. How could it be better than what they were experiencing at that very moment?

The boys were too engrossed in their fun to consider the narrow upper reaches of Soldier Creek. From The Point, the creek was plenty big. Several boats could run around at full speed all at the same time without getting in each other's way. Maps called that area Crystal Lake, even though technically it was part of Soldier Creek. From there, the waterway then turned west for a ways, then made a jog to the north and stayed wide enough to ski for about a mile. Then boats entered The

Narrows, where Soldier Creek became a thin meandering river, about as wide as a dirt road and twenty feet deep in places.

Because the creek was spring fed it got fresher and colder the farther up river they went. Fishermen even caught fresh water bass up there, along with mullet and trout that could tolerate both salt and fresh water. The Narrows looked like an Alabama Amazon, a place where alligators roamed free in decades past. Local hunters had killed all of the gators but occasionally one would find its way up there and quickly fall victim to someone's shotgun.

Bushes and trees leaned out over the water and big pine trees were forever getting knocked over by storms and blocking the way. Luckily for the boys, fishermen kept bow saws in their boats to clear the path. Still, all of the sharp curves, cut-off stumps, low-hanging limbs and shifting sandbars, made driving at a high speed perilous. So naturally, Danny pushed the throttle to full tilt. Skidding around blind corners at full speed and nearly losing control was just too much fun to pass up. An added hazard, one that kept the boys on high alert, was the knowledge that a boat might be coming around the next corner. Occasionally it happened. Somehow, their lightning reflexes and driving acrobatics saved them. But all of that was in *Greenie*. They'd never ripped up The Narrows in a boat as fast as the little *Whaler*. Not until that day.

Fortunately, the ride to The Tree was uneventful. That is, if you call speeding up a skinny, curvy river at thirty miles per hour without incident. And, that's not counting the three bushes they exploded through on the tight corners, sending leaves and spiders flying everywhere. A bush branch scratched Trout's shoulder and drew blood but he paid it no mind. Anyway, in a day or so, it blended in with all his other cuts and bruises.

"How long are we gonna stay?" Danny asked as he swung out and casually back flipped off the rope.

"When we hear 'em coming," Will said. "Let's take off."

Between hoots, hollers and splashes, they listened for the sound of *Greenie* chugging up the creek. But it never came. Finally, they decided they needed another dose of speed.

"They must have turned back," Trout said. "They'd be here by now."

"Let's go," Will decided. "And run over to Ono Island to chase some armadillos."

"You wanna drive this time?" Danny asked Will.

"I thought you'd never ask."

Will matched Danny's driving prowess as he stayed wide on the sharp turns, cut to the inside, and slid safely into the straight-aways. The thrill ride had them hanging on tight and laughing like crazy until they came to a particularly narrow corner.

"Look out," Danny yelled as Will yanked back on the throttle. They'd seen it at the same time. A massive bush had fallen in and was floating across the creek. Will threw the boat in reverse and they stopped just inches before plowing into it.

"Where'd that come from?" Will asked.

"I don't know, it wasn't here earlier," Danny said.

All of a sudden, two bodies flew from the sky and landed on each side of the little *Whaler*. Gar and Willy had jumped from a large cedar tree and quickly climbed in the *Whaler*. Without much effort, they pushed Will and Trout in the water then grabbed Danny and slung him ten feet across the creek, inches from the riverbank. Gar took the helm of the little *Whaler* and cruised around the bush where Hunter was waiting in the water.

"See ya later, suckers," Gar yelled as the older boys sped away leaving Trout, Danny, and Will dazed and dumbfounded. For a moment, Danny wondered how they were going to get home until *Greenie* floated around the corner.

"Those jerks!" Will yelled.

"I can't believe they did that," Danny said.

"I can," Trout said. "They couldn't stand it that we had a faster boat than they did."

By the time the boys made it back to The Point, dejected and downright angry, the little *Whaler* was cruising the sandbars at the gulf. The older boys had picked up a couple of gigs, sped across the bay and were busy hunting stingrays and gloating over their perfect ambush.

"Those little twerps never saw it coming," Hunter said.

"They never should have taunted us like that," Gar said. "They shoulda known we'd get 'em back."

"Serves 'em right," Willy said. "They don't deserve a boat this nice."

Mr. Walt was waiting as Hunter steered the little *Whaler* to the pier. A five-foot stingray, with two gig wounds in its head, covered the floor of the bow. The older boys were proud of their kill but they knew they'd crossed the line. With one hand on his hip and the other working the stub of his cigar, Mr. Walt glared at them.

"Uh oh," Gar said. "We're in for it."

"Yep," Hunter said, "big time."

"Maybe I'll just head on home," Willy said.

"Don't count on it," Gar reminded him. "As long as you're in Mr. Walt's world, he owns you."

Will and Danny didn't have much choice. They'd come home and immediately told Mr. Walt the whole story about Danny winning the gainer contest, Mr. Lyons letting them use the little *Whaler* and the ambush up the creek.

"First of all," Mr. Walt said sternly "You boys should have told me about Mr. Lyons letting you use his boat."

"We didn't think you'd mind," Will said awkwardly.

"Will, you know me better than that. You and Danny didn't tell me about it because you were afraid I'd say you couldn't use it."

"Would you have let us?" Danny asked.

"Absolutely not. That was nice of Mr. Lyons but you boys have a boat. There's nothing wrong with *Greenie*."

"Yeah but, the *Whaler* is so fast," Danny said.

"Right. That's another reason I wouldn't have let you drive it. That little boat has too much power for you boys. It's not safe."

"Mr. Lyons thought it was safe enough," Will said defiantly.

Mr. Walt's face turned a deep shade of red and Will knew he'd stomped on his tongue. "We'll Mr. Lyons is not your uncle or your daddy, is he? And Mr. Lyons doesn't feed you your meals or provide you with a place to sleep, does he? And, Mr. Lyons won't take you fishing and shrimping, will he?"

Even though Mr. Lyons had offered to take the boys fishing a few times, Will figured he'd keep that little bit of information to himself. "No, sir," Danny and Will said as Trout sunk down in his chair and hoped Mr. Walt would send him home without putting him to work.

The boys hung their heads and wondered what was coming. For the next few moments, they sat in silence as Mr. Walt chewed on his cigar and contemplated. He was upset that they didn't tell him about the little *Whaler*, but mostly offended at their attitude toward *Greenie*. She was a worthy boat and most boys would be thrilled to have her. He worked hard to provide them with a full life and their appreciation was sorely lacking.

"I tell you what," he finally said. "I'll give you boys a small break. That little *Whaler* sure must have been tempting. I know that. But that still doesn't excuse you from not checking with me first. You're old enough to know better and next time I expect more. Do you understand why I'm upset?"

"Yes, sir," they said.

"Okay then. Y'all gather up all the paper trash and burn it. Stay there until it's all burned and be sure to shoot water on it when it's done. Trout, you help them and when the job is finished, you need go home. And boys, no trips to The Point without my permission. You'll need to hang around here in case I need you for something else."

They knew they'd gotten off easy. Burning the trash was more of a super heated skin toasting than a hard job. Plus, they probably would have gotten that chore anyway. Mr. Walt had just dolled out the work early.

A homemade incinerator had been built in the back yard years before the boys were born. It sat behind a row of scrubby bushes where the sun beat down relentlessly and the breeze never blew. With four three-foot-high brick walls, the caldron held more paper and cardboard than the boys could haul in three loads. Mr. Walt made them poke the fire with long bamboo sticks just to make sure they'd get a feel for how hot Hell must be. They kept the water hose running in case a large spark got away. They also used it to spray each other down every thirty seconds or so. Plus they drank the cool well water to keep from melting into a puddle of flesh and bones.

The fire was raging by the time the older boys arrived at the pier. Gar threw the bowline over a cleat without looking up at Mr. Walt.

"Been to the gulf, huh?" Mr. Walt said.

"Yes, sir."

"That's a nice stingray. What are you gonna do with it?"

"We gonna cut off the tail and keep the barb and spine."

"What about the rest of it?" Mr. Walt asked.

"Probably put it in the crab trap," Gar said.

They weren't fooled by Mr. Walt's chitchat. His irritated demeanor oozed out but he had decided to let them stew in their own guilt for a while. An awkward few moments passed while the boys sat in the boat waiting for Mr. Walt to tear into them.

"So I heard about your little incident up the creek today," he finally said. "That sounded like quite an ambush."

"Un huh," Gar mumbled.

Mr. Walt fueled their suspense. "I'm just trying to figure out what I should do with y'all."

The boys sat quietly knowing their toast was burnt. Nothing they said would help so they just waited and wondered.

"I guess first things first," he said. "I'll take the keys to that boat. Y'all need to get that nasty stingray out of Mr. Lyons nice *Boston Whaler* and haul it out into the bay. Before you scrub that boat down with soap and water, then wax the hull and polish all the chrome, you can go ahead and cut that tail off that ray. Carry it up to that big fire ant hill in the backyard so they'll eat the meat off the cartilage. We don't need anything for the crab trap so y'all need to swim that big ol' thing out into the bay with a couple of cinder blocks tied to it so it'll sink."

They listened painfully, knowing that Mr. Walt was just getting revved up.

"If there is so much as a scratch on that boat, y'all are gonna pay to have it fixed. Once you get it all cleaned, waxed and polished, I'll take it on over to Carlton myself. Willy, you stay here and help Gar and Hunter. I'll let you know when it's time to go home."

Without a shadow of a doubt, their fun was over for a while. With Mr. Walt as judge and jury, their sentence was going to be severe. Not only had they humiliated their younger brothers and taken someone else's property maliciously, they'd embarrassed Mr. Walt. Above all, they knew that was their worst offense. They fully expected to be waist deep in the grease pit and septic tank by that afternoon.

When Mr. Walt returned the *Whaler*, it was cleaner and shinier than the day Carlton Lyons had bought it off the showroom floor with one exception. There were several punctures in the fiberglass floor where the boy's gigs had run too far through the stingrays.

"Carlton," Mr. Walt said, "the boys were just ecstatic that you let them use your boat."

"It was my pleasure, Walt. They're good boys, for the most part, and they deserved it."

"Yes, they are good boys but the thing is, they have a boat. They have *Greenie*."

"Yes I know but I thought …"

"Next time," Mr. Walt cut him off, "ask me before you hand over your fancy things to my boys."

Carlton Lyons was full of himself and regularly rubbed folks the wrong way. Despite his aloof nature, he really did love kids. To him, he'd done a good deed. But he could see that Mr. Walt thought otherwise and he knew from good experience not to cross the man.

"Well that's fine Walt. If I ever have an idea like that again, I'll be sure to check with you first."

"I'd appreciate it," Mr. Walt said. "And just so you'll know, my boys will be down here later to pay you for the gas they used and the damage to the fiberglass."

"Oh, that's not necessary."

"Yes Carlton, it most certainly is," Mr. Walt said as he puffed hard on his cigar, turned and headed back to Paradise Point.

Mr. Walt found the boys playing cards and explained the situation to them.

"It's like this. I want you to pay Mr. Lyons $100 for the gas you used and the damage to his boat."

Danny looked at his daddy tentatively. "You mean, we have to pay for something we didn't do."

"Exactly right."

"But we don't have $100," Will said.

"That's not my problem boys. I know you've saved a little money this summer. You just have to figure out how to get more."

"But what about Gar and Hunter?" Danny asked.

"You let me worry about them. You've got your own problems to solve."

CHAPTER 29

The Worst Job of All

If you want something done right, do it yourself.
—Walt Thornton

Mr. Walt stepped out of the back porch door with his nose pointed skyward. His hand dangled by his side as he fingered a smoldering stub of a cigar. His nostrils were more sensitive than a seasoned bird dog's and he'd caught a whiff of something nasty. As he got closer, he recognized the unmistakable stench—the septic tank was bubbling over.

He'd already doled out a good measure of work to the boys and he'd been ruminating on what further punishment would fit the crime of stealing and damaging Mr. Lyons boat. That morning, fate dealt its hand and Mr. Walt chose to play it—coincidence or not. A household can survive without a lot of amenities but a working toilet is not one of them. Something had to be done.

Will looked out of the window in horror as Mr. Walt poked around the yard with a shovel.

"Danny, come here," he whispered. "I think the septic tank is overflowing."

Danny leapt to his feet, "We've got to get out of here." He knew that the worst job of all time would be handed out to any unlucky souls who happened to be available at the time.

Will's eyes were darting back and forth and he was rubbing his chin anxiously. "I think I have an idea Danny. Follow me."

Mr. Walt had Gar and Hunter hammering nails back into the boards on the pier. When nail heads popped up a quarter inch or so, as they tended to do, they could rip skin off unsuspecting bare feet. Cuts on the bottom of their feet were particularly crippling because they'd get dirty, infected and, because they spent so much time in the water, take forever to heal. Keeping a smooth pier surface was supposed to be Gar and Hunter's last punishment.

"Hey," Will said casually, "how's it going?"

"Okay," Hunter said. "What do you two pukes want?"

"Nothing," Will said. "Y'all need a break? Danny and I can hammer for a while."

"Nope. Mr. Walt wouldn't like that and we're almost finished anyway."

"That's fine," Will said. "Oh, by the way, did y'all know that an armadillo got a hold of that stingray tail last night?"

"You mean the tail's not in the ant bed anymore?" Hunter asked.

"Nope."

"How do you know an armadillo got it?" Gar asked.

"'Cause those red ants flat out attacked that armadillo and killed it dead."

"No way," Gar said. "That's impossible."

"Well they did. Go see for yourself," Will said. "Right Danny?"

"Yep, that armadillo is just covered up with ants and that stingray tail is still in its mouth. It's an ugly sight."

Gar tossed his hammer aside. "I gotta see this."

"Me too," Hunter said as they jogged toward the back yard.

"Hey y'all," Will called out, "Danny and I are going to drain the water out of *Greenie*."

"Yeah," Danny said, "See y'all later."

Hunter and Gar didn't respond. They had their minds on anthills and armadillos. As quickly as they could, Will and Danny untied *Greenie* from her piling, cranked the engine and sped out into the bay. When Gar and Hunter came around the corner of the house, they ran smack into Mr. Walt, who was bringing two shovels out of the tool shed.

"Hey boys," he said. "I'm glad you're here. Follow me."

"Uh," Hunter said, "we're going to check on the stingray tail, it …"

Mr. Walt glared from under the brim of his hat and handed them the shovels, "That can wait," he said. "We have an emergency."

"What?" Gar asked, fearing the worst.

"It looks like the grease trap has filled up and is spilling over into the yard."

"The grease trap?" Hunter's voice shook.

"Yep, we're gonna have to dig it out."

Gar and Hunter stood there motionlessly, hoping that somehow they could disappear into thin air. Those three words, "dig it out," were more gut wrenching than if they'd been told they had to eat a bowl of live earthworms. In the distance, they could hear *Greenie* heading toward The Point. They looked at each other and realized they'd been hoodwinked. Danny and Will giggled hysterically. They might have lost Mr. Lyons's little *Whaler* but they had successfully avoided the worst job in the world.

"What are y'all standing around for," Mr. Walt said. "Get to digging."

Before city sewers reached out into rural communities, in-ground septic systems disposed of waste pretty well. And they were a Godsend for folks who had endured the wretched outhouse. But, unfortunately, lots of things went wrong underground. And, in each case, there was only one ghastly solution: dig it up.

One persistent enemy was roots. They grew - and as one might imagine - grew prolifically in all those nutrients. They blocked field lines. They clogged up the connection between the grease trap and the septic tank. And they caused havoc in the same dirt that created spectacular azalea and magnolia blooms for garden clubs to admire.

The septic process was also bogged down by all kinds of greasy solids, none of which will be mentioned here. Let's just say, therefore, that the grease trap was the first stage in the system. It consisted of nothing more than a two-hundred gallon cement box with a drain hole at the bottom. As the slimy goop floated to the top, the liquids escaped through the lower hole, drained into the septic tank, and eventually dispersed into a network of buried pipes called field lines, which frequently got plugged up by roots. In this case, field lines were not the issue. Mr. Walt had determined the problem. The grease trap was completely filled up with goopy gunk that had stopped up the drain hole. The only way to remedy that disgusting problem was by scooping out the stuff with shovels and buckets and hauling it deep into the woods. Gar and Hunter's future for the next four hours was bleak.

Gar choked as they lifted the heavy cement top from the grease trap. "That's nasty! Will and Danny are gonna pay!"

Mr. Walt returned from the woods. "Boys, I've put up a couple of stakes where I want you to dig the hole to dump all this muck into. Cover it all up with plenty of dirt when you finish."

They looked at him like two beaten dogs.

"Well boys," he said. "Time's a-wasting. Start scooping."

Naturally, there weren't any trees around the grease trap for shade. And the breeze hadn't shown up that day. So the boys baked in the sun and cussed Will and Danny with each sloppy bucket full. They didn't even stop for lunch because working in the same stuff that they'd once had for lunch just didn't sit right with them.

By the end of the day, every inch of their skin was smeared with dark, oily muck. Their t-shirts and cut offs were destined for the fire pit and they smelled like a couple of week-old mullets. The final insult came near the end of the job, when they had to climb knee deep into the most foul smelling, slimiest gunk ever created to scoop out the remaining dregs at the bottom. Then they had to snake the garden hose into the drain hole to blow out any obstructions.

When Mr. Walt checked on the unhappy diggers, Gar looked bad but Hunter was worse. Fair skinned, his face and back were burned a deep shade of red and sweat was gushing from every pour.

"Boys," Mr. Walt said. "Y'all look like you need a break. Maybe a swim in the bay would do you some good."

"Once we're done," Gar said. "I think it's all cleaned out."

"Yeah, we're ready to put the top back on," Hunter said with a hint of hope.

"Okay," Mr. Walt said. "Y'all go cool off and I'll test the system to see how she's working."

Dropping their buckets, they headed toward the bay. Will and Danny were tying *Greenie* to the piling when the two soiled zombies stumbled down the hill.

"There they are," Gar said. "Let's get em!"

With what little strength they had left, Hunter and Gar ran after the boys.

"Quick, untie it," Will yelled to Danny as he jumped in and pull started the engine.

Danny leaped into *Greenie* and Will gunned the throttle a split second before their brothers closed in on them.

"You've got to come back sometime," Gar yelled at them.

"This is not over," Hunter screamed.

Danny and Will laughed nervously at their narrow escape. They knew their brothers would torture them later but for the moment they were free, they weren't covered in goop and they were on top of the world.

CHAPTER 30

A Garfish with a Gator Head

We couldn't tell if Trout was fishing or that fish was Trouting.
—Wallace Flomaton

"That boy will never live that one down," George Randolph said as he dealt out a new hand of pinochle.

"I've never seen anything like it," Wallace Flomaton added while he slurped on his third gin and tonic. "It sounded like that old cannon you shoot off every Fourth of July."

"Yep, I thought the Japs were invading Perdido," George smiled. "Turned out it was just Monroe Miflin."

"I'm not sure which is worse," Wallace laughed.

For a week or more, the talk from one end of Perdido to the other was about The Crash. At Mr. Randolph's store, the men played cards and speculated on Monroe's fate.

"All I can say is it's a good thing he's already in the military. His daddy would have shipped him off to the French Foreign Legion," Wallace said.

"You think the French would have him?"

"Oh sure, they take anybody whether they're blind, deaf or dumb."

George leaned back in his chair. "Well that's good because he's sure got that dumb part all wrapped up."

As the sun set, the boys had gathered on the pier at Mr. Randolph's store for an epic event. Separated from the men inside by nothing but a screen door, they were honored to be allowed to hang around and listen to them chatting about The Crash.

"I hope I never do anything that stupid," Trout said. "I don't want

227

everybody to talk about me like that."

"Me either," Danny agreed. "Will, don't ever let me be that dumb, okay?"

Will didn't hear Danny's request. He had his eyes on one of Wallace Flomaton's lackeys coiling some rope and tying a giant hook at the end. The boys had been invited over to help catch an alligator gar, one of the "strangest creatures God had ever dreamed up," according to Flomaton. With a long slender body covered in silvery scales, typical of any run-of-the-mill garfish, but outfitted with the gnarly head of a gator, the fish was indeed a quirk of nature. The half-fish, half reptile also grew to frightening sizes. Six-to-eight-foot alligator gars were common and catching one was a summer ritual.

"I'll never figure out how a gator and garfish mated," Wallace said, "but their offspring sure did get hit by an ugly stick."

"That's a fact," George said, "ugly *and* mean."

"Kinda like my second wife," Wallace spouted. The folks in the store laughed, like they were prone to do when Wallace Flomaton got on a roll. His stories about fishing and sailing were always outlandish. But when he ranted on about his many wives, all of whom eventually left him, he somehow found humor in what were often heartbreaking circumstances.

After a perfectly timed pause, he said, "Or maybe that was my third wife. I forget." The crowd hooted again as Flomaton smiled and sauntered to the bar to freshen up his drink.

"You sure it wasn't both of 'em," George said.

"Might have been," Wallace said. "In fact, I think it was. Hey George, you're out of gin."

"There's a bottle of vodka under the counter."

"You're a good man George, despite what your supposed friends say," Wallace grinned as he filled his glass with vodka and ice and threw in a puny slice of lemon for appearances.

Every so often when the men wanted more action than a game of penny-a-point pinochle, they'd try to catch an alligator gar. And even though the catching part of the process was relatively simple, the struggle of getting a big alligator gar to the pier was complete madness. That's what made it so much fun.

Wallace pushed through the screen door and placed an old shoebox on the pier. "Okay boys, here's what you do," he explained. "It's as simple as this. Put this rotten mullet on that big hook and toss it in. Any questions?"

The boys scrunched their noses as a rancid aroma filled the air.

"Is that what's in the box?" Will asked. "The rotten mullet."

"Bingo! My boy," Wallace said. "This here mullet has been in the box, sitting in the hot sun for two days. It's so rotten the dogs won't even eat it. But an alligator gar loves smelly old fish meat. The smellier the better. This nasty mullet will get an alligator gar's attention faster than a twelve gage shotgun."

He looked at his devoted follower and pointed to the box. "You hook that mullet through the gills and toss it out there away from the pier. Boys, you watch the rope and yell for me when it starts moving. I'll be inside playing cards."

The young man wondered why he'd joined in that night's fishing expedition. But the truth was, he was happy that the great white fishing god himself seemed to trust him. Of course, Wallace didn't even know the fellow's name, nor did he care. He just knew that he wasn't going to put his hand anywhere near that mullet or they'd never let him back in the card game.

"Yuck," Danny said as the man opened the box.

"That smells worse than rotten eggs," Will coughed. "Quick, hook it and throw it in."

With his hands as far away from his nose as possible, the young man grabbed the squishy fish, pushed the hook through it and quickly heaved it in the water along with ten feet of rope.

"I think I might throw up," Trout said. "That was the grossest thing I have ever smelled."

"Then throw up in the water," Will laughed, "it'll help bring that alligator gar in."

The victim with rotten mullet hands disappeared around the corner looking for some soap. If that didn't work, he was considering dipping his hands in gasoline and lighting them on fire.

Unlike speckled trout, bluefish or marlin—fish that slammed the bait with the force of a jackhammer—an alligator gar was a slow-moving scavenger. Wallace Flomaton called them "garbage men of the sea" because they patrolled the bottom eating anything resembling food, from dead fish to old shoes.

"He might suck on that rotten mullet for a minute or two before he swallows it," Wallace had told the boys. "That's why we have two coils of rope. When he drags out the first coil, it's time to set the hook. Then he'll run like the devil with that second coil."

As the men played cards, drank and laughed continuously, the boys watched darkness creep across the sky. They kept a keen eye on the rope, hoping to see some movement as they relived The Crash.

"How creepy was it swimming inside of that sailboat?" Trout asked.

"Super creepy," Will said. "I was expecting to see her body floating in there."

Danny rubbed on his forehead, "I knew you were gonna go in. I was just scared of getting trapped down there. You know, if something fell on top of us. But cuz, I followed you anyway."

"I wasn't worried about getting trapped, I was just thinking we might save Mrs. Felder's life."

"Yeah, I was thinking that too but I was mostly worried about my own skinny butt," Danny said.

"I didn't think about it. I just went in."

"It's amazing that she got off just a couple of minutes before Monroe hit that sailboat," Danny said. "Talk about lucky."

"Maybe it wasn't luck," Will said.

"Sounds lucky to me." Danny said.

"Yeah but maybe someone was looking after her."

"You mean like her fairy God mother?" Danny asked.

"Yeah. Or a guardian angel."

"I don't know about that," Danny said skeptically.

"Then what about Dr. Felder?" Will asked. "He'd been going out there everyday but that was the one day he didn't."

"Why didn't he?" Danny asked.

"Because," Trout said, "the motor on his dinghy wouldn't start."

"Isn't that a new motor?" Danny asked.

"Yep, brand spanking new," Trout said. "It's been running just fine but he couldn't get it to crank. When he pulled the cover off to see what was wrong one of the spark plug wires had melted in half."

"See," Will said, "That's just weird. Like God knew what was gonna happen and saved them."

"Will, that's called a coincidence," Danny said coolly.

"If it is, it's a pretty big one," Will said. "I mean a wire on a brand new engine melts on the day his boat gets hit. I think it's more than just a coincidence."

"Could be," Danny said. "But motors break all the time. I still think they were just lucky."

"Either way," Trout said, "I'm just glad nobody got killed."

"Except Monroe, when his daddy got a hold of him," Will laughed.

"Yep," Trout said. "I wouldn't want to be in his shoes."

"Hey look," Danny interrupted, "the rope's moving."

"I'll get Wallace," Will said as he scampered inside the smoky store.

The moonlit serenity on the pier was in stark contrast to the party going on inside. Twenty or so folks were milling about, playing tunes on the jukebox and drinking cold beers. Without fail, everyone was puffing on a cigarette as clouds of smoke got chopped up by ceiling fans. In the far corner, four men had their eyes glued on their cards and didn't notice Will bursting through the door. As he slammed his palms onto the card table he yelled, "The rope's moving! We got one!"

"Calm down now Will. I'm right in the middle of a hand here. I tell you what, you boys grab the rope on that second coil. If the fish pulls out that much line, y'all give it a hard yank and drop it. And, stay away from that coil!"

"Yes, sir," Will said breathlessly and ran back outside. "He said we need to set the hook."

"How do we do that?" Danny asked.

"It's not that hard. I know how," Trout said as he reached for the rope. "You just grab it and yank."

"NO!" Will screamed an instant before Trout pulled on the rope. "Wallace said we have to wait until the alligator gar takes out the first coil of rope, then we can set it. We have to let him swallow the hook."

The boys took hold of the rope and lined up in tug-of-war position. Like a snake moving slowly through the grass, the line eased out over the edge of the pier and disappeared into the water. Their moment was approaching.

"I'll say when," Will said, "and we all pull at the same time."

Will looked directly at Danny and Trout. "Y'all stay away from that rope like Wallace said. We gotta let the alligator gar run with it."

When the coil was down to three loops, Will tightened his grip. "Here it comes," he said. "Steady, steady, okay—*pull*!"

With all of their strength, the boys jerked the rope. Fifty feet away, at the business end of the line, the razor sharp hook dug into the soft throat tissue of a huge, hideous alligator gar.

"Lookout," Will yelled as the line began peeling off at breakneck speed.

"We got to slow it down," Trout said as he reached for the line, "or it will break that rope. Somebody needs to wrap it around the piling and put some tension on it."

Will grabbed Trout by the arm and tugged him back. "But Wallace said to keep away from it."

Danny stood silently, wide-eyed and transfixed at the rope ripping across the water. Just then, Trout pulled his arm away from Will and stepped closer to the line. "I'm telling y'all it's gonna break, I know it."

The sound Trout made when his back hit the pier reminded Will and Danny of the blunt puff of breath purging from their lungs whenever they got punched in the stomach. He'd disregarded Wallace's advice and the rope had whipped up around his ankle. Trout dropped faster than a prizefighter. As he skidded past a piling, he made a futile grab at it and splashed in the water. It happened too fast for Will and Danny to react. For a moment, they were frozen in shock. This had to be a first; Trout and the angry alligator gar were *both* hooked up.

"I'll get some help," Danny shouted as he sprinted inside and yelled that Trout was drowning, even though he really wasn't. But Danny figured on the quickest way to get a bunch of half-drunk men into action.

By the time George Randolph, Wallace Flomaton and a host of others made it out to see what was going on, the gar had pulled out all of the line and was thrashing furiously on the surface. Trout was a mere twenty feet from the pier, attached at the ankle and struggling the keep his head above water. With unadulterated fear in his eyes, Trout whimpered, "Pull me in. Please pull me in."

"Somebody cut the line," said an inebriated man wielding a knife, who clearly had no knowledge of alligator gar fishing techniques.

"Hell no you don't!" Wallace yelled. "If you cut that line, that damn fish will take off and really will drown that boy. We got to get him to the pier before the rope breaks!"

"Then God help that boy," the man slurred.

"If there is a God," Wallace said, "he's not gonna pull in that rope.

It's up to us men."

George Randolph had already taken up position and was starting to drag in the line.

"Will, Danny, give me a hand," George said as Wallace stepped in to help.

The four of them pulled but the alligator gar pulled back.

"Owww, my leg," Trout yelled.

"Stop pulling," Wallace said, "his leg's all wrapped up. We might break it."

Even though he'd consumed enough vodka and gin to kill a large farm animal, Wallace moved with skilled precision. In one fluid motion, he untied *Greenie* and jumped in. Danny and Will followed closely behind.

"Grab the rope and pull us over to him," Wallace said as he opened his pocketknife. Trout was beginning to tire. He fought to catch each breath before his head ducked back under the water.

Wallace reached out, caught Trout's hand and pulled it up to the side of *Greenie*. "Trout, hold onto the gunnel," Wallace demanded. "I'll cut this fish loose."

Leaning over the bow, Wallace grabbed a section of the rope between Trout and the fish and sliced through it. Trout felt the pressure on his leg disappear but he was desperate to get out of the water. For all he knew, the alligator gar was coming after him. "Pull the boy in," Wallace yelled to George.

The massive fish had no interest in Trout. Escape was its primal mission. The thing was, Wallace Flomaton had intentions of his own, especially when a monster fish was involved. Determined not to let the alligator gar go, Wallace wrapped the bitter end of the line around his forearm and hung on. The gar headed for deep water with *Greenie* plowing across the creek in tow.

"Give me the bow line," Wallace barked at Danny. "And hurry! I'm about to lose him."

As Danny handed the line to Wallace, the grizzled fisherman tugged hard on the alligator gar for some slack. The boys watched in breathless awe as his hands moved at lightning speed. A split second before the fish slipped from his grasp, Wallace knotted the ropes together and tossed the line into the water.

Wallace sighed heavily. "There we go. Now we just wait."

Until that moment, the boys had never ridden in a boat running on fish power. They sat quietly and wondered how long the thrill ride would last.

"This is the same way we get big sharks," Wallace said. "But we use a gig with a strong line tied to it."

"The shark drags the boat around?" Danny asked.

"Sure does. We cruise the sandbars in the gulf until we see a shark. I stay on the bow with a three-pronged gig. Once we get close enough, I throw the gig. When the barbs go in, the shark takes off and we tie the line to the bow cleat. Sometimes a shark will drag us around for two hours before it finally dies or gets so tired we can haul it in."

"Have you ever caught an alligator gar that way?" Will asked.

"Nope. This is the first time. But it should work the same way," Wallace said as he looked around *Greenie*.

"Say, you boys don't have any cold beer on here, do you?"

Will glared at Wallace. "We're only twelve. We don't have beer."

"Oh yeah," Wallace said. "Well then we ride it out and wait."

Back at Mr. Randolph's store, Trout had been helped onto the pier and given a towel to dry off. He was accustomed to trauma but the thought of getting chomped by an alligator gar still had him shaking.

When he saw how pale Trout's face was, George Randolph headed to the bar with a plan. He filled a large glass with ice, two healthy squirts of cherry syrup and poured in a twelve-ounce Coke.

He handed it to Trout. "Here's something that'll put a smile on your face, an extra-large, ice-cold cherry Coke, on the house!"

Trout wrapped his hand around the chilled glass and took a long, slow drink. "Thanks, Mr. Randolph," he said. "That's sure a lot better than a bite on the leg by an alligator gar."

"Probably better than drowning too, huh?" George Randolph grinned.

"Yes, sir, better than that, too."

Thirty minutes later, they heard *Greenie's* motor crank up and ease slowly toward the store. Danny steered *Greenie* to the pier as Wallace Flomaton, with his signature flamboyance, stood on the bow dragging a ten-foot alligator gar beside the boat. Gingerly he hopped over to the pier and handed the rope to an underling.

"George, that's another state record in the bag. No doubt about it."

"That calls for a celebration," George said.

"I concur. Ya got any more of that vodka?"

"As a matter of fact I do. Lemons, too."

Before they got through the screen door, Wallace and George heard a high-pitched howl. Looking over his shoulder, Wallace saw his disciple down on his knees, hanging on desperately to the rope.

"Damnation!" Wallace said. "That fish got his strength back. Quick, somebody catch a hold of that rope!"

Danny and Will grabbed the line until Wallace and George got there. They tied it around a piling and stood back while the alligator gar went berserk.

"I'm afraid he's gonna snap that line," Wallace said. "We're gonna have to pull him in. George, get ready with the shotgun."

Wallace slowly unwrapped the line. "Boys, get over here and help. You there," he shouted to the fellow whose hands were still stinking of dead mullet, "help us out."

"We're gonna pull that big ol' fish in?" Danny asked.

"Yes we are son. And, you're gonna have to use every bit of strength you've got."

"Yes, sir."

"Okay everybody," Wallace began. "When I say so, start pulling and don't stop until we get that fish close enough for George to shoot him."

In the distance, the alligator gar was thrashing fanatically. Every so often, it would grunt like a wild hog and jump completely out of the water. Danny and Will's knees were shaking but as the youngest protégés of Wallace Flomaton, they kept quiet and followed orders. Trout leaned against the wall and kept sipping on his cherry Coke. He almost felt good enough to help pull but he'd already been in battle with that fish and he'd had enough.

"PULL!" Wallace commanded. "Again! Pull! Again!"

Each time they got that alligator gar a foot or two closer, Wallace pulled in the slack. With a single loop still around the piling, he slid the rope toward him to keep the line taught. And, if the fish happened to jerk the line from the boys' hands, something Wallace had seen too many times before, that rope around the piling would hold him steady.

"Keep pulling boys, we're getting him!"

The closer the fish got to the pier, the madder and stronger it got. They were in a marathon tug-of-war and not making enough progress.

"My arms aren't working anymore," Danny said. "They're too tired."

"Mine too," Will said. "I can't pull anymore."

"Okay, Will and Danny get over here and tend this line. George, put that shotgun down and help me pull this damn monster in."

The men tugged but the fish tugged back.

"We're gonna have to give it everything we've got. This is a state record fish and I'm NOT gonna lose him."

"We are giving it everything," George shot back. "Maybe you can think of something else."

For ten minutes, they couldn't budge the humongous creature. The fish had gone to the bottom and wasn't moving.

"Damn him," Wallace said. "Our only hope is to flip him around if he jumps. We'll just wait. When he jumps, we'll get him."

Suddenly from out of the depths, the state's biggest, and undoubtedly meanest, alligator gar leaped in the air, spun around and soaked everyone on the pier with a monumental splash landing.

"NOW!" Wallace yelled. And with all their strength, the men pulled the vicious beast next to the pier. For a moment, Wallace was relieved but he knew the fight was far from over. There's something amazing that happens to a fish when it has been in a lengthy battle and it finally stares into the eyes of the fisherman. In one last act of survival, it summons strength from deep within its gut, and for a short burst of time, it fights with supernatural strength. Many a fish have broken off the line because a fisherman didn't anticipate that final explosion. For Wallace and the alligator gar, that time had come. Had he been tending the line at the piling instead of Danny and Will, Wallace would have given the animal a little slack. He would have eased the tension so the fish wouldn't snap the line. Unfortunately, Wallace acted too late. Before he could say to the boys, "Let off on that line," the alligator gar landed, thrashed his head back and forth and, just like that, the rope popped. In that spilt second, Wallace thought about his story of the giant blue marlin and almost jumped on top of the fish but his better judgment kept his feet planted firmly on the pier. An alligator gar that big could literally bite his head clean off and Wallace had no intention of tangling with that fiend.

As George, Wallace, Will and Danny stood at the edge of the pier with their hands red and swollen, they couldn't believe that they'd lost a state record fish. Before they could even gasp in disbelief, the deafening sound of a twelve-gauge, double-barrel shotgun, filled with buckshot rang out. Poised at the edge of the pier, Trout fired again. Both shots hit the target dead on. The giant fish shook one last time, grunted and rolled over as dead as a doornail.

"Take that sucker," Trout huffed. "You won't be pulling me in the water again."

"Good shooting, Trout," Wallace shouted. He smiled broadly and patted Trout on the back. "You saved the state record."

"So whose record is it?" Trout asked soberly. "Mine or yours."

Wallace assumed that all fishing records went to him. After all, he was the man among men in all things related to the sea. But as Wallace examined Trout's steely eyes that night, he saw more than just a silly kid. Wallace recognized that this young man had something special.

"I tell you what son," Wallace said. "This is a state record we can share. How about that?"

"Really? You mean it?" Trout asked.

"Sure I do. We're partners, you and I."

"That calls for cherry Cokes all around, I'd say," George shouted.

"All right!" the boys cheered.

"Uh hum," Wallace coughed.

"You can have a cherry Coke too," George said.

"You know bourbon is good in cherry Coke," Wallace mentioned.

"You're hopeless," George said.

"Maybe so. But I'm still one helluva fisherman."

"That you are," George said, "as long as you have those three boys to help you out."

"You know, they're good. They're damn good. Especially Trout here."

Will, Trout, and Danny sipped on their cherry Cokes and beamed brighter than the sunrise. The men let them come inside and get a full dose of jukebox music, cigarette smoke, and even a few off-color jokes.

Six months later, when the new edition of state fishing records came out, it listed Wallace Flomaton and Trout Loxley as holding the record for the biggest alligator gar ever caught in Alabama. At nine-feet, seven inches long and four hundred and fifty two pounds, it's a record that was never broken.

CHAPTER 31

The Spanish Graveyard

Even if you don't see anybody, act as if somebody's watching.

—Kitty Thornton

"Sorry about your family's sailboat," Danny said to Stuart. "That was a real shame."

"Yeah, we're just glad nobody got hurt. My step-mom probably would have gotten killed if she'd been on there."

"We're glad she wasn't," Will said.

"I know. And my dad is really proud of y'all for getting out there so quick and trying to find her. Everybody is."

"It just seemed like the right thing to do," Will said.

"If she'd been in there, I'm sure you and Danny would have pulled her out."

"Yep," Danny said. "We sure would have."

The boys sat quietly for a moment percolating in their thoughts. Finally, Stuart broke the silence. "So, I guess we're going home early this year," he said sadly.

"How come?" Danny asked.

"It's this sailboat thing. Daddy's all upset and he just wants to get home."

"But we never got to take y'all to the Spanish graveyard," Will said.

"That's right," Danny said. "We've gotta do that before you leave."

"I think we're leaving tomorrow," Stuart said.

"Then we'll just have to go tonight," Will insisted.

"We're doing a bonfire at The Point tonight," Danny said.

"That's perfect," Will said. "We'll go to the Spanish Graveyard at dark then come back to the bonfire. It'll work out just right."

"Let me make sure the girls can come," Stuart said.

"Yeah," Will said. "And you have to tell them that Trout and I can't make it."

"You can't? Why not?" Stuart wondered.

Will winked at Stuart. "Just tell them," he said. "But we're not coming with y'all."

Stuart was still confused. "So are you coming or not?"

"No dorkus," Will said with a smirk, "because Trout and I will already be there waiting and hiding. Just don't tell the girls that."

Stuart looked at the sneaky grins on the faces of Danny, Will, and Trout. He wasn't sure what they had planned but he could count on one thing, they were going to scare the pee out of some girls.

Just as the sun was touching the horizon, Danny pulled *Greenie* up on the beach at Witchwood. He could see folks milling around on the front porch. Stuart and the girls were playing cards and keeping cool under the ceiling fan and Lilly Felder had just served them some lemonade. In the master bedroom, Dr. Felder was laid out on the bed, lost somewhere between a wrecked sailboat and his insurance agent. His suitcases were already packed and stacked neatly by the door.

Danny walked up the steps and opened the screen door. "Y'all ready?"

"Ready as ever," Stuart said.

"Good. Then let's get going while we still have some light."

"Danny, would you like some lemonade?" Lilly asked.

"No ma'am but thank you. I'm fine."

"Where's Will?" Lilly asked. "Is he going with y'all?"

"Uh," Danny said, looking at Stuart, "you didn't tell them?"

"The girls know that Will and Trout aren't coming. But I didn't tell my parents."

"Oh, well Uncle Brewton, I mean Uncle Brew, that's what we call him, he's Will's daddy. Anyway, he just came down from Montgomery and Will hasn't seen him all summer so he wanted to stay home and visit. And Trout's in trouble 'cause he forgot to clean out the gutters or burn the trash or rake the yard. I forget which one."

"He always seems to be in trouble," Lilly said.

"Yes, ma'am, that's Trout. He's pretty much been in hot water his whole life."

"That's too bad. He's such a nice boy. Are they coming to the bonfire tonight?"

"I think so."

"Good because I know the girls want to see them before we leave."

"Yes, ma'am, I'm sure they'll see 'em. I'm absolutely sure."

That was the first true statement Danny had made since he walked onto the porch. His white lies were not intended to be harmful. His Uncle Brew actually had come down but he'd never deprive Will of a Spanish Graveyard jaunt. And Trout really was in trouble because he was always in trouble, so that wasn't far from the truth either. But he wasn't actually grounded at the moment. Anyway, like snipe hunting, trips to the Spanish Graveyard needed to be shrouded in a little bit of deception.

"Do y'all need some flashlights?" Lilly asked.

"No ma'am. I have one in the boat," Danny said knowing that less light was better for scaring girls.

"Go ahead and take one," Lilly insisted, "just in case your batteries die or something."

Ellis grabbed the light and clutched it with both hands. "This is the girls' flashlight," she said. "No boys can touch this one."

"Right," Grace agreed. "We don't want to get out in some graveyard and get lost in the dark."

Early Spanish settlers had picked one of the most gorgeous locations on Perdido Bay to lay their loved ones to rest. And why not give them the best? After all, they were beloved parents, grandparents, sisters, brothers and, sadly, children. Back then, in the late 1600s when the area was sparsely populated, they had hundreds of acres of waterfront land to choose from. And fortunately, the graveyard predated by hundreds of years one of the area's most detested varmints—the real estate speculator.

They'd chosen a quiet piece of land set a few hundred feet back from the towering bluff and in amongst humongous oaks trees decorated with an extraordinary mass of Spanish moss. A broad beach guarded the site and an ancient path wound up the soft sandy hillside. From the top, the expansive view of the bay was stunning. From there, the trip to heaven must have been a short one.

A black wrought-iron fence aged with streaks of rust surrounded the graveyard. Over the years the spindles had twisted and bent and the gate was rusted halfway open—or shut, depending on one's perspective. Early wooden grave markers had long since rotted away but some tombstones from the early 1700s still stood. Most of the graves dated back to the 1800s, after which time the graveyard filled up. As the saying went, people were just dying to get in. The last to be buried there was a fellow named Frank Fell, who died in 1898, according to his headstone.

"Fell off what?" they always joked. "That must have been what killed him."

Making light conversation took the edge off because on a dark night there was nowhere on earth as spooky as the Spanish Graveyard. Not even the Widow Woman's house.

"Hey y'all check out that sunset," Danny said as he steered *Greenie* eastward. "It's getting good."

The girls spun around and witnessed yet another fiery Perdido sky while Stuart, under secret instructions from Danny, opened his sister's flashlight and reversed the batteries.

"That's beautiful," Grace said.

"Gorgeous," Georgiana said. "I'm sure gonna miss this."

"Me too," Grace said. "I wish we didn't have to leave tomorrow."

"If that idiot Monroe Miflin didn't hit our sailboat, we'd be here for another few days," Ellis said. "I'm sorry girls."

"It's okay," Grace said, "we understand."

The sunsets weren't the only thing they were going to miss. Having cute, adventurous boys around had been a bonus to their beach vacation. And Georgiana was really getting fond of Trout. She had hoped to spend a few more days with him. Grace was still playing the Danny 'n Will combo. Danny had been as nice as he could to her and she'd eaten that up. On the other hand, Will had been kinda mean. In fact, he'd been a bit of a pill. But his good looks and self-confidence had a way of overshadowing his smart mouth. And those blond curls sweeping across his tanned face made her heart race. At least both boys would be at the bonfire later that night to give her the chance to juggle their emotions one more time.

By the time *Greenie* eased onto the beach, darkness had set in. A partial-moon high in the clear sky lit the path well enough for them to pick their way upward.

"Is this it?" Grace asked.

"Yep," Danny said pointing to the top of the hill. "Up there."

"How do we get to it?" Ellis asked

"We climb," Danny said. "It's not that hard."

The soft sand was easy to navigate and they quickly trekked to the top. With a slight breeze blowing in their faces and the moon sparkling on the bay, they took a few minutes to soak up the splendor.

"I see why they put a graveyard here," Grace said. "It's beautiful."

"Yes it is," Ellis agreed.

"Which way is it?" Stuart asked, anxious to scare the wits out of the girls.

"Follow me," Danny said. "We have to go down this path for a little while."

"Wait a minute y'all!" Ellis said. "My flashlight isn't working."

She clicked the button on and off with no success.

"It was working great when we left."

"That's a shame," Danny said. "Maybe it bounced around in the boat and something shook loose. Y'all better stick close to me."

He didn't have to make that suggestion twice. The girls bunched tight around him with Grace on one arm, Georgiana on the other and Ellis clinging to the back of his t-shirt. Although he knew the way by heart, Danny used his feeble light to shine on the path just to make girls feel better. They followed the single-track as it slithered through the oaks into the near total darkness.

"Hold on a second," Danny whispered and stopped in his tracks.

"What is it?" Grace trembled.

"I'm just listening," he said as he turned off the flashlight. The girls squealed at the sudden profound blackness around them

"Turn it back on," Grace begged.

"I think it's kinda on the blink," he said, flicking it on and off a few times. From deep within the graveyard, Will and Trout saw the signal and smiled. Danny was leading them right into their web.

"There it is," Danny said, shining the light into the distance. "See that fence? The gate is around the other side."

The girls' legs wobbled. Their breathing was rapid and shallow. Panic began to creep up their spines. To say that the boys weren't a little frightened too would be stretching the truth. Even though they'd been to the Spanish Graveyard many times, the place was downright chilling. Not only was there darkness absolute but they were far away from any houses or roads and the deathly silence had goose bumps popping up on top of each other. Occasionally they heard a bird or land critter meandering through the dead leaves and wondered if the mythical hatchet man who escaped from prison was tracking them. Besides images of homicidal maniacs, they could only think about how scared they were. They listened to their own quiet panting and the eerie shivering of limbs swaying in the breeze.

"Follow me," Danny said as he passed through the gate. "We are now officially in the Spanish Graveyard," he whispered.

The five kids clumped together tightly, moving along slowly from tombstone to tombstone. Georgiana could feel her tongue going dry and she wished for a glass of cool water and a giant flashlight.

"Look," Danny said. "Elija Suarez—born 1842; died 1899."

"One more year and she would have made it to the next century," Grace said.

"Yeah," Stuart said. "Look at that one. Larry Resmundo—born 1785; died 1863. He was pretty old."

"Seventy-eight," Grace said coolly. "That was really old back then."

As they read gravestone after gravestone, Danny led them closer and closer to a large oak with two low-hanging limbs. An owl hooted in the distance. Georgiana jerked and whimpered, "What was that?"

"Just an owl," Danny said. "It's okay." Then he flicked the flashlight off to a multitude of squeals from the girls. He tapped on the light but as far as the girls knew, it was broken, too.

"Don't worry," he said. "I know the way out. Keep following me."

"Make it come on," Georgiana begged.

"I'm trying," Danny said, continuing to shake it around. "It's messed up. Just stay close to me."

When they approached the oak tree, Danny stopped.

"Did you see that?" he asked.

"See what?" Ellis asked. "It's too dark to see anything."

"Something moved up in that tree," Danny said.

"Probably a bird," Grace said shakily.

"No, it was too big," Danny said. "Maybe it was the wombat."

Georgiana squeaked. "What's the wombat?"

"It's half ghost, half wild animal. It lives around here and comes out on nights like this."

"Stop it," Grace said. "Y'all are scaring us."

"LOOKOUT!" Danny yelled as Trout and Will, both covered in white bed sheets jumped through the Spanish moss and flew toward the girls. They hooted, shook their sheets, scampered past the girls and disappeared into the woods.

In broad daylight, their sheets would have just looked silly but in complete darkness with Spanish moss wrapped over their shoulders and around their arms, Will and Trout were bona fide, full-fledged wombats.

When Georgiana saw them sailing out of the tree she collapsed to her knees and covered her head. Ellis and Grace hugged each other and screamed at the top of their lungs. Danny and Stuart fought back their laughter. They expected the girls to figure it out but Trout and Will were experienced wombats. In their minds, the girls had just witnessed two ghosts and they sincerely wondered if they were going to get home alive.

"Are wombats good or bad?" Ellis whimpered.

"It depends on if we respect the graveyard or not."

"What do you mean?" Georgiana sobbed.

"Well as long as we just look it's okay. But I've heard of folks coming in here to steal gravestones and stuff and, well, I'll just say nobody ever heard from them again."

"Really," Grace said. "Be honest."

"I am," Danny said. "It's all true."

Georgiana looked up from her knees. Tears were streaming down her face. "Can we please leave now?" she asked.

"Sure," Danny said. Although scaring them was fun, Georgiana was beginning to sob and he felt bad for her. Relieved that this ordeal was over, the girls bunched next to Danny for the trip back to *Greenie*. Little did they know that Will and Trout were waiting at the bluff, preparing for round two.

"I'm really scared," Georgiana said between snivels.

"Just think of marshmallows roasting on the bonfire at The Point," Grace said. "We'll be there before you know it."

"I'll try," she said.

Jumping off the bluff into the soft sloping sand at Pirate's Canyon was perfect practice for Will and Trout's final act at the graveyard. As Danny, Stuart and the girls inched their way down the sandy slope to the boat they heard some commotion above them. With running starts and still draped in sheets and Spanish moss, Will and Trout catapulted off the edge of the hill. The girls collapsed to the ground as the screaming wombats flew over their heads with sheets fluttering in the moonlight.

Trout and Will landed, rolled down the hill and howled in laughter. Danny and Stuart broke up, too. Success was theirs, sort of. Realizing they'd been duped, Ellis turned to Stuart and punched him in the stomach, knocking the wind out of him. He fell to his knees and rolled slowly to the beach, moaning all the way down. Georgiana threw three hard clumps of clay at the giggling ghosts. One whacked Trout square in the back and almost knocked him over.

"Ouch," Trout squirmed. "That's gonna leave a bruise."

"Good," Georgiana said. "I hope it never goes away!"

Upset at the boys' tricks, Grace walked silently to *Greenie* without speaking to Danny or Will. When she climbed into the boat, she blasted the boys, "I'm glad we're leaving tomorrow. Let's go."

"Oh lighten up Queen Elizabeth," Will said.

She ignored him.

"We were just joking around," Danny said. "Don't be so mad."

She ignored him, too.

"We were just following tradition," Danny tried to soften her up.

"Leave her alone Danny," Will said. "She can't take a joke."

Despite the splendid moonlit bay and *Greenie* slicing nicely across the smooth water, the ride back to Witchwood was painful. Each apology was met with ice water.

"Come on girls, we were just having fun," Trout said.

"At our expense," Ellis shot back.

"Sorry about that," Danny said for the fifteenth time. But the girls never softened, and Will never let up.

"Y'all really thought we were ghosts," he said. "Admit it. I've never seen three people so scared. We'll be talking about this night for a long time."

As Will bragged and Danny apologized, Grace began to forget about Will's luscious hair and self-confidence. Even though she was still annoyed at them both, she was beginning to appreciate Danny's sincerity, not to mention those piercing blue eyes. After what seemed like an eternity, *Greenie* finally slid on the beach at Witchwood.

"Okay, all girls off the boat," Will said. "We've got a bonfire to get to."

"Y'all are coming tonight, aren't you?" Trout asked.

"Yeah, we're sorry we scared you," Danny said, "but that doesn't mean you should miss a great bonfire. Especially on your last night."

"We'll discuss it," Ellis said. "Maybe we'll come and maybe we won't."

"Well, we hope you will," Trout said. "Think about those roasted marshmallows."

"If we decide to come," Grace said with a chill, "it'll only be for the marshmallows. It certainly won't be for the company."

"Okay, that's enough yakking," Will said. "Let's get moving."

As Will idled *Greenie* away from the beach, he shouted back to the girls. "See y'all later," he said, "or not!"

CHAPTER 32

Milky Way Kisses

The Big Dipper catches the milk that his little brother spilt.
—Wallace Flomaton

When the boys arrived, the fire was already roaring over six-feet high, throwing an orange glow on the faces of the crowd gathered around. Bonfires at The Point were regular rituals where folks shared stories, songs, food and fellowship. And somewhere between the ages of experimenting with beer and learning how to turn innocent marshmallows into flaming torches, was the mystery of confronting the opposite sex. There was something about the heat of the fire and the glow of red embers that stripped away masks of pretense. The moon and stars; soft sand and warm breezes; and the sound of waves flirting with the beach tended to open young hearts. The purity of it all also seemed to cast a revealing light on those sinners, liars and deceitful characters. Simple bonfires helped to germinate the seeds of love or drive home the nails of distrust. They were magical, mystical and sometimes tragic.

Then again, sometimes bonfires at The Point were none of that. They were as far from anything esoteric as a smile on a little girl's face. Bonfires were simply a place to relax with friends, dig one's toes in the sand, cook a hot dog, squeeze together s'mores, and enjoy the simplicity of a night under the stars while burning up some old wood.

For Will, Danny, and Trout, the gatherings were mostly about being silly and hanging out with friends. They were still too young to think about cold beer, and girls were just beginning to knock on their consciousness. Of course, with Grace, Georgiana, and Ellis in the pic-

247

ture, that situation had heated up.

Trout grabbed a slender stick and slid a long hot dog onto it. "You think the girls will come down?"

"They'll be here," Will said. "They'd be stupid to miss a bonfire."

Danny concentrated on rotating his marshmallow so that it would brown evenly all over. He hated to burn them. Not that a crispy marshmallow tasted bad. It was more the challenge of a uniform browning without any unwanted flame ups or brushes with the sand. When marshmallows were involved, his perfectionism was as obsessive as Dr. Felder's.

"I think Will's right," Danny said. "They've heard so much about these bonfires. I think they'll come. Plus, it's their last night."

"And Stuart's coming," Trout added brightly.

"Right," Danny agreed. "So the girls will come, too."

Although he'd never admit it, Will hoped Grace would show up. She was as pretty a girl as he'd ever seen and he knew she liked him, even though he'd been an arrogant smart aleck. If he could get the chance to be alone with her, he'd ease up and make nice. But showing his soft side when Danny and Trout were around wasn't going to happen. That was completely against his nature.

Every so often, the boys would glance down the dark road toward Witchwood and wonder. Finally, after the girls had showered, fixed their hair, changed clothes three times and even dabbed on a little makeup, they appeared in the soft glow of the fire. Grace took everyone's breath away. She was gorgeous with wind-blown hair and an old t-shirt. But as she stood there with her hair styled, a pink cotton blouse and skin-tight white shorts, she was a vision of beauty. As they stared at her smooth skin and sparkling eyes, Will and Danny felt a strange tingling inside. Neither of them realized they were wearing goofy smiles nor did they recognize the odd emotions overcoming them. At that moment, the sight of her had kick started them into puberty. And there was no turning back.

Trout was fixated on Georgiana. He didn't care if she wasn't the sharpest hook in the tackle box. As far as he was concerned, Georgiana Starlington was his kind of girl. Danny and Will could fight over Grace, while Trout and Georgiana learned about puppy love on their own.

Danny managed to catch his breath. "Wow. Y'all got all fixed up. We haven't even had a shower yet."

"We wanted to look good for our last night," Grace smiled warmly.

"You sure do did it ... I mean ... sure ... did ... do it," Will stumbled. He wasn't used to doling out compliments, especially when his mind was clogged with pubescent testosterone. Grace was somewhat taken aback. That was the first sort-of-nice thing he'd said to her in days.

"Thanks," she said. "I really appreciate it."

"You're not anything. I mean, it's not a thing. Uh ... I'm sorry ... I *mean*," he said finally composing himself, "it's nothing."

Danny cracked up. "You okay, cuz?" he asked. "You got marshmallow stuck on the roof of your mouth or something?"

"No, I'm just ... I'm just ... I'm just ... " Will's mind went blank. Everybody was looking at him, and he couldn't think. Never one to be self-conscious, he was terribly confused. *Why couldn't he think*, he wondered. Of course, the answer was simple. Grace had whipped the poor boy's mind into butter.

"You're just what?" Danny asked.

Will figured the truth was his only way out. "I'm just amazed at how pretty the girls look tonight," he said with a wide smile. "I guess I'm just speechless."

"That's such a sweet thing to say," Grace said.

"Yeah, thanks Will," Ellis agreed. "You're pretty good at being nice when you try to be."

She was right. But he had a problem. He'd already dug his grave with Grace. And she had other things in mind.

Grace stepped next to Danny and smiled. "That's the most perfect marshmallow I've ever seen. How'd you get it so brown without burning it?"

"Well, it takes a lot of concentration, a little luck, and a perfect coat hanger."

"Can you show me how to do that?" she said as she moved in closer.

"Sure I can," he said. "You can use my coat hanger."

Danny showed her his homespun cooking tool. "I made a little handle at one end, so it's easy to hold and I won't drop it in the sand. The only thing worse than a burnt marshmallow is a gritty marshmallow."

"How clever!" she said, pouring on the charm. Danny's heart

might as well have been one of those fat marshmallows, because at that moment, Grace had the power to skewer it, melt it, burn it, squish it between her teeth, and swallow it. "Can you do two at a time?"

"Sure can," he said. "That's why I leave the little squiggle on the end. It keeps them from falling off."

"I didn't know you were so smart."

Pure jealousy pumped through Will's arteries as he watched them flirt. "Yeah," he said, "he's smarter than a coat hanger,"

Stuart laughed, but Danny and Grace barely heard the dig. With the sweet taste of marshmallows on their lips, they'd quickly bonded in the warmth of the fire.

"Let's do two more," Grace said as she reached into the bag. Danny held the coat hanger steady while she skewered them. To help steady the wire, she placed her hand on Danny's and giggled. As her soft fingers brushed against his, he felt his knees wobble.

"There," she said. "Ready to go."

While Trout and Georgiana were engrossed in conversation, Will, Stuart, and Ellis watched what they considered the most sickening display of romantic ogling ever. An ache formed in the pit of Will's stomach, because Mr. Nice Guy was clearly getting all of Grace's attention. He wondered if he'd been too much of a jerk and quickly concluded that he had.

As the evening wore on and everyone stuffed themselves with too many hot dogs and sweets, Danny and Grace melded into one. Before anyone knew it, the 10:30 curfew had drawn near. Danny decided to take one more step. With beads of sweet popping from his palms and his heart racing, he took a deep breath and looked Grace in the eyes.

"You wanna walk out to the tip of The Point and look at the stars?" he asked with a noticeable warble in his voice. "We can see them better out there away from the fire."

"Sure," she said softly.

Although he didn't realize it at the time, he would use that same line with great success again and again in the years to come. As Mr. Walt said, "Don't change the lure if you're still catching fish."

When Danny and Grace faded from the glow of the fire, they held hands and wondered when they'd see each other again.

"I'll be going back to Montgomery in a couple of weeks," Danny said. "School starts after Labor Day."

"Mobile isn't that far away," Grace said, "and maybe you could come over before the swim meet."

Mobile was okay as cities went, but it didn't hold a candle to Perdido. He'd be away from *Greenie*, his freedom, his family, and his playground. Plus, he'd have to wear real clothes and probably shoes. The thought made him shudder.

"I guess I could," Danny said trying to appease her. "But maybe you could come back to Perdido for a day or two."

"I'll ask my parents," she said. "If not, I guess I'll just have to wait 'til Labor Day weekend."

"Yeah," Danny said. "You think Ellis will ask you down again next year?"

"I hope so."

"I just hope they rent Witchwood again after this whole sailboat thing."

"Me too," Grace said as she reached in her pocket. "I have something for you," she said.

"What?"

"I bought it at The Hangout when Mrs. Felder took us to Gulf Shores. It's a friendship ring."

Danny looked at the thing. Was she giving it to him? He'd never worn a ring before. And he wondered what Will and Trout would think.

"It's, uh, nice," he finally said.

"See, it has two circles that are hooked together."

"Oh yeah," he said. "I see it."

"You don't like it, do you?"

"Yeah, I like it," he said.

"Would you wear it?"

"Sure, I guess. It's just that I've never worn a ring before."

"You don't have to wear it."

"No, I want to wear it."

"Really?"

"Yes. But I don't have anything for you."

"That's okay."

"Wait, I have an idea."

Danny reached down and pulled off a hunk of fringe hanging from his cutoff blue jeans. "Hold out your finger," he said.

Grace offered her right hand. Danny held it softly and tied the bundle of white string around her pinky. As his hands shook and he labored over the knot, Grace realized that he was genuinely kind and gentle. Thinking of using a piece of his cutoffs was clever. She liked that, too.

"There you go," Danny said. "Now we both have rings."

"I won't take mine off unless it wears out," she said.

"Same here," Danny smiled.

"So I was thinking about the swim meet. I know Mr. Lyons can get you in, but why don't you come as my guest. And try to talk Trout and Will into coming."

"Trout will be there if he's not grounded, but Will wouldn't be caught dead at a country club."

She grabbed his hands. "As long as you come. That's what matters."

"If Mr. Walt can't take me, I think Mr. Lyons will."

"You think your father will bring you over?"

"I don't know. He's not much for leaving Perdido, and Mobile's not his favorite place to spend a hot day."

"You can talk him in to it. I know you can."

"Maybe, but riding over there in Mr. Lyons's Lincoln Continental might even be better. He is kinda like our coach and everything."

"That's true."

"Then again, he's pretty sensitive about Mr. Lyons after that whole little *Whaler* thingy."

"Yeah, I guess so."

"But you know what?"

"What?"

"Mr. Lyons's car has air conditioning."

"Really?"

"No kidding."

"I'm so excited. It would be wonderful if you came."

"I'll do my best."

Cars and girls. Danny was all boy. As they stood on the beach, their minds spinning with possibilities, Danny noticed how bright the stars really were.

"See that? It's the Milky Way."

"Where?"

"That thick bright group of stars going right over our heads. Those are the stars in the galaxy."

"It's beautiful."

He slowly moved next to her and pointed over her shoulder. "And there's the Big Dipper."

"Wow, I see it right there."

"Do you know how to find the North Star?"

"No, which one is it?"

Danny slid his arm around her waist and she quickly put her hand on his. "Well, see the last two stars in the dipper part of the Big Dipper?"

"Yeah."

"You have to follow them straight up."

"Okay."

He pressed his face against hers and pointed at the star. "Just make an imaginary line going up until you get to that one star. It's not the brightest star, but it's right there."

"I thought the North Star was really bright."

"Not really. It's bright enough, though. Do you see it?"

"I think so. Is that it?"

"Yep. And you know what? The North Star is also the first star in the handle of the Little Dipper. See, there's the handle, and there's the dipper."

"Oh yeah. I see the Little Dipper, too. Neat. How'd you get so smart, Danny Thornton?"

"Mr. Walt teaches me about the stars. He says it helps to navigate in the boat at night."

"Does it?"

"I guess so, but I never go far enough away from here at night. I always know where I am without looking at the stars."

She squeezed his hand and turned her face toward his. Although stargazing helped to keep him calm, Danny's brain was just about to spin out of his head. He'd never kissed a girl. He'd never worn a ring. Doing both within a span of ten minutes was almost too much. But somehow, he mustered the courage to turn and place his lips on hers. The feeling was something he could have never imagined. The soft touch, her sweet smelling perfume, and their gentle embrace sent a warm rush through his body. They stood there for five minutes hugging and kissing, innocent and inexperienced, awkward and stiff. But, nonetheless, they were embracing under the stars and, for the first time in their young lives, they were making out.

By the time they returned to the fire, everyone had left except Ellis, Will, and Stuart. Trout had offered to walk Georgiana back to Witchwood, and she had readily accepted. Danny figured they'd stopped along the way to check out the stars, too. Then Grace hit them with the big news.

"I've invited Danny to be my guest at the Labor Day swim meet. Will it would be great if you'd come, too."

Will sat quietly and stewed. He was miffed on at least three levels. First, she'd given her kisses to his cousin and not him. That alone was enough to keep him away from the Mobile Country Club. Second, as he'd clearly pointed out, he wasn't going to wear any stupid grippy swimsuit. And third, "There's no way I'm gonna hang around with a bunch of country-club sissies, even if I was gonna to win all the trophies in the world. I think I'll pass, thank you very much."

"Come on, Will," Danny begged. "It'll be fun. We'll show Rodney and those country-club weenies how to really dive."

"Ain't no way," Will said. "I'd rather get a fish hook stuck in my eye."

"Just think about it," Danny said.

"I have thought about it."

"Okay."

"Okay is right. Let's go home."

"Uh, I was gonna walk Grace back to Witchwood."

Will threw his coat hanger in the fire and got up to leave. "Fine, then I'll see y'all later."

"I'll go with you, Will," Ellis said.

She saw her opportunity and decided to go for it. Now that Grace had focused in on Danny, Will was on the open market. Ellis knew she wasn't the beauty queen Grace was but, like Will, she was self-assured. At least she could try to cheer him up. As they walked the dirt road to Witchwood, Will didn't hide his disgust.

"I can't believe Danny's all sweet on that girl. And now he's gonna go to that stupid swim meet with her. I just can't believe it."

"I'm surprised Grace didn't pick you, Will," Ellis buttered him up. "You're better looking and a better athlete and everything."

"Ya think so?" he said momentarily breaking out of his funk. "Well, anyway, he can have her and all those stuck-up, country-club pansies."

When they arrived at Witchwood, Stuart patted Will on the back. "I guess I'll see ya next year, buddy."

"Yeah, I hope so."

"I hope so, too," Ellis said, softly touching Will on the shoulder.

"Yeah," Will said, still preoccupied with Danny and Grace.

To her disappointment, Will didn't even notice Ellis's flirting. "Are you going to wait here for Danny?" she asked hopefully.

"Nah, I'm gonna walk on back to Paradise Point. Y'all have a good year."

"You too, Will," Stuart said.

"See ya next summer," Ellis said. "Be good."

A deep sadness swept over Will as he kicked down the sandy path. His cousin had abandoned him for a silly girl, of all things. As inconceivable as that notion was, he didn't recognize that he would have done the same thing. If Grace had sidled up to him at the bonfire, they'd be holding hands now and strolling along the road together. And then Danny would be the one left out in the cold. But his anger blocked that logic from his mind, and he only felt betrayal. For twelve years, he and Danny had been inseparable—until that night. The whole thing was damn hard to swallow, even though the girl was leaving the next day.

Grace and Danny stood at the screen door and kissed one more time.

"Please, please come to the swim meet," she said.

"I will. I promise."

"And send me a letter. I'll write you as soon as I get home."

"I'm not much on writing letters and stuff, but I'll try."

Grace leaned in and kissed him on the cheek. "Just do your best," she said as she spun around and sashayed inside. With a silly grin on his face, Danny stood and watched her until she disappeared around the corner of the porch. He'd had a night he would remember forever, and he could hardly stop smiling. The touch of her hands, the feeling of her lips, and her sweet smell just played over and over in his mind. *This must be what love feels like*, he thought. Then his mind shifted to Will.

Seeing him was going to be tough. Grace had been like another competition for them, and Danny knew Will would take the loss hard. But Danny was logical. Despite his hatred of country clubs, even Will would have accepted the swim meet invitation if Grace had given him the friendship ring and kissed him. Danny just hoped Will wouldn't be too mad. And since Grace was leaving the next morning, maybe Danny 'n' Will 'n' *Greenie* 'n' Trout 'n' everything could just pick up where it had left off.

Will's father watched his son climb the steps with his head hanging low. "Hi Daddy," he said.

"Well, that's no way to greet your old man, who you haven't seen in two months. Come over here and give me a big ol' hug."

"Yes, sir."

"Where's Danny?"

"He's off with some girl."

"Oh, I see. And where's your girl?"

"I don't have one."

"Well, why not? A fine young strapping boy like you."

"I don't want to talk about it."

"Son, talking always helps. You know, get things out in the open and all that."

Will stood silently next to his father.

"Now come on boy, out with it. Every time I come down here, I see lots of girls. Aren't there enough girls to go around?"

"Yeah, there are some other girls."

"Then why aren't you with one of them?"

"I don't know. Daddy, do we have to talk about this now?"

"Yes, we do. It's not good to bottle these things up inside. It'll eat you up like a leech sucking you lifeless. Ya gotta get everything out on the table, son. Now what about these other girls."

"I don't like the other girls."

"Oh, oh, oh! Now I'm starting to see the picture. Are you saying that you and Danny like the same girl?"

"Yeah, I guess so."

"Well now that is a dilemma, isn't it?"

"I don't know. What's a *de-lemon*?"

"It's a conundrum, uh, you know, a difficult problem to solve."

"Yeah, and Danny's the biggest problem of all."

"Hmm, that is a tough one, my boy. All I can say is keep your head up. Don't let it get to you. There are plenty of fish in the sea, so don't get upset over losing one. Do you know what I mean, William?"

"Kinda."

"Son, it's like this. Danny isn't just your cousin; he's your best buddy. Don't be upset at him over a girl. It's not worth it. Trust your old man on this one. I know."

"Did you bring Mama with you this time?"

"No son. I wish I could have, but she's got a household to run."

"I miss her."

"Aren't Walt and Kitty taking good care of you?"

"Yes, sir, but Aunt Kitty's not my mama."

"I know son, but we'll be heading home soon, and you'll get to see your mama every day."

"Can I go to bed now?"

"Sure son. Give your daddy another big hug and we'll chat more in the morning."

"G'night, Daddy. I'm glad you're here."

"Me too, Will. Me too."

Brewton Stapleton, better known to friends and relatives as Brew, was a natural-born salesman. During his careers, he'd sold cars, life insurance, farm equipment, and plumbing supplies. He always made good money, but had never managed it well. However, his latest venture into kitchen appliances was beginning to pay off. None other than General Electric had hired him. That meant good benefits and a territory that covered all of Mississippi, Alabama, and Georgia. So he called on every mom-and-pop appliance store from Savannah to Tupelo and sold truckloads of stoves, refrigerators, and washing machines. The commission money was beginning to roll in, but life on the road kept him away from home most of the time. That suited Will's mother just fine. She stayed home and focused on climbing the social ladder, while her two sons lived at Paradise Point for the summer. As long as Brew kept sending money and the boys were away, Eloise Stapleton was a happy and energetic socialite.

To the great pleasure of his wife, Brewton bought a big new house for the family on upscale Allendale Avenue near the Montgomery Country Club. Of course, he was never there to enjoy it. "One of these days," he said, "I'm gonna make enough money to spend some time fishing with my kids." But they were growing up quickly, and time was slipping away even faster.

The appliance job had another benefit. Uncle Brew had brought down a spanking new washing machine as a gift to Mr. Walt and Miss Kitty for taking care of Will and Hunter all summer. As he and Mr. Walt unloaded the machine, Brew explained what had happened.

"The customer ordered a white one and, for some reason, the factory shipped this brown one. I'd say it's kinda like an old plow mule. It ain't real pretty, but it'll do the job. It's the best one GE makes."

"We don't care what it looks like, Brew," Mr. Walt said, "as long as it washes clothes."

"It will do that," he said. "It's a workhorse."

"Speaking of workhorses," Mr. Walt said. "I've worked the boys hard, and they've played hard. It's been a good summer."

"That's great, Walt," Brew replied. "And you know how much Eloise and I appreciate what y'all have done."

"It's no trouble, really. Danny and Gar love having their cousins to play with, you know that."

"I know, but keeping them all summer is a godsend. Eloise just can't seem to handle teenage boys."

"Teenagers are hard. They take a lot of nurturing."

Brew laughed and slapped Mr. Walt on the back. "You got that right, Walt. And while I'm busting my butt on the road every day, Eloise's only nurturing is with all those stuck-up women at the country club."

Mr. Walt smiled cordially. Brewton joked about Eloise, but Mr. Walt didn't approve of the way she ignored her kids. Raising children was a job he took very seriously.

"Yeah, well, Eloise is welcome to come down and help out any time she wants."

"She'll come as soon as y'all build a Sears at The Point."

"I kinda figured that, Brew, but let her know that the invitation is always open."

"She knows that, but Perdido is like camping to her. Her idea of roughing it is running out of cream and having to use milk for her morning coffee."

The analogy made Mr. Walt chuckle. It didn't do any good to criticize the way other folks lived, especially when he and Miss Kitty had created an idyllic life at the beach. And the truth was, he liked having two more boys to help with the chores.

Will poured a glass of water in the kitchen. The drone of the fan masked most of the conversation coming from the porch, but he heard the tone of their voices. He knew what they were talking about, and he didn't care to hear more reasons why his mother never showed up. He was already depressed about Grace and Danny. As he slipped out to the Back House to go to sleep, he prayed for something good to happen.

CHAPTER 33

Watermelon Mini-Bikes

Two most dangerous things in the world: a doctor flying an airplane and a redneck driving a pulpwood truck.

—Brewton Stapleton

"Wake up, son. I have something to show you."

Will cracked an eyelid and saw his daddy standing over him with a mile-wide grin.

"What is it?"

"Ya gotta come outside and see for yourself."

Will glanced at the other bed. Danny's face was buried in his pillow.

As he stepped through the screen door, Will couldn't believe his eyes. Leaning proudly on its kickstand was a new minibike with a Briggs & Stratton 3.5-horsepower engine.

Will ran to the minibike and jumped on. "Can I ride it?"

"Sure you can, son. That's what it's made for. Let me show you how it works. The engine is the same kind as the lawn mower. Here's the pull cord to get it started. You pull out the choke like this."

Brewton Stapleton had none of Mr. Walt's mechanical acumen, but he knew how to crank a small engine. One yank on the pull cord, and the engine fired to life. Inside the Back House, Danny stirred, but he figured Mr. Walt was cutting some grass, so he put the pillow over his head and drifted back into dreamland.

"It's pretty simple, Will. You have the throttle right here on the handle and the brake pedal right there at your right foot. You know how it works, right?"

Will looked at his daddy with a toothy grin. "Throttle to go. Brakes to stop."

"That's all you need to know, son. Give it a go."

Will twisted his wrist and the minibike took off down the driveway. He tested the brakes once, but hardly slowed down until he stopped at The Point. On the way back, he cut through the woods and terrorized three squirrels and a possum. *Danny can have the girl,* he thought. *I've got a minibike!*

Brewton was waiting when Will returned. "I was wondering if you'd gone into town."

With a humongous smile frozen on his face, Will sat on the minibike and prepared to zoom off again. "I went all the way to The Point, Daddy."

"That's great. Now listen, just like the lawn mower, you have to fill up the oil every time you put in gas. Otherwise, you'll burn up the engine."

"Yes, sir."

"And it's got the extra large seat so you and Danny can ride it together. It's made for two people."

Will was still upset at Danny but he couldn't wait to show him.

"Daddy, how do I turn it off?"

"You push this little lever against the spark plug, like this."

Will sprinted across the grass to the Back House. He flung the screen door open and blew a puff of air into Danny's ear from half way across the room.

"Danny, wake up. Come on, ya gotta come see."

"What is it?"

"Follow me."

Danny poked his head out of the screen door and saw Uncle Brew standing next to the mini bike. Still in his underwear, Danny ran out the door with Will close at his heels.

"Will, is it yours?"

"Yep, sure is."

"Now wait a minute Will," Brewton said. "I'm giving it to you *and* Danny. You boys are both responsible for it."

"Really? Thanks Uncle Brew," Danny said. "That's great."

Will fought back his disappointment. He wanted something he could call his own. But he was too excited to be upset.

Danny hopped on the back. "Show me how it works Will."

"It's easy. Just watch me."

"Don't you think you should get some clothes on Danny?" Uncle Brew asked with a smile.

Will and Danny burst out laughing as Danny ran to the Back House for his cut offs. Uncle Brew continued to grin as the boys sped down the sandy driveway. Feuding over a girl was sticky business but there was nothing like revved-up wheels to bring two boys - no matter how old - back together again.

"Let's go to The Point."

"I've already been there," Will said. "Let's go somewhere else."

"Ya think we can make it up to Mr. Hoover's watermelon patch?"

"There's one way to find out."

More than a mile up the blacktop, the watermelon patch was brimming with juicy melons. In the summer heat, they'd never consider walking that far. But their new toy had quickly expanded their range. With the wind blowing across their smiling faces, they zipped along the pavement. Before they knew it, the watermelon patch came into view.

"Let's eat one," Will said. "Nobody's around."

"Old Mr. Hoover will tan our hides if he catches us," Danny said.

"Then we won't let him. Quick, let's find a good one."

Will grabbed the emergency screwdriver and poked at a few melons until he found one he liked. "This one looks good."

"I don't know about this Will."

Will stabbed the melon and yanked a jagged cut in it. "Come on. Don't be a stick in the mud," he said. With a couple more swipes at the rind, Will cracked into the juicy red meat.

"Well," Danny said, "since you've already broken it open, I guess I'll eat some."

The boys sat at the edge of the five-acre patch and stuffed their faces. Juice ran down their chins and dripped on their tummies as they shot slippery seed missiles at each other. Suddenly they heard a car door slam. They ducked behind a group of big melons and thick vines. Just like every other morning, Mr. Hoover was checking the patch for some ripe melons to sell.

"Stay low," Will said. "Maybe he won't see us. The old fart is practically blind."

"But he's coming this way."

For seven decades, Mr. Hoover had been farming that piece of ground. Pushing ninety-years-old he still drove his beat up pickup truck to the watermelon patch. He'd ramble and weave slowly down his driveway, cruise the quarter mile to his field, pick a few melons and then head back home. The routine was good for him. Even though he was old and frail, farming kept him going. He knew that folks driving by had a tendency to sneak a melon here and there. And those thieves infuriated him. He'd been chasing them off since his horse and wagon days.

As he shuffled closer to the boys, he saw something moving. He set his course straight for Danny and Will and waved his cane in the air. "Hey you there! What the hell are you doing in my patch?"

Will jumped up and pull started the engine. "Let's go before he gets here."

Danny knew he'd better jump on or get cane whipped by old Mr. Hoover. With his heart racing, he grabbed a hold of Will and they sped back down the road.

"And don't ever come back," the old man yelled. "Or I'll fill your backside with birdshot."

Giggling nervously, the boys sped back to the safety of their stomping grounds. A swim at The Point would be ideal for washing off sticky watermelon juice and showing off their fast new machine.

CHAPTER 34

Jellyfish Stings and Rings

A broken heart stings worse than a jellyfish.
—Will Stapleton

As they walked from the pavilion to the diving board, Will noticed something for the first time. "What's that?"

"What?"

"That thing on your finger."

Will's voice was frosty. Danny had dreaded this moment. In all the minibike excitement, he'd forgotten about it.

"It's a ring."

"Duh, I can see that. Where'd it come from?"

"Grace gave it to me last night."

"So y'all are getting married now?"

"No, it's just a friendship ring. It means we're friends."

"Boy friend and girl friend?"

"I guess."

"It's goofy," he said angrily. "All those country-club sissies probably wear rings. What about that Rodney jerk?"

Danny looked confused. "What about him?"

"I thought he and Grace were going steady?"

"Why'd you think that?"

"Because that's what Grace told me."

The hurt from the night before made twisting the truth easy for Will.

"She said she liked him okay but not that they were a couple or anything."

"Well she sounds like a first-class two-timer to me," Will said.

Danny was speechless. Even with a new minibike to bring them to-gether, a girl was threatening their friendship. As he walked to the pier, Will kicked at the sand. He felt like getting on his minibike and riding all the way back to Montgomery. With a sluggish bounce off the diving board, he plunged in. On that seemingly uneventful dive, Will was shocked to spot a jellyfish with three-foot-long tentacles pass within inches of his face. To Will's relief, his momentum carried him past the spineless creature without incident. Realizing he'd dodged a bullet, Will quickly swam to the rope. Migration of the vicious jellyfish was as unpredictable as when a mullet might jump. Sometimes they'd show up in June and hang around for a week. Or they might have a mass appear-ance in August and be gone the next day. No one ever knew, but they always stayed on alert.

Getting stung was not the end of the world. The boys usually got hit a couple of times each summer but it never failed to hurt like the devil. So far, that summer had been wonderfully jellyfish free—until that moment.

For a split second, Will considered warning Danny. But his anger prevailed. *That jellyfish might sting some sense into him,* he thought. Or Danny might just as easily miss it. Despite their lethargic appearance, jellyfish were always moving. The currents and tides dragged them from the gulf to the bay and into the creek but in still waters the jellies could get around pretty well on their own.

Even though Will was down and out, Danny was energized with young love and a fast motorbike. He took two steps, sprung high into the air and shot straight down. His first underwater image was a mass of tentacles as they slapped directly into the right side of his face. In-stinctively, Danny jerked his head to the left and the tentacles slid across his shoulder, down his arm and over his hand. Like octopi, jelly-fish tentacles have myriad suction cups that hold their prey while they inject their poison to slowly kill their next meal. Danny could feel them sliding by and sucking on his arm at the same time. Quickly and vigor-ously, he shook the thing off his arm and stroked safely away. For a few seconds there was only anticipation of the pain about to unfold. Noth-ing could be done except to wait and let nature takes its course.

"Ye-ouch," Danny squealed as he surfaced, "there's a huge jelly-fish down there. It got me on the face."

Will was ambivalent. A jellyfish sting wasn't fatal. The pain would subside in fifteen minutes or so and he'd be fine. He was glad he didn't warn Danny.

"I'll get the baking soda," Will said dryly.

A box of Arm & Hammer baking soda always sat on a shelf at the pavilion. The theory was that the soda counteracted the poison, but in reality, nothing really helped to ease the pain. The merciless jellyfish had shot thousands of microscopic barbed nematocysts into Danny's tender skin and they were doing their job. As he swam for the beach, Danny replayed the horrific scene in his mind. He recalled the tentacles sucking and sliding down his arm to his hand and …

"My ring," he yelled.

"What about it?"

"The jellyfish sucked it off."

"You're lying."

"No really. I felt its tentacles pulling it off. I wasn't about to stop and try to get it back."

"That's too bad."

"What am I gonna tell Grace?"

"Tell her the truth," Will said with an annoyed chuckle, "that you lost it and you can't be friends anymore."

Danny didn't appreciate Will's attitude. He wanted some sympathy and Will wasn't giving it. Danny dumped baking soda all over the right side of his body.

"Just 'cause she likes me doesn't mean that you have to be a jerk about it."

Insulting Will was extremely rare for Danny but the intense pain on the side of his face clouded his judgment.

"Maybe that's why she doesn't like me. Because I'm a jerk and you're a goody two-shoes."

That was enough confrontation for Danny. He focused on his injuries and clammed up. He realized that Will was angry and the conversation could only go downhill. After a few minutes of awkward silence, Will shuffled toward the minibike.

"I'm ready to go home," he said.

"Go ahead. I'll just walk."

Danny didn't realize the depth of Will's declaration. As Will sped off on the minibike, Danny strolled down the road hoping Grace would sympathize with his injury. When Danny arrived, the girls were swinging on the hammock and chatting with Trout. Stuart and Dr. Felder were packing the car while Lilly sat in a rocking chair reading a magazine.

"Hey y'all," Danny said. "Whatcha doin'?"

Grace jumped out of the hammock. "We're waiting for you!"

"Well here I am and I just got stung by a giant jellyfish!"

Seeing the red welts on his face and arm made Grace gasp. "Oh my goodness, you got stung bad."

"That's ugly," Stuart said. "Did it have those long technicals?"

"You mean tentacles?" Danny said.

"Uh, yeah, I guess so. How long?"

"Probably three feet or more. It was big. But Stuart, they're tentacles not technicals. Just like they're barnacles not molecules."

Stuart grinned. "I know. I just get confused sometimes."

"You're goofy," Ellis said.

Lilly was eavesdropping. She decided her husband needed to take a look.

"Honey, can you come inside and check on Danny. He's got a terrible jellyfish sting."

Dr. Felder was still moping about the *Water Lilly* but he looked at the welts. "Did you put baking soda on it?"

"Yes, sir."

"How about vinegar?"

"No, sir."

"Lilly, get some vinegar and pour on it."

"I think we're out of vinegar."

"Well, the only other thing is urine."

"Honey!" Lilly said.

"Well, it helps to neutralize the venom."

"Did you say urine?" Danny asked, "Like pee?"

"Yep. Maybe Trout could pee on it," the doctor said, actually smiling for the first time since The Wreck.

"Sure I'll do it," Trout said.

"Me too," Stuart said.

Danny backed away. "I think I'll be okay. I'd rather be in pain that let y'all pee on me."

"Good call," Stuart said. "Hey so where's Will?"

"Wasn't that him buzzing by on that minibike?" Trout asked.

"Yeah," Danny said.

"I can't believe he didn't stop," Stuart said.

"Yeah, where'd he get it?" Trout asked.

"Uncle Brew brought it down. He gave it to us."

"That's great. But why didn't he stop and show it to us?" Stuart asked.

"I think he had to get back to help his daddy with something," Danny said not wanting anyone to know they were arguing. "I'm sure he'll show it to y'all later."

"I hope so," Stuart said. "But daddy says we're leaving as soon as we get the car packed."

Danny had been hiding his finger. He hoped to get Grace alone and explain what happened. She was proudly showing off the string ring he gave her.

"Hey Grace, can we walk outside?" he asked. "I want to show you something."

"You gonna get her to pee on ya?" Trout grinned and Georgiana giggled.

They walked along the path to the beach and Danny told her about diving headlong into the fiendish jellyfish. "You're not going to believe this but the tentacles dragged that friendship ring right off my hand."

Grace stood as still as a statue for a moment. She reached down and inspected his swollen hand.

"I hope that's not some kind of a sign," she whispered.

"I don't think so. It's just one of those things. You know, a weird accident."

She thought about it for a moment. In her mind, life was predestined. Everything happened for a reason. But she wasn't going to give up on Danny over a silly jellyfish.

"Well," she finally said with a smile, "when you come over to Mobile, I'll just have to give you another one."

"That would be great," Danny said. "Grace, I have to ask you something else."

"Sure, anything."

"Are you and Rodney a couple?"

"Absolutely not. What gave you that idea?"

"Will said you told him y'all were boyfriend and girlfriend."

268

"I did no such thing," she said. "Will and I never even talked about Rodney, except when Will was saying bad things about him."

Danny smiled and took her by the hand. "Okay, I believe you. I think Will's just upset about everything."

"I think you're right Danny. Rodney and I are close but I've never given *him* a ring."

Hidden from the front porch by a large patch of bushes, Danny and Grace took the opportunity for one last kiss. Danny realized how much harder kissing was in daylight. He preferred a starlit evening with a blanket of darkness to hide under. Still, her lips were soft and sweet and he was going to try like the dickens to get over to that swim meet.

When they returned Dr. Felder was loading everyone in the car. Trout pecked Georgiana on the cheek and Ellis asked Danny to tell Will goodbye for her. As they pulled away, Grace spun around in the backseat and smiled at Danny.

"Hey, ya wanna come have lunch with me," Trout asked. "Mama's serving up some of those blueberries for dessert."

"Sure," Danny said.

"Ya wanna go get Will?"

"Nah, I didn't really want to say anything to them but Will's pretty upset about Grace."

"Yeah, I kinda figured that."

"I think I'll let him cool off and visit with his dad for a while before I go home."

After a huge lunch of fried speckled trout, new potatoes, corn and a big bowl of blueberries on ice cream, Danny was stuffed. Just like everyone at Paradise Point, the folks at Trout's house always took a nap after a meal like that. Danny figured the longer he left Will alone the better. Maybe Uncle Brew would talk some sense into him.

"Trout, get up," his mother snapped. "Nap time is over. You need to bury the garbage."

Danny hopped up. "I'd stay and help Trout but I'd better get on home."

As he walked down the driveway to Paradise Point, everything seemed normal. Mr. Walt was tinkering with the lawnmower, Hunter and Gar were raking pine needles off the roof and he could see Ethel and his mama sweeping the porch. Yep, everything was in its place except something new and exciting—a new mini bike parked next to the

Back House.

Danny poked his head in the screen door. Even though he didn't feel like he'd done anything wrong, Danny decided he was going to apologize to Will for spending so much time with Grace. He didn't mind acting regretful if it ended up mending their friendship.

Will wasn't there. As he walked to the main house, Danny realized that Uncle Brew's car was gone, most likely off on another appliance adventure.

Danny bounced up the steps to the porch. "Hey, Mama, where's Will?"

"Oh honey!" she said. "Come here and sit down."

"What is it?"

"When Uncle Brew came down, Will got kinda homesick. And he seemed so despondent, you know, sad."

"Where is he?"

"He went home honey. Your Uncle Brew took him back to Montgomery. They waited for you but they needed to get on the road so they'd get home before dark."

"I can't believe it."

"You'll see him in a couple of weeks, right after Labor Day."

"Yeah but what am I gonna do for the next two weeks?"

"You can play with your brothers and older cousins. It'll be fine."

Danny was distraught. Grace had just left. Will had abandoned him and Trout was leaving in two days to visit his cousin in north Alabama. A few hours before he was on top of the world with a new girlfriend, a new minibike and Will to spend the waning days of summer. In what seemed like the blink of an eye he was all alone. Mobile was starting to sound better all the time.

As they headed north through Bay Minette on Highway 31, Brew Stapleton rambled on about stoves and refrigerators and all the new accounts he had. Will listened half-heartedly and thought about the bad words he'd had with Danny. The thought of Grace stirred up anger inside and he looked forward to reconnecting with his buddies back home. They'd play some basketball, throw the football, ride their bikes and roll mock oranges under passing car tires to watch them splatter.

And, he'd get to see his mama. Although he already missed the beach, the thought of going home made him smile.

Looking out of the window at passing cotton fields and pastures of cows lazily grazing, he closed his eyes and pictured his mama. It wasn't fair that she didn't come to Perdido. Lots of things didn't seem fair to him lately. A tear came to his eye and he quickly wiped it away before his daddy could see it.

"How much further is it daddy?"

"A few more hours, son, and we'll be home."

"I'm glad."

CHAPTER 35

The Legend of Harold Caine

Raccoons aren't smart; they're damn geniuses

—Marlow Loxley

Men folks, whose work schedule only allowed occasional visits to Perdido, always planned to be at the beach for at least one special time: the last week of August. Not only was it a great time to fish, swim and play with their kids before the new school year, but no one wanted to miss the Legend of Harold Caine—an epic Perdido party commemorating a pirate and the coming of fall.

According to local folklore, Harold Caine had once been a trusted captain of pirate Jean Lafitte in the early 1800s. One night during a late summer celebration in New Orleans, Captain Caine and a small band of men absconded with a frigate loaded with gold and escaped to Perdido Bay to attempt a new life of honesty and morality. Lafitte searched for the traitors for years but never found them or the frigate they prudently sank somewhere deep in the bay.

Knowing pirates plied the same waters where they fished, sailed and skied gave the Perdido folks a proud sense of intrigue. Celebrating Harold Caine was bold and defiant at the same time and added spice to the festivity. Tradition dictated that the location of the party change each year. Being somewhat of a historian and secret wannabe pirate Carlton Lyons started it all off by hosting the first Harold Caine function. After that, it moved to Witchwood, Paradise Point, Cantafford, and so on and so forth. As it turned out, Marlow and Lottie Loxley were next in line to put on the Ritz.

Even though Trout's mama preferred to ride herd on her kids rather than mingle with neighbors over drinks and cheese, hosting the Legend of Harold Caine party was an honor no one passed up. The event rivaled Fourth of July festivals and New Year's Eve bashes. Everyone came—children and adults—and brought abundant food and drink. Big Johnny Showers and Freddie had brought two bushels of fresh vegetables and helped Miss Lottie set up the tables and chairs. He was happy to help because she'd kept her promise and had been tutoring Freddie. The boy was catching on to reading and spent more time looking at those books than throwing bones to White Boy.

The party was bittersweet for Danny that summer. He looked forward to the festivities but felt kind of lost without Will or Trout. They always had a good time stuffing themselves until they hurt with barbeque, shrimp, fish, coleslaw, hush puppies, corn and all kinds of desserts. And he was certain Mrs. Loxley would churn out some of the finest homemade peach ice cream ever.

After they'd overeaten to their satisfaction Trout would always say, "Boys, my belly is as tight as a tick's." Then they'd find a strategic hammock where they could stretch out and bet on which adults were going to drink too much and make fools of themselves.

My money's on Carlton Lyons this year, Danny thought, *'cause that Monroe Miflin's pretty much ruined his summer.*

Shaded by a dozen live oaks, the Loxley's yard was a perfect setting for a group of a hundred friends and family. It faced west for spectacular sunset viewing and Mrs. Loxley dotted the lawn with round tables draped in colorful tablecloths and rose-shaped candles. For the most part the yard was level until it finally sloped off to a wide beach decorated in bushy palms and tiki torches. When night fell, they lit the torches and some Coleman lanterns fitted with yellow, red and pink glass. The lanterns simulated the colors of the rainbow and cast a festive glow on the partiers as well as the overhanging tree limbs. A six-piece brass band from Mobile played the Big Band tunes of Jimmy Dorsey, Benny Goodman, Duke Ellington and the like, capping off another wonderful summer.

Guests began arriving as the sun was reaching for the horizon and the smell of barbeque and fish simmering on the grill filled the air. Marlow Loxley had generously stocked his bar with a variety of liquor, mixers and cold beer. Always the first to come and the last to leave, Wallace Flomaton, made a B-line for the vodka and topped off his glass. Predictably, he began the evening telling fishing stories and ended it singing raunchy seafaring ditties that were guaranteed to run off the women. As the crowd gathered—Mr. Walt and Mrs. Kitty, Doc Jordon, George Randolph, Carlton Lyons and the rest of Perdido—Wallace spun a tale about catching giant tuna using rope wrapped around oil drums. Feeling lonely, Danny eased over to listen.

Wallace stopped his story in midstream. "Hi Danny. Where's your cousin Will?"

Danny lowered his eyes. "He went home already."

"Oh" Wallace replied continuing his dialogue without a second thought.

All evening, everyone had the same question for Danny, and eventually, he got tired of answering. Will was in Montgomery and that was that. He was gone for the summer. End of story.

Carlton Lyons picked up on Danny's mood and decided he'd help made things better. Danny was sitting on a stump looking out over Soldier Creek when Mr. Lyons approached.

"Hi Danny," he said. "I'd like you to meet some friends of mine."

Danny spun around and saw a man and woman dressed a lot like Mr. Lyons. She was wearing a pearl necklace and a white linen dress. Her husband sported seersucker shorts, white shoes and silk shirt. Danny thought that must be what country-club folks dress like. In fact, he was correct.

"Danny," Mr. Lyons said. "These are the Farbers from Mobile, and this is their son, Rodney. Y'all are about the same age. We thought you should get to know one another."

Danny tried to hide his shock. "Uh, we actually met a few days ago Mr. Lyons."

"Oh, well that's even better. I figured you might have, since the Farbers have a place in Gulf Shores. That's why I invited them over tonight."

"That's good," Danny said.

"And, by the way, Rodney is on the swim team at the country club."

"That's what I heard."

Mr. Lyons turned to Rodney and his dad. "Danny and his cousin,

Will, and their friend, Trout, are pretty fine divers in their own right. In fact, they might come for the Labor Day swim meet."

A look of shock splattered across their faces. "To Mobile? At our country club?"

"Of course," Mr. Lyons said. "Where else?"

"You don't mean to compete, do you?" Rodney asked. "I mean, they're just going to watch, right?"

"Watch? Well hells bells son. No, they're going to compete. They're good divers. I think membership at the club will be duly impressed."

The Farbers shined their best plastic smiles at Danny. "That's nice," Mr. Farber said. Rodney wore his familiar arrogant sneer and rolled his eyes at Danny.

"Well good," Mr. Lyons said, "since y'all already know each other we'll leave you be to talk about diving and things."

As they walked away, Rodney looked at Danny. "Where's your butt head cousin?"

"He's back in Montgomery."

"Too scared to stay around and face me, huh?"

"I don't think so."

"So you really think you can come to my country club and compete against real divers?"

"We'll see," Danny said coolly.

"That we will. Too bad your cousin is scared of getting beat. I'd sure enjoy showing him up."

"Hey Rodney," Danny smiled. "Guess who invited me to the meet?"

"I was assuming Mr. Lyons did. He's a founding member. He can get anyone in, even country bumpkins."

"Wrong buckaroo. Grace asked me to be her special guest."

That tidbit actually shook Rodney up. For a moment, he was speechless.

"Well then, I'll just have to show her who the best diver really is. Maybe that will change her mind."

Danny's smile grew. "Don't count on it."

Rodney grumbled under his breath, turned and walked toward the Loxley's house. He needed an ice-cold glass of coca-cola. Danny watched him slink away then spin back around. With fire in his eyes he said, "We'll see how you do on my home turf. I'll promise you one thing; I'm going beat your butt in that diving competition. And if your redneck cousin has the guts to come, I'll kick his butt, too."

Danny felt pretty proud of himself for knocking Rodney down a peg or two. As Rodney disappeared into the house, Danny fetched a bowl of peach ice cream and watched the adults get silly. But it just didn't have the same zing without Will and Trout to giggle with so he took to spying on Hunter, Gar and Willie Loxley sneaking beer out of the cooler. They'd been quite successful and had crawled deep into a stand of palmetto bushes where they could swig the cold brew without getting caught. For a moment, Danny thought about hinting to Mr. Walt to check into the palmetto bushes down by the Loxley's tool shed. But he figured the grease trap job was punishment enough for stealing Mr. Lyons's little *Whaler* and ruining a week's worth of high-speed boating. Instead of causing a scene, Danny decided to keep a low profile and go for a solo cruise on the minibike. With Mr. Walt's help and some duct tape, Danny had rigged up a flashlight on the handlebars. He'd also salvaged an old bicycle basket and mounted it up front to hold towels, a sack lunch, a change of clothes, or whatever else he needed to carry. The basket had worked out well, but the light beam bounced around wildly when he zipped along the bumpy dirt roads. Going fast in the dark didn't set too well with Danny anyway. So he ambled over to the minibike for a slow cruise through the woods. On a dark night, that was still exhilarating.

To everyone in attendance, the Legend of Harold Caine seemed to be going along as smooth as silk. What no one knew, except for the Loxleys, was that their house had been plagued by raccoons all week. To make matters worse, one of the coons had babies living under the cottage.

They discovered the problem one morning when some food had been snatched right off the kitchen counter. After interrogating their kids, all of whom denied being the thieves even after a good whipping, the Loxleys determined that coons might have done the deed. The large round hole in one of the screens that had just appeared also pointed to wild coons. Of course, Mrs. Loxley didn't put it past her boys to make the hole themselves as an alibi.

Not being around his kids very much, Mr. Loxley was more trusting. So the next night he had his boys hide the food in the cabinets.

Low and behold, the coons were smart enough to open the cabinet doors with their dexterous little hands, eat until they were full and spread crackers, cookies and bread all over the kitchen floor. Not to be outsmarted by a bunch of varmints, Marlow Loxley fastened the cabinet handles with ropes the next night. When he entered the kitchen the next morning, he was pleased to see the ropes still in place. Coons were wily critters but no match for a good boater's knot and strong rope. However, when the clever little buggers figured out they couldn't get into the cabinets, they simply opened the refrigerator and dragged out an entire ham. All they left was a bone and a puddle of juice.

That's when Mr. Loxley got his dogs involved and his shotgun ready. Coons sneaking into the kitchen and eating crackers and cookies made an amusing story. But when they went after his ham, they had to die.

"Make sure you hang those car keys on a high hook," he told his wife after the ordeal. "Or those damn coons might take our car for a joy ride." At least he kept his sense of humor.

As the party night approached, the Loxleys shuffled their food into the high cabinets and propped a heavy chair against the fridge before they went to bed each night. They sent their dogs under the house to chase the coons away, which seemed to solve the problem. Or so they thought.

Danny slammed on the brakes when his flashlight reflected off two pairs of red eyes.

"It's either a couple of possums or coons," he whispered to himself.

As he eased closer, he saw something he'd never seen before, two young raccoons as cute as kittens, curled up in a stump hole. They were shivering and looking up at him with longing eyes. Abandoned by their parents that either had run off or gotten chewed up by the dogs, the coons were all alone, just like Danny. And they tugged at his heart. As he approached, the babies didn't run. Instead, they reached up, wrapped their hands around his fingers, and let him pet them.

He took off his t-shirt and made a little bed in the basket. "I'll take y'all home and take care of you. I'll name you Will since you're the biggest and you'll be Trout since you look like you might just like to wrestle."

After he got them situated, Danny decided he needed more

padding in the basket for the bouncy ride home. Hanging by the Loxley's outdoor shower were several towels that fit the bill. He eased the minibike slowly to the side of the house and made a cushy bed for the little coons.

It wasn't that Danny underestimated a dog's sense of smell. He never really knew the kind of almighty reaction dogs would have when they caught a whiff of live coon meat. As he flung his leg over the minbike, two giant black Labrador retrievers bolted from under the cottage with their jaws chomping and howling to high heaven. Luckily, Danny had kept the engine running. With a quick jerk, he cranked on the throttle.

Lots of crazy events had occurred at the Legend of Harold Caine parties over the years. At least one person fell off the dock every year and sloshed around like a lame cow. The barbeque grill caught on fire one year and burned up an entire pig. There had even been a few fistfights, mostly between folks who'd had too much to drink. And everyone would always remember the night Wallace Flomaton got knocked out with a paddle when his third wife caught him in the bushes with the woman who eventually became his fourth wife. But no one, not in their wildest dreams, ever expected to see Danny on a minibike roaring through the oaks trees and dodging tables with his legs sticking straight out fending off two yelping dogs.

When the black hounds had jumped out from under the Loxley's house, Danny had two choices—outrun them or outmaneuver them. Unfortunately, a 3.5-horsepower Briggs & Stratton engine didn't have the *umph* to outrun purebred dogs, and Danny knew it. So he elected to race for the lights of the party in hopes that someone might jump on those dogs.

As he rounded a tree, Danny pointed the bike right at several partiers. "Grab those dogs," he yelled as he buzzed right past them. It took folks a moment to realize what was going on. Then one of the dogs jumped up on a table, knocked a lantern over and the tablecloth immediately burst into flames. As one of the labs galloped past George Randolph, it slammed into the man's knees and toppled him over. Wallace Flomaton lunged for the dog but his reaction was four vodkas too slow and he skidded face first into an oak tree root. Somehow, he didn't spill his drink. The band stopped playing when Danny cut a circle around them and both dogs squirted through the trumpet player's legs and sent him flying into the air.

Everything was happening so fast that no one noticed the two raccoons in the basket. Nonetheless, the young coons were apparently having the time of their lives. Standing on their hind legs with their heads sticking up, their eyes bulging wide and their little hands gripping the front of the basket, those little critters were sure enough smiling. With the fur on top of their heads blowing back and the colorful glow of Coleman lanterns reflecting in their eyes, the coons chirped, chattered, and decided that their new mama was a barrel of fun.

Some of the women and children screamed, but most of the crowd laughed wildly at the bizarre scene. Johnnie Showers finally caught one of the dogs by the back of the neck. At the same time, Hunter, Gar, and Willy—tanked up on beer and giggling uncontrollably—jumped on the other dog and wrestled it all the way down to the beach. Danny eventually eased the minibike to a stop, and the coons curled up in their new bed and appeared to go to sleep. All of the action had worn them out.

Mr. Walt threw a bucket of ice on the flaming tablecloth and shot a look at Danny. "What the hell have you got?" he asked.

"Couple of baby coons."

Mr. Loxley ambled over to inspect the coons.

"Those must be the coons that were under our house," he said. "The dogs probably ran off their mama."

With his most pitiful face, Danny looked at Mr. Walt. "Can I keep 'em, Daddy?"

"We can take 'em home and try to save 'em," Mr. Walt said. "But they're mighty young. They might not make it."

"Thanks daddy. I promise I'll take good care of 'em."

"That's fine but once they get healthy you've got to put 'em back in the wild."

"I know. And I will. But how long can I keep 'em?"

"I don't know. We'll have to see."

"Can I go home now? I want to make 'em a bed and get some food ready when they wake up."

"Sure son. When you get home, put that towel in a box with a bowl of water and a bowl of milk on the back porch. I'll check on 'em when I get in tonight."

With a giant grin, Danny putted down the Loxley's driveway. He couldn't wait to tell Trout and Will, the boys not the coons, about his adventure and their new namesakes. Now he had some friends to play with.

"Y'all are gonna be just fine," he said.

The brief period of pandemonium at the party had passed as quickly as it had started. Besides some ruined food, a burnt tablecloth and shocked guests, everything was back to normal except that a new Legend of Harold Caine story was imprinted into the local lore. After watching the scene, the Farbers were even more convinced that bringing these local boys to the Mobile Country Club was an extremely bad idea.

From the front porch, Lottie Loxley surveyed her yard. Marlow and Mr. Walt had dragged the burned up table into the fire pit and folks were crowding back around the food tables and the bar. She walked to the band and instructed them to strike up the music.

"Let the party continue," she announced. "And the bar is open. After all that excitement, Lord knows we need it."

"I'll drink to that," Wallace said, holding a handkerchief up to his bloody lip. "You know, during the war, the English used gin to clean out wounds. Do you happen to have any of that?"

"Right here, Wallace," Lottie said. "Help yourself."

Danny eased through the woods with little Will and Trout resting peacefully in his basket. Whenever he sped up, they'd pop up on their hind legs and get into their riding position. He figured they liked to feel the wind blowing across their pointed noses, just like he did.

CHAPTER 36

Country Club Surprise

Country clubs are for sissies.
—Will Stapleton

Carlton Lyons was directing. The role suited him.
"Cookie," he said with gentle authority, "when y'all finish mowing the meadow, take the tractor and pull those dead pine trees into a pile and burn 'em."

"Yes, sir, are you sure you want me to set 'em on fire today?" Cookie asked.

"Yeah, let's get it done."

Cookie paused respectfully. "Uh, Mr. Lyons, don't you think it's a might windy today. I'd hate to catch all them woods on fire."

Carlton Lyons placed his hand on his chin and gazed into the high branches of the pine trees. Strong gusts from the southeast were whipping the limbs so hard that pine needles were raining down on them.

"You've got a good point there, Cookie. Let's wait for a day when it's not so windy."

"Good idea," Cookie smiled. He knew Mr. Lyons mind was always full, juggling his complex life of family, work, employees, boats, heavy equipment and social obligations. Sometimes he didn't focus on the present task like Cookie did. He looked at every angle, a talent that had kept him as Carlton Lyons's right hand man for many years.

As he buzzed down the sandy road from Paradise Point toward the Lyons' Den, Danny spotted Mr. Lyons, Cookie and his crew ruminating about pine trees. Veering off the road, he pointed the minibike across the grassy meadow.

"He loves that minibike," Mr. Lyons said.

"Yes, sir, he sure does," Cookie laughed.

Danny skidded to a stop next to Mr. Lyons. "Hey, how're y'all doin'?"

"If things get any better I'll have to hire somebody to enjoy it with me," Mr. Lyons smiled.

Cookie glanced at him. "I thought that's why you hired me."

"You're right Cookie. Exactly right," Mr. Lyons laughed. "So Danny, what's on your mind?"

"Well I don't want to interrupt your work."

"Not at all son. Out with it."

"Well, you know how I've been working on my gainers and one-and-a-halfs and all that?"

"Yes, and you're really coming along."

"Well, the thing is, there's this girl …"

Cookie slapped his knee. "You got a girlfriend? You a little young for that, ain't you?"

"I guess I'm kinda young, but she's real pretty."

"Well," Mr. Lyons said wryly, "as long as she's pretty, it's okay."

"Prettier the better," Cookie said. "But them pretty ones is dangerous, too."

"Dangerous?" Danny asked.

"Yep, 'cause all the other boys is after her. You just be yourself, be good to her, and she'll stick by you. If she don't, she ain't worth it anyhow."

"I'll try," Danny said. Talking about girls embarrassed him, but there was no turning back now. "Anyway, this girl, her name is Grace Garland, asked me over to Mobile to their big swim meet this weekend."

"That's wonderful," Mr. Lyons said. "I know the Garlands. They're members of the club. And she's been around The Point this summer, right Danny?"

"Yes, sir. She thinks I can win some trophies, and prize money too, in the diving competition."

"I'm sure of it," Mr. Lyons said. "You're a shoo-in."

"I never been in any diving contests," Cookie said. "But you, Will, and Trout can work that diving board over pretty good."

"Thanks, Cookie. I appreciate that. I hope we're better than that, I mean, better than those boys from Mobile."

"You'll do fine," Mr. Lyons said.

"Uh huh," Danny mumbled trying to figure out how to ask for a ride. "Well, Mr. Lyons, since you're kinda our coach and all, I was hoping that, uh, that maybe, you'd, uh …" Danny stammered, struggling to ask the question.

Carlton Lyons was honored. "Danny, I'd love to," he said, interrupting Danny's stuttering. "I mean, I guess you're asking if I'll come over and help coach you."

"Uh, yes, sir, that's part of it."

"What's the other part?"

"Well, I haven't asked Daddy if he'll take me over there. You know, he hates to go to Mobile."

"Oh, so you'd like a ride over there?"

"Well, you are my coach."

"That's true. But are you sure Mr. Walt doesn't want to go? He might want to see his son compete."

"Yes, sir, he might. But I wanted to have a backup plan just in case he says he can't take me."

Cookie slapped his other knee. "That girl must really be a wild-cat!"

Danny envisioned a bobcat, something he'd encountered a few times in the woods. "I don't know about that Cookie, but she's mighty pretty, like a beauty queen or something."

"I tell you what, Danny. I'll be happy to ride you over to Mobile. However, after that incident with my little *Whaler,* you'd better ask your father first. If he can't do it, then you tell him you want to ask me for a ride. If Mr. Walt is okay with all that, I'll give you a ride and coach you, too."

"Thanks, Mr. Lyons. Thanks, Cookie. I really appreciate it."

Danny yanked on the pull cord, twisted the throttle and took off.

"There sure is a lot going on in that boy's head," Cookie said.

"When girls are involved, there always is a lot going on."

"Yes, sir. That is a fact."

Back at *Paradise Point*, Mr. Walt was doing plenty of directing of his own. When Danny cruised down the driveway, he couldn't understand why their *Glaspar* boat was hanging in midair from a massive oak tree limb.

"Tie those ropes off tight boys," Mr. Walt was saying. "I don't want this boat to fall on top of you and crush you flat as a pancake."

Knowing from lots of experience not to interrupt his daddy during one of his bizarre work projects, Danny sat on the minibike and watched. He figured if he studied on it long enough, he might figure out how they suspended the boat four feet off the ground.

"Y'all get those scrapers and start knocking the barnacles off," Mr. Walt said. "I'll hook up the hose so you can wash it down."

Danny began piecing the puzzle together when he noticed the trailer hooked behind Mr. Walt's car. Apparently, they'd parked the boat under the limb, hoisted it up a couple of feet with ropes then pulled the trailer out so they could clean the barnacles off. That had to be it. They usually scraped barnacles when the boat was in the water but this time Mr. Walt had a grander plan.

"When you boys get all the barnacles off, dry off the bottom with some towels then take this 80 grit sandpaper and smooth out the hull real well."

When Danny spotted the painting supplies stacked at the base of the oak tree, everything became crystal clear. Anti-fowling paint was the latest creation of science. Instead of having to hack at barnacles every few weeks, the toxic paint repelled all forms of sea life, keeping boat bottoms clean for as long as a year. Despite the fact that Mr. Walt had a free labor force to scrape and clean that old *Glaspar* daily, if necessary, he was boldly embracing new technology. Of course, cutting down on the workload had nothing to do with painting the bottom of the boat. For Mr. Walt, it was all about speed. He liked his boat to go faster than everyone else's, especially Carlton Lyons's boat. Barnacles, even a few of them, slowed him down. New-fangled bottom paint not only kept the *Glaspar* barnacle free, but it helped him outrun other boats. And nothing made him happier than passing a fancy, expensive boat.

When Mr. Walt got the four teenage boys laboring on his boat project, he marched forward to the next task—patching a leak in the roof that he and Hunter had missed with the hot tar. Drippy pinholes in a tin roof were part of life at Perdido, but at midday in August, the depths of hell were cooler than melted tar on a hot tin roof. Danny didn't want any part of mopping black tar so he caught Mr. Walt between hanging boats and spreading goop.

He ran up behind Mr. Walt and tugged on his shirt. 'Daddy, can I ask you something?"

"Huh? Oh hi, Danny. What is it?'

"Well, I was wondering …"

As Danny spoke, Mr. Walt was distracted by all the work going on. He looked up at the roof to see if the boys were prepping the area for the hot tar application. He turned back to check on the barnacles scrapers. He checked his watch.

"Un huh," he mumbled.

"I was just thinking about …"

"About what Danny? Spit it out. We have work to do son."

Danny realized that he'd picked a bad time to ask a favor. "I was wondering why the boat is hanging from the tree."

"We're gonna paint the bottom. In fact, why don't you get over there and help them scrap those barnacles."

Danny realized he'd blown it. He had traded wind-in-the-face, minibike fun for bleeding-knuckle barnacle scraping. Of course, life changed like the wind when Mr. Walt was in command. As he chopped at a hunk of barnacles, Danny figured he'd be better off asking Miss Kitty about a ride to Mobile.

That evening when folks were beginning to relax after dinner Danny appealed to his mama. She agreed to ask Mr. Walt but didn't have high hopes. "You know he hates leaving Perdido," she said. "Especially right before we have to pack up and go home."

"Mr. Lyons said he'd take me," Danny said, "if daddy doesn't want to."

The implication irritated Miss Kitty. "It's not that he doesn't want to, it's just that we won't be back down until Thanksgiving and we have a lot to do around the house."

Danny stood up defiantly. "That's fine. Then I'll just go with Mr. Lyons. He'll be glad to take me." The swim meet was his big chance for glory and he'd hoped for a little support from his parents.

"We'll see," she said sternly.

"Whenever you say 'we'll see' it just means you'll say 'no' later," Danny said.

"Not always."

"Every time I can remember."

"That's enough disrespectful talk from you young man. You've had a wonderful summer and your daddy has taken you shrimping and fishing countless times. You need to straighten up right quick or you won't be going to Mobile at all."

Danny sulked away. He knew she was right but missing his best buddies had put him in a bad mood. The next morning Mr. Walt stepped into the Back House while Danny was still sleeping.

"So what's this I hear about a diving competition?" he said loudly.

Danny jerked up in his bed to see Mr. Walt sitting on Will's bed, puffing on a fresh Dutch Masters. The room was half-full of smoke.

"Mama told you?"

"Yep, all about it."

"I really want to go."

"I think you should go. And if Mr. Lyons hadn't offered to give you a ride, I'd be glad to take you myself."

Danny believed his daddy but questioned the depth of his sincerity. Mr. Lyons had given him an easy way out. "I know you would daddy," he smiled. "Thanks."

"So you're gonna get to ride in Carlton's fancy car, huh?"

"I guess so."

"Just be sure to bring us back a blue ribbon and some good stories."

"I will but I wish you and Mama could come."

"Me too Danny but we've got too much to do this weekend. We've got to put the boat in the shed, fasten all the shutters and board up in case a hurricane comes in September or October."

"I know."

"In fact, I was expecting you to help out but you're going to be gone all day."

"I'll do my share before I leave. I promise. And double when I get back."

"That's what I wanted to hear."

When the big day arrived, Danny was more excited about riding in Mr. Lyons's Lincoln Continental than the swim meet. The air conditioning was just the beginning. The car had electric windows, leather seats and a little dial on the speedometer that Mr. Lyons turned to eighty miles-per-hour.

"It's called cruise control," he told Danny.

"What does it do?"

"It keeps the car at whatever speed I set it even if I take my foot off the accelerator."

Danny stared at all the gadgets and gauges, and he wondered if he would ever figure out how to drive a car. Then he spread out on the gray leather and just enjoyed the ride as the world whizzed by. He thought about Will and Trout and wished they were with him. Their companionship was the security blanket he needed right now. As nice as Mr. Lyons was, the two of them were a strange pair—an old man and a kid driving to Mobile together. The whole event was beginning to bother Danny, and his hands started to sweat when he thought about being around all those snotty country-club folks. A weird squeamishness he'd never felt before brewed in his stomach.

Cooling his palms on the cold air blowing from the vents helped but he was having second thoughts about the diving competition. A concrete pool and a fiberglass diving board was a far cry from the old wooden board with a burlap mat he was used to at The Point.

"You worried?" Mr. Lyons said.

"Un huh, I mean, yes, sir."

"It's perfectly normal to be nervous."

"My tummy feels weird."

"That's called butterflies. It feels kind of like they're flying around inside your stomach, right?"

"Yes, sir. Have you ever had butterflies?"

"Are you kidding? When I was competing, I was always nervous. Even when I was Alabama state champion and defending my title, I was scared."

"What did you do?"

"I just thought about how hard I'd trained and how long I'd been diving. I knew I was an excellent diver and I just had to remind myself of that. You need to believe in yourself. That's the key."

"Do you think I'm good?"

"I wouldn't be in this car with you if I didn't. Danny, you do this stuff everyday. It's just diving. You've got to have fun with it."

"But it's a different diving board."

"It's a *better* diving board. You can go higher and spin faster.

You'll love it!"

"If you say so."

"Danny, diving is an individual competition. This is not tennis or boxing where you have an opponent. It's just you and the board. As long as you do your best, you can be proud of yourself."

"But will I win?"

"With the dives you're doing, if you perform well, you will win."

Danny smiled as he thought about getting a trophy while Grace watched and admired him. Mr. Lyons was right. Diving was something he loved. For the moment, his confidence blossomed.

The long, magnolia-lined driveway led to a three-story white mansion with six massive columns. Gleaming, new cars were parked everywhere and a crowd of people streamed through giant double doors. Danny's butterflies took flight.

Grace was waiting at the registration desk.

"Danny!" she squealed as she ran over and hugged him. "I'm so glad you came."

Danny was glad to see her but the foreign environment threw him off. Everyone was all dressed up and it was still summertime. They had their shirts tucked in and they were all wearing shiny shoes. At least Miss Kitty had dressed him in a collared shirt. But Danny had on his signature cutoff blue jeans and an old pair of flip-flops.

"Aren't you going to introduce me?" Carlton Lyons asked.

"Oh, I'm sorry. This is Grace Garland. Grace, this is Mr. Lyons, my coach."

"I met you once at Perdido," she smiled. "Thank you so much for bringing him."

"It's my pleasure, Grace. We're thrilled to be here. In fact, we came to win, right Danny?"

"Uh huh," he mumbled as he ogled at the enormous cut-glass chandelier in the lobby. He felt like everyone was staring at him and, in fact, most of the members were. Neither blue jeans nor flip-flops were allowed in the club. Someone on the Rules and Compliance Committee was going to catch hell.

Grace took him by the arm. "Let me show you around."

"I'll take care of all the paperwork, Danny. You kids run along."

For the next fifteen minutes, Grace introduced Danny to dozens of her friends, parents, and other competitors. For the most part, they were friendly, but friendly in the way folks are nice to puppy dogs. In their narrow minds, Danny was just a country hick. Their arrogance slapped his ego into a tailspin.

"Nice cutoffs," one of the boys said sarcastically. "Did you have to feed the hogs before you came over today?"

A group of teenagers cackled and scrunched their noses as if they had dead shrimp balanced on their upper lips. Danny just grinned and played along.

"Yeah," he smiled, "right after I fed the chickens and milked the cows."

"Don't mind them," Grace said. "They're a bunch of snobs."

"Uh oh, look over there. It's Rodney."

"Danny, don't worry about Rodney. He's been flirting with me a lot but I've just ignored him."

"Didn't he win a bunch of stuff last year?"

"Yeah, he won a couple of swimming races and the diving competition last year."

"He already hates me 'cause I'm with you. And if I beat him, he'll hate me double."

"Don't worry. It doesn't matter."

Trim, cultured and conceited, Rodney looked every bit of fourteen even though he was just twelve. Two years of rowing on the crew team had built an impressive set of muscles in his upper body and he was not shy about showing them off. While Danny's physique was honed by hundreds of hours swimming, pulling in shrimp nets, digging garbage pits and building slides at Pigland, Rodney towered over him. Danny wondered what he'd gotten himself into. The country-club boys didn't look like the sissies Will talked about.

"Guess who else is here?" Grace asked.

Danny turned to see Georgiana strolling over to give him a hug. "Hi Danny, have you talked to Trout lately?"

"No, I guess he's still up in North Alabama visiting his cousins."

"Yeah, I know. I've been writing him letters."

"Really? Has he written back?"

"A couple of times."

"Then you know more than I do."

"I wish he could have come for the swim meet today."

"Yeah, me too. I feel kinda out of place with all these country-club folks."

Grace squeezed his arm. "They're nothing special," she said. "I'll bet they wouldn't jump out of The Tree or go to the Spanish Graveyard at night."

"You're probably right Grace."

"Come on, let's go see the pool."

Danny had never seen anything so spectacular or so many people swimming in one place. With his mouth hanging open, he could only mutter two words. "It's big!"

"Olympic sized," Grace said, "second biggest in the state."

"Where's the biggest?"

"Up in Birmingham someplace."

"Well would you look at that?" Danny said. "It's a real life high-dive."

He'd been to plenty of swimming pools in Montgomery but never one with a high dive.

"Can I try it?"

"Sure," Grace said.

As he climbed the polished chrome ladder Danny's equilibrium was spinning. The height didn't bother him. Heck, The Tree was a good ten feet higher but he wasn't in Soldier Creek any more. Instead of osprey whistling overhead and the wind whispering through cypress trees, all he could hear was the sound of shrieking children echoing off all the concrete. The burning smell of burgers cooking and the sound of lifeguards blowing their whistles at wild kids were giving him a headache.

Standing up there was surreal, like being on display at the county fair. Incredibly limber, the fiberglass board seemed like it might launch him into space. He bounced up and down a couple of times and almost lost his balance.

"Hey Bumpkin," Rodney Farber yelled. "Show us how to do a nice belly flop."

Danny figured he could pull off a monster gainer from up there. That would shut that kid's smart mouth once and for all. But that would be foolish on his first high-dive experience. To play it safe, he decided a jackknife would be better. Plus, he remembered Mr. Lyons advice, "Never reveal your best dive until the end."

When Danny sprung up with all of his might, he rocketed into the clear blue sky. Every movement was exaggerated. Immediately he was off kilter. At the highest point in the dive, Danny began to roll too far forward. He abandoned the jack knife and quickly shifted into survival mode. Three quarters of the way around with his legs kicking spastically, he could hear kids in the pool laughing at him. All he could do was try not to get hurt. His pride was already shot.

Landing almost flat on his back knocked his breath out. A lifeguard dragged him out as Danny gasped for air. Grace waited at the side of the pool.

"Are you okay? That looked like it really hurt."

Danny smiled up at her and coughed twice. Rodney Farber stroked over. "Very nice, Bumpkin," he said. "The judges are going to love you."

"You said you wanted a belly flop," he grinned. "But I like back busters better."

"What a hick," Rodney said as he swam away.

Mr. Lyons strolled over to Danny. "That was quite a show," he said. "I'm glad you got that one out of your system. Now try that from the low board."

"Can I just rest for a minute?"

"Come on son. When you fall off, ya gotta get back on the horse. The competition is from the low board. That high stuff is just for show."

Just then, Rodney soared from the high board, flexing his muscles and performing a picturesque swan dive.

"That's how you do it," he yelled to Danny. "Grace, you better take little Bubba back to the farm before he hurts himself again."

"Shut up Rodney," she shot back.

All eyes were on Danny as he prepared to spring off the low board. The country-club crowd worried what this new boy might do this time. Mr. Lyons told him to relax and have fun. "Imagine you're at The Point," he said. "And you're trying to impress the girls."

That was all it took. Danny flew spectacularly through the air, touched his toes precisely at the peak of his arch, and just for grins, did a half twist at the end. His feet slipped into the water with the tiniest *bloop*. When he surfaced, he noticed an eerie silence. Parents who'd been paying top dollar for diving lessons stared with mouths agape. They realized Danny was going to be a powerful contender.

Rodney shot a stream of water through his front teeth. "He's just a stupid redneck. When the pressure's on, he's gonna choke like a dog on a chicken bone."

Danny spent the next hour getting used to the board and even flew from the high dive a few times. He was just starting to have fun when the loudspeaker crackled with the announcement, "fifteen minutes until the boys' twelve and thirteen-year-old diving competition."

The swarm of butterflies swirled back into Danny's stomach. The fun was over. Reality was setting in. Just barely twelve years old, Danny didn't know he had to go up against thirteen-year-olds, too. Mr. Lyons was smiling widely when he approached Danny with a paper bag. "You're gonna do just fine son. Here, I have something for you. Go put these on," he said.

Danny pulled a navy blue racer's swimsuit from the bag. Red and white stripes cut diagonals across the front.

"That looks real professional," Danny smiled. "Thanks. I like it."

"Look on the side," Mr. Lyons said.

Stenciled in white letters were the words, "The Point Club Diving Team."

"If you've got to wear one, you might as well look good," Carlton Lyons said with a grin.

Grace admired the swimsuit. "I still like your cut offs better," she said, "but that looks really nice. And guess what Danny? I have a present for you, too."

"You do?"

She opened a small cloth sack and pulled out a friendship ring identical to the one he'd lost.

"There are no jellyfish in the pool."

"I'll keep this one safe Grace. I promise."

Grace held her hand up proudly. The string ring was still intact. They touched rings and both giggled. "Good luck," she smiled.

As the competition got underway, Carlton Lyons patted Danny on the back. "Just have fun," he said. "And make us proud."

On his first of three dives, Rodney Farber hit another perfect swan dive. Apparently, that was his trademark. The judges smiled in approval as the crowd applauded. Others divers followed but none held a candle to Rodney. Most just did standard forward dives and some even bent their legs badly. "Frog legs," Mr. Lyons commented. A few kids tried back dives and two did embarrassingly awkward front flips.

When Danny stood on the board, he noticed that the crowd had gone quiet again. Their curiosity ran deep. On Mr. Lyons's advice, he closed his eyes for a moment and imagined *Greenie* pulled up on the beach at The Point along with folks drinking lemonade in the pavilion. Relaxed and confident, he took two steps, bounced and knocked out a textbook jack knife. There was something beautiful in its simplicity that captured the judge's attention. It appealed to classical tastes, illustrated poise and dispelled any notion that he was just a country boy.

For his second dive, Rodney faced backwards and eased out until he was gripping the board with his toes. He bounced up as straight as a flagpole and executed a flawless inward dive. Even more classical than a jack knife, the inward ranked high on the difficulty scale. And coming so close to the board added a twist of danger that the judges admired.

Instead of making him wither, the competition began to strengthen Danny. For their entire lives, he and Will had been trying to beat each other at everything from swimming across the creek to jumping off bluffs to every card game they knew. The competitive feeling was not only familiar but, surprisingly, it comforted him. A calm confidence filled Danny as he realized that this Rodney brat was the best the Mobile Country Club had to offer; yet he wasn't anywhere near as talented as Will. Danny was starting to believe Will's wisdom. Maybe they were just country-club sissies.

With his self-confidence brimming, Danny stepped up, bounced quickly and nailed a one-and-a-half. He held his tuck, opened at the precise moment and entered absolutely straight. The crowd went glacial. The judges were stunned. None of the other kids was even attempting that dive. With one dive left, Danny had bolted into first place.

As Grace beamed, Carlton Lyons cheered wildly, "That's showing them, Danny! Go get 'em son!"

Rodney didn't seem phased by Danny's heroics. On his final dive, the country club's favorite son tried a dive he'd only done successfully once. If he wanted to win, he had no choice but to ride the razor's edge. He calmly climbed onto the diving board and performed an extraordinary one-and-a-half in pike position. As he surfaced to a cheering crowd, Rodney pumped his arms in victory. The level of difficulty and the fact that he nailed the dive moved him into first place.

Danny's heart fluttered as he leaned in close to Mr. Lyons. "Should

I go for the gainer?" he asked.

"Follow your gut Danny. That's always best."

Danny took several deep breaths to build his confidence but his self-assurance was shaky. Rodney Farber had brewed up bad mojo. As Danny tried to focus on his final dive, he heard a strange rumbling in the crowd. He spun around and rubbed his eyes to make sure they weren't full of chlorine. Sure enough, walking right toward him were Trout, Will, Uncle Brew, and Aunt Eloise. Will and Trout were sporting black gripper bathing suits. The entire country-club membership was starring at the peculiar bunch.

"Howdy, cuz," Will said matter-of-factly.

"What's going on, Will? Where'd you come from?"

"Mama and Daddy brought me down. He's got a bunch of customers down here to call on, and Mama wanted to come to the country club."

"But why did you come? I thought you wouldn't be caught dead at a country club, especially in *that*," Danny said pointing at Will's swimsuit and the telltale bulge.

"Yeah, well, that's before I decided to show all these snobs who the best diver in these parts really is."

"But the competition has already started."

"We've got that covered."

"How? I mean, did Mr. Lyons sign you up?"

Will recognized the perplexed look in Danny's eyes. He'd seen it often. "Trout and I are special guests of the Felder's," he said. "Ellis invited us."

Danny spotted Ellis drinking a Coke at the snack bar. "She invited you or you invited yourself?" he asked.

"A little of both. Seems she's kinda sweet on me. Plus, I figured this is the best way to get that money I owe Mr. Lyons."

Carlton Lyons patted Will on the back. "That's mighty thoughtful of you son."

Danny was too young to understand that Dr. Felder's generous annual contributions to the country club gave him plenty of pull. A quick conference with the head judge secured Will and Trout as late entries into the competition. As one of the judges strolled over, Danny had a bad feeling in his stomach.

"Son," the judge said to Danny, "we're going to let Trout and Will here do their three dives since they're late entries. You can do your last dive after they're done."

"Okay," Danny gulped, wondering why he couldn't have just finished. He could feel his palms beginning to sweat and the butterflies flying up a swarm. Now all he could do was wait and watch.

When Danny first saw Will, he'd felt a sense of relief. Maybe he'd come to apologize for acting so childish and leaving Perdido without even saying goodbye. This could be their chance to make up, be best buds again and show everyone their diving skills. But as the pieces began falling into place, he realized that Will's intentions were to put on a show for Grace and whip him in the competition. What had begun as a glorious day had quickly slipped into the gutter.

Trout was up first. Despite Mr. Lyons's best advice, he figured he'd start off with a bang and hit the crowd with the gainer. All was going well until Trout whacked his head on the board so hard it knocked him silly. When he asked if he could take *Greenie* for a spin around the pool, Mr. Lyons decided to withdraw him from the competition. Will, on the other hand, ripped off three immaculate dives in what seemed like a minute and a half—a one-and-a-half, an inward dive and a gainer. With a look of cold intensity in his eyes, Will climbed onto the diving board and, without hesitating, launched into each dive. His performance was all business. The crowd watched in disbelief as this new kid from the country left poor Rodney in his wake. After the gainer, he climbed up the side of the pool, tossed a casual wave at the crowd and sidled next to Ellis. As he walked past Danny, he winked and smiled wryly. "Beat that!" he smirked.

The judges had put Danny in a nearly impossible position. The pressure had his stomach in knots. Mr. Lyons rubbed his shoulders.

"You'll do fine," he said. "Just relax."

Just then they heard more commotion coming from up in the bleachers. When he looked up, Danny's jaw dropped. Climbing toward the top row where Uncle Brew and Aunt Eloise were sitting were Wallace Flomaton, Mr. Randolph and, lo and behold, Mr. Walt and Miss Kitty.

"Go get 'em son," Mr. Walt cheered.

Wallace stood up and held his gin and tonic high in the air. "Hook 'em in the lip and reel 'em in Danny," he yelled.

As the Perdido folks hooted and hollered, the country-club crowd slid slowly away as if they were walking around a rotten catfish on the beach. But the cheers didn't stop. Walt, Brew and Wallace yelped like crazed foxes.

Having a cheering section re-energized Danny. The time had come to prove himself. He stepped onto the board repeating Mr. Lyons's words, "bounce, knee kick, spin and open." He glanced at Grace. Her smile was tense. Danny closed his eyes and replayed the gainer in his mind. In the distance, he heard a seagull squawk. As he cracked his eyelids and focused on the end of the diving board, he stepped forward. In one smooth motion, he bounced and flew ten feet into the air. The audience gasped as he spun slowly backwards, released his tuck and sliced into the water with perfectly pointed toes.

For several seconds the only cheers came from Grace, Mr. Lyons and the ragged Perdido crew. Then the rest of the crowd erupted. They didn't mind so much that their native son had been beaten by two guest divers. They just appreciated the beauty of Will and Danny's performances.

Rodney Farber clinched his teeth and hung his head. Not only was the prize money gone but a third place ribbon was the best he could hope for.

"Hey you!" Rodney yelled as Danny climbed the ladder. "You're still nothing but a hick from the sticks. And if Grace really likes you, she's no better than one of those farm animals you feed."

Danny's performance filled him with an irrational amount of confidence and he didn't take kindly to someone insulting his girlfriend. Even though Rodney was a half a foot taller and twenty pounds heavier, Danny spun around, planted his hands on Rodney's chest and shoved him into the pool.

"Watch what you say about my girlfriend," Danny yelled down at him.

In one motion, Rodney bolted out of the pool but Mr. Lyons was already there.

"Watch it son," Mr. Lyons said. "He beat you fair and square. Remember, gentlemen win with humility and lose gracefully."

Rodney stood up to Mr. Lyons for a moment but backed down when he realized he was causing a scene. As he stormed away, he looked back at Danny. "This is not over bumpkin."

There were no huge surprises when the judges announced the win-ners. Will narrowly defeated Danny to take the first place trophy and money. He bowed to the crowd, even though he still considered them a bunch of twerps. With a slight smile, Will accepted his fifty-dollar prize money and promptly handed it over to Mr. Lyons. The second place trophy was as majestic as anything Danny had ever seen. Even though he didn't win any cash, he was going to love having that trophy on the mantle piece back at Paradise Point.

As Will and Uncle Brew stood under the shade of an umbrella and sipped on Coca-colas, Danny eased over to try and mend a friendship.

"I'm glad you came," he said.

Will set his glass on the counter and moved closer to his daddy. "I'm just here to pay off Mr. Lyons," he said. "Anyway, we gotta go."

Grace glided over and smiled. "Hi Will," she said. "Why don't you bring your trophy inside and show it off to everyone?"

The last thing Will wanted to do was to be passed around the country club like some kind of circus freak. At least he'd showed Grace what he was made of.

"No thanks," Will said, "we're leaving. Come on daddy."

Brewton Stapleton had fully expected the competition to bring the boys back together but he didn't realize the depth of Will's resentment.

"You sure you don't want to hang around for while, son," Brewton said, "and celebrate your victory."

Will turned and walked quickly toward the exit. "No daddy. Let's go!"

Mr. Lyons watched Will and his daddy leave. "What's wrong with them?" he asked Danny.

"I guess Will is still mad at me."

"He'll come around eventually."

"You think so?"

"Sure he will Danny. Just give him some time."

"If you say so, Mr. Lyons."

Waiting in the lobby were Mr. Walt and Miss Kitty. He ran over and hugged his mama. Mr. Walt patted him on the back. "You made us proud, son."

"Thanks Daddy. I feel proud."

Grace hugged him. "That was just gorgeous."

"How about we all go out for ice cream?" Miss Kitty said. "Let's all go together."

"I know just the place," Grace told them.

"I didn't think y'all were coming Mama," Danny said.

"We wanted to, honey, but we had work to do."

"So we got up extra early and got our chores done," Mr. Walt said. "I'm just happy we could make it in time."

"I'm glad too," Danny smiled.

With the closest people to his heart surrounding him, Danny beamed with pride. From that day forward, Will and Danny were known around the Mobile Country Club as those amazing divers from Perdido Bay. And Danny was the kid who stole both second place and the prettiest girl in Mobile from Rodney Farber.

CHAPTER 37

Tumping Over

No good deed goes unpunished.
—Walt Thornton

Mr. Walt's attention to his weather radio was unwavering. He'd heard the alert as soon as they returned from Mobile. A tropical storm in the Gulf of Mexico had strengthened and was expected to become a hurricane soon. But, at that point, its destination was anyone's guess. Predicting the movements of hurricanes was pretty much voodoo science but one of Mr. Walt's credos, "err on the side of caution" was about to take action.

They were planning to leave for Montgomery the day after the diving competition so most everything had already been packed away. The *Glaspar* had been lowered from the oak tree onto its trailer and parked under the shed, the lawnmower was stored in the tool shed and all of the porch furniture had been pushed against the wall. Before he took on the monumental task of boarding up windows and tying down anything that might blow away, Mr. Walt wanted another opinion about where the storm's landfall might be. The closest thing to a mystic at Perdido, not including Ethel, was Wallace Flomaton.

"The wind is already picking up," he said to Miss Kitty. "I want to see what Wallace is thinking. He's usually right on the money, even when he's three sheets to the wind."

"If anybody knows the weather, it's Wallace."

"True. And I know one thing too; we need to postpone our trip home in case the storm comes our way. I want to be here so we can batten down the hatches."

Strong winds from the southeast were blowing twenty knots - no different than a typical gusty summer day. And the clear sky didn't indicate any danger. If he hadn't heard it first hand on the radio and seen the barometer dropping, Mr. Walt wouldn't have believed a storm was on the horizon.

He found Wallace Flomaton at his storage shed sweating like a field hand as he struggled to stuff a huge mainsail into a sail bag.

"Gimme a hand over here, Walt," Wallace said. "This is one unruly-ass-sail."

"Sure thing Wallace, are you just cleaning up or do you think that storm is coming our way?"

"What does it look like?"

"It looks like you're prepping for a storm."

"You got that right, Bub. It's coming."

"What makes you so sure?"

Wallace temporarily broke off his battle with the mainsail and grabbed a towel to wipe his brow. Picking up his coffee cup filled with a dark brew, Wallace straightened up and gazed southward. To someone who didn't know Wallace, they'd think he was just having a morning cup of java but Mr. Walt recognized the purplish concoction as grape juice and vodka. He'd seen it before.

"Ya see those high wispy clouds way out there to the southeast?" Wallace asked.

"Yeah, I see 'em."

"Well, if you watch them for a while, you'll see that they're moving west. That's the counter-clockwise motion of that storm. It's like a pitcher throwing a curve ball. The ball curves the same direction its spinning. So by my calculations that storm is heading west by northwest. That means it's coming right at us."

"But it's still early Wallace. Hurricanes have been known to veer northeast or even slide further west over toward Louisiana and Texas."

"True, but not this one."

"Why not?"

Wallace laughed. "A little birdy told me,"

"Huh?"

"All the birds are flying east Walt. They're getting the hell out of here."

"Then maybe it really will go to Louisiana."

Wallace took a slug of his brew and wiped his mouth with his shirtsleeve, smearing a blue streak across his cheek. "And monkeys could fly out of my butt, too. The thing is I've been watching the barometer dropping and the wind increasing all day. Those are tell-tail signs my friend. You need to listen to this old sea dog. It's coming."

"That's why I'm here Wallace."

"Then follow me. I'll show you something else."

As they walked toward a beat up, thirty-foot tall mast that now served as a flagpole and weather station, Wallace pointed to the wind vane mounted at the top.

"Gusts are almost at thirty knots now," he said. "This morning they were barely twenty. My bet is that we'll start getting hit hard by sundown."

Wallace motioned Mr. Walt to follow as he walked into his make shift office. Dozens of fishing and sailing trophies were strewn around on shelves, under piles of paperwork and across the floor. Some were being used as paperweights and more than a few first-place cups had moldy remnants of limes stuck in them. Hanging on the wall was an elaborate glass barometer mounted on a mahogany plaque—yet another first-place trophy.

"Lookie here," Wallace said as he squinted through his reading glasses. "The pressure has fallen two pounds since this morning. We're in for it, Walter."

As Wallace made his case, Mr. Walt felt his mind racing.

"I'll let you get back to work," he said abruptly. "I've got a lot to do."

"You want a drink for the road?" Wallace asked, smiling wildly. Looking into the sweaty face of a genius alcoholic caused Mr. Walt to pause. The strange drink had stained Wallace's lips and teeth purple and his eyes were blazing red. *If only Wallace could stare into the face of that storm,* Mr. Walt thought, *he might just scare the damn thing away.*

"No thanks, Wallace. I'll drink one with you after the storm."

"Suit yourself. Good luck."

By the time he got back to the house, the wispy clouds had moved considerably further west and the wind continued to pick up. Mr. Walt ripped off a whistle and within seconds, a gaggle of kids came running. Barking out commands like a sea captain, he had kids boarding up windows, moving furniture inside, filling jugs with water, gassing up the

Coleman lanterns and gathering wood for cooking when the electricity went out.

"Danny, I need you and Will," Mr. Walt stopped in mid-sentence, realizing Will was back in Montgomery, "uh, I need you to take *Greenie* around to Soldier Creek so we can pull her out of the water."

Danny was checking out the huge waves that had formed in the bay. "Daddy, I might need some help."

Mr. Walt looked around. Everyone was on assignment. Miss Kitty and Ethel were on the porch stripping sheets from beds. Time was running out and Mr. Walt was out of choices. He hurried over to Miss Kitty. "Sweetheart, can I ask you a big favor?"

"Sure honey."

"Danny has to take *Greenie* around to the creek but he needs someone to ride with him. Can you go?"

In a pinch, Miss Kitty could drive a boat, although it had been years since she had. She didn't hesitate when her husband asked for her help.

"If you need me," Miss Kitty said, "I'll do it."

"I'm going with y'all," Ethel demanded. "I ain't letting Danny and Miss Kitty go out there alone!"

Miss Kitty stood in front of her. "But you can't swim a lick Ethel. You should stay here."

"I don't plan on swimming. I'm just riding in the boat. Now let's go!"

Mr. Walt and Miss Kitty didn't even try talking her out of it. They didn't have time to argue, especially with someone as hardheaded as a mule.

Greenie rocked awkwardly as the unlikely threesome chugged away from the pier toward Soldier Creek. With an extra large pinch of snuff in her lip, Ethel hung on and prayed quietly. Miss Kitty smiled at Danny, "You're doing great, honey," she said calmly.

Danny had negotiated the five-minute ride around The Point into Soldier Creek hundreds of times but never in water so rough. Everything was going well until, in what seemed like an instant, the sky went black, a wall of cold wind slammed into them and the waves grew into giant frothy whitecaps.

Ethel screamed. "Oh Lordy, we gonna die."

Miss Kitty quickly slid next to her and put an arm around her shoulder. "We're not going to die Ethel. Danny can handle this boat."

Under the circumstances, Danny kept his composure. But when Miss Kitty sidled up to Ethel, trouble swooped in quickly. If she'd stayed on the windward side, *Greenie* would have made it. Instead, the boat leaned precariously to one side. Before Danny could tell his mother to move back, both women panicked and grabbed a hold of *Greenie's* railing. Danny tried to even out the weight but his seventy pounds was no match for two plump women in a fit of panic. As a savage gust whipped across the bay and a monster wave broke against *Greenie's* hull, she flipped like a buttermilk pancake on the griddle. The boat flooded with water and the three of them spilled out into the roiling waves. Miss Kitty lost her glasses and Ethel spit her dentures into the sea.

For a brief moment, there were deafening screams of anguish. Death and wretchedness were imminent—until they all realized *Greenie* had tumped over in only two feet of water.

"Gal durn it, boy," Ethel said as she stood up and threw a wet life preserver at Danny. "Can't you drive a boat? I lost my teeth."

"Sorry, Ethel," Danny whimpered.

Fortunately, Mr. Walt had been keeping an eye on the hapless crew. He arrived on the scene within a minute with Hunter and Gar. They dumped most of the water out of *Greenie* and dragged her onshore to try and save the engine. Even with an impending storm, Danny was able to have fun. He bodysurfed to shore on the huge waves, laughing all the way. Miss Kitty and Ethel locked arms but got knocked over repeatedly as they slogged toward the beach. Wet and cold, Danny scampered back to the house to huddle in the safety of a hot shower and hide from Ethel.

CHAPTER 38

Hurricane Beatrice

It's gonna rain harder than a cow peeing on a flat rock.
—Wallace Flomaton

The laws of chance demand that hurricanes strike at night. Daytime storms just don't carry the same impact. Complete darkness stirs up the adrenaline-churning fear that grips those unfortunate souls in the storm's path. Hearing fifty-foot tall pine trees snapping in half and metal roofing flying against buildings is especially frightening when you can't see what's happening. Witnessing destruction like that in daylight can turn your blood cold, but witnessing gnashing devastation on a cobalt night will flat out drive people crazy.

Hurricane Beatrice, as she had been named, followed Mother Nature's nocturnal traditions. Landfall was estimated to be around midnight and by late afternoon, as Wallace Flomaton had predicted, wind gusts were exceeding fifty knots. With water jugs filled, lanterns gassed up, candles at the ready, windows boarded up, boats under the shed, porch furniture pulled inside and ice chests full, all they could do was wait.

Unlike the wary adults, Danny welcomed the excitement. He'd never witnessed hurricane destruction first hand so the awesome rolling waves in the bay and growling winds were his reward for toiling all day. As he stood on the porch watching the onslaught battering at the pier, Hunter and Gar showed up.

"Mr. Walt wants us to try and save the pier," Hunter said to Danny.

"How 'er we gonna do that?"

"As it breaks up, we need to get in the water and pull the boards up on the beach."

"That sounds a little crazy," Danny said. "I'm in!"

Like a piano player starting at the first key and gingerly fingering his way to the other end of the keyboard, the waves smashed into the pier and rippled along its entire length until they crashed into the beach. They'd never seen the waves passing *through* the pier like that, shooting jets of spray up between the spaces in the boards.

"That's kinda neat," Danny said. "But I think some of the boards are starting to get loose."

"Looks like the deck at the end is about to go," Gar said.

"I don't know if we can save it," Hunter said, "but we're gonna try."

The pounding waves had lifted the deck off of the pilings but it stayed wedged in. Still in one piece, the deck lifted and shifted two feet with each passing wave. The boys ran down the front yard with a heavy rope and dived into the melee. They'd never seen the water so deep. Normally it would have been waist-deep but as each wave crested, their feet floated off the sandy bottom forcing them to swim against nearly impossible conditions. Gusts blew across the tops of the waves, whipping spray into their faces. From the beach, Mr. Walt directed them.

"Tie that line around the deck and bring it here," he yelled. "And watch out for nails."

As Gar secured the rope, Hunter pulled it to the beach. Danny clung to the corner of the deck as it rose high in the air and splashed down with a mighty crash.

"Ride it, cowboy!" Hunter yelled.

Outsiders witnessing the scene may have thought that the boys were risking their young lives to save a few sorry planks of wood but they had no fear in Perdido Bay, even in epic weather conditions. To the boys, hurricanes were just another way to milk more excitement out of life. And they didn't let that opportunity pass.

With the rope tied around his waist, Hunter swam to Mr. Walt. They slowly tugged the section of pier, along with Danny, to the beach.

"I'll tie it off to that pine tree," Mr. Walt said. "There's more decking coming off y'all need to fetch."

Once the integrity of the pier was undermined, it broke up quickly. Eight-foot hunks of the walkway were peeling off faster than the boys could retrieve them.

"Get the big pieces," Mr. Walt screamed. "We'll find the rest tomorrow."

And so, as always, they followed his logic. By the time they'd recovered more than half of the pier they were exhausted. The rest had washed down the bay, beyond their realm of safety. Mr. Walt secured the pier scraps to a huge pine tree, knowing full well that even mighty trees have uncertain fates in hurricanes. So he said a little prayer and hoped that God would spare that tree and keep his rope from snapping. The boys trudged up the hill to dry off and watch the last hours of daylight.

As he got to the porch, Danny had an idea. "Let's go up to the bluff and see how strong the wind is." Hunter and Gar looked at each other, grinned, and led the way. The pines were struggling against high gusts and the weaker limbs were beginning to snap. The south wind was blowing an updraft so strong that Gar stood on the edge of the bluff and leaned out over it.

"Look at this! The wind is holding me up."

With their toes gripping the edge of the bluff, the boys looked down at the churning bay forty feet below. They spread their arms and leaned against the wind.

"I think it's going to pick me up and blow me away," Danny yelled.

"Then don't let it," Gar said.

Hunter turned and ran back to Paradise Point. "I'll be right back," he said. A minute later, he appeared with a bed sheet tied to his ankles. He grabbed the other two corners of the sheet and spread it across his body.

"You look like a giant flying squirrel," Gar said.

"That's the plan," he said as leaned out further and further until he was almost perpendicular to the bluff. "Gar, I think I can fly!"

Normal kids who are concerned for their cousin's lives would have tried to talk some sense into Hunter. But if Hunter thought he could fly, Gar wanted to watch.

"Go for it!" Gar said.

Danny watched wide eyed as Hunter took five steps back and crossed his arms to collapse the crude flying machine. Without hesitation, he ran to edge, opened his wings and dived out into space. The sheer force of upwelling winds lifted him ten feet above the edge of the bluff then tossed him back into a giant wax myrtle bush. Even with multiple cuts and scrapes from head to toe, Hunter was proud. "That was so cool," he said.

"Me next," Gar yelped, as he yanked the sheet from Hunter before he could untangle himself from branches.

With considerably more caution, Gar leaned over the edge and jumped out, letting the wind blow him back to solid ground. Weighing half as much as Gar, Danny figured the wind might blow him all the way to Trout's house. He decided watching was enough fun for him. Gar and Hunter traded the sheet back and forth and came as close to flying like a bird as any boy ever had, with the exception of Trout on that parachute. As darkness crept in and the wind continued to build, they scrambled back to the sanctity of home, giddy with their feeling of weightlessness. The afternoon had been wild and wonderful—swimming in mountainous waves, tumping over in *Greenie,* and flying on a sheet in the wind. Yet, the exhilaration had just begun. A long night lay ahead, longer than they could ever imagine.

CHAPTER 39

In the Eye of the Lord

God gave you two ears and one mouth so shut up and listen.
—Ethel Brackin

Folks tend to make a lot of fuss about the eye of a hurricane, especially if they've been in one. Being completely surrounded by a swirling wall of killer winds and knowing there's no way out does not promote tranquility. Mr. Walt was less concerned about being in the eye than whether the eye was going east of Perdido Bay or west of there. As he was ruminating on their situation, Miss Kitty walked into the bedroom.

"What are you thinking about so hard honey?" she asked.

"The path of this storm ... I'm hoping it goes to our east."

She realized she was supposed to know such things but weather just didn't hold her long-term interests. "Why is that?"

"Because if the eye goes west of here, we'll get the full brunt of the winds out of the south. If the eye goes east, the wind will come from the north and we'll be protected by the trees and the bluff."

"Oh, I remember now," she said halfheartedly, hoping the storm conversation was over.

"Plus, if it goes east of us," Mr. Walt continued, "the winds won't be as strong because the hurricane will be moving away from us. Trust me honey, it won't be nearly as bad as getting winds from the south. That's a real double whammy."

"Uh huh," Miss Kitty said shaking her head affirmatively and pretended to understand. The truth was she regularly made a wrong turn on her weekly grocery run to the Winn Dixie, so hypothetical hurricane scenarios sounded a lot like foreign gibberish to her.

"Well then I hope it goes west," she said.

"*West*?"

"I mean east. I hope it goes east. That's what I meant to say."

"Right, we want it to go east," Mr. Walt said. Fortunately, he loved her for her kind heart and natural beauty.

When he walked outside for one final check on items that might need tying down or storing under the shed, Mr. Walt noticed that the hordes of squirrels that usually scampered through the trees had all vanished. Even the trees looked frightened. For a moment, he wondered what all the fish were doing. Probably heading out for deep water, he thought. Too many bad signs were adding up and as he stood in the waning light of day, he prayed for everyone's safety.

Vestiges of pink light disappeared from the horizon opening the door to ten hours of high wind, raging water and black night. Except for the sounds of howling gusts through the trees, they had a fairly calm dinner followed by a friendly game of hearts. Everyone felt relatively safe until they heard a horrendous crack and the house went dark.

"What was that?" Danny asked.

"Calm down," Mr. Walt said. "It was just a pine tree breaking. It must have fallen on the power line."

Danny had some kitchen matches in his pocket so he was first to light his candle. He passed the burning match to Ethel and Miss Kitty, who lit two candles while Mr. Walt got the Coleman lanterns going. Earlier that day, Danny and Gar had cut several jumbo tin cans in half to act as candleholders. With a few drops of hot wax to hold the candle in place, the cans threw off lots of light. They had even screwed old screen door handles on the sides so they could carry their torches without burning their hands. Mr. Walt had shown them the old tin can trick and they built a half dozen to pass around.

Under candle and lantern power, the kitchen and den were illuminated enough to continue the card games and calm everyone's nerves but every so often the wind would scream, another tree would snap and folks would squirm. As the night wore on, they tried to sleep but no one could. The constant noise and fear of the unknown kept their eyes wide. Danny and Miss Kitty, who could sleep through an atomic blast, finally managed to drift off and Ethel's head kept bobbing. But Mr. Walt had Gar and Hunter on high alert in case of emergency. Although the Back

House was not as well built, it was better protected from the wind so the contingency plan, in case the roof blew off of the main house, was to make a run for the Back House and pile in.

"Gar, shine the flashlight at the Back House," Mr. Walt reminded him every half hour. "And see if it's still in good shape."

By midnight, it had become clear that Wallace Flomaton was right. Mr. Walt's hopes of the eye going east were dashed. South winds were battering the shoreline and clocking more to the east. From all indications, Beatrice was knocking on their front door and taking Paradise Point head on.

Danny awoke to a loud banging coming from the porch. He stumbled out to find Hunter and Gar with sledgehammers pounding at the base of the four-by-four posts holding up the roof. He cocked his head for a closer look and realized the posts were pushed in more than a foot.

"What happened," he asked Gar over the screaming wind.

"The wind lifted up this side of the roof," Gar said. "When it came back down, the posts were crooked."

Just then, two more trees cracked in half and one landed across the roof directly over their heads. They all immediately dropped to the floor and, although the house shook, the trees didn't punch through the roof.

"Get inside," Mr. Walt yelled. "That's the best we can do."

As they escaped into the living room, Danny ran to the back of the house to check on little Trout and Will. The coons were sitting straight up with the eyes as big as quarters.

"It's gonna be okay guys," he said as he fluffed up their bedding. "We'll get through this, I promise."

They looked up through scared eyes and he noticed their little hands were shaking. Danny wished the real Will and Trout were there, but his new furry friends would have to do.

"Do you think the storm is hitting Perdido?" Will asked his daddy.

"It kinda looks that way son. It really does," Uncle Brew said.

"Have you ever been through a hurricane, Daddy?"

"Not really. I mean we've had them pass over Montgomery but they're a lot weaker by the time they get up here. I've never been on the coast when one hit."

"Is it gonna be bad? Do you think the house will get blown away?"

"Naw, son. Mr. Walt built that house like a Sherman tank. The winds will probably knock out a lot of screens and it might blow off some of the roofing but Paradise Point will make it through just fine."

"Good," Will said. "I love that house."

"Me too son."

The fact was Uncle Brew was worried sick about Mr. Walt, Miss Kitty, his son Hunter, and all the rest of the Perdido folks facing off against a savage hurricane but he didn't want Will to worry. That wouldn't help anything. There was already too much going on in that young mind of his. Will had been hoping to spend some time with his mama but she'd been so busy organizing the Junior League's fall ball, she didn't even have time to fix him his favorite lemon pie. And even though he had a shiny, first-place trophy up on the mantle—and it looked real nice up there—he was torn up inside over Danny. He kept trying to be angry with his cousin, but all he could think about was the wind whipping through the house, knocking trees over, and maybe killing somebody. Maybe even Danny. Will couldn't bear the thought, especially because there was nothing he could do to stop that hurricane. He just wished he and Danny had made up at that swim meet, but it was too late for that now.

That night, Will knelt beside his bed and prayed harder than he ever had.

"God, please protect my cousins and family at Perdido and, if you think I deserve it, I appreciate it if you'd forgive me for being such a jerk. I'm sorry. Amen."

Wallace Flomaton was trying to do some praying of his own, but he was mighty rusty at it. He wasn't sure he believed in the Almighty and for the life of him, he couldn't figure out how to talk to God without using four-letter words.

As he huddled in the bathtub shivering in fear, his roof creaked and moaned. A sudden a blast of wind ripped off a corner of his roof directly above him and heavy rains poured in. Thinking as hard as he could with a bottle of bourbon in his blood, he struggled outside to his boathouse for a tarp to cover the hole in his roof. The force of the wind knocked him down three times until he could only crawl on his hands and knees while hunks of debris flew over his head. He groaned in pain as sand blew horizontally off the beach and pelted his face. By the time he made it to the boathouse, he realized that he'd made a life-threatening blunder. No sooner had he gone inside did the entire roof rip off throwing sheets of metal into his house fifty feet away. The boathouse shook violently and suddenly the south wall peeled away. Falling rafters should have crushed him but gravity was no match for the wind. Huge pieces of boathouse were sucked into the dark sky.

With all of his might, Wallace hugged a piling and hung on. The fear of death had brought clarity into his mind and, finally, he found some words.

"Please God," he hollered against the howling wind. "Don't let me die here like an old fish washed onto the beach. I know I've done a lot of bad things and I'm sorry. I'm sorry for all of the women I've deceived. I'm sorry for all of the lying and cheating. I'm sorry for treating people like dirt and I'm sorry for being a drunk. That's right: I said it. I'm a drunk. A sorry, lying, cheating drunk."

Showers of water sprayed against his face, and Wallace stared at what he feared the most. Whipping like a severed fire hose, a swirling waterspout danced across the waves spraying a cone of water hundreds of feet into the air. The spinning white mist snaked against the black sky and the roar grew so loud his eardrums nearly ruptured. Helpless and hopeless, Wallace closed his eyes as the waterspout smashed against the boathouse and blew the remaining walls into a million pieces. Splinters dug into his arms and chest as the wind spun him around that piling. Seconds later a wall of water swept him away. As he lost his grip on the piling, he flailed in the raging surge of water and begged for his life.

"If you spare me God," Wallace screamed at the top of the lungs, "I'll never take another drink in my life. I'll be true to my wife and never cheat on her again. But God, just let me live."

And just like that, as if God really was listening, the wind stopped.

"I can't believe it," Mr. Walt said.

"Is it over daddy?" Danny asked hopefully.

"No son. Not hardly. We're in the eye."

Slowly, they all filed outside into the dead calm.

"Look up," Mr. Walt said.

Directly overhead, the sky was perfectly clear. A mass of stars twinkled above them and Orion stretched out proudly in the eastern sky. The air was thick and muggy; so still, that not even one pine needle moved. Danny wondered what it all meant.

"How long will it last daddy?"

"Not too long. Five minutes, ten, maybe more. I really don't know."

"What's gonna happen?"

"Well," Mr. Walt said. "The wind is gonna change. It's been blowing out of the south and east. When the eye passes, we'll get west winds."

"Is that good?" Danny asked.

"Not really son but it's better than south winds. Plus it means we'll be out of this mess by morning."

As they looked in the southern sky, they could see dark clouds swirling into the stars.

"That's it," Mr. Walt said. "Let's get back inside."

Mr. Walt shined the flashlight into a front yard he hardly recognized anymore. Dozens of trees were broken off or uprooted. Instead of a picturesque waterfront view, their cottage was now trapped inside of a pine thicket. Try as he might, he couldn't even see the bay. He figured the pier they'd saved was long gone. Before he went inside a flashlight beam caught his eye.

A voice called out desperately, "Hey Walt, are you there?"

"Over here," he yelled.

"It's me, Wallace."

Wallace scrambled through a tangle of fallen limbs

"I had a helluva time just finding your house," he stuttered.

"Wallace, what the hell are you doing out in this storm?"

"I had to come. My boathouse got washed away … while I was in it."

"Why in God's name were you down there?"

Wallace shuttered when Mr. Walt mentioned God.

"Well, part of my roof blew off, so I went down to get a tarp to tie down over the hole. All of a sudden, the boathouse got hit like a freight train, and a humongous waterspout smashed the place apart." Wallace's whole body was quivering and covered in cuts. A line of blood ran down the side of his face.

"The next thing I knew," he said, "I was tumbling along in the water trying to figure out whether I was upside down or right side up. I was grabbing for something, anything to hold on to, when my hand caught a tree branch. I pulled myself into that tree and hung on for dear life with the water swirling all around me."

"You're lucky to be alive."

"I figured I was on my way to meet St. Peter, or in my case, maybe the guy downstairs, if you know what I mean."

"So how'd you get out of there?"

"When I landed in that tree, the wind stopped and the water went down so I high-tailed it over here."

"Well don't just stand there, let's get you inside and into some dry clothes."

Wallace stumbled into the kitchen dripping wet and as disheveled as a stray dog. Shaking, confused and ashen, he'd lost his shoes and his shirt was ripped apart.

"Walt, ya got anything to warm me up, like uh, some coffee?"

"How about something stronger?"

Mr. Walt grabbed a coffee mug and started to fill it with straight bourbon.

"No thanks Walt," Wallace said. "Just coffee this time."

"You sure."

"Damn sure," Wallace said. "I was a gnat's hair away from being one dead-ass seaman, and I'm just happy to be alive."

"I'm just glad you didn't go down with the ship. We need you around here."

"I need me too," he said as he wiped the blood from him mouth.

Ethel sneered at Wallace. Even though she respected his fishing skills, she didn't like his evil ways. She'd seen him treat a lot of folks bad and, to her, that was downright un-Christian. Truth was, there were baskets full of reasons she didn't like the man.

"You need a towel to dry off Mr. Wallace?" Ethel asked.

"Thanks Ethel that would be great."

"The bathroom's over there," she said with a flip of her hand. "Go get one yourself."

Wallace was too disoriented to catch Ethel's attitude. He just shuffled to the bathroom and wondered if God had heard every one of his promises.

As the eye passed, the westerly winds shrieked for two solid hours. Trees that had been weakened by the first wave snapped like twigs and debris slammed against the house. Everyone had bundled together in the den, huddled under blankets and praying for the mayhem to end.

Finally, the gusts began to ease. Several hours over land had knocked some strength out of Beatrice leaving Perdido Bay on the outer reaches of her grasp. When morning came, a brilliant blue sky unfolded in surreal contrast to the total chaos left behind. Beatrice had wrapped up all of the clouds within two hundred miles and rambled north with the whole bundle. The atmosphere seemed to have been cleansed of evil but the earth was ravaged. Mangled islands of wooden debris—pilings, trees and chunks of piers—sloshed around in the bay and the shoreline had been rolled back like a sardine can. Downed trees numbered in the thousands along with pieces and parts of blown out houses—roof vents, siding, shingles, tin, furniture, clothes and an endless assortment of lawn decorations.

When Danny, Gar and Hunter ventured outside, Mr. Walt was already on the roof surveying the damage.

"Look at all those trees," Danny said.

"Must be fifty or more down," Gar replied.

"At least," Hunter said.

"Hey boys," Mr. Walt called down. "Grab the axes and the bow saw. First we need to get these two trees off the roof and then I want to clear a path to the water."

For the most part Paradise Point had held strong against Hurricane Beatrice. Being on a hill, twenty feet above sea level kept the storm surge from reaching the house. Besides some bent up metal roofing and a bunch of blown out screens, everything was intact. Other cottages, closer to the water, had been completely washed away.

The major effort ahead was clearing the dozens of pines as well as two huge oaks and three magnolias that had been blown over, roots and all. Mr. Walt wasted no time in setting the work force in motion. The boys stopped a few times to eat but spent pretty much the entire day hacking at trees and making humongous piles of limbs to burn later.

Miss Kitty and Ethel set furniture back out, helped take the boards from the windows and swept a million pine needles from the porch.

As everyone pitched in the cleanup effort, remnants of Beatrice's winds cut through the mugginess and gave them some relief from the heat. But as the day wore on the breeze petered out, giving way to oppressive humidity and a constant flow of sweat.

Under normal circumstances, folks at Perdido relied on the southern breezes to stay cool. At night, ceiling fans positioned directly over their beds kept them from melting into puddles of human goop. But Beatrice had stripped them of any and all ways to move air, and while they were happy that the hurricane-force winds were gone, they prayed for even a meager breeze to brush across their moist skin.

The lack of electricity knocked out the pump so running water for showers and toilets was just a pleasant memory. The boys were assigned to fill buckets by hand pumping the well so the women could have water to flush the toilets. Mr. Walt instructed the boys to pee in the woods and only use the toilet for big jobs. To everyone's dismay, the comforts and pleasures of Perdido had vanished. Their beloved Paradise Point had become a cluttered work camp with no end to the labor in sight.

"You boys collect some sticks so we can make some coals for Ethel and Miss Kitty to cook on," Mr. Walt said.

"This must have been what it was like a hundred years ago," Danny said. "No electricity, no running water, no ice, cooking on an open fire—they must have been miserable."

"You don't miss what you never had," Gar said. "They didn't know any better."

"Well, I'll be glad when everything is back to normal."

"Don't hold your breath."

It took several days for Mr. Walt and the boys to clear the trees from the driveway and hack a wide path to the water. That still left dozens of uprooted and broken trees all over the yard that would take years to remove. Mr. Walt had already decided to leave the downed trees in the woods where they fell to slowly rot away and disappear into the underbrush.

The smell of pine permeated the air, and in the distance, they could hear tractors grinding away, moving trees that had fallen across the road. As soon as they could, they picked their way through the woods to check on their neighbors. Witchwood's front porch had been ripped from the house and was half submerged in Soldier Creek. Two feet of water had swept through the Lyons's den, knocking out the front door and ruining all of Mrs. Lyons's fancy furniture. Luckily, the barn and guesthouse stood fast, so Mr. Lyons's equipment was gassed up and ready for action.

His boathouse, like every other pier in the area, was destroyed. Mr. Lyons had pulled his fleet out of the water before the storm hit, saving all his vessels except the little *Boston Whaler.* It had been swept off its trailer and ended up crashing though Doc Jordon's front porch, settling down in her living room. Virtually indestructible, the *Whaler* suffered a few scrapes and dings, but was still in one piece. Only the bow rail was damaged beyond repair from battering into Doc Jordon's house.

"Your damn boat did better than my front porch," she told Carlton Lyons. "I guess since it ended up inside my house, I get to keep it."

Mr. Lyons was at a loss for words. "I'm sorry, Doc," he said. "If that's what you really want."

"I want my house fixed, you old fool," she complained. "Not a beat-up boat."

"Don't you worry," he said, "If your insurance won't cover it, I will."

"I expect the hell you will," she said.

Like most communities in a head-on collision with a hurricane, no one escaped the damage. Some just got it worse than others. Everyone in the extended Perdido family was accounted for and, as it turned out, Wallace Flomaton had come closest to meeting his maker.

The worst destruction was to George Randolph's store. The place had been completely demolished. The pilings jutted up like crooked teeth and part of the roof dangled from a broken rafter. But the rest—all those groceries, gas pumps, the bar, the poker table—was scattered everywhere, wrapped around trees or washed a hundred yards inland. A dozen boats—shrimp trawlers, sailboats, and fishing boats—had lost their anchors and been pushed on shore. A forty-foot yacht that no one recognized was high and dry, mixed among the wreckage of Randolph's store.

When folks got their own houses in order, they pitched in to help their neighbors. Carlton Lyons and Cookie had four other men cutting trees and dragging them out of the dirt road with his tractor. In just two days, they'd cleared the road from The Point all the way to the county blacktop.

Even though the Perdido crowd had survived, they still had no way to contact the outside world. Everyone from Mobile to Montgomery worried that Perdido had been wiped off the map. Without telephone service, news of their fate floated in purgatory.

"I'm gonna try to make it to Mobile tomorrow," Carlton Lyons told Mr. Walt. "And get the word out that we're okay."

"Good idea, Carlton. Anything I can do to help?"

"Yes, if anyone needs my tractor or my crew, just let Cookie know and they'll help out.

"That's mighty generous of you."

"It's the least I can do."

Just then, Carlton slapped at his neck. "Damn biting flies," he said.

Mr. Walt whacked two off his ankle. "Damn it to hell," he said. "Isn't that just our luck? First, a hurricane whipped us. Now those damn biting flies are sucking our blood."

"Is the Lord trying to tell us something?" Mr. Lyons asked.

"Yeah, that we need to get our screens fixed," Mr. Walt chuckled.

"I hope that's all," Mr. Lyons said with a smile. "I'm beginning to wonder when the locusts are gonna swoop in and eat all the crops?"

"Yeah. Or maybe it's gonna rain for forty days and forty nights," Mr. Walt said.

"Or we're all gonna turn to salt," Mr. Lyons grinned.

"Well Carlton," Mr. Walt said. "The way I look at it, we've enjoyed the good life at Perdido for a long time. And we will again. But maybe every once in a while we have to suffer to appreciate all the good things."

"That could be it, Walt. But I'm still gonna keep my eye out for those locusts."

"Let me know if you see any."

CHAPTER 40

The Great Hurricane Feast

Perdido is not just a place; it's a state of mind.

—Kitty Thornton

"Everyone's coming over tonight," Miss Kitty announced. "For a hurricane feast."

"A what?" Danny asked.

"A hurricane feast. We've had three days without electricity. All of the ice is gone and the refrigerated food needs to be eaten or it's just going to spoil. Everybody's coming over and bringing their food, too. We'll have enough to feed an army."

"Who all's coming?" Danny asked.

"Everyone who stayed and rode out the storm," Miss Kitty said. "Mr. and Mrs. Lyons, Doc Jordon, Wallace Flomaton, George Randolph, Cookie and his crew, Trout's parents, Big Johnnie, Freddie ... and anyone else that can make it."

"All right," Danny said. "If Trout's parents are coming, that means lots of blueberries and ice cream."

"Mm, those blueberries are the best thing I've ever put in my mouth," Miss Kitty said. "I'm looking forward to those."

Mr. Walt had cleared an area in the backyard for a bonfire and several grills. "You boys have to gather plenty of wood," he said. "A big bonfire will give us plenty of coals for the grill."

With their minds on hamburgers, steaks, eggs, bacon and everything delicious, Danny, Hunter and Gar set out to get as much dried oak as they could find. Mr. Walt arranged three grills near the bonfire and had two shovels handy to scoop the coals right in.

Hurricane cleanup had been going on non-stop since the storm and everyone needed a reprieve from their labor. Guests arrived early in the afternoon while there was still plenty of light outside. They'd already tried cooking by candlelight and ended up either burning the food or eating it raw.

Mr. Walt packed hot coals into the grills and they loaded them with meats of all sorts: venison, fish, turkey, quail, beef, pork, wild hog—the works. Ethel and Miss Kitty set up a long table with everything that had come out of the refrigerators. There were countless varieties of cheeses, bottles of milk, and dozens of jars of mayonnaise, mustard, ketchup, chopped garlic, horseradish, and whatever was on its last leg. Whether or not anyone wanted horseradish didn't matter. It had to go out that night, one way or another.

At one end of the table, they crowded bottles of warm beer and liquor. But without ice, they had to be creative with their drinks.

"I've never tried a warm gin and tonic," Mr. Walt said. "But there's a first time for everything."

Going without ice didn't faze Wallace Flomaton.

"When it comes to alcohol, ice is extremely overrated," he said as he sipped on a glass of tonic water with a lime. "It just dilutes the true flavor of fine spirits."

"Then why did you always use so much of my ice in your vodka tonics?" George Randolph asked dryly.

"Because the ice helped cut that rock-gut vodka you served."

"You never complained before."

"Because you had ice."

"Yeah, I had a lot of things."

"What does that mean?"

"It means, thanks to Beatrice, I now have nothing," George said.

Wallace slapped him on the back. "Don't you worry my good man," he said. "We will build your store back. We *must* build it back. Your store is an institution and it will be reborn."

"I appreciate you saying that but I had my life savings into that place. I don't have the money to build it back."

"We'll find a way," Wallace said. "Consider it my new mission in life."

Wallace was sincere in his pledge to George and he was staying true to God, too. So far, no one knew he'd quit alcohol. The bubbly water with a twist of lime looked like his standard vodka tonic.

He also didn't tell his friends that the past few days had been hell on earth for him. He'd been tortured with headaches, stomach cramps and seizures. He'd felt like death but was thankful to be counted among the living and breathing in Perdido and not burning at the hands of Lucifer.

The morning after the storm, he returned home from Paradise Point and poured all his booze into his kitchen sink. Then he set the bottles up on a stump and blasted each one with his rifle. It had a cleansing effect but the following days brought nothing but pain and suffering. That night, at Mr. Walt and Miss Kitty's hurricane feast, he finally felt better than he had in thirty years.

"Thanks Wallace," George said. "Helping me out like that is a great gesture."

"Helping you?" Wallace laughed. "I need a place to gas up my boat, hold court over my minions and enjoy a cold drink. I'm doing it for me."

"That's okay, too. As long as I get my store back."

"And as long as you keep plenty of ice, it will happen!"

"I'll even upgrade my vodka," George said.

Wallace smiled at his buddy. "We'll talk about that later."

Miss Kitty tapped a spoon against her glass for an announcement. "After tonight, all the food is getting thrown out for the animals. So let's eat up and be thankful," she said, giving a nod to Mr. Walt.

"Uh, yes. Before we eat, I'd like to say a few words. First off, we're glad to have our immediate and extended family here safe and sound. Second, I want to say that we've all been through a lot these past few days and we still have a long ways to go but at least we're all alive, we have our loved ones with us and we still have Perdido, such as it is right now."

"Here, here," Wallace shouted. "Long live Perdido."

"I know everyone is hungry. So let me bless the food so we can eat," Mr. Walt said bowing his head.

Lottie Loxley tapped her glass. "Excuse me for interrupting your blessing Walt but if y'all wouldn't mind, Freddie would like to give the blessing."

"That would be wonderful," Mr. Walt said. "Freddie, the floor is yours."

Everyone turned to Freddie who was fidgeting with a piece of paper.

"Thank you Mr. Walt. I wrote something up special just for tonight."

Mr. Walt patted Freddie on the shoulder. "That'll be fine son."

Most folks wondered how Freddie wrote a blessing seeing as how he couldn't read.

Freddie cleared his throat. Then he cleared it again.

"Go ahead Freddie," Big Johnnie said. "Take your time but not too much time. We're all ready to eat."

"Okay. Here goes. Uh, Lord bless all the folks here and bless this food so that it makes us strong, especially daddy's okra that he made me pick in the hot sun. Lord, thank you for saving us from that hurricane. And Lord, bless Miss Lottie for teaching me to read. She's a real nice lady and she makes the best ice cream in the world. In Christ's name. Amen."

"Amen," the stunned crowd said in unison.

"Freddie," Miss Kitty said. "That was just wonderful. When did you learn to read like that?"

"Well ma'am, Miss Lottie's been teaching me here and there and I've been picking up a few words."

Lottie Loxley put her arm around Freddie's shoulder. "More than a few words Freddie. Once he figured the letters out, he took to reading like a duck to water."

"The ice cream helped," Freddie said.

"Oh, I bribed him with ice cream. Every time he learned a few words or wrote a nice sentence, I'd bring him some of my peach ice cream."

"I'd learn Russian and Chinese for some of that ice cream right now," Wallace said as he wiped the sweat off his brow.

"Wallace, I'm not teaching foreign languages but when we get more ice, I'll make a batch of ice cream for everyone."

The crowd cheered but none so loudly as Freddie. The ice cream sounded good but mostly he was proud of himself. Now that he could read, he could go back to school.

As the feast began, folks laughed and chatted like they had before Beatrice had scrambled their day-to-day lives. For a while, they even forgot there had ever been a storm. That night, Perdido was once again running on all cylinders.

With his plate brimming with food, Danny sat by himself in deep thought. Despite Will's cold demeanor at the swim meet, Danny still missed his best buddy and wondered what it was going to be like when he returned to Montgomery. Grace flittered through his mind and he thought about Trout but mostly he wondered how his friendship with Will could have gone wrong. How could a girl make that much difference? The world was full of mysteries but the two things he was sure he couldn't figure out were hurricanes and girls.

Danny had suffered plenty during the past few days and to make matters worse, they'd found *Greenie* washed against a tree and cracked in half. Mr. Walt didn't think they could fix her.

"She's mighty old," he had told Danny. "And I've patched her up at least a dozen times. Beatrice might have done her in for good."

Danny wiped a tear from the corner of his eye just as Mr. Walt walked up.

"Mind if I sit here and join you, Danny?"

"Sure daddy, have a seat."

"What are you thinking about over here all by yourself?"

"I don't know. I guess that life's not fair sometimes."

"How so?"

"You know. Will and I are mad at each other, *Greenie* got busted up and all of this hurricane stuff is just hard for me to understand."

"Yes it is Danny but you know what, life is hard sometimes."

"It's like what you always say daddy, 'it's hard but it's fair'. Right?"

"Well yeah. Except sometimes, it isn't even fair. But sulking about it doesn't help anything."

"It's hard not to. I've lost my boat and my best friend."

"I can understand that you're upset about Will but y'all will reconcile in due time. You just have to let go of the past and apologize."

"Yeah but he's the one who started it all."

"That doesn't matter. It takes two dogs to make a fight. Like the Bible says, 'turn the other cheek'."

"I guess so," Danny said.

"Trust me Danny. Just let Will off the hook for his bad behavior. That's called taking the high road. Know what I mean?"

"I think so. If I don't hold a grudge then I'm taking the high road, right?"

"Exactly. And Will will see that and apologize for the way he acted."

"You think so?"

"I can almost guarantee it."

"If you say so, I'll give it a try."

"Good. Oh, and one more thing. Don't worry about *Greenie*. There are lots of boats out there."

"Out where?"

"All over, especially after this storm. You never know where your next boat might come from."

Danny wasn't cheering up. No matter what his daddy said, the boy's mood stayed somber. Mr. Lyons and Cookie had been keeping their distance until Mr. Walt motioned them over.

"Hey Danny," Mr. Lyons said.

"Hi little guy," Cookie smiled.

"Hi."

Mr. Lyons put his arm around Danny. "Uh son, Cookie and I have been thinking about making a deal with you."

Danny looked at them skeptically. "What kind of deal?"

"How about this? If you help Cookie get my little *Whaler* out of Doc Jordan's house and if you help him replace her screens, you can have that little *Whaler*."

"For how long?"

"Forever, I'm saying that I'm gonna give it to you."

"What? Really?" Danny said with a look of shock. "You're kidding, right?"

"Nope. I'm dead serious."

A surge of happiness rushed through him until he thought about Mr. Walt. When he turned to see a big grin on his daddy's face, Danny knew that the offer was bona fide.

"Can I really have it daddy?"

"As long as you uphold your end of the deal I have no objection. It's up to Carlton and Cookie now."

"Well then, y'all have yourselves a deal!" Danny said almost shaking Mr. Lyons's arm out of the socket.

Danny jumped up and gave his daddy a bear hug. Not one to show his affection outwardly, this time Mr. Walt wrapped his arms around his son and squeezed him tight.

"Thanks so much, daddy," Danny said. "I'm going to make Doc Jordon's porch as good as new."

"I know you will," Mr. Walt said.

"Can I start tomorrow? Please daddy?"

"I figured you'd say that. What do you think, Cookie?"

"I'm ready," he said. "We'll have that boat back in the water by lunchtime."

Danny was pumped so full of adrenaline he bounced around the rest of the evening telling anyone who would listen that he was getting the little *Whaler*. Gar and Hunter's jealousy was obvious but, at the same time, they were happy for Danny, especially after he told them they could use it if they helped pay for gas.

The feast lasted late into the night until the last of the fuel in the Coleman lanterns burned out and Mr. Walt and Miss Kitty lit every candle they had. When they couldn't eat another bite, the crowd gathered all of the food, said another blessing and tossed it deep into the woods.

"Well everyone," Mr. Walt said half-jokingly. "Your taste buds can go on vacation. Tomorrow we start in on the canned food."

"What are you talking about? We can still catch fish you know," Wallace said. "And crabs and shrimp."

"Good point," Mr. Walt agreed.

"And I have a dozen bushels of corn," Mr. Lyons added. "And there are plenty of watermelons in the fields."

"True again," Mr. Walt said.

"And when I get my new boat in the water, I'll gig some flounders and pull the shrimp net too," Danny trumpeted. "It's going to be great! Just like before the storm."

And just like that, the Perdido family smiled collectively. Their paradise had been ripped apart at the seams but their love and dedication was building it back. In their hearts they knew that no matter what besieged them, good or bad, Perdido would always provide them with an endless bounty of food, family and friendship. Because, as a wise sage once said, "Perdido is not just a place it's a state of mind." That wisdom was passed on to generation after generation after generation.

EPILOGUE

Friends Again

At Perdido, the story remains the same, only the characters change.

—Kitty Thornton, 1968

That night, before Danny drifted off to sleep, he reflected on another incredible summer. He, Will, and Trout had more fun than any boys could have possibly crammed into three months with all the chasing armadillos, shrimping, fishing, skiing, swinging at The Tree and playing at Pigland, Pirate's Canyon and The Point. And, once again, Mr. Walt had worked them like slaves burning trash, digging the garbage pit, cleaning fish, repairing broken screens, scraping barnacles from the boat and on and on. They'd earned their fun; that was certain.

Then he realized how many brand new experiences that summer had brought. He'd learned to ride a minibike; they'd caught an armadillo and an alligator gar; Trout had flown like a bird; he and Will had won the first swim meet they ever entered; he'd kissed a girl for the first time; and he'd endured a horrendous hurricane. Worst of all, that summer was the first time he and Will ever had a falling out. Even though he'd been blessed with a million smiles, the fact that Will was not there to share the last days of summer hurt him deeply.

As he fell asleep, Danny heard a car door slam and people talking. He lifted his head in the darkness and wondered what time it was. Then he turned over sadly, wishing for sweet dreams and a good night's sleep.

The next morning, he felt a puff of air in his ear and sat straight up in bed. Instantly, he knew who was there. Will was standing over him smiling.

"Hi," Danny moaned. "Where'd you come from?"

"Daddy and I've been on the road for three days trying to get here. The roads are a mess."

"That's amazing. I dreamed you were here and now you are."

Will shuffled across the room while Danny stretched his sore muscles.

"Yeah, well I've got something to say," Will said, his face tightening. "I'm sorry about all that mess with Grace and the diving tournament. I acted like a jerk and I promise never to let a girl mess up our friendship again."

Danny smiled and looked at Will. His lips were quivering as he spoke and Danny noticed how watery his eyes were. Will turned and shuffled to the other side of the room. He stood quietly for a few seconds, rubbing at his eyes.

"It's just that I'd rather be here with you than anyplace else in the world. You're my best friend."

Danny felt his throat tighten up. "It's okay, cuz," he said.

"When that hurricane hit … well, I kept imagining y'all getting washed away and stuff. It kept going over and over in my mind. I just couldn't stop thinking about it. I thought I was going crazy," he said as his voice choked up.

Danny walked over quietly and put his arm around Will's shoulder. "I said it's okay, Will. We're still best friends. We always will be. I promise."

Will wiped the tears from his cheek and gave Danny a bear hug. "That's all I wanted to hear."

The boys stood in silence for a few moments, friends again and ready to get on with more adventures.

"Oh my God," Danny said. "You're not going to believe this. Mr. Lyons is giving us the little *Whaler.*"

"You're a liar!" Will yelped

"It's true. I swear."

"Mr. Lyons is just giving it to us? You mean for keeps?"

"Yeah. We just have to get it out of Doc Jordon's porch and fix some screens and stuff."

"Doc Jordon's porch?"

"It's a long story. I'll tell you on the way."

As they sprinted through the kitchen, Mr. Walt and Uncle Brewton stopped them.

"Whoa boys, where do you think you're going?" Mr. Walt asked.

"I want to show Will the little *Whaler* at Doc Jordon's house."

"Okay, but come back for breakfast. We have a lot of work to do today."

"Yes, sir," they said and sped out the door.

On the way, they combed the beach, discovering lost treasures of the storm. In the short distance between Paradise Point and Doc Jordon's house, they found a broken canoe, a dozen life jackets, three paddles, and a water ski. Suddenly, something caught Danny's eye in the edge of the water.

"Hey, Will," he yelled. "Come see."

"What is it?"

"I found Ethel's teeth."

Will scampered over to see what naked false teeth looked like. Miraculously, Miss Kitty's glasses were there, too, lodged between a molar and bicuspid.

"How'd this stuff get here?" Will asked.

"That's a long story, too. I'll tell you about it later."

When they arrived, Cookie had already extracted the boat and had his men pull it down to the beach.

"Hey, Cookie, we were supposed to help you with that," Danny said.

He smiled at the boys. "Glad to see you two scallywags back together again."

"We're glad to be together again," Will grinned.

"Well, now that you are, do you want to take her out for a spin?" Cookie asked.

"Can we?" Danny asked.

"It's your boat."

"Not until we fix Doc Jordon's house," Danny said.

"Oh yeah. But you can still use it as long as I say so."

"You've got a good point, what do you think, Will?"

"A short ride sure won't hurt anything."

Perdido Bay was a smooth as a millpond that morning. As they sped across the water, Will propped his feet up and leaned back.

"Ah," he sighed. "It's a good day to live."

The End

Gift Your Friends
Buy one book, get another at half price

Book Order Form

My Address
Name _____
Address _____
City State Zip _____
Email/phone _____

Book I _____ **$15.00**
☐ *This book is for me – same address as above*
☐ *This book is a gift, please ship to the address below*

Name _____
Address _____
City State Zip _____

Book II _____ **$ 7.50**
☐ *This book is for me – same address as above*
☐ *This book is a gift, please ship to the address below*

Name _____
Address _____   **+ $5.00**
City State Zip _____   *shipping & handling*

Gift books will include a card with the following message: **$27.50**
This book is being sent as a gift to you from (name of giver).   **total**
Make checks payable to Lost Key Publishing,
P. O. Box 34075 Pensacola, FL 32507. Credit
card orders: please go to *www.lostkeypublising.com.*

PREVIEW

Coming Soon!

PERDIDO—BOOK TWO:

Expanded Horizons

FRED D. GARTH

Lost Key PUBLISHING

Perdido Key, Florida

CHAPTER 1

Sink or Swim

You can shake a politician's hand but you better count your fingers.
—Brewton Stapleton, 1962

The morning sun cut a path across Freddie Showers' face. He cracked his eyelids and peaked through a dirty windowpane at a cloudless sky. The pine needles on the tree outside of his window were motionless. The first day of June was shaping up to be prime fishing weather—no wind, no rain, and based on the tide charts, good water movement.

Before he moved a muscle Freddie whispered, "Rabbits, rabbits, rabbits." Then he smiled. His daddy, Big Johnnie Showers, had taught him that saying, "Rabbits, rabbits, rabbits," on the first day of the month would bring him good luck all month. But it had to be the very first thing he said before uttering, "Good morning," or "What's for breakfast?" That would spoil the whole thing.

Freddie was pleased with himself for remembering to say the lucky words before commenting on the beautiful morning. Talking was something he loved to do, whether he was telling stories, yakking with his dog, or just having a jovial conversation with himself—something he did often, especially on a bluebird day like this one. Before he pushed through the screen door, he grabbed a couple of pieces of bread, his fishing pole and tackle box, and headed to Soldier Creek. Big Johnnie was already loading the skiff when Freddie strolled up.

"It's gonna be a good day, Daddy," he said.

Big Johnnie looked at his son. The boy was growing into a fine young man. His schoolwork was downright impressive and his muscles were finally catching up to his broad shoulders. "I'm glad you think so, Son, because I'd just love to catch a mess of fish this morning."

"We will," Freddie said emphatically.

Lottie Loxley had given Freddie the old wooden boat for finishing the seventh grade with all A's and B's. Everyone was proud of him, because his early attempts at reading had ended in failure. A young doctor had told Big Johnnie that his son had a touch of something called dyslexia. In fourth grade, Freddie wrote a story called, "Jesus was a dog." Lottie wanted to take the whip to him until the doc explained how dog is God in the language of Dyslexic. Once they invented ways to teach him to read, Freddie made up for lost time. Big Johnnie could hardly get him to tend to the crops and feed the animals anymore. All the boy wanted to do was read. He'd even abandoned his old dog, Spooky. The poor mutt spent more time nipping at Big Johnnie's pants legs than playing with Freddie.

Even though the old skiff was small, she was seaworthy. Of course, that was after Big Johnnie patched the leaks, replaced some of the rotten ribs, and put on a fresh coat of paint. Lottie Loxley was generous with things she no longer had use for.

Not the best swimmer, Big Johnnie made sure they stayed close to shore, just in case. That's where the redfish and trout were anyway. No need to venture into deep water when the fish hung around pier pilings and grass beds along the shoreline.

Freddie tied on a Rebel Horse top-water lure. "I'm gonna catch a hoss daddy speckled trout with this."

"I hope you do," Big Johnnie said. "I hope you catch lots of 'em."

With the sun still low on the horizon they paddled slowly along the shore. Big Johnnie was trolling with a double spec rig while Freddie cast the Rebel Horse from the bow. The tiny propeller on the front of Freddie's lure hummed as it spun across the slick surface of the creek.

"It sure looks fishy over there," he said.

Before the last word left his lips, a giant silver fish crashed his lure. Freddie let out of hoot and yanked back on the rod to set the hook.

"That's my hoss daddy spec," he yelled. "It's a beast."

The line spun off Freddie's reel so fast he burned his thumb trying to slow it down. Slowly he tightened up the drag.

"Not too much son," Big Johnnie warned. "You don't want him to break the line."

Freddie had fought plenty of fish and knew how to work the drag to tire a fish out, but he had hooked into a granddaddy this time. It took all his strength to keep his rod tip up. Without much line left on his reel to play with, Freddie cranked down on the drag and held on as the fish pulled them and the skiff straight across Soldier Creek.

Rodney Farber had told his daddy he was going night fishing. That much was true. What he neglected to mention was that he'd snuck a six pack of Busch beer out of the refrigerator and stuffed it into his backpack. He was guzzling the last one as the sun came up and he rounded The Point at full tilt. Rodney hoped to get home and crawl in bed before Judge Farber woke up.

Two years earlier, Judge Marlow Farber had bought a prime piece of land on Soldier Creek. He'd grown tired of the country club politics and decided to build a house where he could be the master. The ostentatious mansion dwarfed the simple beach cottages that dotted the shores of Soldier Creek and Perdido Bay. Even though Judge Farber had tried to escape the country club, the truth was, the country club couldn't escape from him. With white columns and chandeliers, it looked more like a clubhouse than a place to unwind.

Construction was still underway on The Castle, as the locals had begun calling it, but Rodney and his father had brought in some temporary cots to sleep on. Marlow Farber made it his priority to oversee the final stages of building.

Rodney's eyelids were heavy as he pointed his 18-foot fiberglass Welcraft toward home. Freddie had all but worn that fish out, and Big Johnnie had the net in his hand ready to bag it. But when they saw Rodney sliding around The Point and barreling across Soldier Creek, they had a bad feeling. Big Johnnie and Freddie barely had time to stand up and wave their arms as the speedboat rushed at them.

Somehow Rodney heard the sound of Big Johnnie's booming voice over the whining of the 75-horsepower Evinrude. When he looked up, he was about to broadside the old wooden skiff. His reaction was quick and deliberate as he cranked the steering wheel to the left. The stern of his boat whipped into Big Johnnie and mule kicked him out of the boat. Freddie threw himself amongst the ribs at the bottom of his skiff and somehow hung on as the wall of water capsized his pride and joy.

In a panic, Rodney never looked back. He straightened the wheel and bee-lined it home. Back at the boathouse he inspected his hull. No visible marks. Half-drunk and slightly guilty, Rodney ran up to the house and slipped into bed.

Freddie opened his eyes to find himself underneath his boat but un-injured. He ducked under the rail and popped up to a frothy surface. Big Johnnie was nowhere to be seen. As his boat bobbed upside down beside him, Freddie repeatedly held his breath and dived to the bottom looking for his daddy. After thirty minutes of trying, the only thing he found was Big Johnnie's red University of Alabama cap floating nearby.

The screams woke Judge Farber. A south wind had kicked up and was blowing the sound of Freddie's voice clear across Soldier Creek and onto the sleeping porch where the judge had placed his cot. Rodney had free fallen into a deep, drunken sleep.

Judge Farber walked inside and shook Rodney. "Son, wake up. Do you hear that?"

Rodney mumbled but didn't move.

Freddie's hollering for help sparked what little goodness Judge Farber still had inside of him. He took one last look at his nearly coma-tose son and decided to take matters into his own hands. In a half a minute the judge was cranking the Evinrude and heading in Freddie's direction. A man of meticulous detail, Marlow Farber noticed that the engine was hot when he got on board. He also detected the smell of stale beer and found a crumpled can stuffed under the steering console. It didn't take a man of his intellect to piece together that puzzle.

As the Welcraft closed in on Freddie and his overturned boat, the screaming intensified. Freddie saw the death boat coming his way again and figured it was going run him over this time. In a fit of panic he swam to the bottom of Soldier Creek and stayed as long as he could.

Judge Farber was more than perplexed when he saw Freddie disap-pear like a loon on a cold winter day. When Freddie finally burst to the surface he was hysterical.

"You killed my daddy, you bastard. I can't find my daddy. You killed him."

The judge had witnessed plenty of off beat behavior in his years of sitting on the bench. He had a knack for diffusing difficult situations.

"Now hold on there son. Tell me what happened. Get a hold of yourself."

Freddie glared up from the water. It took him a moment to realize that the judge was behind the wheel, not Rodney. The whole situation confused him and deep down in his soul, he knew that his daddy was gone.

Exhausted from the search, Freddie swam to his skiff and held onto the submerged railing. "Daddy and I were fishin' and that boat, you, I mean Rodney came around The Point. We didn't have time. I had a big fish on …"

"You're saying your daddy was with you?"

"Yes sir, he got knocked out of the boat."

"You're sure?"

"I'm sure. We were fishing. I had a big spec on. Rodney broadsided us."

Judge Marlow Farber also knew how to control a situation. He saw Freddie clutching Big Johnnie's cap and realized the gravity of the situation.

"Freddie," he said calmly, "we need to find Big Johnnie, but first I have to tell you something."

Freddie whimpered. "We need to find daddy."

"We will, but I want you to listen to me right now. Rodney did not hit you with this boat. It has been tied to our pier all night."

"But I saw him …"

"Listen to what I'm saying Freddie. I'm the Honorable Marlow H. Farber, a circuit judge for thirty years, and I'm telling you that your boat capsized on its own. My son had nothing to do with it. Do you hear me?"

"But that's not the truth."

"It is now."

Tears streamed down Freddie's cheeks as he looked into the stone-cold eyes of the judge. Why was he saying those things when he should be helping him find his daddy?

With cool precision, Marlow Farber removed his t-shirt and plunged into the water. On his third sweep of the muddy bottom he spotted a fishing net. The handle still had Big Johnnie's huge hand wrapped around it. The man was drowned dead.

The judge surfaced quickly, grabbed an anchor line and swam back down the body. He tied a slipknot around Big Johnnie's ankle and lashed a life jacket to the other end to mark the body. It was the best way to spare Freddie further grief and get away from the scene as soon as possible.

"Let's go Freddie," he said. "Climb in my boat and let me take you home."

Freddie's mind spun into some far off, distant place. Shock had set in and he moved slowly without emotion. He climbed into the Welcraft and huddled in the corner. The judge put a dry towel over him and eased the boat away as Freddie stared at the orange life jacket bobbing on the surface. Suddenly he felt ill and everything inside his stomach spewed out, covering him and the back of Rodney's boat.

Like the rest of the Perdido folks, Trout, Will, and Danny, were oblivious to the horror that had taken place on that stunningly beautiful morning. Will had rallied the boys at sunrise to go water skiing while the creek was still glassy smooth. They'd almost worn themselves out trying to learn to drop the slalom so they could slide along on their naked bare feet. They'd heard about professional skiers at Cypress Gardens in central Florida barefoot skiing, so they figured they could do it too. If confidence were fertilizer, those boys could have grown the tallest corn in Alabama. Problem was, they had no idea how to ski on their feet. As with many of their pursuits, hearsay and grit were their only guides.

Will decided that going full speed was essential. That was just common sense. It made the water harder. But it also compounded their crashes into extended head-over-heals tumbles that invariably ended in hopeless wedgies, blasts of water up the nose, twisted muscles and severe pain. That tended to slow them down, but not much could stop them.

The trick was getting rid of the ski. As far as Will could tell, jumping out of the slalom seemed like the best option. The plan worked well, until he landed feet first on top of the water whereupon he'd face plant and flip for a good five seconds. He took a good beating before he finally gave up and turned the ski rope handle over to Danny.

As they headed toward The Point with Danny in tow, Will and Trout saw Rodney's boat moving slowly across the creek. Trout noticed the orange life jacket floating out in the middle of the bayou but didn't give it a second thought. He wanted to watch Danny wipe out one more time on his last attempt at barefoot skiing.

Danny reached down to loosen the boot and gave Will the thumbs up to go full tilt. Will jammed down the throttle. Danny slowly removed his back foot from the slalom and stepped gingerly onto the water. Slowly, he shifted more weight to his barefoot. As the water rushed by it burned and tickled at the same time. It felt hard enough to hold him up so he put more weight on his foot. Then in a quick motion, instead of jumping out of the ski, Danny slipped his foot out and quickly planted it firmly on the surface. For at least three seconds he slid across the water on his bare feet. Water flew in his face as he tried to settle in. Suddenly and without warning, he caught a big toe and tumbled violently across the slick water.

Will and Trout hooted and hollered. Danny had done it. Sure, he only went about thirty yards before he crashed, but he had clearly skied barefoot. The gauntlet had been thrown. For the next hour they recreated Danny's technique. Soon enough they were all skiing barefoot until their feet burned.

Life was all about trial and error for the boys. When they set their minds on something, they usually achieved it or got completely banged up trying. Sometimes it was the competition between them that drove the boys to great individual accomplishments. Other times they teamed up to overcome challenges. But every time was a good time, because they were always pursuing a dream.

As he putted slowly toward his dock, Judge Farber observed the commotion in the distance. After he'd tied off the Welcraft, he cleaned Freddie up and gave him some cool water to drink.

"I think I know what happened," the judge said.

"What?" Freddie asked, still stupefied.

"You and Big Johnnie were fishing, correct?"

"Yes sir."

"And those boys were skiing wild like they always do, correct?"

"I guess so. I'm not sure."

"And they came too close to your boat and the waves tumped you and Big Johnnie over."

"No sir, it was Rod …"

Judge Farber grabbed Freddie by the arms. "Now you stop that kind of talk right now. You hear me? That is not what happened. As I told you earlier, neither this boat nor Rodney have left the house since yesterday, except just now when I came to rescue you."

"But judge …"

"Don't 'but judge' me boy. I'm telling you how it happened and that's final."

Freddie was shaking out of his fog and starting to figure what was going on. His dyslexia never had fogged his view of the way life worked. The rich folks did what they pleased, and the poor folks did what they were told. The anger began to well up inside him. He didn't care what kind of judge the man was. His son was guilty, as guilty as Al Capone.

Freddie looked at the judge through fiery eyes. "It's a lie. I won't lie. Your son's gotta pay for this."

A wicked smirk spread across Judge Farber's face. "Son, you don't want to go down that road. I'm making it easy on you. Just blame those boys and their wild skiing, or you'll bring more hurt to you and yours than you could load into a 20-yard dump truck."

As best as he knew, his daddy was freshly dead and Freddie wondered how much more hurt there could be. He sneered at Marlow Farber. "I won't lie. It ain't right."

"I'll tell you what's not right," the judge shot back. "Your mother going to jail for writing bad checks and then the state sending you off to some foster home in Texas or North Dakota to live with a bunch of misfits. That's what's not right."

"My mama paid back that money. She's an honest woman."

"Is that right? Son, you don't know much about the law, do you? As a judge, I have the power to reopen that case and put her in jail while we set a trial date. She could be in there for months, maybe years."

"You can't do that."

"Oh I can, and I will. See, here's what I'm telling you plain and simple. I'm a judge and you, well you're really nothing but poor white trash. So unless you want to live in North Dakota you just tell everyone about those boys skiing wild and kicking up all those waves that capsized your boat. It's a story everyone will believe and understand, because those boys are always an inch away from disaster. But if you try to say that my son had anything to do with it, then I suggest you have a suitcase packed with some warm clothes. Do you understand?"

A cold fear crept up Freddie's backbone as he saw, once again, how power could prevail over righteousness. He hung his head and

339

whimpered. "What now?" he said without looking up at the judge.

"Well I have to take you home and tell your mother the bad news. Then we have to get Big Johnnie out of the creek. Go get in my car and I'll be out directly."

The judge literally kicked Rodney out of bed. The cot broke into three pieces.

"What the hell?" Rodney yelled before he knew who was kicking him.

"That's my question son. By my reckoning you have caused a man to drown this morning. We have a dead man in Soldier Creek."

"We do?"

"Yes we do. Big Johnnie Showers is lying in the mud at the bottom of the creek, and it looks like you put him there."

Rodney rubbed his head. The beer headache throbbed. "I guess I came close to them ..."

"Freddie said you hit them."

"Freddie? Is he okay?"

"He's in shock. His daddy's dead. So no, he's not okay. But at least I have the situation under control for the moment. I have to leave for a few minutes. Under no circumstances do you tell anyone that you left this house last night or this morning. You've been right here working on the house since yesterday afternoon. Is that clear?"

"Yes sir!"

Rodney had learned to follow his father's instructions implicitly or pay dearly. This was one time he wouldn't deviate. As the sound of his father's car faded up the driveway, Rodney pulled a blanket over his head and fell back to sleep among the wreckage of his cot.

Trout wondered why that orange life jacket hadn't blown across the creek.

"Hey y'all," he said, "what's up with that life preserver?"

Danny and Will spotted it too. "Haven't seen it before," Danny said. "Maybe somebody's marking a crab trap."

Will laughed. "With a life jacket?"

"Maybe they ran out of buoys."

"Could be," Trout agreed. "Let's go check it out."

Being orderly was not part of the boy's fabric. At sixteen-years-old they were overflowing with stupid, and they rarely colored inside the lines of life. Nevertheless, when something or someone was out of place on their home turf, they investigated.

Trout leaned over the bow as Will eased back on the throttle. "It's marking something," he said as he snatched up the life preserved and pulled on the rope. "Feels like a crab trap. I bet Wallace or Big Johnnie ran out of buoys like Danny said."

"See if they caught any," Danny said.

The first thing Trout saw was the shadowy outline of a rubber boot. The other end of the rope was tied to it. He froze as he felt a shiver run through his body. Then he dropped the line and backed away. Will and Danny figured he'd just seen an empty crab trap and let it fall back to the bottom.

"Nothing?" Will asked

Trout didn't move. "Uh, not nothing," he finally said.

"Then how many crabs?" Will asked.

"Not sure."

Will was getting irritated. "Then why'd you drop it, Goober?'

"I saw something weird. Looked like a boot."

Will was already pulling the rope back in with Danny standing by. "Move out of the way, Trout," Will said. "Let's see what's down there."

As Trout eased toward the back of the boat, he tried to shake the image from his mind. "I don't think we want to see it, Will."

Big Johnnie's body was in plain site before Will tossed the rope away. Danny's let out a high-pitched yelp but couldn't take his eyes off the body. There was no doubt that they were looking at Big Johnnie. As his thick black hair washed away from his face two eyes bugged out as big as hard boiled eggs.

"What the hell?' Will said.

Trout couldn't look. "Is he dead?"

"Dead?" Will shot back. "The man is deader than a doornail."

"Then why the heck is he marked up like a crab trap?" Danny asked.

Will stared into the depths. "Beats me, Cuz. I guess somebody's gonna come collect him later."

"We gotta go tell Mr. Walt," Danny said. "This ain't right."

For a moment the boys lost track of their role in life and acted responsibly. As quickly as the boat would run, they headed back to Paradise Point to spread the bad news.

N O T E

A Sign of Good Character

The three-hour drive from Montgomery, Alabama to Perdido Bay on Interstate 65 is generally boring. A stop at Bates Turkey House in Greenville is one of the few ways to break the monotony of pine trees, small towns and cop cars tucked into the woods.

I was heading south on I-65 a few years back (as I have done so many times over the years) and passed the Grace Garland exit. *Grace like Kelly and Garland like Judy*, I thought, what a great name for one of my characters.

After that epiphany, I thought about exit 114, Georgiana Starlington, and another character was born. Exit 69, Wallace Flomaton and so on. I also named a lot of my characters after small towns in Baldwin County, Alabama (in bold on the map at right).

Not all of the character's names come from road signs or small towns but I had fun with the ones that do. Brewton Stapleton, Lottie Loxley and Monroe Miflin are all inspired by classic southern towns that are as warm and complex as the characters they represent.

- Fred Garth

Baldwin County

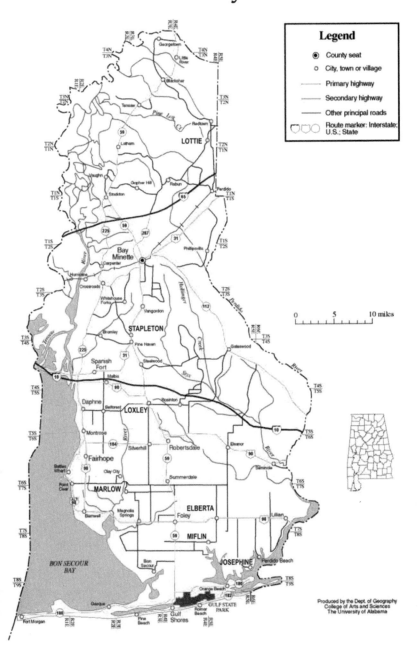

Produced by the Dept. of Geography
College of Arts and Sciences
The University of Alabama